Jack Be Nimble

Jack Be Nimble

Chris Palmer

TSB

LONDON AND NEW YORK

Jack Be Nimble

© 2021 Christine Palmer

9 8 7 6 5 4 3 2 1

First published by TSB, 2021

TSB is an imprint of:
Can of Worms Enterprises Ltd
7 Peacock Yard
London SE17 3LH
United Kingdom

www.canofworms.net

Cover design: James Shannon
Text design: Henry Iles
Cover image: Copyright 2020, Wayne Brittle Photography

ISBN: 9781911673040 (paperback))
ISBN: 9781911673057 (ebook)

Printed and bound in the United Kingdom
British Library Cataloguing in Publication Data
A catalogue record for this book is available from the British Library

Library of Congress Cataloging-in-Publication Data
A catalog record for this book is available from the Library of Congress

ABOUT THE AUTHOR

 Christine Palmer was born in Derbyshire an 'enfant terrible' of the sixties. She has lived and worked in Canada and America returning to England to go back to University. Christine then took up a career with the BBC as a documentary maker. She is now a full-time writer and lives with her husband in a medieval house in France or on their canal-boat in London.

Dedication – To Renella, Charles and William

Find Christine on Instagram @chrispalmerbooks

Acknowledgments – My thanks to Alice Ahearn, Graham Battye, Lynda Davies, Imitiaz Dharker, Tobias Steed, Josie Walter

Other books by Christine

NON-FICTION

Walking Back to Happiness, Eye Books, 2011

"Succumb to Christine Palmer's charm, spirit of adventure and huge sense of fun. I'm already shopping for my walking boots."
– SUSAN RAE, RADIO PRESENTER

CHILDREN'S BOOKS UNDER THE NAME CHRISTINE BATTYE

Cowardy, Cowardy Custard, Can of Worms Kids Press, 2009

Cowardy, Cowardy, Custard and the Scary Tunnel,
Can of Worms Kids Press, 2018

Cowardy, Cowardy, Custard and the London Adventure,
Can of Worms Kids Press, 2021

These charming picture books in both French and English, make them ideal for children learning either language as the translations appear on adjoining pages.

The delightful illustrations, by renowned artist and production designer, Christopher Hobbs, are imaginative and amusing, bringing the Custard and his Clan story alive.

All of Christine's books are available either directly from the author, or via www.canofworms.net and/or your local bookshop or online retailer.

PRODUCTION AND PUBLISHING CREDITS

A considerable number of people are involved in realising an author's work as a finished book on the shelf of your local library, bookshop or online retailer. TSB would like to acknowledge the critical input of the following individuals:

Text design, layout TSB/Can of Worms has worked with Henry Iles on a variety of book and online projects since becoming his neighbour in the late '90s when Henry was designing for the Rough Guides and others. For *Jack Be Nimble* Henry has undertaken the typography and layout design.

Cover design TSB/Can of Worms has benefitted from a longstanding relationship with James Shannon on book production and website development for many of its own titles as well as some of Can of Worms's consultancy clients. For *Jack Be Nimble* James has undertaken the cover design, further examples of his work can be found at: www.jshannon.com

Cover Photography The image of a Derbyshire landscape was taken by Wayne Brittle of Wayne Brittle Photography. More examples of his work can be found on his website and Facebook page at: www.waynebrittlephotography.com FB: www.facebook.com/ waynebrittlephotography1

Editorial Editorial development and editing has been provided by Alice Ahearn. Alice has worked with TSB/Can of Worms on a freelance basis over the last few years and is a copyeditor and proofreader based between London and Oxford. She is currently studying for a PhD in Classics at the University of Oxford, researching women's English translations of Latin poetry. She is currently working on Christine's next novel, *Shape*. For further information please visit her website at:

Athena Literary Services www.athenaliterary.co.uk

Publishing Publishing has been provided by Tobias Steed, publisher of TSB/Can of Worms. Tobias's career in publishing has spanned forty plus years having started as an editorial assistant for Johns Hopkins University Press in Baltimore, co-founder of illustrated travel guides publishing company, Compass American Guides, Oakland, California, Associate Publisher and Director of New Media at Fodor's/ Random House, New York, founder and publisher of Can of Worms Enterprises, and most recently has acquired the Leapfrog Press, New York where he is president and publisher. www.canofworms.net www.leapfrogpress.com

Sales and Marketing Sales and Marketing for *Jack Be Nimble* and all other TSB/ Can of Worms titles is overseen by Garry Manning of The Manning Partnership. Established in 1997, The Manning Partnership provides a complete Sales, Marketing & Distribution solution for TSB/ Can of Worms and other publishers to the UK and English language export markets. Garry also oversees the TSB/Can of Worms relationship with our distributor, GBS/ Penguin Random House. www.manning-partnership.co.uk

Publicity All publicity enquiries should be directed to Tobias Steed. info@ canofworms.net. Further information can be found at: www.canofworms.net

FOREWORD

Some things are meant to be.

Many years ago at school I wrote a synopsis of Christopher Marlowe's play *Tamburlaine the Great*. When the teacher returned my effort, she had merely written on it, "Your synopsis is longer than the play." In writing this foreword I am aware that, since *Jack Be Nimble* fascinates and intrigues me, this effort could end up longer than the book if I'm not as nimble as the author, as nimble as Jack.

Chris Palmer has created a story which is both episodic and a single entity, confidently and comfortably existing entirely in the present. Her canvas is large, her cast considerable, but she bestrides her creation like a colossus. A debut novel, yes, but needing no apology; there is no hesitancy, no uncertainty. Chris paints word pictures in full colour, images of varying size and intensity, illustrating everything from the smallest instants, not 'memories' because all is in the moment throughout, to whole episodes, short stories in their own right, now intimate, now familial.

When you're at the end, should you wonder what you have experienced, let your mind take a step back and suddenly, as with a mosaic or a pointillist painting, all the fragments, the disparate regions of colour, become one single picture, a tapestry revealing one unique story: without doubt an adventure, a thriller, a mystery, a tragedy, but essentially a joyous and fulfilling love story.

Thank you, Chris. May your readers enjoy their journey with *Jack Be Nimble*.

Jean Gemmell FRSA

The title is from: "Can't Help Falling in Love" by George David Weiss, Luigi Creatore & Hugo Peretti sung by Elvis Presley in the film "Blue Hawaii" (1961)

Part One

CHAPTER ONE

We used to build civilizations.
Now we build shopping malls.

– BILL BRYSON, *NEITHER HERE NOR THERE*

BELPER, DERBYSHIRE, 2014

It was August. There had been no sky for several days, just a matte grey. At times it darkened; 'black over Bill's mother's' was the local expression. Occasionally, a sudden breeze lifted the dust. Discarded sweet wrappers mingled with dried leaves spiralled and twirled, finally dropping to the ground when the wind subsided as if they were tired of the game.

Jack rushed across the car park. He could see the blue light of the ambulance flashing above the parked cars, but he found it difficult to negotiate his way between the loaded shopping trolleys. The ambulance was blocking one of the entrances, causing major annoyance with drivers trying to reverse between the lanes of parked vehicles. He could hear horns being sounded, and a medley of overheated voices.

As he approached the ambulance a small group of people started to drift away, leaving him space to observe Nancy. She lay slightly twisted on the ground, one arm partially tucked under her back. One of her many berets clung awkwardly to her riotous hair, secured by two white grips. As the paramedics slipped their arms under her, the breeze showed no mercy, billowing her skirt above her head and revealing to Jack's dismay beige pop-socks, mottled white legs, and ample silk underpants. He hastily bent forward to grapple with her errant skirt and for a split second he was twenty-two again, in love for the first time with the beautiful enigmatic Nancy.

'Careful, sir, let's move her. There we go.' The ambulance team slid her gently across to a stretcher, then secured her limp body with strong webbed bands.

'Are you a relative?' the paramedic enquired. 'We think it's possibly a stroke, heart seems strong and she's breathing ok. Will you be coming in the ambulance?'

Thunder grumbled in the distance. Large leisurely drops of rain made patterns in the dust. Ten minutes ago, Jack had been contemplating which of the exotic fruits on offer he would buy this Saturday. It was a petty game, a sad little ritual, aimed at provoking a response from Mary. Any kind of response, even 'What have you bought those stupid things for?' would have been better than no response at all. Now, the ritual mainly resulted in either him preparing a fruit salad for one, or leaving them in the fruit bowl until a cloud of fruit flies hovered above.

This morning he had chosen 'exotic fruit of the week', a dragon prickly pear, reputedly highly prized in its native country for its citrus flavour with overtones of honey, and its anti-inflammatory properties. Avoiding the prickles, he selected three, joshing privately to himself as to whether you ate them or rubbed them on.

As he placed them in the bag, he had spied Charlie rushing towards him. Jack usually tried to avoid Charlie at all costs. He was one of the new breed, or perhaps old breed was a better description, of supermarket assistants. He was in his seventies, and proud that he could be of service in the new branch of Dennison's that had opened on the outskirts of the town. The uniform involved a white and yellow overall, a jaunty white hat reminiscent of a fifties spiv, plus shiny black shoes. He'd explained to Jack that he had wanted to wear his Nike trainers, but the company had objected, saying they didn't want their more senior staff to look like 'old people in trainers', whatever that was supposed to mean.

Charlie was popular, but he over-explained everything. Ask where the HP sauce was hiding, and Jack felt as if you had engaged him to take you to the foothills of Everest. Everything was articulated, even the short cuts from meat through tinned vegetables. When you eventually reached your goal, one felt congratulations were in order. But Jack couldn't avoid him this time, as he bore down on him.

'It's that friend of yours, the one with the dog,' he cried, rushing down the aisle. 'She's had a funny turn in the car park.'

'You mean Nancy? What kind of a funny turn?'

'A proper funny turn,' replied Charlie.

Jack succeeded in stopping himself asking if there were different degrees of funny turns. Whilst he revelled in the richness of the spoken word, he was aware that not everyone enjoyed his irony, particularly Mary, who would on occasions call him 'too clever by half'.

'We've phoned for an ambulance. Better come quick, Jack, she looks right poorly,' Charlie continued, taking control of Jack's trolley with its one bag of exotic fruits.

The journey to the hospital would take around forty minutes. Jack had hesitated before climbing into the ambulance. Mary would not take kindly to being left at the hairdressers. But Charlie had arrived on the scene again, shouting, 'Go on, Jack, I've paid for your shopping.' He thrust the bag of dragon prickly pears into Jack's hand. 'I'll pick you up at the City Hospital in a couple of hours if you want? It is the City Hospital you're taking her to?' he asked the ambulance driver.

'No, sorry guv, it's the weekend. It's the Royal Infirmary. Come on gentlemen,' he continued, 'make your minds up, this lady is in need of some attention.'

The promised rain was short-lived, leaving the oppressive heat to rise. The air-conditioning in the ambulance fought to keep the temperature down. It seemed completely unreal, Jack thought as he looked around the vehicle. A whole miniature medical world, cut off from the outside, equipped to deal with life and death, racing through the lunchtime traffic along the twenty-mile stretch from Belper to

Derby. Nancy murmured, a low groan with a rustle of vomit. The nurse lifted her head gently.

'Steady, love,' he said, 'you're going to be ok. Your friend… what's your name, sir?' he enquired.

'It's Jack. I'm here, Nancy, it's Jack.' He couldn't reach her hand as he was restricted by the seat belt, but he was able to lean forward and gently squeeze her shoulder.

'Speed up, Alan,' the young male nurse shouted to the driver. 'She's ok,' he reassured Jack, 'but her pulse is a bit low.'

Jack nodded, attempting to steady himself as the ambulance now sped up, picking its way through the traffic. He remembered how at the age of five his grandson Tom had demanded to know why ambulances made that noise. 'Is someone going to die?' he'd asked. Once it had been explained to him that it could just as likely be a lady getting to the hospital to have a baby, he had joyfully cried when he next heard an ambulance siren, 'It's another mummy going to get a baby.' What nonsense, Jack reflected as he reached forward again to comfort Nancy, but at least it had satisfied Tom at the time.

The siren was loud, and although he had his back to the driver, he was impressed how safe the journey felt even at this breakneck speed. He half expected it to screech to a halt, but it stopped slowly, negotiating a three-point turn so as to be able to park at the Accident and Emergency entrance. A young male orderly opened the door, his thick black dreadlocks looking as if they would at any minute burst from their ponytail and cascade onto his shoulders.

'Hello, my lovely,' he said cheerily to Nancy. 'You just relax, darling, we'll get you sorted no time.'

Alan, the driver, came around the ambulance to help Jack out.

'You don't have to rush, mate,' he said. 'They'll take a while to make her comfy like.' He reached into his pocket for a packet of cigarettes, as they watched the two young orderlies guide the stretcher through the rubber doors. They were both laughing, and from the back Jack could see an assortment of highly coloured beads threaded through the dreadlocks.

'He's a case, that one,' Alan said. 'But a heart of gold, he's a real gent, married with twin girls. He's well-educated as well. The lads call him Marley.'

Jack smiled, offering the driver his hand. 'It's the first time I've been in an ambulance with the lights flashing.'

'You're the guy that works at the Regal Cinema in Belper, aren't you?' Alan asked as he edged his way around the side of the ambulance, indicating Jack should follow. 'Out of prying eyes,' he explained as he lit up a cigarette. 'I've seen you there a couple of times. When they're busy, don't you serve on the till?'

'I'm the general dogsbody,' Jack replied, eager now to follow Nancy into the hospital.

'Lovely place, the Regal, great that it reopened,' Alan continued. 'Rubbish films though sometimes. Now that *Last Year in Marienbad*, now what was all that about? Thank goodness they showed *Le Ballon Rouge* as a double bill, great little film that, stands the test of time, unlike that Marienbad rubbish.'

Jack suddenly felt light-headed, astonished that Alan, who was now coughing irregularly as he dragged on his cigarette, was a regular visitor to the Regal Cinema, which had a reputation for avant-garde films. But even more astonishing that he mentioned *Le Ballon Rouge*, one of Nancy's favourite films. He and Nancy had been to see it three times in the sixties, each time involving a motorbike ride to Nottingham to the only cinema that showed foreign films at the time.

He had been rather overwhelmed when he first met Nancy that they shared a taste for avant-garde cinema. He could rarely persuade any of his mates to go with him to see anything remotely foreign, unless there was a suggestion of some implicit sex or Brigitte Bardot, or both. With Nancy it was different. She used cinema as her window on the world. She would quite often sit on the edge of her seat, her chin in her hands, completely absorbed by the film. If it was sad or poignant, she would lean back, resting her head on his shoulder, accepting his offer of a handkerchief if needed. If the film was amusing, she would laugh loudly without embarrassment, clutching his hand and turning to check his reaction matched her own.

On their first meeting she had seemed more serious and sophisticated then his usual female friends, but as their friendship developed the seemingly worldly façade diminished a little to reveal tantalising glimpses of a more exuberant Nancy, eager to embrace a shared relationship together.

As he took his leave of Alan and walked down the hospital corridor, past the tired-looking vending machines, the well-meaning collages of children's drawings and the endless coloured strips and arrows indicating which way to go, he was astonished so many memories came tumbling back.

The Derbyshire Royal Infirmary had been on the verge of closure for many years. It was a large Victorian building with an impressive portico which led by way of several steps to what used to be the main entrance. The double doors were locked with a large sign placed across them announcing the entrance was now at the east end of the building. The statue of Florence Nightingale remained, but minus her lamp which had been constantly abused over the years by groups of young men attempting the Derby Mile, a notorious pub crawl that took place most Friday nights.

Jack felt slightly annoyed that Alan had delayed him, and he was now finding it difficult to pick his way through the labyrinth of corridors to locate the A&E reception. The August heat seemed to have taken its toll on the building. A few listless patients tethered to drips wandered about, but there was no sign of a helpful medical professional he could ask for directions. Eventually, more by accident than design, he found the waiting room. He understood the newly built City Hospital on the other side of the ring road resembled a first-class hotel, with flowers gracing the reception, a comfortable seating area, television, easy access to a tea bar, and a large play area for children. This waiting room had the air of having passed its sell-by date long ago. The vending machine had a handwritten 'out of order' sign on it, and the selection of magazines placed on a stained coffee table looked grubby and uninviting.

There were only four others waiting: a teenager who regularly jumped up, raising his fist in the air and shouting 'Fuck!' then collapsing quietly back into his chair, and a young couple with a toddler, who sat on the floor playing listlessly with a selection of toys from a cardboard box. The nurse took Jack on one side, explaining that the doctor was already with Nancy, and he would come and talk to Jack as soon as he had finished examining her.

'I'm not a relative,' Jack explained, 'just an old friend. As far as I know she has no relatives. In fact, she only moved to this area about three years ago.'

He saw the nurse's shoulders sink slightly. Her uniform stretched tightly across her chest, bearing the signs of perspiration. Her name badge announced she was Nurse Flora McDonald. Jack started to make a friendly comment, but stopped when he became aware of her weariness, and the need to concentrate on what was now a slightly more complicated case.

'So no next of kin, you think? Do you know her address, age, a neighbour who can perhaps help?'

'I know her address, but even she didn't know her exact age. I guess she must be in her late seventies or early eighties. I think her doctor is Dr Walton at Allestree.'

Nurse Flora's spirits visibly lifted as she started to fill in the details on her form. 'We have her handbag, which just contains house keys and a purse,' she said, 'but unfortunately we can't pass those over to you as you are not a relative.'

'Well, someone needs the keys to see to her dog,' Jack replied. 'It's a scorcher today, so I expect that's why she left him at home. He'll need water.'

As she left, asking Jack to wait, his mobile rang. *Shit*, he thought, *I haven't phoned Mary.*

'Hello, is that Jack?' the caller asked.

'Yes, speaking,' whispered Jack, trying to moderate his voice so as not to annoy the others in the waiting room. 'I guess that's Mavis from the Cut Above?'

'Oh thank goodness,' Mavis replied. 'We've been worried about you, Jack, you're never late. Is everything all right?'

'Yes fine, I had a bit of a problem with the car, is Mary still there?'

He could imagine Mary standing at the reception desk, her beautifully crafted blow-dried hair smelling of hairspray. Mary had what she described as 'baby-fine hair', which each Saturday morning Mavis shampooed and teased into a curly bob. The colour was touched up monthly, and every three months it was subjected to a cut and perm.

Since she had retired, or 'taken early retirement' as Mary preferred to phrase it, the Saturday morning ritual was for Jack to drive her to the Cut Above. He would then forage for the shopping at Dennison's, returning two hours later to collect her. Then they would normally go and have lunch with their daughter Sheila and her family.

Mary had been a client since Mavis had taken over the hairdressing business from her mother twenty years ago. The salon, as Mavis like to refer to it, stood in a line of uninspiring shops built in the early sixties on the edge of a large housing estate. Only the Cut Above and the fish and chip shop remained of the several family businesses that used to sell groceries, hardware and haberdashery. Over the years they had been replaced by a pound shop, a betting establishment and a rather desperate-looking charity shop that was only open on the whim of its elderly volunteers.

In the past there had always been plenty of good-natured banter when Jack went to pick Mary up. She scathingly accused him of winding them up when he teased the gaggle of Mavis's ladies and staff about their devotion to the various television soaps and talent shows they enjoyed.

Whilst he had a great deal of affection for the salon, he always felt that it was trying to be something it wasn't. Most years it had a little makeover, new mirrors perhaps, dried flowers, and a much-discussed change in products. The turnover in staff was predictable. The young fat ones stayed, the young slim attractive ones left after completing their apprenticeship. But it served a purpose, Jack acknowledged, as useful as any social service. The elderly felt comfortable under the old-fashioned dryers, and for an hour or more the regulars could enjoy the camaraderie that Mavis generously dispensed.

'He's a bit posh is your Jack,' Mavis would say to Mary, as she berated him when he feigned to know who had won *The X Factor* or the names of the contestants for *Strictly Come Dancing*. But recently as they left the salon and walked towards the car, the silence between him and Mary had intensified. A moment before, they were engaged in cheery goodbyes, then as they stepped outside Mary's unspoken displeasure engulfed them. One Saturday he had just sat in the car waiting for her to emerge. He had expected a rebuke, but instead she remained silent as they drove to their daughter's.

'Your hair looks nice,' Jack had ventured, desperate to pierce the balloon of discontent that constantly seemed to divide them.

'Does it?' was her curt reply as she turned away from him and looked out of the window for the rest of the journey.

His mobile went silent for a moment and Jack could sense his wife's reluctance to take the phone from Mavis and speak to him. As he expected, Mavis came back on the line, and this time her voice sounded a little hesitant.

'She says that she'll take a taxi to Sheila's and see you there.'

'That's fine, Mavis,' Jack replied, 'but please tell her it's probably going to take some time to get the car sorted, but I'll phone her later at Sheila's.'

There was more hesitation, and then Mavis's voice again.

'Ok Jack, she says that's ok. Take care my luv,' she added before the call ended.

The young man in his beanie hat leapt out of his chair again, punching the air and shouting, 'Fuck, fuck you!'

'Why does he do that?' Jack enquired to Nurse Flora who had just come to take him to Nancy.

'I don't know. Quieten down, Lee, you're disturbing everyone, and it's not nice for the toddler.' As they left the waiting room, she explained to Jack, 'He's a bit of a regular. He's harmless, and not on drugs, possibly autistic. We let him stay for an hour or more if we aren't too busy, then give him a cup of tea and a Kit-Kat and off he goes. Breaking the rules a bit, but I know his mum, she's got her hands full with several other kids so it's something of a break for her. You'd be surprised how polite he is, always comes up to the desk to thank us for his tea. But God knows why he shouts out like that.'

As they entered Nancy's room, she explained that the doctor had had to rush off, but he thought it had been a stroke aggravated by a weak heart.

'We'll take her to the ward shortly and they will probably do some more tests, but you can stay with her now if you want. Would you like a cup of tea?' she enquired. 'We're just making one. You can have the other half of Lee's Kit-Kat.'

'I'd love one. And thank you.'

They both laughed as Jack pulled the only chair in the room closer to the bed so he could touch Nancy. She looked peaceful, and her breathing was even. One hand had a drip attached so he moved the chair to the other side of the bed to more easily hold her free hand, which rested on a neatly folded sheet. The room was cool; the two windows which looked out on to the back of the hospital were open. Jack was surprised to see a small park with a variety of old trees, some of whose branches swept the grass. A little girl set loose from her pushchair ran around one of the ageing trees shouting and laughing, as a young woman sat on a bench watching her.

The room was small, clean and almost completely devoid of any kind of decoration except for a framed picture of a group of small children fishing amongst the rocks at the seaside. Nancy was dressed in a white cotton gown with the emblem of the hospital machine-stitched across the front.

Jack spoke softly. 'I'm here, Nancy, you just relax, darling.' A deep sadness swept through his body. Surprising even himself, he whispered, 'Never stopped loving you, Nancy, you know that.'

It was only recently that they had been reunited after forty years, but it was as if nothing had changed. His love for her remained, as he knew hers did for him.

'You concentrate on getting better. No dying on me, Nancy,' he implored, gently squeezing her hand. 'I've got all those raspberries in the allotment still to pick, and you did promise to make jam.'

There was no response, although her head did move slightly, but her eyes remained closed.

'Your hair looks lovely as usual,' he continued, twisting one of the curls between his fingers.

Nancy had always had a love-hate relationship with her hair. When he first knew her, she had devoted a great deal of time trying to tame the mane of light brown pre-Raphaelite curls into a respectable ponytail, or an elegant French pleat. He in turn would try to release it, insisting that she looked her best when it fell haphazardly onto her shoulders. Now, her hair was a mixture of salt and pepper, but the curls remained defiant. Her face had become rather angelic and chubby, with a web of wrinkles around her eyes. It bore little resemblance to the face Jack remembered from his youth, but the hair remained the same. His Nancy's hair.

He sat quietly holding her hand, sipping the tea and eating two fingers of the Kit-Kat that Nurse Flora had quietly left by his side. He had never met Seamus, Nancy's partner of many years. Nancy had eventually found contentment with him, and judging from the several photographs of them together on her desk, theirs had obviously been a happy partnership.

'He's sitting on a cloud waiting for me,' Nancy had once remarked, 'smoking his pipe. He had your sense of humour, Jack,' she had confided.

'How in heaven's name can you remember what my sense of humour was like, forty years ago?'

'Well I couldn't,' she had replied, 'until we met again and then it came back to me in a flash. You were always ironic, a bit naughty, different to the rest of the crowd.'

The sound of the door opening broke through Jack's memories.

'We'd like to move her now,' Nurse Flora explained, 'and your friend Charlie is waiting for you in the car park. I've checked and if you have a problem with the dog the police will help.'

'I'll try and contact her neighbour,' Jack replied. 'It's so hot she probably left the dog in the garden.'

He rose, and bending forward he nuzzled his face in Nancy's hair and murmured, 'I'll be back soon, luv.'

As he walked down the corridor to the exit, stopping to help a young man battling with his drip as he tried to use the vending machine, he heard the nurse calling, 'Mr French, Mr French!'

He ran back along the corridor. 'It's ok,' Nurse Flora said, 'but she became very agitated when you left.'

They entered the room. Nancy's eyes were rolling, and beads of moisture had collected on her top lip.

Nurse Flora gently wiped away the moisture. 'She kept saying something like – well, it sounded like "Take care of…" but I couldn't quite understand the rest.'

'I think I know what she said,' Jack replied, taking Nancy's hand to his lips and kissing her fingertips. 'Were you saying – take care of Nimble, is that it, Nancy?'

Her eyelids gently flickered, but her hand gripped his firmly for a second.

'Of course, Nancy, goes without saying,' he said kissing the tips of her fingers again. 'Of course, you know I will always take care of Nimble.'

Nancy opened her eyes for a second, their gazes met and a faint smile swept across her face. He replaced her hand on the bed covers, remaining for a minute to reassure himself her breathing was even.

'Who's Nimble?' enquired Nurse Flora.

'He's the dog,' he chuckled, content that she would understand, and they could both laugh together in the shared friendship that they had effortlessly slipped into during the sleepy summer afternoon.

As he walked towards the car park, he was aware that his prickly pears were also suffering from the heat and beginning to leach through the brown paper bag. He sensed a kind of sadness coming from the vehicles in the half-filled hospital car park, as if like him they were patiently waiting for the inevitability of some life-changing event.

While he scanned the area for Charlie, a ripple of memories from the past interrupted his thoughts of the present. His father, also named Jack, young, not even thirty, tall and proud as they walked home from their allotment, laughing as he had begged him to relate for the umpteenth time his adventures during the War.

'The War's over, Jack. You remember, young man, you have to live for what's happening now. Don't look back, look forward.'

He'd only been about eight, but strangely those words had lodged themselves in his memory, as did the feel of his small hand clasped in his father's as they ran down the steep hill that led from the allotment to the village where they lived.

As he saw Charlie approaching, he was touched by his unwavering kindness.

'I've parked on the road,' he shouted cheerily. 'Can't be doing with these newfangled parking meters, doubt we'll get a ticket on a day like today.'

CHAPTER TWO

---

*There are times when I doubt everything. When I regret
everything you've taken from me, everything I've given you,
and the waste of all the time I've spent on us.*

– DAVID LEVITHAN, *THE LOVER'S DICTIONARY*

Jack was in the shower, so he didn't hear the phone ring. He hadn't really spoken to Mary about the previous day, relieved she had accepted his excuse about having problems with the car. He gently turned the heat up as the water cascaded over him, enjoying a feeling of calm as it soothed his body.

Deep inside, he had to admit that he didn't expect Nancy to pull through. He'd phoned the hospital the previous night and had received a guarded reply that she was comfortable.

Over the intervening years the few photographs of Nancy and him together had disappeared, not for malicious reasons, but just lost in the jumble of photographs of family life. Nowadays, he thought, as he towelled himself dry with a large blue bath towel, you didn't have the same problem; technology did it all for you. Nancy's unexpected exit from his life had, for a while, consumed him with an agonising grief, from which he'd thought he would never recover. But as time had passed, the pain had faded.

As he tidied the bathroom to leave it immaculate for Mary, he remembered a snap of Nancy he had carried in his wallet for many years. He'd forgotten about it until his mother had given him a new wallet for his birthday, not long before she died. He discovered the photograph in the old one, tucked behind a couple of supermarket loyalty cards and a dilapidated National Insurance Certificate. The photograph was yellow and dog-eared, but charged with memories.

He and Nancy had stayed in Derbyshire for a week; part holiday and part escape from the nightmare of Bill. It was the only real holiday they had ever had together. A farm that did bed and breakfast tucked away in a peaceful idyllic spot in the Derbyshire Dales, not too far from Ashbourne Cottage Hospital where he had been born. The young couple who owned the farm had four children, and an assortment of dogs, cats, ponies and farm animals. It was the start of the sixties and they were at the forefront of being 'green' before it became fashionable. The large Aga that graced their kitchen was constantly in use, with a kettle on the hob wheezing in the background.

Like his father, Jack's passion was photography, and he had just treated himself to a new camera, prompting Nancy to remark that perhaps he saw himself as an up-and-coming David Bailey. She hated to pose, but he caught her off guard as she helped the family to pick apples. She was wearing a simple cotton blouse and shorts, which showed off her long slim legs and, as usual, her hair was a mass of unruly curls. Perched at the top of the ladder, she hadn't seen him, but when she did, she had reached into her basket and aimed an apple skilfully at his head.

When he had changed everything over to his new wallet, he'd initially thrown the photo away, but then retrieved it, unable to let go of the bittersweet legacy of their relationship that had lasted through the years. He wished now that he had taken a 'selfie' of himself and Nancy last week when they were in the allotment. He'd toyed with the idea, but then rather despised himself as he had always maintained 'selfies' were rather pointless. Nancy would certainly have been up for it. Perhaps if she was feeling better, he could take one at the hospital.

He finished towelling himself dry, grateful for the neat pile of underwear left on his bed. He paused for a moment, considering what to wear. Something reasonably smart, he decided, if he was going to the hospital.

Regardless of the fact that he felt refreshed by the shower, he continued to be annoyed with himself for not explaining to Mary months ago about accidentally bumping into Nancy in the supermarket. At eighty-two, and an interval of forty-odd years, his former girlfriend could hardly be seen as a threat, and yet something had stopped him. Despite all his efforts, life with Mary had become suffused with a veiled unpleasantness that was hard to penetrate. He acknowledged that he preferred an easy life, rather than confronting her with anything that might cause conflict.

As he left his bedroom, he could hear her talking on the telephone.

'It's the Royal Infirmary,' she told him as he came down the stairs. 'She's dead.' She passed him the phone.

The voice at the other end sounded startled. 'Hello, Mr French, we are very sorry. I was just explaining to your wife. Miss Dupray died earlier this morning. It was very peaceful. She never regained consciousness after you left.'

'I was just on my way,' he replied anxiously, like a child making an excuse for being late. Then he hesitated as memories began to rise, not of the Nancy he had left in the hospital, but the Nancy of his youth: beautiful, vibrant, full of life. In the last few years it had become a joy having her living close by again. In spite of the intervening years, he acknowledged that she had always remained in his life. The elusive shadow, sometimes present, sometimes not.

'Well, there's no urgency,' the nurse continued, 'but if you could come in later to help with the details, that would be very useful.'

Grief began to seep through his body with the realisation that she had finally left him for ever. 'I'm so sorry,' he mumbled, half to himself. Then more robustly he replied, 'I'll be in shortly. Was it a stroke?'

'No,' the nurse replied, 'her heart just gave out. There was nothing we could do. I was there. Nurse Flora told me to talk about Jack and her dog. I didn't know his name, but I kept on telling her Jack would take care of him. I hope that was right.'

'It's Nimble. And yes, you were right, I'll take care of him. I'll see you in about an hour, and thank you again.'

'So, what was all that about?' Mary demanded as he put the phone down. 'When did Nancy Dupray come back into your life?'

Jack walked into the kitchen and put the kettle on. 'Let's have a cup of tea in the garden,' he suggested, 'and I'll explain.'

He made the tea, pausing for a second to decide whether to use mugs or cups and saucers. Smiling inwardly, he chose cups and saucers, in homage to his mother. Then, arranging them on a tray with a plate of biscuits, he walked outside and placed it on the garden table.

'It was nearly three years ago. I literally bumped into her in the supermarket. I didn't recognise her at first. She is – was – coming up for seventy-seven then.'

Mary did not look at him but directed her gaze towards the roses that tumbled over their neighbour's fence. She remained silent.

'Hand on heart, I tried to avoid her. But Betty and Brian had also met her by accident just before Christmas. She'd bought a house in Allestree, not far from them. Well, you know what Betty's like. They'd taken her under their wing straight away. Betty tore me off a strip afterwards for being offhand. It was a shock. I'd never have recognised her, and I was surprised she recognised me.'

He knew he sounded as if he was rambling, and stopped for a moment to bend down to stroke their neighbour's cat. There was something comforting about its presence as it rubbed its coat against his legs.

'After a while I bumped into her again and we had a coffee. She told me her partner had died, that she'd had a couple of hip operations, the usual stuff. I didn't tell you because I didn't want to upset you, and I think Betty and Brian felt the same.'

He poured the tea, his hand hovering over the sugar as he tried to decide whether sugar was something Mary had given up for the umpteenth time. Unsure, he cautiously edged the sugar bowl in her direction. There was so much more he wanted to say, an acre of missed opportunities stretching between them. Surely none of it mattered now that Nancy was dead.

With some difficulty, Mary rose from her garden chair. 'Be honest, Jack, you always loved her, didn't you?' She didn't wait for a reply as the words hung awkwardly in the air; it had been a statement, not a question. She returned to the house leaving her tea untouched.

Jack sipped his tea, inhaling the delicate fragrance of the sweet peas as they absorbed the warmth of the morning sun. They were getting to be past their best. Leaving his tea, he went into his shed to find some scissors, then, returning, he cut a small bunch to give to Mary. His father had always grown sweet peas for his mother, and he had continued the tradition after Mary had remarked how much she liked them. Before his mother had died, he had made sure that they both received regular bunches during the summer, often teasing them that the pale silk-like colours of the blooms reminded him of ladies' silk underwear.

He returned the scissors to the shed, considering that it might be a good place to house Nancy's dog for the time being. Mary loathed dogs, and could barely tolerate cats, but he had made a promise. He walked back to the house and through the kitchen into the lounge. He put the flowers in a vase on the coffee table, with the rest of the sweet peas he'd picked the day before, next to the fruit bowl with the three prickly pears.

Mary watched him as he arranged the flowers. Then, as he finished, she stood before him. Her voice was soft but tight with emotion as she declared, 'She was a whore, you know. A whore, Jack. Everyone knew, everyone talked about her. It might be forty years ago, but I remember she even lost her job because she was carrying on with black men, you know she did. Don't forget, I was there.'

He stood for a moment, unsure of how to respond. 'How could you, Mary, you should be ashamed of yourself. Good God, they were Nancy's friends, their wives and kids too.' He felt weary but continued. 'I'll tell you about Nancy, if you'll let me, or you can ask Betty.'

'I can't believe Betty took up with that woman behind my back,' Mary spat, her voice rising from its former softness towards a shrill scream. She drew her face close to his, exuding her familiar odour of deodorant and hairspray. 'She was a whore, Jack. You were a fool. Or did you pay for what you got?'

Jack stood rigid, for a second startled. Mary didn't do passion, hardly even anger. He reached out and took her gently by the shoulders.

'You're wrong, Mary. She was a lovely, kind, compassionate woman and in old age she was lonely.'

Mary's body tightened, and bringing her face even closer to his she hissed, 'She was a whore Jack, and liked a bit of black, whatever you say.'

Jack had never hit Mary, even though her words could hurt as sharply as any blow. But as she hissed in his face, he felt a sudden revulsion and pushed her away. It wasn't violent, barely enough to move her shoulders, but as she stepped away her leg caught the edge of the coffee table. She half turned to save herself from falling, but lost her balance and fell over the table, breaking one of its spindly legs. The vase of sweet peas overturned, spilling water and flowers over the carpet, together with the fruit bowl, sending the three prickly pears rolling clumsily under the sofa. The side of the sofa broke her fall, but she hit her head on the wall behind.

Alarmed, Jack stepped towards her, offering her his hand. 'Come on, Mary, up you get.'

'Don't touch me,' she cried. 'Get out, get out!'

Jack looked at her. 'Come on, Mary, don't be so silly.' He offered her his hand again.

She straightened up a little, then shouted at him again, 'Don't you dare touch me!'

He stood for a moment, shocked by her anger. 'I won't,' he replied, standing back. 'Don't worry, Mary, I haven't wanted to touch you for years. You actually disgust me, full of your petty-minded prejudices, jealous over an eighty-year-old ex-girlfriend. You're just like your father. He thought the world revolved around him. Well, it doesn't, Mary, believe me, it doesn't.'

With that he ran upstairs to his room. They hadn't shared a room for years, so it was easy to gather a few clothes into a bag before returning downstairs. Mary had gone down to the far end of the garden and was standing with her back to the kitchen window. Yet again, that familiar feeling of compassion for her swept through him, but then his anger returned. She was her own worst enemy, he thought.

He left the house, slamming the door with so much force that when he looked back, he could see a tiny crack working its way down the glass.

The car was stiflingly hot as he backed it out of the drive. He opened the windows, but he was aware that his hands were shaking. For a minute he thought he was going to faint. He turned the ignition off and lowered his head for a minute until he felt himself recover. He sat for a moment. His familiar surroundings felt unreal. He twisted around to see if he could see Mary, but only the neighbour's cat looked curiously at him as it sat defiantly on the mat by the front door. He started the car again and set off down the road.

He turned into the housing estate, despising its delusions of grandeur, as he had done since they had moved there. Brick pillars, false porticos, stone gateposts without gates, all jostling with the plague of green plastic wheelie bins standing to attention on every drive. The whole place looked self-conscious, with its continuous stream of 'For Sale' boards from Raj Estates, Frank Innes and the rest, all vying to sell their clients the standard middle-class dream.

His faintness had disappeared, to be replaced by a sudden euphoria. He relished the fresh air from the open windows as he drove out of the estate and towards the hospital.

'She wasn't with us long,' remarked the nurse as he led Jack down the hospital corridor to the door marked 'Mortuary'. 'Sad really, but at least it was quick and peaceful, and not a bad innings. My mum died six months ago, she was eighty-two, and hers was quick as well, a bit of a blessing when it's like that.'

Jack hadn't been sure he wanted to see Nancy, but after signing various forms and taking possession of her handbag, it seemed impolite just to leave. He was relieved to be met by the young man with dreadlocks, who assured him that if he wanted to see her it was no trouble.

'She looks…' He paused, as if to weigh up Jack's likely response. 'She looks like an angel. It's her hair, very beautiful and unusual for a lady of her age.'

'Well, you obviously know about hair,' Jack countered, gesturing to his remarkable hairdo.

'Well, kind of,' he chuckled, 'I've been growing mine since I was a kid. At first it was a kind of black statement. School hated it but my mum said if I wanted it, there was no way she was going to have it cut. But now I'm frightened to cut it off, bit like Samson, my wife reckons I'd lose all my strength. They call me Marley here at the hospital because of the locks.'

Jack was about to ask him his real name, but he stopped abruptly before opening the mortuary door.

'Just wait a tick; I won't be long getting her ready. I'm going to wheel her into the little Chapel of Rest next door.'

He was right, Jack thought, she did look like an angel in a white shroud, her hair illuminated by a strip light above her head. He bent and kissed her cold fingers.

'You still look wonderful, Nancy. And would you believe it, even in death they're still talking about your hair. Rest in peace, my love. Nimble and I will take care of one another.'

He started to leave, but then turned back. With the scissors on his pen-knife, he snipped a piece of her hair and wrapped it in his handkerchief.

'I've taken a lock of her hair,' he confessed to the nurse as they returned to reception. 'A bit sentimental and against the rules, I'm sure.'

'No problem man, sentimental is good, and there aren't any rules in death. I once went back to the Chapel of Rest and found that a relative had put a fag in the deceased's mouth. Only problem was that it was alight.'

Jack chuckled.

'You know,' the nurse continued, 'I think my mam and dad knew Miss Dupray, that's if she used to live around here years ago. I was little, but my mam had a special friend we called Auntie Nancy. She was a white lady and I can remember they used to say she had a French name. Dad's almost ninety but when I mentioned her to him last night, the first thing he said was, "Did she have curly hair?"'

'Is your dad called Louis?' Jack asked in surprise. 'Because if he is, I remember him and your mum – and you, come to think of it. I only knew them briefly. Don't you have a brother, Amos, and a sister? I can't remember her name.'

'Lizzy, and I'm Josh, I'm Josh!' he cried, embracing Jack in delight. 'Amos is a doctor in Jamaica and Lizzy still lives in Derby. Small world, man, Dad will be chuffed. He said Miss Dupray disappeared and they all lost touch. Shame Mum's not still about.'

For a second Jack felt guilty. After Nancy had disappeared he'd contacted them to find out if they knew where she was, but that had been all.

'Does your dad still live in the same house, was it Carlton Street?' he asked.

'Yeah man, they bought it in the end. It was tough for them at first, but at least there was none of the old Rachman stuff around here. Mum was a real mover and shaker, she worked as a social worker for years, and ran the local residents' association. She didn't take shit from anyone. Loads of people at her funeral, even the Mayor came.'

'Well, you tell your dad Jack and Nancy found each other. You tell him it all worked out well in the end.'

The heat was now unbearable, and Jack sat for a moment in his car with both the windows and door open. Everything including the sky looked bleached by two weeks of constant heat. He wanted to cry, to release the baggage of emotions he had kept tucked away for years. But more than that, he wanted to be held, to be comforted like a child. If Nancy had been sitting beside him, she would have sensed his mood and held his hand, suggesting they had a cup of tea. Two teas, he thought, one breakfast tea and an Earl Grey for the lady.

He started the car and picked his way through the traffic towards Nancy's house and Nimble. The calmness that had embraced him as he bid farewell to her in the Chapel of Rest began to disperse, to be replaced by a feeling of rage and indignation. He reached for the radio in the hope of calming his nerves, but all Classic FM could offer was a selection of anodyne melodies, which only exacerbated his mood.

His relationship with Mary in the last few years had deteriorated, but not for one minute had he thought that she still bore a grudge against Nancy. To suggest she took money for sexual favours was ludicrous.

He fumed as he felt more memories returning. Mary had deliberately or otherwise got everything wrong about Nancy and his time with her. It hadn't been like that at all.

CHAPTER THREE

I'm singin' in the rain, just singin' in the rain
What a glorious feeling, I'm happy again

– 'SINGIN' IN THE RAIN', FROM *SINGIN' IN THE RAIN*

DERBY, 1968

Nancy hadn't seen Jack at first. Her head was tucked into her umbrella. The classic April shower picture, head down, battling into the wind. With her free hand she clutched her bright yellow beret. In one erratic gust, the wind snatched the umbrella violently from her. At first it tossed it high into the air, and then as the gale dropped slightly, it began cartwheeling down the road.

Jack, walking towards Nancy, had watched this with amusement. Turning, he followed the errant umbrella, eventually bringing it to a halt when the wind subsided for a moment. Nancy ran towards him, but as the rain slashed horizontally across them, Jack guided her into a shop doorway where they could shelter. The yellow beret had held firm, but it was so wet that Nancy removed it and then, laughing, started to wring it out.

'I'm afraid it didn't make it,' said Jack, attempting to twist the umbrella back into shape.

'Thank you anyway,' Nancy replied, 'it was most gallant of you.'

He hadn't seen Nancy for a while. Every Friday lunchtime Rolls-Royce, the engineering company on Nightingale Road where he was employed as a trainee draughtsman, opened up one of the big reception rooms near to the canteen so that all their younger employees could get together. With only the possibility of buying coffee or a soft drink, it hadn't been very popular, until someone had had the bright idea of setting up a record player and two impressive speakers. There wasn't a lot of choice along Nightingale Road for entertainment during the lunch hour. There was one pub, although officially if you were an apprentice, you weren't allowed to go there.

Until recently Nancy had been a regular at the gatherings, occasionally dancing, but usually standing with a group of fellow secretaries. There was something about her, the way she appeared to distance herself from the crowd, and he had never plucked up the courage to approach her.

'You want to keep your eyes off that one,' Brian had told Jack, 'she's got form.'

Jack had gone to school with Brian. They'd both opted for apprenticeships rather than university. They had an easy relationship, forged when Jack's father had died; Brian's family had offered Jack a place where he could escape from the grief that had engulfed his own home.

'What exactly do you mean by form?' Jack asked.

'In fact more than form, she's not averse to a bit of black, I'm told, besides countless affairs. Someone says you pay for what you get.'

Jack didn't even reply. Ridiculous, he thought. Another one of Brian's many fantasies. He didn't even bother to ask later about Nancy, knowing that if he had done, Brian would have spun one of his entertaining stories laden with gossip and hearsay.

He felt he knew instinctively that there was something special about Nancy. She was different. Her hair was a mass of unruly curls, similar to the women painted by the Pre-Raphaelites at the turn of the century. It was usually tamed into a ponytail or French pleat, but he sensed it wanted to break free. There was no evidence of makeup, apart from a dull red lipstick. Classic clothes: a pencil-slim skirt, wool twinset, a silk blouse with a touch of lace. She was tall and elegant, but with an air of vulnerability that Jack found disturbingly erotic.

Manipulated by Brian's anxiety that his friend was still a virgin at twenty-two, Jack had somewhat unwillingly lost his virginity to Brian's girlfriend's best friend. A delightful but clingy young woman, he'd spent the following few weeks trying to satisfy her constant demands for attention, until, confident that she wasn't pregnant, he'd brought the whole affair to a clumsy conclusion by declaring himself in love with someone else. He'd been truly mortified by her heartbroken response, but relieved and wiser when he encountered her with another young man only a few days later.

The whole area revolved around the engineering works. Dreary red-brick offices ran the length of one side of the road, housing most of the draughtsmen and tracers. Further along there was a series of large factory workshops that made small components for aeroplane engines, with the foundry at the far end. On the other side was a far more impressive building, the Head Office, with the name 'Rolls-Royce' emblazoned in large gold letters high above the entrance.

Behind this imposing façade was the legendary Marble Hall, reminiscent of a stately home, with stairs on either side leading up to an enormous stained-glass window. The window was very stylised, portraying a young and classically handsome pilot standing on the three-bladed propeller of a Merlin engine, with rows of grey factory buildings beneath his feet. In this hallowed environment the Chairman, chief engineers and directors of the Company had their wood-panelled offices.

Outside, everything was grimy, with the constant smell of grease and metal filings. During the week, there was the continual banging and whining of machines. But this was Saturday and the whole area seemed to be resting, with only a low hum from the factories.

'You probably don't remember me, but I used to see you at the Friday lunchtime get-together,' Jack shouted over the wind. It continued to drive the rain relentlessly, and they turned their backs against it as they stood in the shop doorway.

'I don't work at Rolls-Royce any more – long story,' she yelled back. 'Thank you again,' she added, preparing to launch herself into the storm. He gently stopped her.

'So where do you work now?' he asked. He knew Brian would have had a great quip or line in a situation like this, but he just felt deflated as he sensed her eagerness to escape.

'I work at the pie shop.' She smiled, waiting for his response.

'Do you make the pies?' he replied, realising immediately how ridiculous this sounded.

But she was laughing, and for a split second, she rested her hand against his chest. Then, continuing to laugh, she stepped out into the rain, shouting as she ran down the road, 'You mean like Sweeney Todd?'

He stood in the shop entrance for several minutes. A bedraggled dog joined him, sitting close to his leg.

'I am a prat,' Jack said out loud, feeling a delayed flash of embarrassment sweep over him, 'a stupid prat!'

The dog looked up and Jack bent down to stroke him. He was a terrier with a wonky eye and half an ear.

'What would you do, mate?' he enquired of the dog. Sensing it had been asked a question, it looked up, hesitated as if considering its reply, and then, braving the rain, it tripped quickly down the road in the same direction as Nancy.

'Hmmmm, follow her, you think? Could be a plan,' Jack mused. He watched it for a minute, before it disappeared down an alley between the terraced houses.

The wind caught the damaged umbrella again. It tumbled down the road, snagging itself eventually in a metal grid, where it rested looking somewhat forlorn. A few cars passed by, creating slicks of black water along the pavement. Jack pulled his collar up, bracing himself against the rain, and headed towards the Drawing Office in the opposite direction to Nancy.

A bank of warm air hit him as he walked into the cloakroom. It always reminded him of being back at school. Rows of coat stands, a comforting smell of sweat, mingled with steam pudding and stale cigarette smoke. A bouquet of assorted umbrellas was bunched in the far corner. Where normally sixty-odd coats hung, the Saturday workforce looked to amount to fewer than a dozen. He could spot that Brian was in, as his much-admired Gannex raincoat still dripped unceremoniously on the floor.

The Drawing Office was vast, forty or more drawing boards in regimented lines, with a balcony above on three sides which gave space for several more drawing boards and an opportunity for the senior draughtsmen to observe their domain below. Jack walked down the centre aisle, approaching Brian who was leaning over his board.

'See the Gannex didn't let you down,' he said.

The Gannex had been a standing joke for a couple of months amongst the group of fellow draughtsmen he and Brian went around with. 'Who wants to look like bloody Harold Wilson?' they had remarked, after the Prime Minister had taken to wearing the same raincoat in support of British products. But Brian saw himself as something of a follower of fashion and enjoyed the notoriety. They were all used to this kind of good-natured humour, allowing it to sustain them through their working days and the Friday 'boys' nights out', a ritual Jack wasn't quite sure he really enjoyed, but Brian was passionate about.

'It's more about making a stand against the girls,' Brian explained, 'show them who wears the trousers.'

Occasionally, much to Brian's disgust, one of their girlfriends would arrive and join the group, and Brian would be forced to take her offending partner outside and explain, 'It's not on. If we start bringing girlfriends, they'll have the upper hand straight away. My Betty wouldn't dream of joining us.'

But today, Jack could see immediately that Brian was not his usual self. During the previous week of constant rain, he had kept everyone amused with his 'Singin' in the Rain' routine, coyly peering around the rows of boards with his black umbrella. By Friday all the draughtsmen, and even Wendy the office girl, were word perfect. Mary, one of the secretaries, being rather shy, took a little persuading, but when Brian pointed out that the senior engineer was also singing, she relaxed and joined in with the rest. Brian was well-liked, and an excellent draughtsman who, in Jack's opinion, was destined for promotion. Jack had decided he was going to share his Nancy encounter with him, until he saw his face.

'My God, what's up, Brian?' he asked. 'You look like you've seen a ghost.'

Brian stepped back from his board, checking from right to left for other draughtsmen who might hear their conversation. 'It's Betty, she's pregnant. Well, she's three weeks over.'

'Bloody hell, Brian, I thought you were the one that was super careful.' He was surprised, when he looked at Brian more closely, to see that he had quite clearly been crying.

'Bloody nightmare,' Brian said, 'she'd never said a thing until last night. She met me out of the pub really upset. Fuck me, Jack. I don't know what to do.'

Jack hesitated. Physical contact was not their style, but his time he put his arm firmly around Brian. 'More to the point, what does she want to do?'

'She says I haven't got to marry her, but she'll have the baby. Like that frigging *Alfie* film with Michael Caine, everyone's shit scared of an abortion.'

'Come on,' Jack replied, 'you wouldn't let her do that, you know you wouldn't. She has every right to be shit scared.'

'Well, if I thought it was safe, I might, but no, you're right.' He lit a cigarette, blowing the smoke expertly into the air.

'Come on,' Jack said, 'you know you can't smoke in here.'

'I don't fucking care,' he replied.

'Well, you're stupid,' argued Jack. 'You know you're in line for promotion, don't spoil it. I can't believe you've cocked it up, pardon the expression. All those man-to-man lectures you gave me. Betty's a lovely girl. Christ, she must be upset.'

Jack was deemed to be picky when it came to girls, but he genuinely liked Betty. She was straightforward and kind, and refrained from taunting him about his lack of girlfriends.

'She is lovely, Brian,' he repeated, 'not common like some of the girls you've worked your way through. Thank your lucky stars it's not one of them. Do her parents know?'

'No, not yet, God knows what her old man is going to say. I don't know what it's fucking all about, Jack. What are we bloody here for? Work, have kids, die? My grandad did that and died in the War. My dad sits glued to the telly every night now he's retired. None of them have moved further than twenty miles from around here, their bloody horizons are nowt bigger than a dinner plate. I like Betty, no, I love her, and she's a great girl.' He stopped, looking directly at Jack as if he had the answer.

'It's a baby,' Jack said, 'a baby, your baby. Anyway, it could be a false alarm.'

Brian perched on his stool. 'Yeah, I know, she says she's been willing it to start, even secretly finished off half a bottle of gin one night. Christ, she never said a thing to me.'

'Is the canteen open?' Jack asked. 'I'll get you a cup of tea.'

'Yes, B block's open,' Brian replied, stamping his cigarette out, then picking the butt off the floor and tossing it into the waste bin. 'Can you get us some chocolate as well, a Mars Bar, something like that, I need the sugar.'

'You need a bloody kick up your backside,' replied Jack, as he headed for the canteen.

When he returned, Brian was calmer. Jack felt there really wasn't any more he could say, so in order to lighten the situation, he embarked on relating his meeting with Nancy, embroidering the story a little in an attempt to raise a smile out of his friend.

'Can you imagine my chat up line?' he asked when he'd finished. '"Do you make the pies?"'

Brian laughed, patting his friend on the back.

'She is beautiful though,' Brian replied wistfully, 'but you have to be careful of the brother, or half-brother, I'm not sure what relation he is to her. But you know him? Big guy from the Foundry, he works in Germany half the time. His name is Bill, Betty's dad knows him, says he's a right scheming bastard.'

'Oh, Nancy and Bill,' Jack remarked, enjoying the Dickensian reference. 'Gets more interesting. I wonder why she left Rolls-Royce. She worked as one of the secretaries in the Marble Hall, didn't she?'

'Yes,' replied Brian, 'one of the posh dollies. I heard she was sacked. But why don't you buy her a new umbrella, then you can ask her?'

'Why don't you buy Betty a big bunch of flowers, not crappy ones from the corner shop, but the proper job from the market hall,' Jack countered.

'Well, if I turned up at her place with a bouquet that would certainly let the cat out of the bag.'

'Well, yes, you could be right,' Jack admitted, 'although they've got to know sometime. How about two bunches, one for her mum as well.'

'Fine bloody friend you are,' Brian replied.

Jack patted him gently on the back. 'Eat your Mars Bar. It helps you work, rest and play.'

Buses from Nightingale Road were frequent during the week, but on Saturday only the trolley bus ran. Jack rarely caught it as his preferred mode of transport was a Triumph motorbike. When he bought it, his mother had struck up a deal that he didn't ride it in bad weather. However, he had managed to get through the winter without too much trouble, even though from where he lived in Belper to Derby was twenty-two miles. But the unending wind and rain had eventually taken its toll, and this morning he had opted for the bus into Derby, followed by the dreary trolley bus to the factory. The local newspaper had announced the previous year that the trolley system would be terminated very soon, to be replaced by a new fleet of buses adopting the same routes. But for now the trolleys still continued in operation, their overhead lines sparking and spitting at each junction.

Looking through the steamed-up windows he had to congratulate Brian for his grand idea, an umbrella, the perfect present. He would deliver it to the pie shop on Monday in order to facilitate a brief chat. He realised their recent conversation had not been under ideal circumstances, but even so he still sensed a kind of reserve, the vulnerability he'd observed at the Friday get-togethers. She wouldn't reject his gift, he was sure, although she might of course refuse his invitation to have a drink. 'Faint heart never won fair lady,' he mused.

He'd learned to like shopping after his father had died. He and his mother would create special things to do in order to dispel the grief that hovered over them in the first few years. Shopping was one of them. A small item such as an electrical appliance or a new set of towels would be given the status of a project. So searching for an umbrella for Nancy was a pleasure, not a chore.

When he was a boy there had been three department stores in Derby. The one Jack had liked the best, with its old-fashioned money system rattling overhead, had closed down, shortly followed by a family-run business that his mother always frequented when she wanted quality goods. It was now Boots the Chemist, and stood opposite the only department store to have weathered the changes, the Midland Drapery.

Nothing of course compared to shopping in Nottingham, but that involved an hour's journey on the bus each way. When his father was alive, the three of them always went to Nottingham to the annual Goose Fair in November, a gathering of tinkers, gypsies, merry-go-rounds, hot dog stalls, candy floss and dodgy-looking characters selling even dodgier-looking goods. His father had likened it to a complete chapter from a novel by D.H. Lawrence. Elizabeth hated it, and usually arranged to spend the day Christmas shopping, whilst her two men enjoyed the spills and thrills. But the year after his father had died, Elizabeth had unexpectedly said, 'Shall we go to the Goose Fair?'

Jack had said yes, just to please her, despite finding it unimaginable to think about not being there with his dad. On arrival they had wandered around for half an hour before Elizabeth had asked, 'This isn't working, is it, Jack?'

He'd agreed and together they had caught the bus back into the city centre. The bus was crowded, but they managed to get a seat, sitting quietly side by side, distancing themselves from the Goose

Fair revellers. He was barely ten, and the embarrassment of seeing his mother softly crying had a lasting impact on him. Taking her hand he had said, 'Don't cry, Mum, Dad wouldn't want you to cry. We'll have a cup of tea when we get into town. We'll have a flapjack too, Dad's favourite.'

'Never stop talking about him,' his mother had replied.

'Never,' replied Jack, sealing their pledge to always keep his memory alive, with a squeeze of his hand on hers.

But he'd wanted to say the unspoken words, *if I hadn't made Dad go out it might not have happened…*

Worse, a couple of kids at school had taunted him by saying his dad had 'topped himself'. When he had asked his mum what that meant, she had been quite angry, and said that was ridiculous, his dad would never take his own life. He'd wanted to ask how you 'take your own life' but didn't want to upset her, and so he never asked again.

The young assistant in the Midland Drapery explained there had been a run on umbrellas, especially the new collapsible ones. 'But perhaps, sir, I might suggest one from the new Mary Quant range?'

'You might,' Jack replied solemnly.

She replied immediately, 'Are you making fun of me?'

'No, no,' Jack laughed.

'Well, that's what they tell me to say,' she replied, peering out from under the weight of a hairstyle that would have done credit to Marie Antoinette. 'I know it's a laugh,' she continued, 'but it's the best Saturday job I've ever had. They've even kept me on after Christmas. Now, if I was buying a new brolly, I'd buy this one.'

'Is it a Mary Quant?' Jack asked, looking at the pattern of blue and yellow daisies embellishing its white background.

'Of course,' she said. 'Now might I suggest, sir, you buy it, and I parcel it up immediately for you?'

Jack soon discovered that even wrapped, a full-sized umbrella was not an easy thing to disguise. His mother had noticed it straight away, allowing for some light banter between the two of them about who the lady might be.

Monday morning was equally tricky, with several colleagues spotting him with it in the car park. Starting to enjoy the intrigue, he hung it over the side of his drawing board. Then at lunchtime, he marched out of the office with it over his shoulder.

At noon the pie shop already had a queue outside. The choice of pies never varied, meat and potato, steak and kidney or chicken and mushroom; gravy was optional. There was also a selection of fresh sliced bread sandwiches, teetering in huge piles, various cakes usually involving coconut, icing and crystallised cherries, and a small counter devoted to cold cooked meats, black pudding, haslet and sausage rolls. The sign outside announced, 'Cowlishaw's Pie Shop – everything made on the premises to the highest standard'. Usually by half past one they had run out of pies, and by mid-afternoon only a few sticky buns and sausage rolls were left in the window.

Nancy and another woman were serving at the counter, both wearing white nylon overalls piped with blue and emblazoned with a large letter C on the top pocket. The ensemble was completed with a soft white paper cap. Jack stood in the queue watching with interest while Nancy dealt with the customers, mostly men from the adjoining factories, whilst the other assistant, probably Mrs Cowlishaw he guessed, was loud and familiar.

'Meat and potato, Fred, no gravy? There's a luv, if you can manage the right money that would be great.'

Nancy was fast and efficient, only looking up occasionally in response to some remark when it interrupted her concentration. Negotiating carefully so that he was in Nancy's line, Jack reached the counter. He very rarely bought a pie, as whilst they smelt good, the reality was that they were cheaply made, a thick pastry surrounding poor quality meat. He felt nervous, but was pleased she hadn't spied him until she finally looked up waiting for the next order.

'What do you recommend?' he asked.

Her response went from annoyance to confusion and then recognition.

He passed the umbrella over the counter quickly, saying with a laugh, 'It's a gift for another rainy day.'

It would have been awkward not to have accepted the unwieldy package, and Nancy accepted it happily.

'Oh, you shouldn't,' she responded, 'that's really so kind.'

The queue behind was already beginning to sound restless, so buying a little more time, Jack ordered a chicken and mushroom pie, with no gravy.

'A wise choice,' she remarked, slipping it across the counter and whispering, 'it's on the house.'

Responding to her warmth, he found it easy to pose the question, 'Would you like to meet me for a drink one night?'

'Come on, Nancy,' he heard a cry from the middle of the queue, 'he's not that good-looking.'

Not letting the comment faze her, she took the next order for a meat and potato with gravy, whispering as she wrapped it, 'I'd love to. Tonight? The Dolphin, do you know it? It's near the Cathedral, down Sadler-gate.'

'Great,' replied Jack, amazed that it had been so easy. 'Seven thirty?'

'Make it eight,' she replied, 'and not in the main bar, in the back, they usually have a fire.'

Jack left the shop amidst a lot of ribaldry. He felt exhausted, but took some comfort by wrapping his hands around the warm chicken pie she had placed in the brown paper bag for him.

He was early arriving at the pub, but she was already there, the only person sitting in the back room. There was a small bar space, and a fire struggled to get going in the grate nearby. He was surprised to see she was wearing glasses, absorbed in a book. When he approached, she rose immediately, kissing him on either cheek.

'Thank you again for the umbrella,' she said, 'it's far too nice to take out in the rain.'

Startled by the kisses, he regained his composure by asking what she was reading.

'Zola,' she replied, 'very tough and depressing.'

'In French?' he asked in amazement.

'No,' she laughed. 'I only know a smattering of French, but I have to confess I am a Francophile, even though I've only spent a short time there.'

'My dad bailed out over France just before the War ended,' Jack explained. 'When I was nine, he and I went back to stay with the family who had sheltered him.'

'So you like France?' she asked with genuine interest.

His reply was lost as the barman appeared. 'What would you like, ladies and gentlemen, or should I say lady and gentleman?'

'I'd like a glass of red wine,' Nancy volunteered, looking at Jack.

'I'll have one too,' Jack added, 'but don't ask me what kind, so long as it's red and preferably French. That will be fine.'

'I'll see what I can do,' the barman replied.

'I'm sorry, Nancy,' Jack said, aware of using her name for the first time, 'you probably know which red you prefer.'

'You must be joking,' she replied, 'I've no idea. To be honest, I will be surprised if he can come up with any wine, French or otherwise.'

But to their amusement, the barman returned holding a bottle of red. He was a big man who looked as if he was going to get wedged in behind the bar. His Derbyshire accent was delivered in a rather theatrical drawl.

'I've sourced one bottle of red wine in the cellar.' Here he hesitated for maximum effect. 'It's probably there for some special occasion, but as the guv'nor isn't here, I'm offering you the whole bottle for one pound.'

'Please let me pay?' Nancy jumped up.

'Certainly not!' the barman said, coming to Jack's rescue. 'Let your fellow pay. He looks like he can afford it. Never let a lady pay, that's my motto. Well, only for the second round!'

Their conversation together was blissfully easy, unlike anything Jack had experienced before with other girls. Later he tried to analyse it. What was it that made them such comfortable companions? They had many shared interests, but it was more than that. She revealed very little about herself, apart from her time in France, but seemed eager to listen to him.

When he jokingly asked her again about making pies, she batted it back quickly, revealing that her actual job was keeping all the accounts and working her way through a backlog of neglected paperwork. She also asked him not to question her about why she left Rolls-Royce as it was still too painful to explain. All she had to say was that the Cowlishaw family were all delightful. When she had told them that Jack had asked her about making the pies, they had said to tell him that she was head of everything, apart from the pie-making.

As the evening wore on, the snug bar filled up, mainly with elderly couples, often accompanied by their pet dogs. Their corner, however, remained an oasis, until Nancy put her hand on Jack's saying, 'I have to leave.'

Jack had established she lived on her own, only two minutes' walk from the pub. He felt heady from the wine, but gathered himself together and asked if she would like to see him again. Still holding his hand, she looked directly into his eyes, and using his name for the first time she confessed, 'Jack, I guess I am quite a lot older than you, and with that goes… well, a life, I suppose.'

He interrupted immediately, 'Nancy, I don't care about age, and what has gone, has gone. We've all had lives. Let me put it this way. My mother says I am "an old soul". Does that make sense? Let's not agonise over it now, let's get to know one another a little.' He was surprised how confidently he had delivered this enticement to meet him again. But he knew it was important, a hair's breadth between acceptance or refusal.

'Very well,' she replied quite formally, 'Sunday afternoon. This has been lovely, but I never feel really comfortable in pubs.'

'How about motorbikes? Providing it's not too cold, we could go to Dovedale. Perhaps find somewhere for a cup of tea?'

'I'd like that, but I'll come to Belper on the bus, and you can pick me up from there. I'd rather do it that way.'

By now they were standing outside the pub. Nervous that she might change her mind, he sealed the agreement with, 'I'll bring some sandwiches and a helmet for you.'

He could sense she was beginning to feel unsure, so taking the initiative, he drew her gently to him, and kissing her on both cheeks, whispered, 'My surname is French, so this is allowed.'

'Coincidence, how strange, mine is Dupray, or I think it's Dupray,' she added mysteriously. 'We have the start of a French Connection,' she laughed. Then, returning two kisses in a similar manner on his cheeks, she left him and ran slowly down the street. As she turned the corner, he waited for a while, savouring the sound of her high heels as they clicked against the paving stones.

* * *

'Penny for your thoughts, Nancy,' Jack whispered in her ear. He felt at a loss with his emotions. They had slipped so easily into bed. No uncomfortable foreplay, just an overwhelming desire to seal their relationship for better or worse. The wind blew hard against the window, gently lifting the curtains so that Jack could see the outline of Nancy's body under the sheet for an instant. Released from its band, her hair spread across the pillow in an ocean of curls.

'My feet are cold,' she replied. 'My feet are cold because I stupidly tried to impress you by wearing shoes rather than boots. Our first rendezvous I know, but I should have thought!'

She was tempted to add 'at my age', but sensed their relationship was too fragile to sustain any irony, as yet.

'I was impressed,' laughed Jack, 'and flattered that you looked so chic on our first...' He was about to say 'date', but felt that her use of the phrase 'rendezvous' embellished their time together.

When they had met as arranged that afternoon, the weather had not been good. However, they continued their plan to drive through the Dales. He guessed that she had ridden a motorbike before, as she had shown no nervousness, gently holding him around the waist and leaning alongside him into the bends. At Tissington Ford he had hesitated, to be sure it was low enough, and then sped through it, delighted by her laughter as the water splashed her feet.

The countryside was still bleak, not ready to concede to the onset of spring. Only the splashes of yellow daffodils and the occasional hedge of forsythia broke up the grey landscape. At Dovedale, they were the only ones to park next to the stepping stones. It was raining a little, but Jack managed to persuade Nancy to negotiate the twelve large flat stones across the river, where they sheltered under an outcrop of rocks and drank tea from a flask that she had provided. His mother had been out before he left home, leaving him to be resourceful and make banana and sugar sandwiches.

'Not a good idea,' he confessed, as they laughingly confronted a brown slimy sludge in the greaseproof paper wrapping.

But the tea was good, warming them as they nestled against each other, sheltering from the wind. They did not embrace, but just allowed themselves to enjoy an intimacy untouched as yet by the future. As the weather deteriorated, Jack headed back towards Derby, not questioning the fact he was taking Nancy all the way home, rather than leaving her at Belper where she had wanted to meet that afternoon.

When they arrived, Nancy asked him to park his bike in the pub car park as it was only a short distance from her flat, which she described as her 'nest'. It was just one large room on the first floor of a double fronted Victorian house. Its redeeming features were two large sash windows that overlooked an attractive street of similar period houses. At one side of the room was a small modern kitchenette, and in the other corner a rather mean-looking boxed-in toilet and shower, which Nancy had partially disguised with a decorative screen. There were two sofas either side of the fireplace, which was obviously unused as the grate was filled with pebbles and stones. Assorted candles were placed around the room and a large desk was graced with a vase full of daffodils. The room was lit by a selection of table lamps, which skilfully illuminated several large cinema posters hanging from the walls. Against the wall opposite the window was an old double bed with a matching wardrobe. As he looked around, he felt a sense of déjà vu. The bed was similar to the one he remembered sleeping in aged ten when he and his father had gone to France.

'Why the love of France?' he asked Nancy as they lay together.

'Because,' she said, her head still partially buried in the pillow, 'because it was the happiest time of my life.'

'Aren't you happy now?' he asked. 'I don't mean, right now,' he added, slightly embarrassed, 'I mean with your life. Well, you know what I mean!'

'Yes, I do, but my life has been complicated.' She paused. 'Well, not I suppose that complicated, just difficult at times.' She paused again. 'I don't wish to be rude, Jack, but how old are you?'

'Twenty-two, going on forty, as all my friends will tell you.'

'I'm thirty-four,' she replied. Her words hung in the air, until she added, 'Going on twenty.'

'The perfect match. Now, please tell me a little bit about your complicated life. Warts and all.'

'You mean, why I was sacked?'

'Well, yes, if you want to talk about it, but I'm far more interested in before Rolls-Royce, and of course, France.'

She had only ever wanted to share the intimacy of her past life with very few people, and never with a partner. So why was Jack so different? Why did she suddenly want to pour it all out? He was so much younger, but had none of the cockiness that often came with that age.

He sensed her unease. 'Trust me,' he whispered, 'you can trust me as I can trust you. Let's share a little bit of our past lives.'

She leapt out of bed.

'Where are you going?' he cried.

'To the bathroom,' she giggled, 'and also to put on my pyjamas.'

When she returned, she snuggled up to him, her feet now encased in a pair of fluffy pink socks.

'Once upon a time,' he started.

'Once upon a time,' she continued, 'there was a little girl found wandering around the Railway Orphanage with a five-pound note pinned to her cardigan.'

'Are we doing Brontë or Dickens?' he asked, a little startled.

'Both,' she replied sombrely. She uncurled herself from his embrace and, sitting up, she turned so she could look directly at him. 'If,' she emphasised the word, '*if* I tell you my story, Jack, I fear I might drag you unwittingly into it.' Sensing his disappointment, she smiled and gently rested her hand on his face. 'I'm sure you're brave,' she laughed. 'But you must promise me that if I tell you my story, you'll be brave enough to tell me yours.'

He clasped her hand, then, kissing her palm, he replied, 'I promise.'

CHAPTER FOUR

What are little girls made of?
What are little girls made of?
Sugar and spice and all things nice.
That's what little girls are made of.

What are little boys made of?
What are little boys made of?
Snips and snails and puppy-dogs' tails.
That's what little boys are made of.

– NURSERY RHYME

DERBY, 1939

Bill couldn't take his eyes off Nancy; she was the prettiest little girl he had ever seen.

'Leave her, Bill, let her take her time,' Edna had said. 'When you first came to me, you were a bit like that.'

In that area, in the terraced streets behind the Rolls-Royce factory, they called Edna the Foster Queen. She had taken in so many children, some of them going back home eventually, others, like Bill, being left when no one returned. He couldn't remember a time when he hadn't lived with Edna. He'd never know what to expect, a crying kid with a runny nose screaming for its mother, tiny babies that had to be bottle-fed, or, on one occasion, sickly twins with pinched little faces. Occasionally, as in Nancy's case, they would be referred to her from the Railway Institute Orphanage. Edna took them all in for a few shillings. Her reputation was good, and even the medical profession would call on her when families were struggling to cope.

Her house was small with an outside toilet, but everyone managed to cram in, sharing beds and sleeping on the floor. When Bill had started work, he negotiated with Edna for sole occupancy of the back room for 'a few bob' extra.

'Bloody witch!' he remarked when he passed it over each week, only to be reminded he got his washing done for that. They had an easy relationship, built on years of living together. Whilst basking in Edna's reputation of having a heart of gold, he was a little more realistic and knew she was canny and that each additional child in her care represented a few more shillings in the tin.

But they survived, despite the damp, the peeling wallpaper and the constant stocking up of coal to keep the fires burning. No one went hungry, and miraculously, everyone got to school on time. Edna created a home and was not above giving the children in her care affection and an ample bosom to cry on if necessary. She enjoyed a drink and would pop down to the pub on Nightingale Road every Friday night, but Bill had never seen her drunk. She had promised years ago to adopt him, but it never came to anything. She'd been married once, but that was all he knew of her life. It was enough that she introduced everyone to him as 'my son Bill'.

No one was really sure how old Nancy was when Edna took her under her wing. Edna guessed around four years old. For the first few days she just sat on the floor, even eating whatever food they could tempt her with from that position. Bill would often sit next to her, just quietly talking to her. Nancy always maintained that she couldn't remember anything about where she had come from, although sometimes a sense of unease would sweep over her, pinpricking her memories, such as a cry, a noise, a feeling of loss, but as time passed, even those disappeared.

She had been found abandoned in the grounds of the Railway Orphanage, and although there had been an extensive search for any clues that might indicate her background, nothing was ever found. Her clothes were good quality, and the only clue to her identity had been a name tag sewn into the back of her cardigan saying 'Nancy Dupray' and a five-pound note pinned to the front.

After two weeks in the Orphanage, the Matron became increasingly concerned as she refused to eat, drinking only a little warm milk before she slept at night. One of the staff suggested Edna might be the solution to the problem as her reputation for fostering was well known. When the little girl arrived, she had a small bag of hand-me-down clothes, plus a ten-shilling note to cover her stay for the first few months.

Bill was in his early twenties and had just started a new job at the Foundry, which was bringing in some extra cash and allowed him to buy Nancy some little treats, sweets, a few toys, anything that might bring a smile to her face. But what finally woke her from her trance was when he arrived home one Friday night with a toy dog. He'd bought it from the mother of one of his mates, who made stuffed toys for the local church bring and buy sales.

By this time Edna had persuaded Nancy to sit at the table for supper, and Bill placed the dog in front of her. It was made out of a piece of black velvet with an embroidered mouth, button ears and a large tartan collar. She looked at it carefully, pausing to turn to Bill to check it really was for her. Then she lifted it up so that she could bury her face in its side. Bill watched as she remained like this for some time.

As he whispered, 'It's your dog, Nancy, it's for you,' she slipped off her chair and raised her arms up to him. Responding immediately, he lifted her into the air, whirling her around, causing her to giggle for the first time since she had arrived. 'It's for you, Nancy,' he repeated, 'your own special friend.'

From then on, Edna would tell the Matron at the Orphanage that Nancy became just an ordinary little girl, a little reserved at times, but nevertheless seemingly happy in her new surroundings.

The Railway Orphanage had been founded just for children of railway employees, and as there was no evidence that Nancy's family had ever worked on the railway, the Matron asked Edna if she was prepared to foster the girl. With the help of the five pounds, they would contribute towards her keep until she was thirteen, providing Edna brought her to the Orphanage every year so they could ensure she was thriving.

Bill readily became her protector. If Edna chastised her, or she was tormented by other children, Bill defended her. It was natural that Nancy took comfort in Bill and in the toy dog, which, due to its squat body, short legs and tartan collar, they called Mac.

Bill found a new dimension in his life. He would often take her to the market on a Saturday to buy herrings with soft roes for Edna's tea, something she adored. The next stop would be the pet section, where you could buy mice, rabbits, dogs and kittens. Nancy didn't much like the smell of it, but she loved stroking the animals.

'Buy us a dog, Bill,' she'd often demand, knowing full well the reply would always be the same: 'What, and upset Mac?'

Nancy knew there was something called the War going on, but what that meant she wasn't really sure. Now and then Edna would get a bit nervous, but the air raid shelter at the bottom of the garden was only ever used after the War as a place to play.

Soon after Nancy's arrival, Edna stopped fostering children as she found it more lucrative to mind toddlers and babies for women who worked at the Celanese, a factory that made material for parachutes. Pushchairs and prams would arrive around seven in the morning, and whilst Nancy would be grabbing a slice of bread and a cup of tea before she went to school, Edna would be juggling her brood. Mums were supposed to bring their own nappies for their babies, but for a few extra pence, Edna would wash them in a copper boiler, which was constantly kept going outside. All year round the yard was filled with lines of towelling nappies. In the winter they would freeze on the line like pieces of white cardboard, causing Nancy's hands to chap as she battled to unpeg them.

Each mother was instructed to sew a coloured thread through their nappy so that it could be distinguished, and Nancy's year-round job was to fold them, stack them and, under Edna's instructions, 'fluff 'em up a bit'. They tried to get everything clear by the time Bill arrived home, often bringing with him a 'lassie', as Edna referred to his girlfriends.

'Look at little green-eyes,' Edna would say to Bill, 'our Nancy's jealous, she doesn't approve of your goings-on.'

But Nancy usually liked Bill's girlfriends, especially if they made a fuss of her, playing with her curls and allowing her to try a bit of much sought-after lipstick. She was just rather shy, not as fast as they were with the backchat.

Edna revelled in the fact that Bill seemed to always have a bit of spare cash through his wheeling and dealing, and occasionally during the summer, he would borrow a car from a mate and take them for a spin to Skegness, the nearest seaside town, less than a hundred miles from Derby.

'I'm not sure where he gets the petrol from,' she'd say as she settled into the front seat, leaving Nancy and one of his lassies in the back. 'Probably one of those American buddies, I bet. Is that right, Bill?'

The journey was always conducted with good-natured banter, and for Nancy it was one of the most exciting events in her life.

Edna, whose legs were now as she described 'proper poorly', would walk slowly to the beach, before descending heavily into a deckchair provided by Bill. She would then hold court for the rest of the day, wrapped in an old blanket if the weather was nippy. People would stop and chat, occasionally being offered a cup of sweet tea from the large thermos flask, which she kept in a big wicker basket with their picnic of sandwiches and Huntley and Palmer biscuits if Bill had managed to buy a packet.

If the tide was out, they would hardly see the sea all day, but if it was in, Bill and Nancy would run along the beach screaming as the waves splashed over their feet. Nancy never remembered the sea being warm, even on hot summer days. Mac always went with them, perched on the back ledge of the car for the journey. As an integral part of the group he was constantly consulted.

'Are you all right, Mac? What do you fancy for lunch, Mac?' This allowed the person posing the question to reply on his behalf, 'Oh, so you fancy a few cockles, do you?'

On one occasion Nancy asked on Mac's behalf for candy floss. After Edna had been persuaded to open up her ration book and part with a coupon, Bill bought her one, which she pretended to share with Mac, but it left an indelible sticky patch on his nose.

The Foundry had started to send Bill away for weeks at a time. His expertise in casting and his ability to grasp new processes being developed in the north of England facilitated his rise at the Foundry, and not being called up.

'They think a lot of him,' Edna would announce proudly. 'But I've warned him he needs to dress proper, those bloody brothel creepers he's started wearing. I've told him we don't want any of that East End Teddy Boy nonsense up here.'

Although they were not related, bizarrely he and Edna looked very alike. Built like brick shithouses, as the local expression would have it, they were both of medium height, square, solid and with thick black hair that refused to be tamed. Edna often wore a hairnet to keep hers in control, whilst Bill slicked his back with Brylcreem.

Before a foray to the pub or out with one of his lassies, Nancy would watch with interest as he stood in their cramped kitchen, bending over the sink so he could see his reflection in a little mirror balanced precariously on the window-ledge, as he battled to create a fashionable quiff.

'You wouldn't describe him as handsome,' Edna would say, 'but he has a way with the girls. He can be a real gentleman when he likes.'

Nancy always accepted that Bill was more important to Edna than she was, but it didn't matter; Bill represented family life as much as Edna, and constantly demanded a say in her wellbeing.

'I've told you, Edna, she's not to go down the Cut.'

'Oh don't be so daft, Bill, all the little 'uns play down there. You did when you were no more than five or six. The banks are so mangled, you canna fall in.'

'I was a lad, you silly cow, makes a difference. She's not to go down there. Remember that bloke we found? Drowned or pushed in, God help us, all bloated, he was. Some very unsavoury things happen, you know that, Edna.'

'Well, you know better than me,' retorted Edna, her dignity ruffled. 'Any ways up, who's in charge of Nancy, you or me? Tell me that, Bill? In fact, if anyone had their dues, I'm guardian to both of you.'

Nancy was used to these arguments; they never really amounted to much and Bill always won. She knew Edna adored Bill, and Bill took care of Edna, not always willingly but ready to help out, if she needed anything.

The Cut was only about a ten-minute walk away, down the jetty at the back of the house. It had been closed for years. Bill reckoned it had never really been used a lot.

'It was finished a bit too late, canals were nearly over by the time it were done,' Bill had explained to Nancy.

But for Nancy it remained a magical place. She didn't have a lot of friends, and whilst she'd play in the street with the other youngsters, she always felt a little bit apart, and given a chance would try to be with Bill whenever she could. She'd wait for him at the corner under the streetlight in the winter, or venture to the bus stop further down the road if the nights were light.

The Cut was usually a treat at the weekends when he wasn't away or working, and they'd walk there together. The canal was stagnant, and both banks were overgrown. But this played host to a variety of insects, often with jewel-coloured wings, hovering above the water. Things rustled in the reeds, and iris and a mixture of plants flourished on its banks. In the distance you could see the railway sidings, and the occasional goods train passing by. In the week, the clanging and banging spoilt any sense of tranquillity, but often on a Sunday there was no work on the railway and it was peaceful and calm. Occasionally, a swan would glide by with his mate.

'Got more sense than to stop here,' Bill would say as they watched them from the bank.

If the weather was fine Bill would find a place to sit and light a cigarette, as she raced up and down the tow path, searching for flowers, mice, anything that moved. In the spring she and Bill would search for frogspawn, taking it back to the house in a jam jar, to the disgust of Edna.

'Bugger me, Bill, what you brought there? Keep it outside,' she'd cry. 'I don't want bloody frogs jumping all over the kitchen floor.'

But then when they'd start to grow, with their tiny legs, she would be as enchanted as Nancy watching them swim around in the jam jar. Eventually the water would become green and murky, and Edna would empty them down the drain, assuring Nancy they would have plenty of mates down there.

Bill wasn't interested in the flora and fauna, but would happily help Nancy gather a bunch of wild flowers to take to Edna. When she was small the treat was that he piggybacked her home, making her yell as he jumped about pretending to be a circus horse.

In her teens they would still walk along the tow-path together. Not saying much, just dishing a bit of dirt, as Bill would have it, about their neighbours in the street.

Feeling old enough at around thirteen, she would disregard Bill's instructions when he was away and would often disappear with a book she'd borrowed from the library. Finding a warm dry patch on one of the banks she'd curl up and read for an hour, well out of Edna's way.

Years later Nancy was to think that if she'd had a special friend at school, her life could have been different. Whilst she would confide in Bill, her relationship with Edna revolved around the day-to-day trials of making ends meet.

'You spoil her, Bill,' Edna would remark when Bill bought her a new dress, or a cardigan for school. Unlike her school friends she always had shoes that fitted, and a coat that wasn't a hand-me-down.

Vera, who was the same age and lived two doors down, would tease her calling her 'Lady Muck' or 'Miss Lah-di-dah', and her nickname at school was 'Froggie' in reference to her French-sounding surname.

'The curse arrived yesterday,' Vera announced as they walked to school one morning. 'Mam was right bothered, she said I'd started way too soon, our Dot didn't start until she was fifteen. She made me lie down and gave me a drink of Indian brandy, bloody awful.'

Nancy was constantly in awe of Vera and her seemingly bottomless knowledge of what was going on around her. Mystified, Nancy remained silent, hoping to pick up a few more pointers about what 'the curse' was before having to admit to Vera she didn't know what she was talking about.

But just like so many times in the past, Vera sensed her weakness.

'Blood hell, Nancy, you're so bloody gormless. Don't you know what the curse is? It's your usual, you know, your period. Hasn't Edna told you? You know, blood in your knickers.' Then she added, 'You know where babies come from, don't you?'

'Of course I do,' Nancy replied, 'out their mummy's tummy.'

'Out their mummy's tummy,' mimicked Vera. 'Come on, Nancy, how did they get in there in the first place? There's not buttons and eyes on mummy's tummy,' she mimicked again. 'You push 'em out yer fanny.'

As they approached the school gate, Vera greeted a group of their friends.

'Hey, Nancy here doesn't know about the birds and bees,' she announced triumphantly, 'do you, Nancy?'

One of the older girls, sensing Nancy's embarrassment, put her arm around her. 'Naught wrong in that, Nancy,' she said kindly. 'You have a word with your Edna.'

'Or her Bill,' Vera added, to the amusement of the group. 'He knows what he's talking about.'

Nancy spent the rest of the day worrying, with the term 'gormless' ringing in her ears.

When she arrived home, Bill was making a fuss with Edna about 'chitlings' for tea.

'I know we like 'em,' he shouted at Edna, 'but Nancy hates 'em, don't you, Nancy?'

'They look like dead people's insides,' she admitted, sitting down at the tea table. 'I'll have dripping instead.'

'Well spotted, that's exactly what they are,' Edna replied, 'but go on, I'll open a tin of spam, just to keep Bill quiet.'

Nancy tried to avert her eyes as Bill and Edna doused their chitterlings in salt and vinegar, mopping up the juices with slices of white bread. Spreading the dripping on her bread she confessed, 'Vera says I'm gormless.'

'Mm, she's got room to talk,' Edna said, 'her mum's as thick as two short planks. Thinks she's summat special now the Celanese has changed over to making nylon underwear, rather than stuff for the War.'

'Why did she say you were gormless, Nancy?' Bill asked, 'and shut up, Edna, Vera's mum's ok, you don't mind having a drink with her on a Friday night, I notice.'

'I didn't know what the curse was, or she called it your "usual",' Nancy replied. 'I said babies came out of their mums' tummies and she thought that was funny too.'

Bill folded his paper and purposefully wiped the last of the chitterlings off his plate with a remaining slice of bread.

'You're laughing,' Nancy cried at him. 'Bill, why are you laughing? That's not fair. They said I should ask Edna and even you.'

Joining in with his laughter, Edna cried, 'Christ, Bill, they've got the measure of you.'

'Over to you, gals, count me out of this one.' He lightly kissed the top of Nancy's head. 'Go on then, Edna luv, birds and bees, if you can remember that far back.'

A year later, Nancy woke to find blood on her bedsheet that had gone through to the mattress.

'Never get that out,' Edna had commented, and then regaled her with the various options with coping with her period. 'You can buy sanitary pads, but they're expensive though. Most people round here wear pieces of cloth, you can boil them like we did with the nappies. Hold on a minute, I might have some nappies still you can cut up.'

But a few days after 'the curse' had arrived, Edna was eager to greet her as she came in from school.

'Go upstairs Nancy, look on your bed what Bill's got you.' Edna followed her. There were three boxes on her bed. 'Open 'em up luv, I don't know how he does it.'

Inside Nancy found what appeared to be twelve cotton pads.

'They're sanitary towels,' Edna announced triumphantly. 'Bill got them, you can get them at the chemist but they're not cheap, and I can't believe he asked for them. But these look a bit special to me. But ask no questions. There's a belt with them as well, you just hook them on. You burn 'em, Nancy, bit of a waste, but we can burn them outside in a bucket or on the fire in the winter if Bill's not about.'

With Edna's help Nancy fitted the belt and one of the pads.

'They feel a bit funny, Edna,' she confessed. 'Comfy though.'

'You'll get used to them. I wish I'd had them, it's a bloody curse for half your life, might as well be comfy. Don't forget to thank our Bill.'

'Thanks, Bill,' she said quietly that evening as he was reading the paper.

'My pleasure, sweetheart,' he'd replied, not looking up. 'Remember they're not like a box of chocolates, you don't eat them all at once.'

CHAPTER FIVE

*You will see a state of prosperity such as we
have never had in my lifetime – nor indeed
in the history of this country. Indeed let us
be frank about it – most of our people have
never had it so good.*

– HAROLD MACMILLAN

DERBY, 1951

A few years after the War, Bill went to work in Yorkshire for a couple
of months. The house was quiet without him, coupled with the fact
that Edna had given up fostering. She had gained weight after the
ulcers on her legs started to cause her pain and impaired her ability
to walk around. Nancy, now aged sixteen, did most of the shopping
at the local Co-op, whilst Edna attempted to keep the house clean in
a rather half-hearted way, just about continuing to get Nancy's tea
ready when she returned from school.

In the old days, Edna had taken pride in sporting a clean pinafore every morning, but since the onset of her 'poorly legs' she only
changed it when Nancy provided her with a clean one. Bill bought
her a two-bar electric fire, which she sat in front of for most of the
day, roasting her legs until they had turned a mottled purple. When
the electricity ran out and she couldn't 'be arsed' to find another coin
for the meter, she would retire to bed with a hot water bottle, leaving
Nancy to fend for herself when it came to mealtimes.

This new-found freedom enabled Nancy to hang around with her friends more after school. She was popular, but never built up a camaraderie like some of the girls. She was taller than average and somewhat gauche, always more comfortable standing at the back of the school photograph in an effort to disappear. However, her outrageously curly hair, which obstinately defied being restrained, drew attention to a face with features that were both classical and refined. To her amazement, one of her schoolmates, a young man called Jimmy, started to chat her up, telling her he thought she was beautiful.

He was also sixteen and in a special class for bright students who were being encouraged to try for O-levels, even though the school was a secondary modern. They met after school, perhaps stopping in the park or walking to the local Co-op where they could buy sweets and biscuits. Unlike Nancy, Jimmy lived on one of the new estates built just after the War, and his journey to and from school involved a bus ride. At weekends they started to meet in Derby on a Saturday afternoon followed by a trip to the cinema in the evening.

Their tentative lovemaking in the back row of the cinema usually involved Jimmy fumbling to stroke Nancy's breasts plus a series of awkward kisses. Nancy liked Jimmy, but the whole ritual seemed furtive and she agonised about how far she should let him go. Should she allow him to just feel her small breasts through her cardigan, or let him unclip her bra and feel them properly? She longed for a best friend who could have advised her on these matters, but fortunately Jimmy wasn't the pushy kind. He had once directed her hand towards his erect penis, but sensing her horror had spent the rest of the evening apologising.

He knew he had gone out on a limb asking Nancy out as she didn't come from the same mould as most of the girls he came into contact with at school. She was always simply dressed, wore flat shoes and barely a trace of lipstick. His friends demanded other attributes from their girlfriends, like tight-fitting sweaters, high heels and artful makeup. They quickly became self-sufficient, to some extent enjoying being apart from the crowd. Nancy never met his mum, dad or brother Tony, but she felt they sounded nice when Jimmy talked about them.

'Mum says you must come over for tea,' he told Nancy on several occasions, but she was reluctant to say yes, knowing it might mean a return visit. Guiltily she acknowledged for the first time that she was a little embarrassed about Edna and Bill.

Bill arrived back late one Sunday night. He'd stayed in Leeds for most of the weekend and was particularly annoyed that he had spent so much money wining and dining one of his lassies.

'Honestly, Edna,' he reported back, 'you'd have thought she was Lady Muck the way she messed me about.'

'What do you expect, Bill?' she replied, 'those fur and no knickers girls are all the same. Now then, Nancy has got herself a boyfriend whilst you've been away! As yet we haven't been graced with his presence, but Madge up the road says he's a very nice lad, and his Dad is a white-collar worker at the Building Society.'

Nancy immediately sensed a change in Bill, but overcame her unease in delicately taking the wrapping from the first pair of nylon stockings she had owned. After a trip away, even if it was only a week, Bill always arrived home with gifts for the 'ladies of the house'. This time it was two scented soaps in a box for Edna, 'and use them, Edna, no leaving them in a drawer. You're starting to whiff a bit at times, you know.'

'Cheeky bugger,' Edna retorted, unwrapping one and lifting it to her nose.

Nancy let the stockings slip through her fingers. Some of her friends wore stockings to school but Nancy didn't even own a suspender belt.

'Perhaps you're a bit young,' Bill said. Then, taking them off her, he continued, 'Yes, definitely too young, particularly for a boyfriend, my girl. Don't you let me catch you with him.'

Nancy grabbed the stockings back. 'Don't be stupid, Bill; he's only a schoolmate. I'm going to need a suspender belt,' she continued, aware that she needed to steer the conversation away from Jimmy.

Bill gently took the nylons away from her for the second time, but this time he wound them round her neck, crossing them at the front so he could pull her face closer to his.

'Nancy, I'm telling you, not asking you, no boyfriends.' He tightened the stocking around her neck, as if to emphasise the seriousness of his words. 'No boyfriends, you're not ready yet.'

'Don't be silly,' Edna started to say.

But Bill interrupted, releasing the nylons and turning towards her. 'Shut up, you old cow,' he shouted. 'Given a chance you'd probably have her on the streets if it made a bob or two! I'm telling you Nancy, no boyfriends, do you understand?'

Nancy was about to protest but Edna intervened. 'Leave it, Nancy, no use arguing with a bear with a sore head.'

The following few days were a bit strained but they soon picked up the threads. Bill went to work at seven in the morning, Nancy to school at eight. It was her last term before she left for the summer. She had wanted to go to the Further Education College to learn secretarial skills, but Edna had said no, she had to find a job.

She continued to see Jimmy after school, but was careful she only went to the cinema with him if she knew Bill wasn't about. She had been surprised by Bill's anger; the only time she could remember him being that upset was when she was little. They were getting on a bus and some man had pushed her clumsily to one side trying to get on first. Bill had grabbed him by the collar and shouted so loudly at him that Nancy had covered her ears in terror. 'You bloody well mind where you're going,' he'd shouted, 'or you'll be running behind.'

He'd picked Nancy up and to her embarrassment she had cried on his shoulder as if it had been a seriously traumatic experience.

On occasions he and Edna would have slanging matches, instigated by what Edna saw as his less than generous contribution to the housekeeping. But it never resulted in any violence, just a silent stand-off for one or two days. Eventually, Bill usually gave in, slipping her an extra ten shillings. But this time Nancy felt uneasy, as if she was on shaky ground and her actions might affect not only her, but Jimmy and Edna as well.

The following Saturday evening she met Jimmy in Derby. It was one of those warm evenings, so instead of going to the cinema they opted for sitting by the river with two other couples from school who had joined them. There was much good-natured horseplay, with Nancy discovering that Jimmy had a natural talent for impersonating those around him.

'Give us Mr White again,' they kept insisting, delighting in his irreverent take on their hated French master. Nancy felt oddly proud of Jimmy, especially as the more she laughed at his antics, the more she sensed he wanted to perform for her benefit. Instead of catching the bus they all started to walk home. It was less than two miles, with the opportunity to stop at the newly opened fish and chip shop. Nancy never usually had any money, apart from the odd bit of change left over from the weekly shopping, but tonight she had five shillings, earned when she had taken care of a neighbour's little boy for a day.

'It's on me,' she said to Jimmy when they approached the chip shop. 'Have what you want, my treat.'

They both had fish and chips, overlaid by a layer of bright green coloured mushy peas and a pickled egg. The complete blowout, thought Nancy as she liberally doused hers in salt and vinegar. Later she remembered that she was conscious of feeling happy, as if she was on the brink of something, she knew not what. It was as if this wonderful balmy evening had unlocked her ability to see the world, not just through Edna and Bill's eyes, but opening up to her new opportunities where she could pick and choose which path she should follow. She was also content that the other two couples seemed to enjoy her company, accepting her happily as part of the group.

As they rounded the corner before tackling the long drag up the hill, Bill appeared, as if from nowhere. Dusk had fallen quite suddenly, so at first she was unsure if it was him as he barred their path.

'Bill!' she cried out, somewhat startled. Then regaining her composure, she announced to the group, 'This is my brother Bill.' But it was immediately obvious that Bill wasn't in the mood for formal introductions.

'I fucking told you Nancy, no boyfriends.' He turned on Jimmy, snatching his fish and chips and scattering them on the ground. Both the other lads rushed at Bill, but he swung round, scattering a greasy array of chips and fish over the pavement.

The girls were screaming. One of them tried to grab Bill's coat before her companion pulled her back, imploring her, 'Leave the bastard alone!'

'Fuck off,' Bill kept repeating, 'fuck off, all of you!'

Jimmy was standing bewildered, his arms outstretched in order to protect Nancy. He was taller than Bill, but Bill had all the advantages. He grabbed the boy by the shoulders, then, raising his knee, he brought it viciously into Jimmy's groin.

Nancy leapt forward, but it was pointless. Bill just dragged her along the road, leaving Jimmy bent over in agony, surrounded by all his mates. She continued to struggle, digging her heels into the ground until Bill stopped and slapped her sharply across the face.

'Shut up, Nancy,' he threatened, 'or I'll go back and sort them out proper. He got off lightly, but next time it will be within an inch of his life.'

When they arrived home, Edna was sitting by the electric fire. She didn't look up as Nancy escaped Bill's hold and scrambled up the stairs. Nancy flung herself on her bed, trying to stifle the wave of emotion that flooded through her body.

When she heard the front door close, and Bill's footsteps fade into the distance as he left the house, she rushed down the stairs screaming at Edna, 'You told him! You told him! He's nearly killed Jimmy!'

Edna remained calm, reaching forward to switch off one bar of the electric fire. 'He told you no boyfriends,' she replied weakly. 'He got back early and asked where you were. I didn't know what to say.'

'But why, why?' shouted Nancy. 'I'm sixteen, why no boyfriends?'

''Cos he loves you, Nancy. You'll always be his little girl. He loved you from the minute he saw you. Now go to bed, there's a good girl. He's gone to the pub, it'll be all right in the morning, you'll see.'

'I won't go to bed. It's not fair. He's got no right,' she cried, violently pushing her fingers through her unruly hair.

'Mark my words Nancy, you will never win. I've seen it coming, I'm telling you better to give in now than try and fight a fight you will never win. Believe me, he'll take care of you, and I mean really take care of you. I wish I'd had a man who cared for me as much as Bill cares for you.'

'No,' shouted Nancy, bending a little so she could hold Edna by the shoulders and look directly into her eyes. 'No, no,' she repeated.

'Gerroff, you young madam! Leave me alone, I'm an old woman. I've done my bit, more than my bloody bit for you. I'm going to bed, and you'd better go to yours before he gets back from the pub. I tell you it will be all right in the morning, but watch out, my girl, you watch your p's and q's. He can be a bugger when he wants summat, you watch out.'

Later Nancy lay on her bed. It had started to rain, bringing a chill to the air. She heard Bill come in. As he climbed the stairs, she could hear him repeating her name. Later she recollected that she hadn't really felt afraid, just angry with him. She'd never considered he might love her – well, not in that way. It seemed stupid, he was her Bill, a mate, a kind of older brother; in fact she'd quite naturally called him her brother sometimes when people asked. It was repulsive just to think about it. Edna had got it wrong.

The light from the landing shone through as he opened her door and entered her room. He'd always knocked before, usually shouting, even when she was a little girl, 'Are you decent Nancy?' He stumbled, then sat awkwardly on the side of her bed. For a moment she thought he was going to fall on the floor. But he clutched at the quilted eiderdown to steady himself. He leaned forward. His breath was hot with the smell of alcohol as it wafted towards her face. Normally he drank beer, but she knew this was hard spirits.

Her room suddenly felt different, isolated from the sound of the trains in the sidings, isolated from the rain falling against the window. This was her home; whatever the difficulties she had always felt safe.

Bill had decorated her room with pink floral wallpaper, paying for Edna to have some matching curtains made. Most mornings she had woken to the sound of Edna or Bill making a cup of tea. The smell of gas as the kettle boiled, toast being made in the new toaster Bill had brought back from Germany. Their own little world. She never thought of Edna as her mum; they had a warm, easygoing relationship which as she became older she often thought was a lot better than some of her friends who were always at loggerheads with their mums.

But now a sudden panic gripped her. Bill reached under the bed-clothes for her hand.

'Nancy, I'm sorry,' he mumbled, pressing his lips against her warm hand. 'I'm sorry, Nancy, I'm sorry. You know how I feel about you. You know you're my little girl.'

He continued mumbling, holding her hand against his face. He stared at her with mournful bloodshot eyes, but the grip on her hand now seemed like a vice.

She struggled to sit up, trying to pull her hand away. 'Edna,' she shouted, 'Edna, help me, it's Bill!'

He continued repeating the words, 'You're my little girl, Nancy, come on, you know how I love you, I'll give you the world, you know that.'

She waited for a second, then cried for Edna again. But as his face approached hers, she screamed, fighting to get out of bed.

'Well I hate you, you're disgusting!' she shrieked. 'You're fat, ugly and old. Why would I want someone like you when I could have someone like Jimmy? I'm not your Nancy. Stop it, Bill, please stop it.'

She remembered very little after that. He had struck her face, and she was conscious of falling out of bed. She'd fought as he had held her down whilst he raped her. She had kept on fighting until she felt the full weight of his body relax onto hers. But then everything else was a blank.

The surgeon explained that Bill appeared to have kicked her several times in her abdomen. 'In your tummy,' he added when he saw her confusion. To save her life it had been necessary to remove her womb. Edna had apparently left her in a pool of blood for a day until she had panicked, and a neighbour had called for an ambulance.

'I thought it was her usual,' she told the ambulance driver, 'she only started a couple of months ago, and it was always heavy.' Edna hadn't accompanied her to the hospital, but after the police had contacted her, she had arrived the following afternoon.

The surgeon insisted on seeing Edna and had explained that Nancy was very lucky to be alive.

'I find it hard to understand, Mrs Blore, that Nancy was obviously unconscious with multiple bruises on her face and body, and yet it was twenty-four hours before you asked a neighbour to call for an ambulance. Apparently she was still in her nightgown with a pillow placed between her legs? What were you thinking?'

'I told the ambulance driver,' she replied, 'I thought it was her usual. I don't know anything more. I need to speak to Nancy.'

'It remains to be seen if Nancy wants to speak to you, Mrs Blore. This is a very serious matter, and the hospital report will be part of the investigation by the police. I assure you that I will make it very clear that it was far more than Nancy's period that caused such devastating damage to her body. You of course realise she will be unable to have children of her own now.'

Nancy was in a large gynaecological ward. Her bed was surrounded by two screens, and when Edna arrived clutching a bunch of flowers, there were already three people standing around the bed. A small woman with a briefcase was taking notes, alongside a policewoman and a nurse.

Her mind at first had been a complete blank. She vaguely remembered being wheeled down a long corridor with lights set in the ceiling. Several voices spoke to her; she sensed they were kindly, and she had told them her name, but that was all.

'Is this your mum?' the police woman asked Nancy when Edna appeared from behind the screens.

'No,' Nancy replied. 'No, not my mum.' She started to cry. 'Not my mum.'

The policewoman checked her notes. 'My apologies,' she said, appearing to address all those present around the bed.

She addressed Edna. 'Can I confirm you are Nancy's foster mother, Mrs Edna Blore?'

'Well, I've brought her up since she was five. She always called me Edna, but, well, yes, I am her foster mum. The Railway Orphanage asked me to help out with her years ago, it's all above board. We've always been a happy family, haven't we, Nancy?'

Nancy remained silent. The nurse passed her a tissue to wipe away her tears.

'Nancy has told us as much as she can remember, Mrs Blore, about Saturday night and the early hours of Sunday morning. We have also spoken to the young man, Jimmy, and his parents. We are now trying to contact Mr William Dodd, who Nancy said perpetrated this crime and the attack on Jimmy Watson. If you have any idea of where he is, I suggest you tell us immediately. We will need a statement from you anyway, but that can be done at the station.'

Edna stood her ground, placing the flowers on the bed.

'Oh Nancy, how could you squeal on our Bill?' she asked.

'Please take her away,' Nancy softly implored the young woman taking notes. Then she gently moved her head, taking in the confines of the space around her bed. The screens were covered in a floral pattern of mauve flowers, and next to her bed one of the nurses had placed a bottle of Lucozade and a small plant left behind by another patient. The ward smelt of disinfectant, combined with a savoury smell lingering from the lunch trolley that still remained in the corridor. Gathering her thoughts, but as if in a trance, she directed her appeal at both the young woman taking notes and the policewoman.

'Take her away, please!' she repeated quietly. 'I never want to see her again. You won't let him get me again, will you? Please, I never want to see them again.'

The nurse, obviously moved by Nancy's outburst, reached for her hand. Then, holding it tight, and without waiting for anyone's approval, asked Edna to leave immediately.

Edna hesitated. 'All I've done for you, my girl. All I've done for you,' she repeated.

The policewoman took her arm. 'Please, Mrs Blore, Nancy needs to rest. We will need a statement from you and Nancy will in due course decide whether she ever wants to see you again.'

CHAPTER SIX

*Life is always a rich and steady time when you are waiting
for something to happen or to hatch.*

– E. B. WHITE, *CHARLOTTE'S WEB*

DUFFIELD, DERBYSHIRE, 1952

Nancy sat silently in the front of the car while Miss Agnes Sevier drove expertly through the evening traffic. She had remained in hospital for two weeks, and then in a convalescent home for nearly a month. In that time, she and Agnes, in spite of the difference in their ages, had become friends. Agnes was the Almoner at the hospital where Nancy had been taken after being attacked by Bill.

She was a neat little woman who was always attired in a Harris Tweed suit, crisp blouse and flat shoes. Now in her early forties, she had accepted the fact that she would never marry, but was content in the knowledge that her position in a large city hospital gave her constant opportunities to pick up the baton passed on to her by her mother and suffragette grandmother, who had devoted their lives to helping women less fortunate than themselves. The War years had been particularly hard for working-class families, both their relationships and their health. Nancy wasn't unusual in her plight, although botched abortions were the more common threat to young girls' lives.

Agnes' heart had gone out to Nancy as soon as she had met her. Nancy had told the nurses she didn't want any visitors. But they reported to Agnes that she still remained terrified at visiting times in case Edna or Bill might appear, and during the night would often be found crying into her pillow. Agnes tried to visit her every day, sometimes arriving at visiting hours just to alleviate the loneliness she thought the girl must be feeling when visitors crowded around the beds of other patients.

As Nancy's trust in Agnes grew, Agnes in turn came to develop a huge respect for Nancy. She was intelligent and had an undefinable manner which made her seem poles apart from other working-class girls who Agnes had come into contact with over the years. Agnes discovered she liked reading, and kept her well supplied with books from her own stock. She had tried on a couple of occasions to talk about Nancy's past life, but Nancy had told her she didn't wish to discuss, or even think about it. She admitted that she had a horror of Bill returning, and thought her best option was to move a long way away.

It was beginning to rain and as she reached in front of Nancy to switch on the windscreen wipers of her little Morris Minor, she touched her hand.

'You'll like them, Nancy,' she said, 'trust me, you'll like them, and they will like you.'

Agnes drove out of Derby. As she looked across at Nancy, she realised just how fond she had become of her. She had done some careful investigation of her own volition by contacting the Railway Orphanage. Whilst the Orphanage had been as helpful as possible, there was no trace of Nancy's parents, apart from a suggestion that she was possibly related to a group of Huguenots who had lived in Derby for a number of years. They had run a small French polishing establishment, but it had run into financial difficulties and it was presumed they had left England in a hurry. But nothing was confirmed, and she was relieved when Nancy didn't appear to want to pursue any further investigation as to their whereabouts.

Nancy had made it clear that she didn't want any more involvement with Edna, and had calmly stated that she was capable of taking care of herself. She appeared to be neither bitter nor angry, but continued to confess to having a horror of meeting Bill again. The police had, in Agnes's opinion, only half-heartedly tried to trace him. He had vanished, and she thought it was unlikely he would turn up in Derby again. She had encouraged Nancy to press charges against him, feeling this might give her some protection in the future.

It was clear that Nancy had very little experience of life. Since she was five, she had lived with Edna and Bill in one of the poorest areas of Derby. Things had improved gradually since the War ended, but the camaraderie and culture found in this working-class environment often out of necessity remained the same. Wages were still low, and better housing and schools were only just starting to emerge that would eventually make a difference.

Working slightly outside her accepted code of behaviour as an Almoner, she was taking Nancy to a family she knew in Duffield, a village ten miles outside Derby on the edge of the Pennines. It was a large village with a long, distinguished history. A few stones remained of a castle built in the Middle Ages, and one or two seventeenth-century stone houses, once home to farmers who bred sheep. Duffield had become popular at the turn of the century when the Industrial Revolution had engulfed the area, feeding off the River Derwent for its power to drive machines. The Derwent ran through the centre of the village with rolling hills and dales either side, the perfect location for the newly rich to build attractive homes. It had the reputation of being 'the place to live', and whilst Nancy had heard of it, she had never been there. Agnes indicated left and dropped her Morris into first gear before attempting to climb the steep hill.

'It's a nightmare in the winter,' she remarked.

Solidly built Edwardian houses occupied both sides of the road, their small front gardens alive with foliage and colour. Large established trees, their roots erupting through the pavement in places, were already turning an autumnal gold.

'Right, this is it,' Agnes indicated as she stopped the car.

She felt a little nervous. This was after all a little unorthodox, a private arrangement that might be frowned upon by the hospital. Professor Sloam and his wife were old family friends. They were

German Jews who had managed to leave Germany before it was too late. They had two children and several grandchildren, but Agnes understood that they had lost many members of their family in the Holocaust. Both were now in their seventies, and while Professor Sloam appeared in good health, his wife Ruth suffered from arthritis and walked with a stick. The arrangement was that Nancy would help Mrs Sloam around the house and the Professor in his study, although no one was quite clear as to what that would mean. There was a cleaner who came in every weekday, and Agnes had arranged that twice a week, Nancy would travel to Belper to attend the Further Education College for lessons in shorthand and typing. She was to receive full board, plus one pound a week pocket money. As Nancy turned to reach for her suitcase, the door of the house opened, and when she went to squeeze out of the car, the Professor was already there to help her.

'Welcome, welcome,' he said, 'mind those damned tree roots, they seem to be invading the whole pavement.'

As she followed behind him, Agnes embraced Mrs Sloam. Nancy felt nervous and completely out of her depth, but she wanted this to work as much as Agnes. The fear of meeting Bill haunted her, but she knew as soon as she reached Duffield that this wasn't Bill's natural environment, and it would be unlikely she would accidentally bump into him.

The semi-detached house was large with four bedrooms, the smallest of which had been prepared lovingly for Nancy. There was fresh linen, a pile of white towels, a dressing gown, even a washbasin just for her use. The room was at the back of the house, overlooking a large well-kept garden. She had never been in a house like this before; her only reference points were films she'd watched on the television, usually with Edna on a Sunday afternoon.

She looked around her room, opened the door and walked along the corridor. At the end was a round table on which had been placed a large bowl of autumn flowers. Something rang a bell in her mind, a kind of déja vu, as if she had been here before, walking along the corridor, descending the stairs with its woven carpet. It puzzled her for days, but then she remembered a film that she had actually seen twice, a film that Edna really loved, about an English family in the War. Edna didn't like American films very much, and Bill only seemed to enjoy action films, but strangely this one had gripped them all, and Edna in spite of herself had cried with Nancy at the end.

Eventually, she remembered it had been called *Mrs Miniver*, and there had been a housekeeper in it called Gladys, a bit like Carol, Ruth's cleaning lady. The Minivers lived in a house bigger than, but similar to the Sloams', and in spite of the War raging around them seemed to live comfortably in beautiful surroundings, and, Nancy remembered especially, with flowers in every room. 'Another bloody world,' Edna had described it. Mrs Miniver had a car, she was smartly dressed, kind, brave, gliding from one sunlit room to another. Nancy had agreed with Edna; another world that she hadn't even aspired to, just perhaps been comforted to know that it was there.

But now she too walked from one often sunlit room to another, admiring the flowers on the table so carefully arranged by Ruth, with the warm smell of coffee pervading the house. To her delight pictures hung on the walls, some quite modern, others just photographs of family or friends, she guessed. She would catch her reflection sometimes in a mirror, amazed that it reflected not just her face, but a backdrop of elegant surroundings of which she would never have imagined she was now part.

From the minute she arrived, she was content in feeling that she was wanted, but nervous that she must live up to Agnes's expectations. Over tea and cakes shared with Agnes, Ruth explained that because of her arthritis she needed help with all kinds of chores. She insisted that she was to be called Ruth, rather than Mrs Sloam. Her husband, she added laughingly, preferred to be addressed as Professor.

'Nonsense,' he argued, 'I'm just as happy with Jacob. It's you, my dear, that likes to add a bit of dignity to my title. I need help in my study, Nancy. Are you a reader?' he enquired.

'Well, sometimes when I can,' Nancy replied honestly, 'but English was my favourite subject at school. Well, it was the one I did best in. I used to like doing précis, because you read a really interesting bit from a book and that would make you want to read the rest of it. I did go to the Carnegie Library sometimes at the end of our street. I remember finding *Jane Eyre*, I loved that. The lady at the library told me it was one of the most read books in the world.'

Nancy stopped, realising she was chatting away, but Agnes encouraged her, relieved that the trauma she had gone through was starting to pass.

'Go on, Nancy, what did you think of *Jane Eyre*?'

'I loved it,' Nancy replied quietly, remembering sitting in her bedroom with the noise of the railway sidings clanging in the background, and the smell of the local chemical works leaching through the half open window. Edna would frequently disturb her by shouting up the stairs, 'Head in a book again, have you? Come on, Miss Bookworm, there's work to be done.' She knew this was never meant unkindly, but on the other hand she was never encouraged to read.

'We read *A Christmas Carol* at school,' she continued. 'I got into trouble because I finished it first and spoilt it by telling everyone the ending.'

'We're going to get along fine,' Professor Sloam remarked, 'I will prepare you a reading list.'

'Hold on a minute, Jacob. Now can you cook, Nancy?'

'No,' she replied, 'well, bacon and egg, that kind of thing.'

Ruth leaned over and patted her hand. 'Never mind, I can cook, but I can't stand. So I will teach you to cook. Jacob can supervise your reading and you can help him with his papers. You can give Carol, our cleaner, a bit of a hand and do a little shopping in Belper after you have finished at college. Does that sound all right?'

The room was warm and everyone was glowing from cups of tea, cakes and sandwiches.

'It sounds lovely,' Nancy replied, 'thank you so much.' She felt overwhelmed and nervous that if she said any more the spell would be broken.

'I told you,' said Agnes, aware of her confusion, 'this is a remarkable family.'

Nancy presumed she would continue by saying, 'And you're very lucky,' but to her surprise she said, 'And you, Nancy, are a remarkable young woman, you deserve to have this opportunity.'

The room went quiet. To break the silence, Professor Sloam bent forward and offered her another cake. 'Go on, Nancy, help us out, they are bad for my waistline.'

Feeling relaxed, she had replied 'No ta, I'm stuffed,' then embarrassment swept over her and she felt her cheeks turn red. 'No thank you,' she murmured, 'they were delicious, but I've had enough.'

She knew they had all sensed her embarrassment, but she also knew instantly she would change, to diligently immerse herself into their culture.

True to Agnes's words, the Sloams were remarkable, drawing Nancy into their life with ease and elegance. She marvelled at her bedroom every time she entered it. Her own space with a wardrobe and a dressing table. Just too good to be true after the cramped, often damp surroundings she had grown up with. Social services had provided her with money for some new clothes, and Agnes had given her a bag full of underwear from Marks and Spencer, explaining she could change it if it wasn't suitable.

The Sloams had two sons who lived in London with their wives and families. If they came to stay, as they did fairly regularly, Nancy was included in all the family events. If they entertained, she was always introduced to all the guests, so within six months, she was completely integrated into the household, confident enough to make suggestions about the day-to-day running of the house.

Carol, the cleaner, who was about as arthritic as Ruth, often let her do a bit of 'whizzing around', whilst she and Ruth had a cup of tea. The Education College she attended at Belper twice a week gave her a sense of independence, but she instinctively kept herself apart from her fellow students. When her classes were finished, she would leave immediately, armed with her shopping list from Ruth, before catching the first available bus home. Occasionally, Carol would meet her and they would go to the cinema together for an afternoon matinee.

Agnes, who often visited, had explained to the Sloams about Edna and Bill, but it was never referred to. The only thing the Professor teased her about was her surname, Dupray, the name sewn onto the back of her cardigan when she was found wandering about the Orphanage.

'You're probably from some aristocratic family,' he would suggest, 'don't you want to find out?'

'Why?' she had replied. 'I'm sure the mystery is better than the reality. They abandoned me.'

She had remembered years later that he had replied, 'You should read *Les Misérables*, not now, but one day you'll be ready. Then you will know what it is to be truly abandoned.'

But she did want to improve herself. Her Derbyshire accent had never been strong, but now she tried to sound a little more posh, much to Carol's delight. 'A bit of Derbyshire, a bit of London lah-di-dah and a bit of German Jew, they'll never guess where you came from.'

After a few months, Agnes arrived with a cardboard box, which she explained had been left at the hospital by Edna.

Nancy nervously took it up to her room to open it in private. The box smelt musty and when she opened it, the selection of clothes that Edna had forwarded on had the lingering smell of stale cigarette smoke and chips. At the bottom of the box lay Mac, his stuffing hanging out and the candy floss sticky patch still in evidence on his nose. Beneath him was a letter that had been typed out and signed by Edna. It read,

Dear Nancy
I hope you are well.
Please come and see me.
I need to talk to you.
Yours sincerely,
Edna Blore

Nancy felt chilled. She wanted to get rid of everything. It felt as if the contents of the box were invading the room. That the clothes, the smell, would grow and spread, smothering what she had established and ultimately destroy what she had achieved.

She removed the letter and Mac, repacked the rest of the things into the box and tied it with string, forming a handle so she could leave it by the front door to be taken away. Then rejoining the others in the drawing room, she passed the letter to Agnes.

'Edna wants to see me, but I don't want to see her,' she explained. 'If she's worried about me continuing to press charges against Bill, please could you tell her I won't do anything, providing he never attempts to see me. If he does, I will.'

'I'm not sure that's the right thing,' Agnes replied. 'The longer these things go on, it might be too late to get any justice.'

'I agree,' said Nancy, 'but if Edna feels she can protect Bill, she will, and that in turn will help to protect me. Honestly, Agnes, I couldn't bear to go through any more.'

She turned to Professor Sloam. 'May I burn this on the fire?' she asked, holding Mac in front of her.

'A bit dramatic,' he replied. 'Just a bit symbolic, is it? He looks to me as if he might have been loved. But do as you wish, my dear, this is your home.'

Nancy felt she wanted the dramatic gesture to demonstrate her obliterating her past. The conversation continued, but everyone was aware of Mac's demise. He took only a little time to burn, and at one point Nancy felt she needed to jump up and rescue him from the fire. In the morning she searched the ashes and found his two button eyes, which she placed in her purse.

The Sloam family weren't Orthodox Jews, but they did celebrate all the main festivals and happily embraced some of the Christian ones as well. One of their sons had married a Muslim, so it felt a completely liberal household.

'Any excuse for a celebration,' Jacob would say. He was a tall man who walked with a slight stoop, his white hair falling into his bushy eyebrows.

He had a very droll sense of humour, seeing a delicious irony in most situations, which at times upset both his wife and Carol the cleaner.

Nancy, however, sensed a deep sadness in both Ruth and Jacob, and occasionally Jacob would say, 'Leave us, Nancy, today we are in a bad place, but we will return soon.' They would then shut themselves away, with Jacob holding Ruth's hands as he puffed his pipe.

'I don't ask questions,' Carol once told her. 'I know they lost a lot of loved ones.'

But in general the house was lively, with laughter and good humour.

Nancy learned to cook the basics, and several Jewish dishes that avoided using pork. However, Jacob would often demand crispy bacon for breakfast, which outraged Carol. As a Roman Catholic, she felt if you signed up for a religion, you had to keep to the rules. So fish on Friday was a must, and giving something up for Lent was obligatory. In order to tease her, Jacob suggested that he and Nancy also give something up for Lent.

'It has to be something you like,' Carol explained seriously, 'otherwise it's no good. Now if you gave up your pipe for Lent,' she challenged Jacob, 'that would be worthwhile.'

However Jacob was reluctant to give up his pipe. Instead he and Nancy settled on marmalade and chocolate, something they both liked. But for Nancy it was far more than giving something up, it was the realisation that she was accepted lovingly as part of the family.

Two years passed quickly. The two days a week at the Further Education College gave her a Royal Society of Arts Diploma in secretarial skills. Jacob had meticulously supervised her reading, and occasional visits to London had helped to widen her horizons. Ruth's arthritis had become worse, leaving Carol and Nancy to organise most of the domestic tasks. Nancy felt completely content, acknowledging how fortunate she was, strengthened in the knowledge that she always had Agnes to call on. Embraced by this loving family, her fear of Bill had largely diminished. She learned to laugh again, to return Jacob's teasing at times, and to be constantly aware of ways to help both Ruth and Carol with their aches and pains.

Just after Christmas, when the friends and families had returned home, she heard a commotion in the hall. Professor Sloam was talking on the phone, with Ruth interjecting every few seconds.

'My God, I can't believe it, of course we'll go. You can join us, it's not that bad a journey from London.'

Standing at the bottom of the stairs, Nancy was eager to know what had instigated this friendly commotion.

'They're going to Paris,' Carol explained. 'Professor Sloam has been asked to work at the International University from now until October.'

'How did you know?' asked Nancy indignantly.

'Never you mind, miss,' she said, touching her nose. 'I knew before Christmas that there was a likelihood, but they didn't want to say anything to you until they got the final offer, which came this morning.'

Jacob put down the phone.

'Well, the children are pleased. Jane is already planning when they can come over. We're going to Paris, Nancy,' he shouted, grabbing her hands. 'You are going to love it, isn't she, Ruth?'

Nancy felt such a sense of relief that she was part of the adventure that she had to steady herself by sitting down on the bottom stair.

'I'm coming too?' she whispered.

'Of course,' Ruth replied, 'I couldn't do without you.'

CHAPTER SEVEN

*I don't photograph life as it is, but
how I would like it to be.*

– ROBERT DOISNEAU

PARIS, 1955

Only their cleaner Carol seemed to rise above all the turmoil of the Sloams' departure for Paris. Each day she studiously added to two large trunks the items she felt would make her much-loved employers comfortable for their stay. Jacob and Ruth had to renew their passports, whilst Agnes took on the challenge of obtaining one for Nancy without her having a birth certificate.

The phone seemed to be constantly ringing, with calls from across the channel, plus advice from family and friends. Jacob retired mostly into his study, where the smell from his pipe would eventually leak under the door, causing Ruth to demand why he needed to take so many books with him, and had he finally arranged their travel tickets. Nancy revelled in the whole upheaval, helping whoever called on her first.

She knew nothing about Paris, although the two years living with the Sloams had widened her horizons somewhat. But apart from a few very elementary lessons at school about France, her only tangible references were a cobalt-blue bottle of 'Evening in Paris' perfume that Bill had given Edna one Christmas, explaining he had bought it for one of his lady friends and then changed his mind, and the recently released film *An American in Paris* that she and Carol had seen one afternoon in Belper.

Ruth's daughters-in-law would frequently bring her old copies of *Vogue*, and she and Carol would often while away the time looking at them over a cup of tea. So she was familiar with the 'New Look' and the name of Dior, but that, she acknowledged sadly, was about the sum of it.

'So what is Paris like?' she had challenged Jacob one afternoon as they listed the documents going into his trunk.

'It's all of a piece, Nancy. Unlike London, it doesn't turn its back on the river. The Seine is like a satin ribbon thrown carelessly on the ground, with the city embracing it on either side. Unbelievably beautiful, reflecting the seasons as no other city I know. Look.' He reached down into the trunk and retrieved a large book. 'Look, you only have to look at the Impressionists to get a sense of what I am talking about.'

'You sound romantic,' she laughed, taking the book and slowly turning its pages.

'I make no excuse, Nancy. I am romantic. Ruth and I met in Paris. We fell in love in Paris. It's been traumatised by the War, I admit, but it's recovering, and recovering fast, I understand. It's been adopted by the American writers and artists. As I said, I think you'll love it.'

Again he reached down into his trunk. 'Try this, I haven't read it yet. You'll not find it easy, too much angst I suspect, but if you really want a get a feel of modern French culture, it's probably a must. *She Came to Stay* by Simone de Beauvoir, she and Jean-Paul Sartre have been partners for years. It's a kind of 'ménage à trois' I believe, subversive possibly. Anyway, give it a go and let me know what you think.'

She was mildly shocked by its surreal graphic cover. 'I don't know what you are talking about, Jacob,' she laughed, confident in his total lack of disapproval if she owned up to her ignorance on any subject.

'Don't try too hard, Nancy, you're like a sponge – a very beautiful sponge, I admit. You'll just soak it up. You'll be café society before you know it.'

Before they left Agnes gave her a Brownie camera. She admitted her brother had given it to her for Christmas, but she knew she would never use it.

'When I read an article that "street photography" was very popular in Paris, I thought of you. Don't ask me how to use it, I've no idea, but the instructions are in the box.'

It was that smell of coffee, cigarette smoke, perfume and urine pervading the Metro, cafés and bars that first made its impact on Nancy when she arrived in Paris. Within days she was completely seduced by the city, loving everything about it, even though when they arrived at the end of January, it was bitterly cold. She had never been sure about the difference between a flat and an apartment, but Ruth had been quick to point out that an apartment indicated that it was larger and more elegant than a flat. And that was what they found on their arrival, a large Art Nouveau apartment, on the top floor of the main building of the International University. It had a terrace that ran the whole length of the building, which overlooked the campus with all the other various Universities from around the world.

There was a Metro stop very close, so getting into the centre of Paris took less than half an hour. On closer examination the building was a little run down but full of *objets d'art*, paintings, and a melange of old and modern furniture. But despite its fading grandeur, it felt like home, which in fact it was to a Professor Jennings, who Jacob was standing in for. Nancy wasn't quite clear why Jacob had been offered the post, but he seemed to be delighted, telling everyone he was flattered that at his age he could still be of use to the students.

Ruth loved the apartment but found it cold, so Nancy's first job was to create an area where Ruth could sit comfortably and be reasonably warm. The boiler, which served the whole building, including the lecture hall, burst noisily into action at seven in the morning, rattling and wheezing until all the old iron radiators were piping hot. But by midday, it appeared to switch itself off, and by the evening there was barely any warmth left in the system. By moving a little of the furniture around and placing a large comfortable chair in direct contact with one of the radiators together with a two-bar electric fire, similar to the one Edna used to have, Nancy achieved her goal of keeping Ruth warm.

Everyone missed Carol, as their cleaner in Paris only appeared for one morning once a week. Never in any way trying to extend a hand in friendship, she moved noisily around the place, her main consideration seeming to be to polish all the floors, which, when she left, smelt headily of linseed oil. But Nancy coped, finding she didn't have time to be intimidated by her new environment and lack of French. In fact, encouraged by Jacob, she thrived. At first she remained in the area surrounding the University, sourcing the best butcher, grocer and boulangerie. However, in March, the weather burst into an early spring, bringing not only warmth but also a plethora of friends and relatives, eager to enjoy visiting the Sloams and post-war Paris.

This allowed her time to escape a little and explore the city. Jacob had explained that she had to learn the art of French life. The first thing to understand was that she must have the confidence to sit in a café, preferably outside, and watch the world go by. She should take a look in every church, museum and art gallery that crossed her route. She should visit the Louvre regularly, but most importantly, to only allow one hour for each visit, otherwise it became exhausting, and in Jacob's opinion, unproductive.

He advised her to use the Seine, the Eiffel Tower and various parks as her geographical references, adding that she must practice asking for directions, but more importantly, learn the key words in order to understand the reply. To this list of *joie de vivre*, Nancy added the sheer pleasure of wandering along some of the chicest streets. For a girl brought up in the back streets of Derby she soon adapted, and acquired a taste for gazing into boutique windows and confidently ordering a cake, or a small selection of handmade chocolates to carry home as a present for Ruth.

When the family came to visit from London, she accompanied them all to the ballet, the cinema and, on one occasion, to the theatre. As everyone spoke French effortlessly, offering her a swift translation was never an issue. They entertained small groups of lecturers and students on a weekly basis. Advice was always on offer from Jacob.

'Don't be nervous,' he explained. 'In my opinion, most people enjoy a little intrigue. If someone asks about your background, and you tell them you were found as a little girl wandering around in an orphanage, you will have them eating out of your hand immediately. As Ruth constantly points out, I often embellish my stories a little,' he confessed, 'but no bad thing if you stick basically to the truth. You are beautiful, Nancy, something which I think you have not as yet realised. Your outrageously unruly hair is something of a showstopper already.'

She found it wasn't quite as easy as he suggested, as she remained reserved. But after a while, she realised that with the help of his tuition she was becoming quite well-read, and her confidence increased. Many of the young students offered friendship and it would have been easy to have slipped into a relationship with one of the many young men who attended the weekly soirées. But the memories of Bill's attack had left indelible scars, and she preferred to gravitate to the security of the Sloam household.

She adored Jacob, who would constantly provoke her, happy to share his unorthodox view of life in order to make her laugh. As spring developed, the boxes and pots that had lain dormant on the terrace erupted into a riot of colour, with pale blue wisteria overflowing over the balustrade to the gravel drive below.

Now confident on the Metro, she became eager to wander further afield, and as Jacob had suggested, the river became her main landmark. She became familiar with the bridges and the streets with their hidden passages, preferring them to the grander Avenue des Champs-Elysées and Boulevard Haussmann. Occasionally, she would lose her way, and as she described to Jacob when she returned, she felt that she had for a moment scratched the surface to reveal another Paris. One that shocked her with its poverty, which she found it hard to believe still remained so long after the War. The terraced house she had lived in with Edna and Bill was luxury compared to some of the dereliction she saw only a short distance from the centre. She never lingered for long, only perhaps to take a couple of photographs of a lone cat, or a group of children playing amongst the rubble.

If the weather was fine, she would sit outside one of the many cafés, savouring the smell of coffee, treating herself to a pastry or small baguette stuffed with ham and cheese. Self-consciously at first, and often with Ruth's help, she started to develop her own look. A pencil slim skirt, a black polo-necked sweater teamed with a three-quarter length linen coat that the Sloams had treated her to when the weather had turned warmer. Ruth gave her a beret, and there had been much laughter when she had tried it on, but it tamed her unruly hair, and as Jacob observed wryly, 'She knows she looks good in it.'

At first she hadn't used her gift from Agnes, but once she had found how easy the Brownie was to use, she carried it everywhere. As she never had any of the rolls of film developed whilst she was in Paris, she wasn't really sure whether they would turn out, but that didn't deter her from having fun trying to record her love affair with the city. When she heard it click as it snapped a photograph, she was confident the scene would remain in her mind. On one occasion when she was sitting in a café, she was conscious that the young man opposite had surreptitiously taken a few photographs of her. As he left, he smiled, declaring in French, 'I am taking photographs of a beautiful woman,' and placed his card in her saucer. Seeing her confusion, a woman on a nearby table shouted across a translation in English.

'How did you know I'm English?' Nancy shouted back.

'Because you look so French,' the woman replied. 'I'm American and we all want to look French,' she laughed, walking over with her elegant French poodle, who disdained to acknowledge Nancy even though she tried to stroke him.

'The beret is classic. Unbelievable on your hair. "Don't change a hair for me, not if you care for me,"' she sang, to Nancy's embarrassment, before turning to cross the road to join her male companion who stood waiting for her. Nancy guessed the dog was his, as it greeted him excitedly. The woman waved a final farewell, and Nancy watched with amusement as they walked away, the dog trotting happily next to its master.

Nancy pondered whether to remove her beret. No, she decided, cliché or not, it would remain her signature, her homage to Paris.

Ruth's arthritis was now becoming a real problem, and she had reluctantly accepted that on some occasions, a wheelchair was her best option. Clutching a street map, Nancy would wheel Ruth through the local parks and along the river. Jacob would sometimes join them, which invariably led them to walk too far so that they had to hail a taxi for the journey home. As summer faded into autumn they reluctantly started to pack in readiness to return to England.

On their arrival back, they all felt subdued, declaring that they would return again the following year. But for Nancy, Duffield had now become her home, and in spite of it feeling provincial at times, she was contented to have returned.

DERBY, 1968

Nancy stopped speaking. Struggling to free her legs from the blanket on the bed, she stood up and walked towards the window. Apart from the glow of a streetlight her flat was dark, and she stumbled a little to find the switch for one of her table lamps. As it illuminated the room, she turned to Jack.

'Forgive me, Jack, I'm exhausted. It's the first time I've ever really told my story to anyone. Parts are so painful, and parts are so wonderful. But come on, you promised. It's your turn, warts and all.'

'Come back to bed,' he insisted, 'it's cold out there.'

She returned to the warmth of the bed and he embraced her, laughing as she intertwined her body with his to absorb his warmth.

'I suppose a lot my story is dominated by the death of my father. I was born when he was hiding out in France just before the end of the War. My mother didn't know whether he was dead or alive, but she always maintained she thought he had survived.' He reached up and touched Nancy's hair. 'Your hair is so beautiful, you know,' he whispered.

'Cut the compliments,' she cried. 'We aren't talking about hair, we are talking about Jack, and your father – what was his name?'

'He was Jack too. Apparently, he had been adamant that if I was a boy he didn't want me to be named after him, but Mum said when she didn't have any news, she had instinctively called me Jack. Dad hated to be referred to as Jack Senior, so he was always Jack and I was young Jack.

'I just remember him as being the perfect dad, if there is such a thing. Kind, funny, adventurous. He'd parachuted from a plane over Burgundy. The crew thought it was going to crash, but after he leapt out, the engine spluttered back to life and landed safely back home. He was found by two brothers, who took him back to their farm and hid him for about six months. He loved telling the story, and I used to lap it up as a kid.'

He stopped, considering how much he should reveal to Nancy, and how much he could honestly bear to examine himself.

'Go on,' Nancy cajoled. 'Be brave, young Jack.'

'It was a truly happy childhood. Perhaps I'm romanticising it, but it was a bit like the Ladybird books. You know, with the handsome young couple together with their perfect children. The boys wearing short trousers and their sisters in smocked frocks.'

'What do you know about smocked frocks?' Nancy laughed.

'But then something changed. I can still feel that change now. Mum and Dad stopped being the Mum and Dad I knew. They started to be unkind to one another, not in a violent way, just silent. It was like they just stopped communicating. Then there was the storm, and that changed everything.'

CHAPTER EIGHT

What good are words I say to you?
They can't convey to you what's in my heart..

– FRANK SINATRA, '*TIME AFTER TIME*'

BURGUNDY, FRANCE, 1944

It was dark but he could see the ground coming up to meet him, then nothing.

When he opened his eyes he felt no pain, just extreme cold, despite being covered by two large coats. He was able to move slightly but the effort made him feel sick, unlocking the pain, which started to penetrate his body. He lapsed in and out of consciousness. His waking moments were troubled by the knowledge that he must hide his parachute; it took him a while to realise that it was no longer attached to him.

Eventually he became aware that he was on a stretcher. When he lifted his head slightly, he could see the back of a tall man. Conscious of his movement, the man turned. His eyes were just visible through the gap between a mass of scarves and a woollen hat. The piercing eyes met Jack's, communicating as effectively as his voice.

'Don't make any noise!' he said in French, then continuing in English he whispered, 'You understand?'

'*Oui, je comprends*,' Jack replied.

The man's eyes softened a little. The stretcher, Jack realised, was merely a wooden board cushioned by blankets. Two pieces of rope tied across his body secured him to it. He could see they were walking along the edge of an open field. The frozen grass crackled beneath their feet. There was hardly any moon, and at times they stumbled, causing him to groan. After a while they rested, lowering him gently to the ground. Lifting his head and shoulders, they encouraged him to drink from a small bottle. '*Doucement*, slowly,' they cautioned, as the brandy seared down his throat.

Soon they reached a track, and their progress became a little easier. At times a white owl hovered above their heads as if leading the way. The icy silence of the night was only interrupted by the sound of the two men's feet on the gravel. The brandy helped, but before the drowsiness took over, Jack heard a third voice as they moved him off the stretcher.

When he awoke it was light. A young woman was asleep on a chair in the corner of a small but well-furnished room. A book rested on her knees, ready to fall to the ground at the slightest movement. A fire had been lit in the grate of an elaborate stone fireplace, so the room, whilst not hot, had lost its chill. The painted wooden desk, which stood against one wall, looked well used. Its stencilled flowers were faded by the sun, as was a matching chair positioned in front of it. On every wall there was a selection of paintings and prints, mostly depicting flowers and birds. The wallpaper that covered not only the walls but also the door and cupboards was decorated with tiny green sprigs of foliage scattered between narrow strips. The air smelt sweet from whatever oil had been used to polish the floor.

To wake in such a room after the trauma of the night before seemed to Jack like waking up in a kind of paradise. As he moved, his leg brushed against a stone hot water bottle. He found he couldn't straighten his right arm, which had been strapped against his chest. He sensed his right ankle was also bound with some kind of support attached to his leg. He wore what appeared to be a large nightshirt, but with only his uninjured arm in one of the sleeves. His feet felt cold.

Hearing him move, the girl stirred, causing her book to fall to the ground. She stared at him for an instant as if remembering where she was. After a second she sprang from her chair, a look of alarm spreading across her face. She spoke hurriedly, and although Jack's French was schoolboy stuff, it was sufficient to understand she was going to fetch someone called Jean-Baptiste.

'What is your name?' he asked her in French.

She stopped at the foot of the bed. 'You speak French?'

'*Un peu,*' he replied.

'My name is Françoise, and you must be very quiet,' she added seriously.

'I promise to be very quiet,' he agreed, 'just like a mouse.'

'Mice can be very noisy,' she replied. 'Quieter than a mouse, please.'

Within minutes Françoise returned with Jean-Baptiste, who Jack presumed was the hooded man of the night before.

'My name is Jean-Baptiste,' he announced, his voice tinged with arrogance, 'and I present to you my parents.'

He indicated the two people standing to one side. He had thick black hair like his mother, but there the resemblance stopped. She was even taller than him, with a startlingly square jaw. She wore a spotlessly clean all-enveloping apron, and a woollen shawl around her shoulders. Her expression was severe, but Jack sensed no animosity, just the realisation that the situation they had found themselves in was unquestionably dangerous. Jean-Baptiste's father was short and wiry, and probably, Jack thought, some twenty years older than his wife.

They stood in a group but in deference to the older man they let him speak first. He began slowly articulating each word, but then glancing at his son, he started to speak faster so that the words ran together. Jack raised his good arm, indicating he couldn't understand. Jean-Baptiste placed his hand on his father's shoulder in order to stem the stream of words, then he continued to speak at a slower pace, throwing in the occasional English word here and there. He explained that Jack's presence placed his family in a very dangerous situation. '*Vie en danger*, life threatening,' he repeated several times. The Germans would shoot anyone who was part of the Resistance, or anyone, male or female, who gave protection to the Allies.

Jack struggled to understand everything, but he grasped the fact that Jean-Baptiste thought that the war was now drawing to an end. However, he made it clear that he thought this didn't make the Germans any less dangerous. As he spoke, a large man of indeterminate age came into the room, ducking his head slightly under the door lintel.

'I present to you my brother Bernard,' Jean-Baptiste said in halting English. Then, continuing in French, he added, 'He helped carry you last night.'

Bernard was even taller than his mother, but with softer features. He looked down all the time, which gave him the air of being simple. His hands were huge, and as Jack noticed later, each finger was the same size, with hardly any nail. Like his father he wore thick working clothes and sturdy leather boots. In stark contrast to the room with its feminine touches, they carried in the earthy smell and feel of the farmyard.

'It's finished,' he said. 'Françoise is tidying up.' He extended his hand towards Jack, and nodded awkwardly as Jack returned his grasp, thanking him for his assistance the previous night.

'We have to hide you,' Jean-Baptiste explained. 'Do you understand? It's not going to be easy, but I can't risk the lives of our family. If you don't stick to the rules, I'll shoot you!' His mother gasped, clutching Jean-Baptiste's hand, but he brushed it to one side and repeated in English, 'You understand?'

Jack indicated he understood, explaining in his broken French that they must not feel that they had to hide him. He would surely survive as a prisoner of war.

'It's too late to hand you in,' Jean-Baptiste said ungraciously. 'Blame my father, if he hadn't been checking our traps last night we wouldn't have found you. I heard a plane falter, but then it regained power. Why the hell did you jump? And I am hoping, for God's sake, that you were the only one?'

He repeated the last question, giving Jack the chance to understand it properly and to be able to reply honestly that as far as he knew he was the only one. He too had heard the engine spring back into life. He had half expected it to crash. When that didn't happen, he felt confident they had continued.

Françoise appeared at the door with a tray bearing a saucepan of thick chicken soup, accompanied by a large chunk of grey bread. They all watched and partly assisted as Jack struggled to eat with his only useable hand. He was suddenly ravenous, and had to check himself from not causing offence by gobbling the food down too fast.

'*C'est délicieux*,' he said to Jean-Baptiste's mother.

'You would like some more?' she replied timidly in English.

'*Vous parlez anglais*?' Jack enquired.

She laughed. '*Un peu*,' she replied.

The tension in the room relaxed, until Jack felt his stomach contract. 'The toilet please, I am sorry, I need the toilet!' he cried.

Bernard and Jean-Baptiste lifted him out of the bed and half carried him down to the large bathroom at the end of the landing. As they lowered him onto the toilet his insides exploded.

'I'm sorry, I'm sorry,' he murmured.

Bernard left the room, but Jean-Baptiste remained leaning against the wall. He lit a cigarette. After a while Jack raised his head and the two young men looked at one another. The tension that had surrounded them in the bedroom diminished and they started to laugh.

'Silence!' the father shouted, 'silence!'

Jean-Baptiste continued to laugh, replying, 'There are no Germans around, and if you see one ask him to come and wipe his bum!'

Jack barely understood the nuances, but he heard Bernard and Françoise laughing outside the door. As he curbed his laughter and out of necessity accepted Jean-Baptiste's help, he marvelled at their generosity. He wondered whether he and Elizabeth would have done the same thing. He smiled, conjuring up his wife's face. Yes, he thought confidently, I am sure she would, despite the danger. This war had brought with it not only pain and suffering but a genuine camaraderie, a desire to help your neighbour.

The two brothers moved him that night. He had lost all sense of time, but he guessed it must be late as the fire in the grate was just a mound of grey ashes. Jean-Baptiste stood over him, then, bending, he lowered his face to Jack's. His hot breath smelt of wine and stale cigarettes.

'Silence,' he said, 'silence, you understand?'

There was no warmth in his words, just the sense that if he disobeyed, Jean-Baptiste was capable of inflicting a lasting and deadly silence on him. He braced himself for the pain as the two men lifted him onto the stretcher. His breathing became increasingly laboured. He guessed that he had broken ribs as well as injuries to his shoulder and leg. Bernard offered a small towel, indicating that he should put it between his teeth. He closed his eyes, biting into the towel so that he could direct the pain into it whilst they negotiated getting him down the wide, shallow stairs. Halfway down they took a turn, which involved a difficult manoeuvre but at the bottom they rested the stretcher on three small chairs.

By the faint light of an oil lamp, Jack was able to see he was in the hall. A large clock stood in one corner, and a boar's head and a collection of small antlers were clustered on the wall above an upright piano. Below the window stood a chest adorned with a large pewter jug full of holly. He felt a complete sense of helplessness. He was an intruder, an uninvited guest who could destroy all their lives. As their father opened the front door, Jean-Baptiste and Bernard took control again, conveying him into the freezing air.

The journey across the courtyard was swift and silent, their footsteps muffled by a carpet of falling snow. He sensed by the sound and smell of livestock that he was entering a large cattle shed. Jean-Baptiste had extinguished the lantern, so it was difficult for Jack to know exactly what was happening. Without warning they lowered the stretcher and in one movement, Bernard cradled him in his arms and, with Jean-Baptiste pushing from behind and half supporting him, they mounted the ladder into the loft. Françoise was already positioned above to help Bernard as he gently lifted Jack off the ladder. They slid him onto a blanket, and regardless of being half-conscious, Jack realised he was being dragged across the floor. This took some time, but finally Bernard lifted him again and, half kneeling, he awkwardly placed Jack on a narrow bed. He guessed they had given him more of the dark brandy to drink, because in spite of the searing pain which wracked his body, he slept.

When the morning light penetrated his hiding place, he realised why the manoeuvre had caused such a problem. His new bed was no more than four feet wide, wedged between two walls, one a stone exterior, the other appearing to be constructed from wooden planks. When he tried to lift his head he felt nauseous. He reached out and touched the stone wall; it felt deeply cold. He lay still for a little longer, willing the sickness to pass, clutching the towel Bernard had given him to his mouth in case he vomited.

Eventually, he raised himself onto his elbows, striving to make some sense of where he was. He could see no sign of a door, and the only light came from an opening high up on the end wall some twenty feet away. He lay on a mattress covered in an assortment of blankets with one pillow for his head and a further two placed either side to protect him from the cold.

As the light continued to filter through, he could just see a small table and two chairs. The only other items were a bucket and two large jars on a small shelf next to his bed. One for water and one for urine, he guessed. If they had taken this much trouble, he reasoned, they hadn't planned to abandon him. He peed into one of the jars, struggling to replace it back on the shelf. The nausea passed.

Relaxing a little, he became more accustomed to the gloom. Dictated by the wind, puffs of snow burst through the opening at the end of his narrow cell. He could see his breath in the bitingly cold air, but he felt reasonably warm swaddled by his mountain of covers. He watched, mesmerised, as one minute the wind would die down, and then a further gust would send a flurry of snowflakes into his room.

Some survived the descent and landed on the table, others melted as they fell.

He sought comfort in allowing himself to remember being sent home from school one day with the rest of his class. It had been snowing heavily, and when he approached his street, he was startled that it looked so different. The pavement and road had merged into one. Great flakes of snow fell majestically to the ground, their intricate patterns illuminated by the afternoon light. He remembered walking with his head turned up towards the falling flakes, enjoying the way they landed gently on his face. Later, in the early dusk, he and his father had built a snowman. It was rather wonderful, he remembered, with a carrot nose, pebble eyes, a scarf, two sticks for arms, plus the final touch: one of his father's pipes.

He soon realised, as he continued to watch the snow swirling into the cell, that Bernard had built a false wall in a loft space in what he thought must be an ancient outbuilding. It was intensely claustrophobic, although this was slightly alleviated by the opening where the snow tumbled through. Raising himself was difficult, but even using his good arm to sit up, he was still unable to discern where the door might be.

Not long after, he heard a noise from behind the partition and was relieved but somewhat surprised to see, rather than a door, a long, floor-level hinged flap open up, through which Jean-Baptiste emerged like the delivery of an oversized letter. As he rose to his feet, the flap closed noisily behind him. He was still wearing the same ensemble from the previous night. The dust from the floor had streaked his thick navy coat with its embossed brass buttons. As he brushed it off with his woollen scarf, Jack reflected that Jean-Baptiste did not have the look of an artisan, as did his father and brother. He sank unceremoniously on to Jack's bed.

'What do you think?' he demanded somewhat arrogantly.

'Incredible,' Jack replied, 'truly incredible. Did Bernard build it?'

Jean-Baptiste nodded. 'Listen to me,' he spoke slowly, completing each sentence with, '*Comprenez vous?* Do you understand?'

He was never to open the flap and go outside into the other room. He would bring Jack an oil lamp, but he was only to use it when he could sit at the table, not near his bed. The bucket was his commode, which would be emptied every day. He should continue to wear his nightshirt, as it made ablutions easier. 'Trousers come later,' Jean-Baptiste remarked wryly.

He lit a cigarette, shrugging with a mixture of surprise and annoyance as Jack refused his offer of one. He continued to explain slowly that the Germans were everywhere. Their base was in the local town of Avallon, nine kilometres from the village, where the majority of them were billeted. But he cautioned there were some in the surrounding villages, and most of the officers occupied a large chateau three kilometres away. Each village town hall was subjected to a visit from them at least once a week, and each morning two or three German soldiers arrived to collect milk, eggs and anything else they could plunder from the farm where Jack was now being hidden.

When they first occupied the area, the Germans had tried to be friendly, but his family had found it hard to respond in a similar fashion, particularly his father. They were one of the largest farms in the area, and to a large extent this had protected them as the soldiers relied on them for food. However, a week ago one of them had tried to shoot Françoise's cat, which had been caught drinking from one of the milk churns. Fortunately he had missed the cat, but the churn had fallen over and the garrison in Avallon had run short of milk as a result. His mother and sister had both been present when it happened and had not disguised their horror that a gun had been used in an attempt to kill their cat.

The ambience was not good, he concluded, and if Jack were to be discovered, he felt they would show very little mercy, even to the women. Three young local men, last seen walking from Avallon to a neighbouring village, had disappeared recently. Their distraught families had pleaded with the Adjutant for information, but none was forthcoming.

Jack sensed, when he asked about the Resistance, that Jean-Baptiste was guarded in his reply. They operated in the Morvan, he explained, a large forested area south of the town. They did a good job, he admitted. But sadly, he thought that no one was to be trusted. He stressed that Jack must play close attention to his injuries. His father had dressed and strapped his shoulder and leg, but they must be kept clean to avoid infection, as there was no possibility of contacting a doctor. He would help him each evening, and Françoise or his mother would bring him breakfast and some bread for midday, pushing it through the flap. He and Bernard would bring him dinner.

Food was scarce, he was quick to point out. The Germans would consume everything given half a chance. It was, he acknowledged, easier for his family because of the farm. They tried to hold a little back to help the villagers, but even that posed a danger. He reached into his pocket, producing a small French-English dictionary; it had been his mother's when she taught years ago at the village school. 'Do your homework,' he instructed Jack gruffly.

As Jean-Baptiste made ready to post himself through the flap, Jack managed to string together a halting expression of thanks. Jean-Baptiste shrugged, his shoulders hunched up with weariness. Hesitating for a moment he finally turned around, and facing Jack again, he asked with a touch of compassion in his voice, 'Ça va, Jack?'

Jack responded quickly, 'Ça va, ça va merci. Vous êtes très gentil. You are very kind.'

Jean-Baptiste threw back his head and broke into a short burst of laughter, before he negotiated his way clumsily though the exit to the cell.

Jack could hear the storm continuing outside, buffeting the external wall. He marvelled at how extraordinary life was. What was Elizabeth thinking? Had she been told he was missing? Did she think he was dead? To avoid worrying her he hadn't mentioned his mission when they were last together; it seemed pointless to distress her unnecessarily. As an officer in the RAF he was normally office-bound, there to support the bombing crews with precise information, photographs and maps. Occasionally he was asked to join them as he specialised in night photography. He admitted to himself that these missions gave him the extra frisson of feeling he was risking his life like countless other comrades, and not just sitting safely at a desk.

It was a relief that he was not allowed to talk about these trips to anybody. Elizabeth would have naturally worried. In spite of their happiness together, the spectre of her two miscarriages continued to haunt their lives. It hung over them, regardless of the fact she was now eight months pregnant again. Occasionally she had placed his hand on her stomach, asking him excitedly, 'Can you feel it move?'

They were an intelligent, rational couple, but the fear of having their hopes dashed yet again caused them to avoid discussing their longed-for child, fearing that just mentioning the subject might turn fate against them. In the past, baby clothes had been made, or bought with precious coupons donated by other members of the family. Then everything had been packed away in a drawer when she had miscarried. He thought how easily it could have damaged their marriage, but, whilst heartbroken, Elizabeth picked herself up quickly, confident they would eventually produce a child. *This time*, he thought, *we are so close, closer than we have ever been before.* 'Please, God,' he thought, 'keep her safe. Don't let this drama destroy our child.' He lay on his bed willing her to know he was still alive.

His courtship of Elizabeth had been brief. She was training to be a teacher. He was a civil engineer working for the local council, but about to join the RAF for the duration of the War. They met in the library, both reaching for the same book. There had been much laughter, resulting in an agreement that Elizabeth would read the book the following week, after which Jack would read it and then they would meet to discuss it over tea. They stuck to the plan and over tea they discovered that not only did they have the same taste in literature, but a shared interest in other subjects too.

They were both only children born to middle-aged parents, who were both delighted when they announced their intention to marry. Their wedding had been simple. Elizabeth dressed in a tailored suit that complemented her classical features and slim figure. Jack thought how beautiful she was, but in a totally understated way, elegant in both mind and body, with a heart-warming optimism about their future life together.

The austerity of the war dictated that there was little time or money for a honeymoon. Nevertheless they had managed to steal a heady few days alone in their new home. Shy to begin, with neither having much experience of the opposite sex, they had tentatively explored each other, until an overwhelming passion engulfed them. For a while they became a single entity, hardly needing friends or family to share their life. When Elizabeth became pregnant she gave up her teacher training, promising herself she would continue with it one day.

These images of Elizabeth flooded his mind as he lay in his narrow bed. He suddenly recalled the Christmas cake. He'd cut a chunk to take back to base last time he'd been home, and a slice of it had been in his pocket when he bailed out. He had no idea where they had put his uniform, but the thought of the cake wrapped in a piece of grease-proof paper was strangely comforting.

Regardless of the cold and cramped conditions, he soon fell into a routine dictated by visits from Jean-Baptiste, Bernard and their sister, who delivered his meals and assisted him with caring for his injuries. Ablutions were difficult but Jean-Baptiste helped on some occasions, joking to Bernard that they'd better keep the Englishman clean. On the instructions of Claude, Jean-Baptiste's father, the bandages had been removed and a foul-smelling cream that Jean-Baptiste reckoned was for the horses was administered every other day by one of the brothers, Bernard being by far the gentler of the two in this regard. Jack considered that Jean-Baptiste enjoyed inflicting a little pain on his captive, possibly seeing it as part payment for the risk they took in hiding him.

Prior to Christmas he'd spent a whole day creating a simple card for the family. Although painful at first, he was soon able to lift his arm and creep his fingers up the wall until it was fully extended. Holding a pencil was difficult, but as Françoise had supplied him with paper, and several pencils, he was able to draw an imaginary Christmas scene. Battling with an attempt to create a crowd of carol singers, he felt the style was Dickensian, with a hint of Picasso. Taking no chances, he wrote the Happy Christmas in French. On Christmas morning when Françoise delivered his breakfast through the flap, he posted the card in return. He heard her giggle, and was relieved that he had made the effort when he saw that his *petit déjeuner* contained not only bread but an egg and a piece of cheese.

He was surprised that he did not feel depressed; impatient, yes, but not morose. He felt confident that Elizabeth and their baby were safe and well. He would be reported missing, but thank God not dead. He respected Elizabeth's inner strength and her resolve, that even after two miscarriages, they would eventually have a child. He could imagine her distress, especially at Christmas, but he knew she would not contemplate the possibility of his death, at least while hope remained. Wrapped in his tangle of blankets, which barely protected him from the cold, he contemplated how fortunate he had been in finding a young woman he not only felt passionate about, but who he also admired and respected for her intelligence and enthusiasm for life.

After Christmas each day became a minor battle. He devised a routine that he rigidly stuck to despite the cold and frequent lack of light. He washed, studied French, aided by the dictionary that Jean-Baptiste's mother had provided. He exercised and walked up and down his bleak corridor for hours at a time, often softly humming a piece of music or reciting a poem remembered from his school days. His ankle had improved, although he continued to wear the crude brace that supported it.

Most evenings Jean-Baptiste would bring his supper. Sliding the flap, he would light the oil lamp and then after Jack had eaten they would play cards. Jack was impressed to see that he appeared to have an endless supply of tobacco, enabling him to roll his own cigarettes. He would also usually arrive with some kind of alcohol, which was shared in equal measure. Sometimes Françoise would join them, but Jack sensed that perhaps her parents did not approve of her visits. But when she did arrive, wearing several layers of clothing, plus hat and gloves, she immediately lifted their spirits by provoking her brother whom, Jack observed from the outset, she unashamedly adored.

Jack found it hard to access Jean-Baptiste's feeling towards him. One minute they shared a kind of camaraderie, another Jean-Baptiste would appear sullen, even angry, pushing his thick black hair away from his face to reveal a deep scar on his forehead. Jack had at first fantasised he had received it in a fight, but Françoise said it was the result of falling out of a tree when he was a child.

He was the same height as Jack, but thicker set. His dark complexion and piercing brown eyes reminded Jack of a portrait of a young Italian Count he had seen in an art gallery he had visited with Elizabeth. He couldn't remember the name of the artist, but he remembered being disturbed by the way the young man's eyes were full of arrogance and challenge. Elizabeth had laughingly thought that it was just a young man revelling in his masculinity, but Jack had continued to be unsettled by his gaze, as he was occasionally by Jean-Baptiste's unfaltering confidence in himself.

After sharing a particularly strong bottle of home-made wine with Jean-Baptiste and Françoise one evening he had tried to explain this resemblance. It was meant as a jest, a back-handed compliment, but their limited understanding of each other's respective languages made it virtually impossible to explain properly, and it ended up with them all laughing hysterically. Françoise had discovered that both Jack and Jean-Baptiste were the same age, twenty-eight, although Jean-Baptiste was the elder by seven months, and would thereafter call Jack 'our little baby'. In truth that was how Jack felt at times, helpless and reliant on their goodwill for his survival.

Françoise was nineteen, a disturbing mixture of pretty and plain, depending on her mood. She was aware that Jack had a wife, but that did not stop her flirting with him. Jean-Baptiste tormented her about not having a boyfriend, but she defended herself robustly saying that all men in their village were stupid. Jack tried not to respond to her, but his young spirit made it difficult not to engage in some coy banter at times.

One evening she explained the dynamics of the family. Her father's first wife had died, leaving him with an only child, Bernard. Her mother's first husband had also died in a farming accident, leaving her with a young son, Jean-Baptiste. Scandalising the village, in her opinion, she had married Claude, twenty years her senior, 'and nearly half her height!' Jean-Baptiste had added. Françoise was born shortly after the marriage, described by Jean-Baptiste as the 'little love child'. Françoise retorted that she accepted that as a compliment, and was quick to endorse Jean-Baptiste when, through the haze of smoke, he proposed a toast to his stepfather. 'The jolly Papa is a good man, a good father, and if I am to believe my mother, a good husband,' he added with a wink to Jack.

When Jack probed for more information about the family, Jean-Baptiste was adamant the less he knew the better. Françoise begrudgingly agreed, explaining that her father constantly worried about the situation.

When they left, still stifling their laughter as the effect of the wine made it hard to negotiate their exit through the flap, Jack considered whether Jean-Baptiste's accolade to his stepfather held perhaps a touch of irony. He rarely saw them together, but when Claude did accompany Jean-Baptiste to check on his injuries, he sensed their relationship was cordial but not warm. Jack acknowledged that possibly, being an only child, he was fortunate to have a very close and loving relationship with his parents. His father's good sense, humour and love for his mother had given him a happy childhood.

Most nights, regardless of the amount of alcohol he and Jean-Baptiste had drunk, he found it difficult to sleep. The cold was relentless, creeping through his blankets to penetrate his body. Often he would resort to pondering on what it would be like to have a child of his own, using these thoughts to combat the cold and ease him into sleep.

CHAPTER NINE

Germany calling, Germany calling.

– LORD HAW-HAW (WILLIAM JOYCE)

BURGUNDY, FRANCE, 1945

January remained icy and bleak. There was little news of the war. Listening to the radio was forbidden, but snippets of information filtered through from the villagers who, Jean-Baptiste explained, recklessly ignored the ban. It was reported that some German troops had already left Avallon, but it wasn't clear if this was a retreat or a regrouping.

February brought driving rain; worse than the cold, it seeped through the walls into his bed. He became obsessed by the flap, gazing at it for hours, trying to imagine what lay beyond. He was aware that Jean-Baptiste dragged something in front of it whenever he left. As the month progressed, he developed a painful sore throat, then a tight feeling across his chest, which in turn culminated in a rasping cough. The cough wracked his body, leaving him weak and listless. Afraid of the noise he was making, he would bury his head under the pillow, his sweat mixing with the dampness that dripped onto his bed from the exterior wall.

At night he started to dream he was being dragged from his cell by the Germans and forced to watch the family being butchered in the mysterious room on the other side of the flap. Each morning became something of a continuing nightmare as he tried to keep himself in check, determined that the family would not become aware of his fragile state of mind. His daily routine started to falter as his failing health took its toll. Jean-Baptiste's visits became less frequent as he and the rest of the family were suffering with similar symptoms. Bernard was now his main courier who delivered his meals.

One afternoon he sensed that Bernard had not dragged the unknown object back after placing his lunch through the flap. Rising awkwardly, he sat on the end of the bed contemplating his next move. He had agreed to abide by the rules set down by Jean-Baptiste. He knew they were fair, made to protect his survival and also the safety of the family. He thought of Elizabeth, acknowledging that any foolish decision could also affect her future. But his exit route beckoned.

He knelt in front of the flap and then tentatively pushed it open a little. Nothing appeared to be obstructing it, but as he extended it to its full height, he heard a crash and the sound of something rolling across a floor. Overcome with guilt, he retreated, unable to muster enough courage to progress into the space beyond. He knew what a fine line he trod. For a while he lay on top of the bed, gazing at the opening at the end of the corridor. He welcomed the cold as it acted as a penance for his reckless behaviour. Perhaps Bernard would not notice when he returned. But later he heard Jean-Baptiste approaching on the other side with his supper.

'A bloody big rat has tried to escape!' the Frenchman shouted. 'If it tries again, I will hack it in two!'

Jack heard the object pulled back into place. He listened hard, in an effort to decide if Jean-Baptiste had left without delivering his food. All was quiet for several minutes, then the flap opened, his supper appeared, followed by Jean-Baptiste. He was prepared for anger, but there was none. The evening continued in its normal fashion, without any reference to the 'bloody rat'. However, his cough had worsened, not helped by Jean-Baptiste's constant smoking. When he left, earlier than usual, Jack rolled fully clothed into bed, only to be disturbed a little later by Françoise who delivered two stone hot water bottles, together with a glass bottle full of a potion that she explained her mother had made to help his cough. Although she didn't scramble into his space, she spoke clearly to him.

'It's ok, Jack, no one is angry. We are just sorry that it has to be this way.'

She extended her hand through the opening in an attempt to wave, then dragged the object back and sealed him in for the night. The potion tasted like thick plum juice, laced with brandy and possibly a little vinegar. He felt a mixture of shame and relief as he drifted off into a good night's sleep.

The day after the incident with the rogue 'rat', the rain had stopped. A blue sky now filled his tiny window, through which he could catch the occasional glimpse of a bird in flight. The hot water bottles were stone cold, and as he removed them, he wondered how on earth Françoise had managed to carry them from the house to his den. The homemade potion had released some of the tightness across his chest, allowing him to cough and sit more easily. His spirits revived as he waited for his *petit déjeuner* to arrive. He resolved that under no circumstances would he let them down again.

His hiding place allowed in very little noise, but this morning seemed particularly quiet, and he guessed it was Sunday and the family had gone to church. Trapped between the two walls, he had no knowledge of the surrounding countryside. When the wind was in the right direction he could hear the faint chiming of a church clock. He had asked Françoise to describe the area and she had offered to draw a map, but Jean-Baptiste had been adamant that the less he knew the safer it was for them all. Chastised by Françoise, Jean-Baptiste had on several occasions expressed his contempt for any form of religion, so Jack was not surprised when the flap opened. What did unnerve him was that he didn't hear the typical cursing that usually accompanied Jean-Baptiste's arrival. Instead he heard Jean-Baptiste shouting.

'*Bonjour Monsieur* Rat, time for your debut. I invite you to join me.'

Jack didn't hesitate, although he felt nervous, like a child being asked to do something for the first time. The younger members of the family had learnt to swiftly negotiate the manoeuvre through the flap, but his first attempt was clumsy, especially as he found he had to keep his head down as he emerged under a large table.

Jean-Baptiste roughly grabbed his arm as he finally managed to right himself. In a kind of disbelief, he tried to take in his surroundings. Far from being in a hayloft as he had imagined, it was a fully furnished studio. On the far wall two identical tall bookcases stood side by side. They had elaborately carved tops that incorporated swags and shells. Books of all shapes and sizes fought for position in the right-hand case. The large ones were stacked horizontally, together with piles of newspapers and magazines. The other bookcase held an untidy array of ornaments, several unfinished sculptures, jam jars filled with brushes, and several masks, one with a long sinister nose. Two enormous trestle tables, pushed end to end, dominated the centre of the room. Their tops were daubed and splashed carelessly with different coloured paints. Next to them was an empty easel.

Jack turned back towards his hiding place in an attempt to piece together the geography of the room. Disguising the entrance to his flap wasn't a table, as he had originally thought, but a huge impressive desk with a solid chair that he guessed hid the flap. Behind that was the false wall that Bernard had so masterfully constructed. It was covered in a haphazard patchwork of pieces of paper, newspaper cuttings, lists and notes as well as family photographs. The desk was littered with books, a typewriter and a bulky stone paperweight in the shape of a pig's head.

As Jack looked up he could see numerous birds' nests tucked in between the gnarled wooden beams that supported the roof. A long cylindrical chimney rose from a wood-burning stove to one side of the room. In front of the stove rested a shabby but uncompromisingly elegant sofa, and a large leather armchair that had seen better days. Piled against the remaining two walls were canvases of various shapes and sizes. They were all turned inwards apart from one. Jack stood back to examine it. It was a haunting illustration of a man standing on a beach. Most of the composition was the portrayal of a vast rolling grey sea, with a turbulent sky filled with heavy clouds. Without permission, he started to turn round some of the other canvases, but before he became too engrossed, he turned to Jean-Baptiste and asked, 'May I?'

Jean-Baptiste nodded, and lighting a cigarette, he sat down in the armchair.

As Jack examined the canvases, he thought of his parents. When he was a boy, they had taken him regularly to art galleries. His father loved the Pre-Raphaelites, whilst his mother preferred the Impressionists. Quite often she would buy a postcard of one of her favourite paintings and timidly try to copy it at home. For a moment he could see her sat at her small rolltop desk, intent on recapturing the magic of the original image. He knew she would have admired most of the canvases, as he did, but possibly not the more contemporary and violent portrayals of the occupation.

'So, what do you think?' Jean-Baptiste finally asked.

'You are the painter?' Jack responded.

Jean-Baptiste's reply was tinged with humour. 'I am the artist.'

'You are good,' Jack continued admiringly.

'Do you know about these things?' Jean-Baptiste asked laughingly, sending a spiral of cigarette smoke above his head.

'I know what I like,' countered Jack, 'and these are really good.'

'Yes, I am good, I am very good.'

For a second, Jack felt embarrassed, then he turned to Jean-Baptiste, offering him his hand and adding honestly, 'You are an artist, a cocky one at that, but a talented artist nevertheless.'

Jean-Baptiste shook his hand, then pulling him closer he kissed him robustly on both cheeks. As he released Jack, he demanded, 'What is "cocky"? Like a *coq*?' Not waiting for an answer, he continued, 'Yes, I am cocky. You are in Burgundy, haven't you heard of Burgundy cocks?' He repeated the word "cocky" several times, obviously enjoying giving it a French resonance.

Jack laughed, suddenly in awe of this man. He had recognised that he was a courageous man, educated and practical, but to discover he was also an accomplished artist was a surprise.

The only light that filtered into the studio was from a small window that overlooked the courtyard and the entrance via the ladder from the barn below. Jack felt strangely dizzy for a moment, as if his senses needed time to re-establish themselves. The sound of cattle moving below and the sweet mixed odour of manure and hay that hung in the air felt for a moment like an invasion into his previously cloistered existence. He steadied himself, startled by Jean-Baptiste's cry to 'stand back!'

Then to his amazement, Jean-Baptiste reached up, unbolted two massive shutters and flung them open with dramatic effect. The sun burst through, obliterating the gloom and highlighting the millions of dust motes caught in its rays. An ancient mechanism, reminiscent of a hangman's scaffold, hung on the outside, its worn rope and hook swinging in the breeze. Having been holed up for five months, any view would have satisfied him, but this filled him with an intense feeling of joy.

Two ploughed fields dotted with trees gave way to a small road, and beyond Jack could see a long fortified stone wall rising up to a row of ancient houses. Several of the houses had turrets, and one slightly further back appeared to be a small chateau. Beyond the dwellings the land continued to rise dramatically to a medieval arch, and finally to a church at the top of the hill. When he had heard the muffled chimes of the clock, he had expected the church to have a spire, but instead it resembled an abbey, its towering honey-coloured stone walls reflecting the light as it towered above the village. He drew closer to the opening, but Jean-Baptiste restrained him.

'Enough beauty for one day,' he remarked solemnly as he closed the shutters.

For the rest of the morning they sat together in the studio. When the family returned from church Françoise joined them. She was dressed more stylishly than Jack had seen before, her face bearing the hint of rouge and lipstick. She coyly offered Jack a large woollen blanket to wear around his shoulders, laughing happily when he complemented her on her outfit. She insisted that Jack sit cosily in the leather armchair whilst she and her brother started to battle with the stove, a tall cylindrical affair with green metal sides that had been moulded to create a circular design depicting a group of statuesque, classical women bearing plates dripping with fruit and flowers. Bernard arrived with a stack of logs and took over the task of coaxing the fire into life.

As they hovered around the stove, warming their hands near the metal, Jean-Baptiste explained that all the family were privy to his release. His mother had been adamant that his routine must change, otherwise his health would deteriorate. 'She is determined you will return to your Elizabeth, and hopefully that brat of yours, in good health.'

'Jolly Papa was not so sure, but eventually he endorsed the plan,' Françoise added. 'In future we suggest you leave your hiding place later in the afternoon when any stray Germans have usually returned to base. The villagers are used to seeing a light and smoke coming from Jean-Baptiste's studio, so no one should be suspicious.'

Bernard murmured something to Jean-Baptiste.

'Yes,' Jean-Baptiste added, 'and Bernard rightly says that you must practice getting through the flap, in case there is an emergency. We'd make as much noise as possible if we did think the Germans wanted to search the place, but you would need to move fast. I've reluctantly done some sign painting for them, so they know I'm an artist of sorts. The fact that the studio feels warm should not be a problem, but make sure the flap is closed. Fortunately, now the rat has finally escaped, there is no need for objects on the other side.'

Suddenly the immensity of the situation registered with them all.

'You understand?' Jean-Baptiste asked in English. Normally he stuck to French, throwing in the odd English word or gesture if he thought Jack didn't understand, but this time he repeated the instructions again slowly, adding, 'This is deadly serious.'

Françoise broke the mood by demonstrating her very personal way of coping with the flap. Wrapping her skirts tightly around her legs, she pushed her feet through first, twisting from her back to her front, so that when she reached the other side, she was on all fours. Everyone cheered, and Jack gallantly offered her a little assistance on her return trip.

When they all left to have lunch with their parents, Jack stayed close to the fire, experiencing a feeling of well-being. After lunch, delivered by the faithful Bernard, he slept until Jean-Baptiste woke him in the early evening. They played cards by the light of an oil lamp. When Jean-Baptiste guessed that he had plied him with enough wine he encouraged him to take up his place again for the night in his cold cell. He felt no temptation to return to the warmth of the fire. He knew they had pushed the boundaries as far as they dared, and he was grateful.

Apart from a few blustery showers, the weather remained mild for the rest of March. Jack could feel his strength returning. Each afternoon he enjoyed the opportunity of exploring the studio. Jean-Baptiste explained that his mother had received a good education in Dijon where she was born, and she had qualified as an infant-school teacher before she had married. Most of the books on the shelves were in French, but he discovered piles of illustrated magazines, even a few copies of *Punch*. In another smaller cupboard he unearthed a selection of classical records, together with a pile of damp but legible theatre programmes.

However, most of the time he spent engrossed in studying Jean-Baptiste's paintings. He was particularly fascinated by his sketchbooks, which depicted in gruesome detail scenes of some of the cruelty that was being inflicted on local people. One showed a young man hung upside down from a tree, his body swinging violently to one side as two German soldiers, roughly the same age, thrust their bayonets into his stomach.

Some he found later painted in oils on large canvases stretched on wooden frames. One showed a young woman being raped, her hands clutching her skirt in an attempt to preserve a kind of modesty. It was only a small painting, but clear enough to convey the revulsion in the woman's eyes as the soldier held her down with one hand, using the other to force his penis between her legs. Close by, an elderly man sat on a bench ignoring her distress. Another showed a man trying to protect his wife as a German soldier knocked her to the ground, her basket tumbling down the road, spilling fruit and vegetables. The backgrounds were mainly pastoral, reflecting the calm, rolling Burgundy countryside, in stark contrast to the violent scenes portrayed as their central theme.

Jack had questioned Jean-Baptiste one evening when they were sitting in front of the stove. Jean-Baptiste usually lay full length on the sofa, whilst Jack continued to sit in the armchair wrapped in the blanket that Françoise had given him. It smelled vaguely of her, or perhaps it was just lavender, he chided himself. Whatever, it evoked a feminine aroma that reminded him of Elizabeth. Leaning towards Jean-Baptiste he enquired, 'Aren't you worried someone, a German soldier, might see some of your more controversial paintings? And why would someone want to buy something so distressing?'

Jean-Baptiste considered his question, which had been asked in the usual melange of French and English.

'Controversial? What do you mean?' He thought for a moment. 'Ah, *controversé*, difficult. You are right, I should be more careful, but it is unlikely anyone would come up here, and if I tried to hide them and they were discovered, that would make them, don't you think, more *controversé*? What goes on is bad, Jack, but half of France stands by and lets it happen. Can you really blame them? We all want to live for our families, we want to survive. Hitler is apparently plundering art from just about everywhere, perhaps he would be interested in one for his collection,' he added bitterly.

On these occasions Jack felt by far the younger of the two. Apart from the war, his life had been predictable, pleasant even. When he met Elizabeth, he was eager to marry, to settle down in the same mould as his parents. But Jean-Baptiste was different; he could play the peasant farmer, but his passion was in his art. Jack guessed he was a radical eager for change, to make things happen. Jack admitted to himself that he was not only in awe of him but envied him his distinctive aura of masculinity. He wondered what Elizabeth would make of him.

Sometimes, she surprised him in the way she could embrace the world. Months after they were married, she told him that she had something to confess: that she was not a virgin when they married, as he had thought, but that she had slept just once with a young man from her school when she was sixteen. She explained it had been an uncomfortable fumbling experience, and she was as much to blame as the young man. No one knew, and she had had the presence of mind not to share the information with her girlfriends, partly as she was deeply ashamed confessing.

'I thought I would never tell you, Jack, but my love for you is – well, it's happily taken over my life, but this pointless sordid act nags at me, telling me I need you to know, to understand and to forgive. Not for the stupidity of the act, but that I should have told you before we were married.'

He had been more shocked than he cared to admit at the time, not knowing quite how to react, but impressed by her dignity. This was a young woman not asking for forgiveness, but for understanding.

'Was he better than me?' he remembered asking, taking her in his arms, 'because if he was, out the door, young woman.' They had laughed, and whenever he saw her pensive or sad in the following months he would kiss her, declaring his love. When the pregnancies started it was all but forgotten, and he'd made a promise with himself that under no circumstances would he ever use it as a weapon to hurt her.

A further sketchbook and a half-finished canvas were devoted to a young woman. Her face was slightly obscured, so it was difficult to define if she was beautiful. In most of the sketches she lay stretched out on a bed, with her arms above her head. Her body was caught up in a single sheet that swirled around her body like a turbulent sea, highlighted by the watery light of the moon, which was just visible in a small window above, in the corner of the room.

'I would hang that on my wall,' remarked Jack, 'but I am not sure that Elizabeth would approve.'

'Of course she would disapprove,' replied Jean-Baptiste, 'it's another woman. But if you allow me to paint her naked as a gift to you...' He hesitated. 'In my experience, all women like to be painted naked, even the fat ones. Legs apart, they are suddenly liberated.'

'Complete nonsense!' Françoise cried, throwing a magazine at Jean-Baptiste. 'What do you know about women?'

'Is it his girlfriend?' Jack asked Françoise.

'It's his muse,' she replied, winking at Jean-Baptiste.

'Yes, she's right,' he replied, jumping from the sofa and gently grabbing his sister's arm and twisting it behind her back. Adele is my beautiful muse. She's a girl from the village, but unfortunately her parents have stopped her "musing" for me. What do they say, Françoise? I am a bad influence?'

Françoise escaped his grasp, flinging herself onto the sofa, and laughingly declared to the two men, 'I've told him I will be his muse, but I'm not taking my knickers off.'

'I should certainly think not, frightfully bad form,' Jack replied in a phoney upper-class English accent, which to his surprise seemed to be understood by them both.

In the weeks since Jack had been released from his hiding place, he and Jean-Baptiste had fallen into an easygoing relationship. They were constantly amused by the 'franglais' they both used and, encouraged by Françoise, they spoke openly about their lives. Jack had told them about what he thought of as his happy childhood, his career as an engineer and photographer. But more importantly, he spoke of Elizabeth and his impatience to return home to see if all had gone well with the birth of their first child.

Jean-Baptiste was reluctant at first to speak of the past, but aided by his sister, he explained that he had studied art in Paris just before the war. His mother had fostered his interest in the subject, encouraging him with his drawings since he was a small child. His stepfather hadn't been convinced it was a suitable career for a man, but in deference to his wife he had financed Jean-Baptiste's studies. However, when the war finally took hold, he made it clear that Jean-Baptiste should return home and work with Bernard on the farm.

'To be fair, he also wanted to ensure I was safe,' Jean-Baptiste explained. 'I know he cares for me, and although we don't often see eye to eye, I have respect for him, and Bernard too. He is a bear of a man, but the kindest person I know. I feel he is my brother in every sense of the word.' As Jean-Baptiste finished speaking, Françoise moved closer to him, and taking his hand, she held it to her face. 'Oh yes,' he concluded, 'and I love my annoying little sister too!'

They filled their glasses, laughing and joshing. Years later, Jack was to remember three young people whose thirst for life could not be dampened by the imminent danger that stalked their daily lives. For a brief heady moment, they rejoiced in a loving and uncomplicated friendship, unsullied by the war and what might lie ahead.

DERBY, 1968

The late afternoon turned to evening and then to night. They only interrupted their tales with a bottle of wine and a hurriedly made sandwich. Eventually they lay silent, drifting in and out of sleep, but both fully aware that there was much more to reveal about their pasts.

The wind was still gusty, and a dustbin blew over, its lid rolling noisily down the street. Jack woke, for a second unsure where he was. Then as reality took hold, a huge wave of anxiety swept over him.

'Nancy,' he said loudly to wake her. 'I have to go home. Please forgive me, I told you, my father died on a night like this.' He started to search for his clothes. 'Mum and I waited up all that night willing him to return, but he didn't, and I know she'll be lying awake now, waiting to hear the sound of my bike. I was just ten and I sensed they'd had a row...'

Nancy lay for a second watching him dress. Later she was to tell him that that was when she fell in love with him. Half-dressed, his tall muscular body silhouetted against the wall had reminded her of the pilot in the stained-glass window in the Marble Hall at Rolls-Royce: a young man who looked compassionately at the world beneath him. She rose from the bed, and without speaking helped him into his clothes.

As he struggled into his father's old flying jacket, she held his face in her hands, then kissed him lightly.

'Take care, Jack,' she whispered. 'On a night like this you'd be safer to stay here. But I can understand how your...' She hesitated for a moment.

'Elizabeth,' he said softly. 'My mother's name is Elizabeth.'

CHAPTER TEN

I woke to the sound of rain.

– SYLVIA PLATH, *THE BELL JAR*

BELPER, DERBYSHIRE, 1968

Elizabeth sat on the side of the bed, straining to hear the sound of Jack's motorbike through the gale. She had secretly done this many times before, berating herself each time. But the pain, the anxiety, was all-consuming. It wracked her entire body.

She hadn't responded immediately when Jack had suggested buying a motorbike. He was nineteen at the time and it did make sense as it was a more efficient way of getting to work.

She knew Jack instinctively understood her unspoken fears. They were a pair, they had survived as a little team together, overcoming the loss of a husband and a father. A motorbike was, she knew, the start of her son's rite of passage to becoming his own man. She had to allow him to start to loosen the knots that bound them together. If she was careful, she knew she would retain not only his love, but also his respect.

The storm had started to subside. A lighter breeze ebbed and flowed, and she thought she heard the sound of his bike in the distance. Her whole body stiffened, willing it to be him. When she was confident it was, she quickly turned out her bedside light and slipped between the cold sheets. Burying her head in the pillow, she sobbed, her body releasing a surge of relief.

She heard him come up the stairs as soon as he entered the house. Knocking gently on her door, he whispered, 'Are you awake, Mum?' But not waiting for a reply, he continued, 'Sorry, I hadn't realised it was so late.'

'The girl with the umbrella?' she replied, her voice straining for a lightness she hardly felt.

'Could be,' he replied. 'Are you OK?'

She hesitated for a moment, wanting to leap out of bed and hug him, but instead she replied, 'Lucky girl, but what a night. I thought it would never stop raining.'

Endeavouring to banish their unspoken thoughts, Jack replied softly, 'Yes, a horrible night, Mum, it's good to be home.'

She relaxed. Her son was safe. Yet, although she was warm and comfortable in her bed and with Jack safely home, her thoughts still remained cold and vivid. She turned restlessly in her bed, trying to dispel the memories that came flooding into her mind, as if she was in need of being cleansed before sleep was possible. Her mind kept returning to that Christmas all those years ago when her life started to fall apart.

WIRKSWORTH, DERBYSHIRE, 1956

It was unusual for their phone to ring on a Sunday evening. Everyone was in the kitchen helping with the Christmas cake, which Elizabeth thought was not going to be up to her usual standard, having left it very late in the making. Ten-year-old Jack had chopped all the walnuts he and his father had brought back from France in the summer, giving him yet another opportunity to happily ramble on about the wonderful holiday the two of them had had.

Since as long as he could remember, he had helped plan and pack the annual Christmas parcel to Jean-Baptiste and his family. Tins of salmon, a small Christmas pudding, a piece of Stilton. One year the parcel included a selection of bulbs for their garden and another some hand-knitted scarves. Everything was carefully wrapped in a box, then again in brown paper, tied with string. The bit that Jack enjoyed the most was sealing the knots with red wax. Then there was the trip to the post office, where there was the ritual of telling the story of why they were posting a parcel to Burgundy.

In later years, they received a return parcel of gifts too, together with an invitation for everyone to come and spend a holiday on the farm. On the mantelpiece above the fireplace in Jack's bedroom, he proudly exhibited a pottery snail, an Eiffel Tower, a Statue of Liberty, a pencil box with a French flag and several birthday cards painted by Jean-Baptiste. But his pride and joy was a black pottery poodle with a proper blue leather collar.

Each year they discussed a visit, but Elizabeth had finally made the decision after Jean-Baptiste had unexpectedly phoned them. Neither family had phones until after the War, but that had changed in the mid-fifties, and Elizabeth had written their phone number on the previous year's Christmas card. Elizabeth had never spoken to Jean-Baptiste before, but his infectious laugh and amusing English accent facilitated a charming conversation over the phone between the two of them. Her French was not good, but she sensed he was flirting with her, and understood he was inviting them to a family party to celebrate his engagement to a young lady from the village, whose name was something like 'muse', she thought. Jack laughingly explained that he thought her name was Adele, the girl Jean-Baptiste had described as his muse.

Elizabeth had always sensed that Jack was reluctant to return, but this time she was determined they would make the trip. She had the full support of young Jack, who started making plans straight away. A neighbour occasionally lent them their rather unreliable Singer sports car for the day, so they could all drive into the Peak District for a Sunday afternoon picnic. This prompted Elizabeth to suggest that Jack try to rent it for a couple of weeks so that they could take time over the journey and stop in Paris for a couple of days.

Young Jack revelled in the notoriety of being the first person in his class to be spending a holiday abroad. Forgetting his natural modesty, he talked constantly to both his teacher and school mates about the trip. Elizabeth encouraged him to compile a school scrapbook with all things French in it such as maps, photographs and stamps, together with a small vocabulary of French phrases and words.

But at the last minute Elizabeth's mother was taken ill. Jack suggested that they postpone the trip until the following year, but Elizabeth immediately sensed her son's disappointment, and insisted that they continue their plans without her. 'There will be another time,' she assured them both.

Young Jack remembered the holiday as a magical experience. He and his Dad had set off in the old Singer sports car, armed with a big toolbox and several spare parts in case anything went wrong. Elizabeth had packed gifts for everyone, including the mysterious Adele. Their plan was to make straight for Burgundy and spend a night in Paris on the way back. They had shortened their holiday to ten days instead of the original fortnight so that they didn't leave Elizabeth too long. Apart from their having to fit a new fan belt, which they fortunately had had with them, the car behaved itself very well, and as the weather was fine, they usually had the top down.

On arrival, Jack and his son were overwhelmed by their welcome. All the family were there to greet them, including many villagers that Jack hadn't met whilst he was hiding in the attic. Françoise took charge of young Jack, showing him around, explaining that the bedroom he was to share with his father was where they had first put Jack.

At first he was in awe of Jean-Baptiste as he seemed a little gruff. He had practised his French with his mother, but found whilst he could say a little, he could never understand the replies. But as soon as Jean-Baptiste realised his problem, he gave him a little sketchbook and together they would interpret things through the aid of a drawing. Often Jean-Baptiste's were very funny, in fact sometimes even a little rude, like the sketch of a pig doing a poo, or a dog sniffing a cat's bottom.

Jean-Baptiste's parents completely spoilt the young Jack, planning picnics and special treats, such as riding in the donkey cart, or being allowed to collect the eggs and choose the biggest, most speckled one for his breakfast.

It was hay-making time, so everyone was busy during the day. In the evening there would be a big meal outside, and much to Jack's delight, he was allowed to stay up as long as he wanted. Jean-Baptiste and his father worked in the fields most days, and Jack watched admiringly as his father's pale skin turned a golden honey colour. Adele, the muse, usually joined the family gathering in the evening, but there was no special event to celebrate an engagement as Jack and his dad had been expecting.

One afternoon Françoise joined them in their car and they visited Avallon and several of the surrounding villages. Even at the age of nine, Jack could sense the emotion his father experienced as they visited various places, including the spot in the forest where he had been found. He began to see his father in a different light and felt proud when he was introduced to everyone as 'le jeune Jacques'.

Just before the end of the holiday, Jean-Baptiste had returned to Paris unexpectedly. The weather had turned, with thunderstorms sweeping across the landscape. Fortunately, they had finished hay-making, but everyone was concerned about the wheat and corn crops, which had to be harvested later that month.

Before taking their leave, Jack and his father had said many emotional goodbyes to the family and friends they had spent time with during their stay, promising to return with Elizabeth as soon as they could. Their little car was piled high with gifts of wine, cheese and delicacies from the region.

Before his unexpected departure, Jean-Baptiste had left a small painting for young Jack. It was unframed, and so there was an unfinished feeling about it, but Jack loved it as it showed him perched on top of a hay wagon pulled by Artos, an old carthorse. In the background his 'uncle' Jean-Baptiste had painted several of the farm workers, including his father, working in the fields. In the right-hand corner, barely visible, were two mice nervously observing the scene.

The journey back to Paris had taken much longer than on the way there, as the rain continued and the roads were often flooded. He remembered that his father was unusually silent. It was late afternoon when they arrived in Paris, and as the rain had stopped, they put the roof down and drove around looking at the sights.

They stopped to buy Elizabeth a present, and then his father had searched on the map for Jean-Baptiste's address, which was just north of Montmartre. They parked outside a café and his father went inside and bought him a drink and a baguette filled with ham and cheese. He had told him to wait there whilst he found the address and promised that he would be back shortly. Jack had remembered eating the baguette hungrily and watching the people coming and going in the café.

His father seemed to be a long time, so he curled up and went to sleep. He only woke when the car door opened. It had fallen dark, and for a moment he was confused. 'Where is Uncle Jean-Baptiste, are we going to see him?' he had asked.

'No, not this time,' his father had replied. Then, starting the car, they had fought to find the right road out of Paris and headed towards the coast. The journey through the night was long. They had stopped twice to find petrol and to rest before they reached Calais.

'I never said goodbye,' he had remarked to his father, but his father hadn't replied, appearing to want to concentrate on the road ahead.

* * *

Jack returned to the kitchen after the phone call from Françoise. The Christmas cake was complete and ready for the oven. Young Jack was wiping his finger round the large earthenware mixing bowl.

As Elizabeth looked up, she was startled by the look on her husband's face. His complexion was completely sallow; his eyes appeared sunken, as if some emotional force was sucking the life from them. He sat down unsteadily, grasping her outstretched hand across the table. In that moment their lives changed irreversibly, never to be the same, she thought, never to find peace again.

They had persuaded young Jack to go and search for the Christmas cake decorations in the sideboard in the next room, whilst Jack related his brief conversation with Françoise. Jean-Baptiste had been brutally attacked in his apartment. He had died on the way to hospital. It had happened shortly after his exhibition in Paris. Françoise had explained the exhibition had been a huge success, but had brought with it a lot of controversial publicity. She promised to let them know about the arrangements. But Jack told Elizabeth later that Françoise had advised him then that it would be unwise to attend the funeral.

Elizabeth had known that Jean-Baptiste had become quite well-known as an artist, but little more. She hadn't known anything about this latest exhibition in Paris and was surprised to hear it described as controversial.

When young Jack had returned with the box of Christmas decorations, they had all sat quietly picking off last year's marzipan and icing from their bases, so that Father Christmas and his reindeer, the pine trees and the little house, which would eventually have a path made from cocoa leading up to its door, would be ready to take their place on the cake the following day.

Without any discussion, just lingering looks across the table, Jack and Elizabeth had agreed not to tell their son about the tragedy until after Christmas. They were only just recovering from the recent death of Elizabeth's mother, and felt it was unfair to burden young Jack with more sorrow.

When Françoise eventually contacted Jack again, she had been adamant in her advice not to attend the funeral, as her brother's death was a major story in the French national newspapers. It was a murder investigation, and it would therefore be weeks before everything was arranged. She would keep him informed, but stressed it was better if he kept away.

That week, Elizabeth had become unwell. She had woken with severe stomach pains, which usually heralded the start of her period. Their longing for another child never went away; despite young Jack having just celebrated his tenth birthday, they still held out hopes that eventually she would become pregnant again. Jack insisted that he stay home from work while she rested on the sofa in front of the fire surrounded by hot water bottles, and he would collect his son from school later that afternoon. She remembered how cold the weather had turned, and Jack deciding to walk to the allotment to rescue the last of the Brussels sprouts, before setting out to collect the boy.

A short while after he had left there had been a knock at the door. Over the years she had often thought that maybe if she hadn't answered it the nightmare might never have overtaken their lives. With the help of the caller she had had to wrestle open the front door as the damp weather had made it stick. With her pulling and the caller pushing, the door finally conceded, revealing a somewhat embarrassed, but seemingly charming young man from the *Derby Post*. As she ushered him into the hall, he announced that he was from the local paper and would like to speak to Mr Jack French.

'It's about the artist Jean-Baptiste Dupont,' he explained. 'We understand he has been murdered in Paris and that he was the man who saved your husband during the War. It's a big story in all the French papers.'

Searching in his briefcase, he revealed an old article that had been written in the *Derby Post* just after Jack's return. It explained in detail how fortunate her husband had been to be hidden by the Dupont family. It mentioned Jean-Baptiste, describing him as not just a farmer, but a talented artist who surprisingly had sold some of his work to a German officer just before the war finished.

Elizabeth remembered quite clearly feeling a sudden sense of unease, and had hesitated before inviting him into the sitting room. After tidying the sofa and removing the hot water bottles, she turned around and saw to her annoyance that without being invited, the reporter had removed his coat and chosen to sit in one of the armchairs near the fire.

'It's a big story in France,' he continued. 'As you know, of course, Jean-Baptiste was queer.' He let the word hang in the air for a minute, in order that its full impact could register with Elizabeth. 'I'm sorry, I mean homosexual. Of course, I expect you know some of his paintings are very controversial, but in the right circles they go for big money. Homo-erotic art, they call it.'

Even all these years later, she still experienced a similar tightening of her stomach, as she fought to make sense of what he was saying. Confused, she had grappled with his explanation, aware that it was being delivered in a vaguely triumphant fashion.

'Homo-erotic art,' she repeated, conscious that she hadn't ever heard the expression. 'I'm not sure what you mean.'

'Of course, forgive me, I am not in any way suggesting that your husband is, well, that way inclined, but many of the paintings found in his apartment after his death are, I understand, portraits of your husband. The triptych that caused all the fuss at his recent exhibition is, well, not the kind of thing you would put in a church, but it is entitled *Mémoire de Jack*. We would just like to…'

Before he could continue, her husband had burst into the room. Instantly she could see he was consumed with anger. He had returned home from the allotment, using the back door to enter the house, and had obviously heard the tail end of their conversation. He had grabbed the journalist, pulling him from the chair, and then shaking him violently like a rag doll, he had dragged him out of the room towards the front door.

She distinctly remembered Jack saying in a voice that was calm, but deeply threatening, 'Get out of my house. If you ever return here, or publish anything about M. Dupont or myself, I will sue you and your paper for every penny it's got. You are despicable, coming into my home when I presume you thought I would be at work. How dare you pester my wife! Jean-Baptiste was a good, brave man and I will mourn him.'

'Yes, I expect you will,' she heard the journalist reply, 'I expect you will.'

She remembered little else apart from stupidly wanting to warn Jack that the front door was sticking. She sensed he was going to hit the man, but a cloud of blackness enveloped her.

When she regained consciousness, the journalist had gone and Jack was kneeling in front of her. He was looking deeply into her eyes, as if holding their love together with the power of his gaze. It was minutes before she broke the silence.

'Is it true?' she asked uncompromisingly, holding his gaze. 'Did you ever... did you ever... you know what I mean, Jack.'

The shock and tone of her question registered immediately, completely obliterating any carefully-thought out response he might have been harbouring. His eyes, she remembered, admitted his guilt far more eloquently than words.

He had falteringly tried to explain. The War, the fear. But she hadn't listened, enclosing herself in a shell that, no matter how many times he tried to prise it open, remained tightly closed.

She had been consumed with anxiety that something would appear in the local papers, but nothing did, apart from a short article with the barest details. She sensed Jack was relieved when he saw it. But she continued to worry, aware that the inquest was not yet over and Jack's handling of the journalist could have made him keener to pursue the story.

'What if he takes it further?' she had demanded after Jack had read the article. 'Did you hit him?'

'I just threw his coat at him. Most of my energy went on opening the front door, it was stuck if you remember. If he publishes anything else, I warned him I'll sue the paper.'

'And Jack, what good will that do, apart from telling the rest of the world? Can you imagine if they published some of the pictures he'd painted? Homo-erotic art. What does that mean? I can't bear to think. But I'm not stupid, not as gullible as you seem to think I am. Can you imagine, Jack, what that would do to us, to our son and me?'

They managed to survive most of December, breaking the news of Uncle Jean-Baptiste's death to young Jack when the festivities were over. Each night she lay next to her husband, longing to embrace him, to wrap her body round his as they had always done. They used to share a joke, saying they fitted together like two spoons in a drawer, but now the intimacy was gone. They clung to separate sides of the bed.

Her world felt shattered. She had shared everything with Jack, all her emotions, her fears, dreams and plans for the future. She had good friends, aunties, uncles and her elderly father, but how could you discuss such a taboo subject? When she demanded to know if he had posed for Jean-Baptiste, he in turn became angry, denying all knowledge of the paintings. Isolated by her fears, she felt utterly alone. She wished that, just once, he would tell her not what he wanted her to hear, but what he was truly thinking.

CHAPTER ELEVEN

We may allow ourselves a brief period of
rejoicing; but let us not forget for a moment
the toil and efforts that lie ahead.

– WINSTON CHURCHILL

BURGUNDY, FRANCE, 1945

Easter was early that year, but the continuing good weather had woken the countryside from its winter slumber. Small lizards raced between the cracks in the stone walls of Jack's cell, dislodging tiny plumes of dust to fall on his bed. A lone beetle paraded cautiously along the edge of the room, the rays from the sun turning its green coat of armour into a glowing jewel.

On Easter Sunday he knew the family would go to church. He expected that Jean-Baptiste wouldn't go, so he wasn't surprised when he knocked on the flap and demanded he came out. To his amazement, Jean-Baptiste was wearing a thick leather motorcycle jacket.

'*Vite, vite*! Quickly! We're going out! Follow me,' he cried, returning to the ladder.

Jack was completely at a loss. He tried to imagine what emergency had given rise to this sudden idea of throwing all caution to the wind. As he climbed down the ladder for the first time, he wasn't surprised to find a large cattle shed, with the door wide open into the courtyard. As he entered the yard Jean-Baptiste stood before him. In one hand he held an oversized coat of Bernard's while the other steadied a motorbike.

'What's happening?' Jack shouted, genuinely distressed.

'We're going out,' laughed Jean-Baptiste. 'Trust me, there are no Germans about. They've gone. It's Easter. Everyone is in church. Come on, just half an hour. I want to show you my mistress, my beautiful home.' He rested the bike back on its stand, then gripping Jack by the shoulder, manhandled him roughly into the enormous coat. 'I want you to see my countryside. She is fickle like a woman, all the time changing, teasing and demanding to be admired under any circumstance.' Jack hardly understood, except he caught Jean-Baptiste's fervour when he held him, declaring, 'Don't you realise Jack, she is my passion.'

'But we can't,' Jack begged, 'it's too dangerous. How can you be sure the Germans have gone? It's blood stupid, Jean, you know it is.'

'Trust me,' Jean-Baptiste replied, 'trust me. Life is dangerous, Jack, but it will be all right. Share this with me, please.' He looked firmly into Jack's eyes. There was an air of anger in his stance as he stood with his bike waiting for Jack's decision.

Jean-Baptiste mounted the bike, then powering it into life, he indicated with a nod of his head that Jack should take his place behind. They exited the courtyard, turning left along the road leading to a long winding bridge. After the bridge they turned left again along a narrower road. For the first few seconds, Jack was blind to his surroundings as he battled with fear and the conviction that this was a reckless and stupid thing to do.

But as he positioned himself more comfortably against Jean-Baptiste's back, he finally started to take in his surroundings as they flashed by. They twisted along the lane, and he saw the church from a variety of angles, although only now could he appreciate its stature. As they climbed a steep hill leaving the church behind, the view across the valley unfolded. Soft rolling hills, a meandering river, small woods and the start of a forest. He felt a shot of exhilaration as they sped along, his lungs filling with fresh air. *Yes*, he thought, *he's right, it is magnificent.*

At the top of the hill was another village. Its square was resplendent with a large war memorial and a town hall, flying the Nazi flag. He could see a mixture of ancient houses, some with turrets and others with iron balconies. At the end of the road was another church, where an old man sat on a bench, as if waiting for the service to finish. As he heard the sound of the motorbike engine, he raised his hand and waved in recognition.

As they descended the hill, Jean-Baptiste stopped and pulled over to the grass verge. 'See that?' he shouted, pointing to a large castle in the distance. 'See that chateau? Destroyed by you English.'

Jack didn't respond, but leaned forward, shouting above the noise of the engine, 'That old man, he saw us.'

'No he didn't, he's blind,' retorted Jean-Baptiste, putting the bike into gear and continuing their descent down the hill.

As they continued, Jack prayed they were not too far from the farm, and that this intoxicating lunacy would end. But no, Jean-Baptiste crossed the road they had originally left by, and changing noisily down a gear, climbed to the other side of the valley. This revealed yet another view of the church, a massive door with a rose window towering above. Turning again they made their final descent, past a field that was being ploughed by a man on an ancient tractor.

At the crossroads, Jean-Baptiste slowed down, then, looking both ways through the avenue of trees lining the road, he raced over the bridge and back into the courtyard at last. Without waiting for Jean-Baptiste to turn the engine off, Jack leapt off the bike, discarded the coat on the ground and then mounted the ladder back to the safety of the studio. He heard the bike stop, for a moment smelling the petrol fumes seeping into the room. Falling onto the sofa, he waited for Jean-Baptiste to join him. When he saw him heaving himself off the ladder he cried, 'You bugger, you bugger! What about the man on the tractor?'

Jean-Baptiste collapsed onto the sofa and for a moment held his head in his hands. 'The man driving the tractor is one of the fathers whose sons have disappeared recently. He will not go to church, and he will certainly not volunteer anything to the Germans. That's if there are any Germans left.'

'What about the flag on the town hall in the village with the old man?'

'Perhaps they forgot to take it down,' replied Jean-Baptiste, 'but shit, Jack, maybe there are one or two still about.'

'You're mad, bad and dangerous to know,' Jack retorted, presuming that Jean-Baptiste only understood the tenor of his voice. 'Mad, bad and dangerous to know,' he repeated.

'But life is like that Jack, if it's not "mad, bad and dangerous to know" at times it's not worth living,' he said in their normal franglais.

'You're familiar with Byron,' laughed Jack.

'*Merde*, Jack, don't be so condescending, I am not just a peasant. Bloody arrogant Englishmen,' he countered. Haltingly he tried to explain his view that if you didn't get your adrenalin going once in a while life wasn't worth living.

'When you fly, Jack, I'm sure you feel truly alive. You have to take risks. But you understand, my mother and father are not to know of our adventure. Like me they are convinced the Germans have left, but they would view our tour as...' He searched for a word that wasn't forthcoming. Instead he continued by saying, 'They invite you to share in our Easter lunch. Papa agrees there is very little risk. The garrison in Avallon has not sent anyone to collect provisions for several days. It is Easter, a holiday, so he will lock the gates. Françoise and mother have laid the table with the best cloth, which reaches to the ground should you wish to hide under it.'

Jack knew immediately as he arrived to join them for their family lunch that this was an occasion he would cherish for the rest of his life. The old farmhouse was a mixture of styles. The main house had been built in the Middle Ages and was graced by a large turret that served as a second staircase. The remainder of the house had adopted several other styles with shuttered windows and carved lintels, stolen, Françoise explained, from the remains of the castle that had been demolished hundreds of years ago. Various climbing plants clung to the walls, fighting for prime position. The yard was large with outbuildings on all sides, housing cattle and farm equipment. Two black spotted pigs reclined in a stall on an untidy heap of straw, whilst several chickens pecked at the gravel under the watchful eye of a majestic bronze-coloured cockerel.

As the weather was mild most of the livestock was already in the fields, apart from two lambs locked in a pen with their attentive mother. He had seen very little of the house before, on the evening when they had carried him across the courtyard into the barn. Then he had been an intruder, but now, as Jean-Baptiste's mother greeted him formally and led him into the dining room, he felt like a welcome guest. The dining room was long and narrow. Either side of the oblong table were two impressive oak dressers that displayed a selection of china and porcelain figures. Several paintings hung on the walls, but nothing he recognised as by Jean-Baptiste. The window at the far end was open, revealing a vegetable garden and an orchard. Most of the trees were only just in bud, apart from two cherry trees laden with blossom. A few sparse daffodils rose bravely above a carpet of dense grass and windblown petals.

The dining table was elegantly laid with blue and white china decorated with a simple design of flowers and birds. A graceful glass vase filled with daffodils sat in the centre of the table and at each place setting there were two wine glasses and a crisp white napkin. At first the atmosphere was a little strained as Claude and Bernard made no attempt to speak English and Sylvie, Jean-Baptiste's mother, seemed a little embarrassed to try out the English she had learnt at college. Jack had anticipated this and had brought his dictionary along. To break the ice, he explained that his surname was 'French', and after a laboured exchange with the old man, he gathered that there had been a General French serving in the British army during the First World War. Perhaps, Claude had suggested, it was a relative of Jack's.

The meal was far from simple. Jack knew vaguely about foie gras, but was in awe of the reverence with which it was served as their first course. Claude poured a sweet wine that Jack understood he had been saving for a special occasion. Roast lamb was then set on the table with redcurrant jelly made by Françoise some years before, when sugar was more readily available. The lamb, flavoured with rosemary and garlic, was presented on a bed of lentils and small purple tinged turnips. To follow was cheese, one a goat's and the other made from cow's milk, Françoise explained. They drank a bottle of red wine, and then after a family discussion, Bernard was dispatched to the cellar, returning with another bottle of red and a half full bottle of brandy. There was much laughter as Bernard had had to move a mountain of logs to reach the alcohol, which had been carefully hidden from the Germans. The wine and food soon worked their magic, and everyone relaxed. Even the cat, sensing it was welcome, sat on Françoise's lap licking the soft white cheese from her finger.

During the meal, Jack had been moved by the affection Jean-Baptiste's parents demonstrated for each other. Often she would rest her hand on his shoulder as she passed his chair, returning to the kitchen for yet another delicious dish. He, in turn, would hold her hand for a second in order to caress her fingers. In his church suit, Claude looked less of an artisan and rather more like the pictures he had seen of Voltaire. The conversation became very animated, politics, art, crops, keeping Françoise constantly consulting the dictionary, dismayed as she raced to find a translation, only to discover that many words were very similar in both languages. It was just the pronunciation that made them difficult to understand.

To complete the meal Sylvie had prepared a splendid *tarte tatin*, which she was at pains to explain to Jack was an upside-down apple dessert. It was greeted with as much admiration as the first course of *foie gras,* for it had taken the last of their sugar and a good deal of butter. When Jack expressed how delicious it was, Sylvie took delight in explaining to him how it was made so he could pass on the recipe to Elizabeth.

As the light faded and the windows were closed, Sylvie slipped into the kitchen and reappeared with something wrapped in a napkin. Gently she placed it on the table and asked Jack to uncover the contents. For a moment he was bewildered before he realised that it was the large slice of Christmas cake he had placed in his pocket just before his flight to France. Most of it was in crumbs, but one piece remained intact. All the thoughts of home that he had tamed over the last few months came rushing back. He fought tears, but he could not control the emotion in his voice as he explained about the Christmas cake and the last time he had seen Elizabeth. Sylvie rose and hugged him, resting her head against his shoulder.

The drama was suddenly broken by Bernard noisily blowing his nose, as if he too had been touched by Jack's story. With everyone now laughing at Bernard's expense, Jack suggested they pour just a tiny drop of the brandy over the cake and all share it as his contribution to the meal. When all the cake and the brandy had been consumed, Bernard heaved a slightly inebriated Jean-Baptiste from the table to help with the cattle. Jack took his leave shortly after, embracing both Claude and Sylvie. He was effusive in his thanks, declaring it would give both he and Elizabeth enormous pleasure to return their hospitality.

'One day,' he shouted, waving his arms dramatically in the air, 'one day this will all be over!'

Aided by Françoise he negotiated the ladder back to the studio, where he collapsed on the sofa while Françoise lit the fire. Jean-Baptiste joined them with yet another bottle of wine, and together they played cards. Jean-Baptiste was not a good loser, frequently throwing his cards onto the table and declaring he was destined to have bad luck for the rest of his life.

Around midnight, Françoise descended the ladder and Jack slipped from the sofa onto the floor, nearer to the stove where he fell asleep immediately.

He was startled and disorientated for a second when he awoke, then, as he focussed, he found he was gazing into Jean-Baptiste's eyes. Jean-Baptiste held his gaze, and for a second, Jack felt as if his heart had stopped. His breathing became laboured as he slid his arm under Jean-Baptiste's neck, drawing his face close so that he could embrace him gently. Jean-Baptiste responded with a passion that engulfed them both.

He would think afterwards that it would have been so much easier not to remember the details of their lovemaking, but the memories of the violence and the confusion as they fought to remove their clothes would pepper his thoughts constantly. He would always remember the heat of their bodies, the sweat, the agony and finally the penetration. When it was over, they lay silently side by side.

Jack's thoughts were filled with disbelief that they had uncaringly spoiled what had been a perfect day. His mind found it hard to cope with the enormity of what had happened. Why, he questioned, had he in that instant desired Jean-Baptiste?

Without looking at Jack, Jean-Baptiste gathered his clothes, only putting on his trousers and boots before leaving the studio.

Jack lay in the darkness. His body felt chilled and damp. He reached for his shirt to wipe the dampness away, then clutching it to his face, he sobbed quietly.

When it became light, anger seared his body. He felt an all-consuming hatred for Jean-Baptiste. He'd never for one moment thought of Jean-Baptiste as homosexual, but then, he reasoned, he'd never experienced any feelings for a man before. Friendship, affection, admiration, yes, even envy at times that he felt ill at ease and unable to join in when some of his friends in the RAF entered into risqué banter that often accompanied an evening out. He'd always stood back, he accepted, from that kind of thing; even at school he preferred cricket, rather than the rough and tumble of a rugby game.

As his mind fumbled for clues, he remembered that his mother used to say with some pride, 'Our Jack likes to always be clean and tidy.' But good God, surely that didn't make him queer, he thought.

Searching for an excuse, he told himself that Jean-Baptiste had seduced him. But he knew that was untrue; he could have turned away from Jean-Baptiste's gaze, but that feeling of desire had overwhelmed him, a brutal passion that he had never experienced before. The reality, he knew, would haunt him for ever.

He reached for the wine bottle, gulping the remaining dregs. Despair weighed him down as he searched the cupboard for anything to take away the pain. Finding another bottle of liquor, he drank the whole contents in one go, forcing it down in huge gulps that tore at his throat. Falling back on the sofa, the room pitched and swirled until he finally closed his eyes. Blocking out the nightmare, he fell into a deep sleep.

The sound of voices eventually pierced through his stupor. Reluctantly, he acknowledged he could hear Jean-Baptiste's voice coming from the courtyard. It sounded loud and animated. He listened more carefully. Why was he trying to speak German?

The crash of a falling bucket brought him to his senses, and he rushed for the flap to his cell. As he heard someone start to climb the ladder, he flung himself under the table, conscious that every split second counted. He tumbled through the flap, but had the presence of mind to lower it gently closed. He lay, not daring to move a muscle. For some inexplicable reason he wanted to cough.

Taking deep breaths, he gradually took control of his body. He strained to hear what was happening beyond the wall. A muffled conversation filtered through, together with what he thought must be the sound of someone moving one of the stacks of paintings. Now and then Jean-Baptiste's voice became louder. For long periods there was silence, but then, when he was about to move, the conversation continued together with a little laughter.

His body became stiff, but he dared not move, unable to even look at his watch. The nightmare of the previous night began to diminish as a desperate state of self-preservation took primary place in his emotions. Unbelievably, he heard what he thought was the sound of Françoise's footsteps. The flap lifted and he heard her whisper, 'It's all right Jack, he's gone, you can come out.'

As he rolled out from under the table the first thing he saw was Jean-Baptiste, head in hands, hunched on the sofa sobbing. Françoise and Jack immediately ran and knelt next to him. Françoise encircled him in her arms. Jack felt unnerved at the sight of Jean-Baptiste in such distress. He had unwittingly admired his confidence, seeing in his rather arrogant behaviour the honest and devil-may-care view of the world that he lacked himself.

As they huddled together Claude came in. He remained standing, but placed a hand on his stepson's shoulder. They were joined by Bernard and Sylvie, who fell to her knees and embraced her son, saying firmly, 'We're all safe, thank God. No harm has been done.'

Hearing her voice, Jean-Baptiste rose and hugged his parents in turn, then Françoise, then Bernard, finally stopping for a brief moment before turning towards Jack. Jack didn't hesitate, but grabbing him to his breast he declared, 'You are a brave, brave man.'

The tension broke immediately. Jean-Baptiste threw back his head, laughing. 'It's crazy, he just wanted to see my paintings!' he cried.

'For God's sake! Explain!' Jack retorted. 'How did he know about your paintings?'

Jean-Baptiste sat down on the sofa, insisting his parents join him on either side.

'Apparently he had heard about me in one of the bars in Avallon. A couple of them have some of my early paintings, mostly landscapes, but some portraits, which he said he admired.'

He stopped the explanation to clasp his mother's hand. Then turning to his stepfather, he put his arm around his shoulder. The old man leaned gently towards him and nodded as Jean-Baptiste continued.

'They're for sale, but no one has ever bought one, unless he did, I'm not sure. Jacques Prost, the man who owns the *Café Rouge* in Avallon, apparently told him where to find me.'

'He was an officer,' his mother added. 'When he drove into the courtyard asking for you, I nearly fainted. But he was polite and spoke good French. But I was shaking all over when I spoke to him. It must have been obvious how nervous I felt. He even apologised for disturbing me.'

She looked up at Jack and, disentangling her hand from Jean-Baptiste's, she offered it to Jack, pulling him to the floor so he rested at her feet.

'I was convinced it must relate to you, Jack, but I couldn't work out how anyone knew. But then Jean-Baptiste came and started talking to him. I could sense by the way you were speaking loudly and trying out your German that it was to alert Jack. That's why I knocked the bucket over. Then I saw Bernard out of the corner of my eye, standing in the shadows near the barn. You had a gun, didn't you, Bernard?' She looked up at her stepson. He remained silent, then nodded and walked away.

'Don't go!' Françoise cried, 'Mama isn't cross. I'd have shot him if they had discovered Jack.'

Claude rose and walked over to his son. He appeared nearly half his size, but his stature did not diminish his authority. 'You did the right thing, Bernard. Who knew what would happen? We might have had to shoot him.' He hesitated. 'And we might have had to feed him to the pigs,' he concluded.

'A pig for a pig,' Jean-Baptiste remarked, but then added, 'but he wasn't a pig. He knew about art and he knew what he liked. He looked at everything, even the sketchbooks,' he paused for dramatic effect, 'and he bought three.'

'He bought three!' Jack uttered in amazement. The horror of the previous night started to diminish; how could he hate this man who had saved his life? 'My God, Jean, that's unbelievable.'

Jean-Baptiste looked up and extended his hand towards Jack. Their eyes met and Jack saw a tenderness he hadn't seen before. He smiled briefly, holding his gaze for a second before releasing his hand.

'He bought three,' Jean Baptiste repeated. 'He started by asking how much they were. I was shocked. I said rather foolishly, I thought the Germans took what they wanted. I thought he was going to leave, but then he replied, "Not all Germans take what they want without paying." He offered me 300 francs.'

He turned to Françoise, adding, 'He even asked me to wrap them. All I could find was your old shawl. We wrapped them together, using that string from the desk. I just prayed that you wouldn't move, Jack. But you know, thinking about it, he wasn't on a mission to discover anything, he even volunteered that most of the troops had left the area. God knows why he was still around. I am afraid he bought that portrait of you, Françoise, the one I did when you were seventeen. Surprisingly he also bought that picture of the elderly couple being intimidated by the soldiers.'

'And the third?' asked Jack.

Jean-Baptiste walked across the studio to the desk, and before answering, he removed a sheet from his sketchbook.

'He bought this,' he replied, offering Jack a rough sketch he had made of him. 'I never told you I was doing it, as my sitters often get quite difficult about how they are portrayed,' he joked. 'It was finished, and rather good I think. Little did he know he was buying a painting of an officer in the RAF. I said it was one of my best friends, but I didn't mind selling it as I could do another.'

Jack looked at the sketch. He was hunched up in the same armchair, a blanket around his shoulders. One bare foot rested on the floor, the other on the seat of the chair. The bare feet gave it a feeling of intimacy.

'I would have liked to have seen the finished one,' he remarked quietly.

'I hope one day you will, Jack, not quite the same, but another nevertheless,' he replied, returning the sketch to the desk.

After they had left, Jack lit the stove and dozed uneasily in front of it. Later Jean-Baptiste returned alone, bearing a jug of hot milk and cinnamon Sylvie had made. Their eyes met again, but Jean-Baptiste raised his hand to silence him when he started to speak. They played cards without speaking. The only noises came from the crackling of the fire, and the sound of the occasional screech owl. When Jean-Baptiste came to leave, they hugged each other briefly, in the manner they had always done when bidding each other goodnight. Jack returned to his cell. He felt strangely at peace, as if the extraordinary day had cleansed him of all the events of the previous night.

The next few evenings they were joined by both Françoise and Bernard. To everyone's surprise, Françoise was flattered that the German officer had chosen her portrait. She justified it by remarking that he was obviously a gentleman and it would probably grace his drawing room.

'Well, I doubt it will hang in a brothel,' her brother had teased, 'you're not brothel material, that's for sure.'

Some days later, Françoise delivered Jack's breakfast. He now ate it in the studio with Françoise chatting away in French, which he was now beginning to feel comfortable with. She was telling him that Bernard and Jean-Baptiste had decided to venture into town to discover exactly what was happening. Their conversation was interrupted by the noise of vehicles moving some distance away. As they stopped to listen more attentively, a commotion erupted in the courtyard. Jack flung himself under the table, leaving Françoise to scramble to the window.

'Jack!' she screamed. 'It's all right, it's all right!'

He rolled back from under the table and joined her, amazed, to see Sylvie and Claude shaking hands with a group of soldiers. Two jeeps and a lorry blocked the entrance to the yard. Jack grabbed Françoise's arm, pulling her towards the ladder.

'It's the Americans,' he cried, 'it's the bloody Americans!'

Jack picked out the officer in charge immediately. Saluting, he declared with pride, 'Jack French, RAF, sir. Parachute drop about six months ago.'

'Well I'll be damned,' the Major replied in a southern drawl, not saluting, but shaking Jack's hand firmly. 'I'll be damned.'

His emotional appearance gave rise to the whole group cheering. Clutching Sylvie and Claude, he explained the accident with the drop, but more emphatically, how his survival had been dependent on the bravery of the family.

The Major introduced himself as Major Mulgrade of the 3rd Battalion. He had been on his way to Dijon, but then was recalled to Paris. They were short of rations and looking for milk, cheese and bread too, if there was any available.

'Is your French good enough to explain to the family? We are in a hurry. I need to be half way back to Paris by tonight. Please tell Madam that we can pay.'

But Sylvie had already understood and assured Jack that she would do her best.

Most of the soldiers were around the same age as Jack. He felt as if he had stepped out of one world into another. The jokes were familiar, the references to the French, and especially to the girls, were predictable. From the corner of his eye he could see Françoise watching him laughing. He reached out, encouraging her to join in, but she turned away and went back to the house, accompanied by the Major. When the Major returned, he instructed two of his soldiers to load two boxes of food into the lorry.

'Well, Madam has provided very nicely. Now, young man, I suggest, no, I order you to join us. We will deposit you in Paris in two days' time at the most. I need to make haste, and your French will help. Now be ready in less than half an hour. Do you have a uniform?'

Jack was about to reply when Sylvie arrived with it in her arms. It had been hidden under the floorboards in the kitchen, she explained. He made his way through the bustle in the yard to the studio to change. The uniform was clean and bore no signs of blood.

It seemed like a dream. After the languid last few months everything now seemed to be moving too fast. He needed to see Jean-Baptiste before he left, but in reality, he knew that was unlikely, unless he and Bernard were back within the next half hour. Removing his RAF belt from his trousers, he wound it in a coil and left it on the table together with a note to 'My dear friend Jean-Baptiste, from Jack'. He wanted to add more, but instead he tore his portrait from the sketchbook on the table, then folding it he put it in his pocket.

Returning to the yard, he held each member of the family in a tight embrace, shaking unashamedly with emotion. When it came to Claude, he asked him to embrace Bernard and Jean-Baptiste for him. Claude rebuffed the hand held out to him and instead gathered Jack into his arms, the tears trickling down his wrinkled face.

'I have another son,' he cried. 'God bless you.'

From start to finish the Americans' stay had been less than an hour. The Major invited Jack to share his jeep, and as they crossed the narrow bridge, he thought he could hear the sound of a motorbike. He turned swiftly to look over his shoulder, but his view was blocked by the lorries following behind.

He remained in France for two more weeks, but in that time he was able to speak briefly on the phone to Elizabeth. The line was bad, but he could hear her shouting, 'You have a son! I've called him Jack!'

CHAPTER TWELVE

*There is no trouble so great or grave that cannot
be much diminished by a nice cup of tea.*

– BERNARD PAUL HEROUX

WIRKSWORTH, DERBYSHIRE, 1956

Elizabeth's family had somehow got through January, her husband
and son making aeroplane models together. The *Daily Express* was
giving one away free each week, and Jack had faithfully collected
them for his son, apart from the last one. He had forgotten to buy the
paper on the way home. Young Jack had become obsessed with them
and was upset when his father returned empty-handed.

Her emotions, she had called to mind, had been swinging dramatically. One minute she wanted to join in with them both, and then the
next, resented their camaraderie. She freely admitted her husband
looked ill. His spirit seemed broken, and somewhere in her mind she
kept thinking, all this will end. I will embrace him, we will continue
our lives together; we have to. But she feared and resented making
the first move.

As she sat by the fire patiently darning a sock, she heard young Jack
crying.

'They'll all be gone by tomorrow. I wanted the full set, you know I
did! You promised, everyone's collecting them at school. You promised, you promised!' he repeated, running from the kitchen and
noisily climbing the stairs, and finally slamming his bedroom door.

The weather had been terrible for over a month. First snow, and then torrential rain, which caused flooding all over the county. Belper had been flooded twice, and as the rain dashed against the window, it was more than likely it would happen again over the weekend.

As her husband entered the sitting room, she refused to raise her head in acknowledgement, even though she wanted the familiar comfort of him joining her and taking his place by the fire.

'I'm going to cycle into town,' he said. 'I bet Harry's newsagents will have a copy left with the blasted model in it.'

She didn't reply, and for once Jack appeared angry, repeating, 'Did you hear me, Elizabeth? I'm going out.'

When the police had arrived the following morning, she had tried to obliterate her last few words to him, but she knew they would haunt her for the rest of her life. Instead of saying, 'Take care,' she had said, 'I don't care what you do.'

She hadn't begun to worry about him until around nine o'clock, thinking he had probably stopped at the public house on the corner for a drink. They rarely visited pubs, but recently he had called in there more often. By eleven she was seriously worried. At around half past, young Jack had stumbled downstairs, heavy with sleep, to see if his father had returned with the aeroplane model. She had tried to make light of the fact that his father had not come back yet. However, by midnight, Jack was crying, sensing something might have happened. She phoned the police and they agreed to put out a search. The two of them sat waiting together in front of a fire that refused to be revived.

At six in the morning, the local bobby arrived accompanied by a young policewoman. Jack's body had been found a mile or more downstream from the bridge. It was unclear, they said, how he had fallen into the swollen river.

'You're the man of the family now.' Jack heard this constantly after his father died. The bobby had been the first to say it when he came to break the news. He had meant it kindly, but Jack had wanted to shout, 'I don't want to be the man of the family. I want my dad to take care of me and Mum.'

He turned to Elizabeth for comfort, but she looked frozen, staring into the dying embers of the fire. The policewoman gently touched her shoulder.

'Come on, love,' she whispered. 'Who can we contact to be with you? Let me make you a cup of tea.'

Elizabeth didn't respond at first, then as if startled she cried, 'It was such a wild night, I should never have let him go.'

As his mother's words sank in, panic overcame Jack. His stomach churned, releasing a bitter taste into his mouth. He raced upstairs and flung himself on his bed. Normally, his room offered him comfort, with its toys, train set and walls adorned with posters of aircraft his father had encouraged him to collect. But as he lay crying on the bed, beating his fists into the eiderdown, he felt no comfort from the familiar things around him, only the realisation that if he'd not demanded the cardboard aeroplane, his dad might still be alive.

He sobbed uncontrollably, angry that he couldn't change the sequence of events. It wasn't fair, he reasoned. His dad had forgotten, broken a promise, but even at his young age, he instinctively knew that he had acted selfishly, and that the memory of this night wouldn't go away.

Days later, when he went to get his bike, he found the clothes his dad had been wearing on the night he had been drowned, neatly folded in the garden shed. His coat was draped across a bench. He ran into the house to ask his mum why they were there, but his aunt stopped him.

'The undertaker left them, Jack. He said they were all dry. I didn't want to upset your mum, so I left them in the shed. Now there's a good boy. Don't mention them to her, will you?'

Hours later when everyone was busy, he returned to the shed. He hesitated, his heart beating as he finally reached into the pocket of his father's old air force jacket. The leather was dry, but the sheepskin lining was still damp. Neither pocket was very deep, but he searched them vigorously, willing them to surrender even a tiny piece of a cardboard plane. Disappointed, he carefully removed his father's corduroy trousers from the pile to check the pockets. Grief overcame him as he found that they too were empty.

Folding the trousers, he returned them neatly to the pile. Then, finding an old hessian sack, he vigorously stuffed his father's jacket into it, and hung it from a nail at the back of the shed where he hoped it would not be discovered.

The inquest recorded accidental death. Jack's bike was found tangled up in the branches of a tree not far from the bridge. It had been such a bad night that there had hardly been anybody about, although a couple of drivers had said they thought they had seen a man on a bike battling against the elements.

Harry's newsagents, where Jack had been heading, had been taken over a few years previously by a Pakistani family. They had kept the name and, according to many people in the town, ran it more efficiently than Harry ever had. Where Harry had stocked papers, sweets and tobacco, the Raj family had expanded into a small grocery shop.

Jack had been a regular customer once they had started stocking quality papers. Most Sundays, he and his son would cycle into town together to pick up a newspaper and a women's magazine for Elizabeth. Young Jack was allowed to choose a treat, usually a Crunchie bar. His Dad would have a Mars bar, and Elizabeth always liked a Fry's Peppermint Cream. Then they would stop at the allotment to pick up vegetables.

The last part of their outing was to race each other home. Elizabeth had become used to the screeching of brakes as they hurtled to a halt outside the kitchen door, joshing each other about who had won.

'One day,' she would reprimand them, 'one of you will have a nasty accident travelling at that speed.'

A few days before Jack's funeral, she had walked to Harry's newsagents with the realisation that those precious Sundays would never return. The previous few days were a complete haze. Everyone, both relatives and friends, suddenly seemed so busy making arrangements. She had shut herself away in her room, not wanting to speak to anyone, not even her son. Angus, their doctor, had given her a strong sedative and she had slept most of the time.

But the funeral had been delayed because of the inquest, and whilst she didn't want to venture out, she knew that regardless of her fears she had to ask Mr Raj one question.

When she entered the shop a delicate waft of curry filled her nostrils. She knew some customers complained about the smell, but she loved it. During the last year, she and Jack had talked about going to Pakistan one day, and with a little encouragement from the Raj family they had made a simple curry with rice, which she and Jack had agreed was far superior to the curry sauce that was now a rival to the mushy peas served at the chip shop.

Mr Raj's teenage son Singh was standing behind the counter. He greeted her politely but was obviously unsure what to say. Shepherding his younger brother Mo, who was arranging the newspapers on the shelves near the till, he made for the back of the shop, explaining that they would let their parents know she was here. She was touched by the concern on their faces as they disappeared.

Mr Raj appeared, shortly followed by his wife.

'He was a good man, Elizabeth,' he said. For a second Elizabeth was surprised, as it was the first time he had used her Christian name. 'A good man,' he repeated. 'I had much respect for him.'

His wife nodded and, coming from behind the counter, she briefly took Elizabeth's hands and enclosed them in her own.

'We often discussed politics, family life and even music,' Mr Raj continued. 'He was surprised, no, astonished that I, like him, love Mozart. He even insisted on lending me a couple of his LPs. A good man, Elizabeth, and you and Jack must keep his spirit alive.'

'And how is Jack? Mrs Raj enquired. 'Mo says he is continuing to go to school. Very brave of him, such a terrible tragedy.'

Elizabeth was comforted by their warmth, finding it easier to ask the question that gnawed at her being every moment of the day and night.

'On the night of the storm, the night Jack died, did he come to the shop to buy the *Daily Express*? The one with the aeroplane models the children were collecting?'

The couple looked surprised. No, they had already explained to the police, when they asked if they had seen Jack that night, that they had closed the shop a little early as it was such a violent storm and nobody was about.

'You know, Elizabeth, we keep the shop open usually until nine o'clock, in case someone wants a pint of milk or something to last them over until the morning. But we asked the boys to close the shop at around half past eight whilst we did some stocktaking in the warehouse round the corner.'

'I know,' said Elizabeth, 'but Jack wanted to get an *Express*...' Her voice tailed off.

'Yes, the police explained,' Mr Raj replied, 'but sadly we didn't see him, nor did the boys. When we got back, they were watching television, and shortly afterwards we lost electricity for a while.'

Elizabeth felt as though someone had delivered a cruel blow to her body. Had it been the final straw when he'd found the newsagents closed? If he had returned, she knew her response to him would have been the same, a show of painful indifference. And young Jack, they had been careful not to spoil him. But he was an only child, and he was, she reasoned, only just ten. In normal circumstances she would have reprimanded him for being rude to his father and indulging in a tantrum about the plane. But she hadn't. In fact, she had ignored the incident, knowing that her lack of concern would underline her indifference, and cause her husband more hurt.

Was it possible her husband had taken his own life?

He had tried to explain so many times, to discuss that what had happened with Jean-Baptiste had not altered his desire or feelings for her. Just once, she had rallied after he had been talking to the back of her head as they lay in bed one night. She'd turned, gripping him by the shoulder and demanded, 'Did you sleep with him again when you stayed there last summer?'

She felt his body shudder. Then she gripped his face, holding it cruelly between her hands.

'You can't lie, can you, Jack? You've never been able to lie.'

He hadn't replied, but just leapt out of bed. As he made to leave the room she had cried, 'You disgust me, you have been unfaithful, not just with a woman, but with another man. Can you imagine how I feel? You have ruined our life. We have nowhere to go.'

He'd retorted for the first time, reminding her that she had kept a secret from him before they were married. 'I forgave you,' he pleaded, 'we all make mistakes.'

'It's not the same thing,' she had screamed. He'd tried to calm her, nervous that Jack would hear, but she struggled from his arms. Turning away from him to her side of the bed, she whispered, 'You're queer, Jack, it's not the same thing.'

Had those words rung in his ears as he went out into the storm? Had the fear of exposure by the press, the shame it would bring on her and Jack, had that tipped the balance, and settled the decision to take his life?

A huge wave of regret swept over her, as she remembered how Jack had lovingly accepted her youthful misdemeanour with both humour and compassion. The stark reality of her inability to even try to understand his dilemma, she knew, would rest uneasily on her for the rest of her life.

Now, standing with Mr and Mrs Raj in a newsagents smelling of curry and family life, she wanted to have her husband by her side as it had been before, happily talking on the way home about a trip to Pakistan, or the possibility of buying more spices for their curry-making. But none of that was to be. So she said goodbye and accepted a small gift of a Crunchie bar and a Peppermint Cream.

She pondered as she slowly walked home. Had she really listened when he tried to explain?

Sex was something that was never alluded to in her childhood home, and she learned the facts of life in the usual way from friends at school, and some less than explicit biology lessons. But this surely wasn't the same; this was a criminal offence.

Jack had constantly said that his brief relationship with Jean-Baptiste had never for an instant altered the way he felt about her. But even now she thought that was nonsense. Yes, she accepted and could have possibly excused that when he was being hidden by the family, the emotional strain might have tipped the balance. But on holiday with his son, she still couldn't understand.

But what she did realise that she continued to love him. She constantly missed his kindness, his humour, the loving friendship he had offered her every day. He was a wonderful father, always generous with his time when Jack demanded attention. How they would have repaired their relationship had he come back safely, she didn't know, but she longed to turn the pages back so they could try to find a way. Mr Raj had said he was a good man, and she knew that to be true.

The whole town seemed to embrace Elizabeth and young Jack's sorrow. An obituary was written about the young RAF officer who had survived the War, only to tragically lose his life in one of the worst storms for years.

Young Jack had passed the Chapel of Rest frequently on the way into Derby, and now he understood where his dad was, having overheard Elizabeth and her cousin Alfred discussing that perhaps it wasn't a good idea for him to go and see his father. His mother had gone on her own, coming back so distraught that he was nervous of upsetting her by insisting he wanted to go.

He continued to go to school, trying to ignore the embarrassing kindness that engulfed him wherever he went. On the day before the funeral he complained of being ill and was immediately given permission to take the day off school. His mum seemed aloof to all that was happening around her, but an army of friends and relatives seemed to be engaged in a frenzy of activity, organising the funeral, flowers and a wake afterwards.

He was told to go to his friend Brian's house, but he decided that as Brian would be at school, that wasn't a good idea. Sitting alone in his bedroom, he realised that the most important thing he wanted to do was to speak to his dad. He had also overheard that the coffin had to be closed and it seemed wrong to him that he hadn't said goodbye.

Quietly he left the house and set out for the Chapel of Rest, relieved when the bus conductor just punched out the ticket without making any comment.

The building was small and modern, standing next to the funeral parlour. He felt slightly intimidated when he realised he couldn't just walk into what he thought would be a little church. Instead a young man asked him at the reception desk if he could help him. Hesitating, Jack asked, 'Please may I see my dad?'

The young man looked startled and asked, 'Please may I have your name, sir?' The 'sir' was said kindly, but made Jack feel even more nervous.

'I'm Jack French,' he announced. 'My dad is Jack too. They said they are closing the coffin and my mum's seen him, but I want to see him too please.'

'I understand,' the young man replied. 'Now let me just go and get someone who can help.'

Jack sensed that this was all getting far more complicated than he thought it would be. This was confirmed when the young man returned with a middle-aged man, whom Jack recognised as the undertaker, Mr Jackson, who had visited their home a few days previously.

'So you've come to see your dad?' he enquired. 'Can I just ask, does your mum know you are here?'

'Mum's seen him,' Jack replied. 'I just wanted to say goodbye.'

As he uttered the words, a true sense of loss swept over him and he fought back the tears that he knew were gathering in his eyes. Gently grasping his hand, the undertaker led him to a chair and indicated he should sit down.

'Listen here, young man, I think it's a very fine thing you have done to come and see your dad. He'd be proud of you, but I tell you honest-ly, I think he wouldn't want you to see him.'

Jack lowered his head. 'Why not?' he mumbled.

'Because,' Mr Jackson continued, 'that's not really your dad in there. It's, well, like a shell, an empty bag, with all the lovely things gone. What did your dad like to do? Did he like football, or car racing?'

Jack thought seriously about the question and then finally replied, 'He liked gardening. We've got an allotment.'

'Well, there you are then,' the undertaker replied, 'I bet you've got a shed. You go in there and you'll be with your dad. You talk to him in there, or whilst you are planting out the potatoes or picking flowers with your mum. Then you'll remember your dad as he really was, not some empty body in a coffin in our Chapel of Rest.'

Jack thought about this for some time. He desperately wanted to touch his dad for one last time, but he knew the undertaker was right. He'd seen dead animals and when they found their cat Moggie after she had died, she had looked all stiff and wrong. He hadn't really liked the look of the Chapel of Rest. It was modern with cheap coloured windows. He paused, realising even at ten that this was a decision he would have to live with for the rest of his life.

'Ok,' he conceded, 'but can I just say goodbye through the door, please?'

Jack wasn't aware of the intense emotion that passed over Mr Jackson's face, but he heard his robust reply, 'Of course you can. We'll go together and you can shout. You can even tell him you will be there looking after your mum tomorrow.'

Taking his hand and gesturing to his young assistant to put some lights on in the Chapel, he led Jack to the entrance to shout his last goodbyes. He could sense the lad was a little embarrassed, but as he moved away, he heard him shout, 'I love you Dad, I'll take care of Mum. I'm sorry I made a fuss about the plane.' He hesitated, then shouted again, 'And I promise to take care of the allotment.'

Later, after giving the boy a fizzy orange and a piece of Victoria sponge cake, Mr Jackson took him home in his pale blue Vauxhall.

'Got to have something a bit cheery,' he explained, 'the wife gets a bit tired of black.'

Jack was impressed by the car, especially as it had a column gear change, like the ones he had seen in American movies. On the way back he relaxed a little, and he and Mr Jackson agreed that perhaps this should be their little secret for the time being. To that end he dropped Jack at the end of the road so he could return undetected.

Later, Jack realised, it had made the day of the funeral a little easier for him to cope with. As he sat with his mother behind Mr Jackson in the black funeral car, he kept imagining him in his pale blue Vauxhall, and when Mr Jackson nodded to him at the church, he felt his dad would have approved and probably said something funny about the whole occasion. When he commented to his mum at the tea afterwards that Dad would have liked the pork pies, he was pleased to feel her squeeze his fingers in agreement.

CHAPTER THIRTEEN

Here's one I made earlier.

– *BLUE PETER*, BBC TV

When Elizabeth and young Jack eventually returned home after the funeral, they endeavoured to pick up the threads, but they eluded them. Nothing felt the same and they spent most of their time circling around one another, fearful of evoking memories.

Elizabeth knew she must eventually emerge from this stupor to confront their circumstances, if only for her son's sake. Well-meaning advice came from all quarters. The consensus seemed to be that she should continue her training as a schoolteacher. It made sense as she had already completed nearly two years when she had first met Jack. After the War she had felt the need to be at home with her son, but now it seemed the obvious way to proceed. She avoided thinking of herself as depressed, patiently waiting for her energy to return so that she could plan for the future. In the end, however, it was the anger that fuelled her spirit, giving her the momentum to start afresh.

Death, she soon found, brings with it a mountain of paperwork. Drawers had to be emptied, death certificates registered. As Jack had been an assistant to the Chief Engineer at the Mill in Belper, Elizabeth would receive a small pension. Brian's dad had also reminded Elizabeth that she had a life insurance policy, explaining that when the Three Counties paid out, she could expect a sizeable sum.

She had nearly forgotten they had signed up to the policy, just after Jack had been born. She had felt at the time that it was expensive and unnecessary but had been in awe of Jack's argument that it would mature on his sixtieth birthday, leaving them with a nest egg. The last Friday of each month had heralded the visit of Mr Drew, the man from the Three Counties. He always called at the back door around seven o'clock, and whilst they were model customers with their instalment ready on the window ledge, he would always try to elicit, by a catalogue of observations on the weather, an invitation to stop for a cup of tea. 'Bitterly cold out here, bloody rain, if you'll pardon the expression.' Or in the summer, 'Hope there's a storm tonight, this heat is getting me down.'

Elizabeth just agreed with him, paid the instalment and wished him goodbye, whilst Jack was always reluctant to turn him away, and invariably offered him a cup of tea. Eventually he became a kind of family joke. Elizabeth described him as 'that oily little man' who she imagined had escaped from a Dickens novel. Jack argued he was just lonely, as he could always be found on a Saturday night sitting in the local pub, usually on his own.

He did call shortly after Jack's funeral, coming to the front door for the first time as if to mark a difference in their usual circumstances. He proffered his own sympathy together with that of the company. In reverence to Jack, she offered him a sherry. He accepted and then proceeded to sit down in Jack's favourite chair. Elizabeth felt uncomfortable, wanting to tell him to move, but instead she listened as he broached the subject of how much the insurance company would pay out. Sipping his sherry slowly, he seemed to take pleasure in informing her that it would probably take months before everything was sorted. He was also bound by company policy not to suggest a final settlement.

Elizabeth had not given it any thought, but now this oily little man was sitting in front of her she felt a sense of indignation. She was just about to ask, 'Why should it take so long?' when her son entered the room. He seemed startled for a moment. Without thinking or conferring with his mother, he blurted out, 'You're in my dad's chair!'

Smiling his oily smile, Mr Drew turned to Elizabeth and said, 'But I am sure he wouldn't mind, would he, Mrs French?'

Young Jack turned to his mother and was delighted when she replied, 'Well, actually, Mr Drew, I think he might.'

Mr Drew left shortly afterwards, stuffing his papers in his bag and leaving by the back door.

'You realise we've both been very impolite,' she told her son. 'But on this occasion I think Dad would have approved.' Later, though, she acknowledged to herself that she had been unnecessarily rude, and probably made an enemy.

The insurance claim was dispatched the following week and to Elizabeth's surprise, Mr Drew arrived at the end of the month. She had assumed that as no payments were due, any further business would be done by correspondence. He came to the front door again, but this time was accompanied by a young man who explained he was from the Regional Office. Could they come in, they asked. 'It will only take a few minutes; we just need to clarify a few points.'

Elizabeth sensed that whatever the few points were, they were not going to be in her favour. Inviting them into the small sitting room, she gestured towards the sofa to indicate that they should sit down. She sat facing them in her husband's chair, amused to see how uncomfortable they both appeared, wedged into a two-seater sofa with their coats still on.

'What few points are we talking about, Mr Drew?' she asked. 'I thought the claim was quite straightforward. I'm surprised you didn't phone for an appointment.'

'Well, yes,' he replied nervously, 'it's just…'

'Let me explain,' the young man intervened. 'You have to understand, Mrs French, we realise these are extremely difficult times for you. The company do not wish to cause you any unnecessary distress, but it has been brought to our attention that your husband was possibly depressed prior to his death.'

'What exactly do you mean?' Elizabeth asked, aware that the luxury of remaining in a kind of limbo since Jack's death must start to come to an end. She had happily relied on him since they were married, content that on the whole they shared the same principles and very rarely argued over anything.

'When an accidental death is recorded,' the young man continued, 'the company is bound by law to investigate. If there are any...' He stopped and turned to his colleague. Mr Drew inhaled sharply, then bending forward as if to touch Elizabeth, he continued in a tone that suggested confidentiality.

'It has been brought to our attention that your husband was very upset after the death of his friend Jean-Baptiste Dupont. They were very close friends. In fact we are given to understand that your husband was often one of his, how can I say...' again he hesitated, searching for a suitable word, 'the subject of some of his paintings. We of course know the story of how the Dupont family hid your husband, protecting him from the Germans.'

Elizabeth felt an icy coldness penetrate her body. Only the firmness of Jack's chair held any comfort for her. Measuring her words carefully, she asked, 'Are you suggesting that my husband may have committed suicide?' Her words hung in the air as if floating above their heads.

After a few seconds Mr Drew continued, 'Well, you must understand the company has a duty to be thoroughly sure that your claim is completely valid.'

She found it difficult to formulate her thoughts. Her own doubts overwhelmed her.

Behind the sofa where the two insurance agents huddled together was a large mirror. It was far too grandiose for the room, she thought, but it had belonged to Jack's parents. Jack had always remarked that it was as good as a picture as it reflected their little sitting room. But on this occasion it reflected a far more surreal scene. The back of the two men's heads, one balding, one neatly cut. Then, slightly obscured, Elizabeth could see herself. She was gripped in amazement for a moment. She looked desperately tired; her complexion was pale, but even more distressing than that, she realised she looked completely defeated.

In the background she could hear her son in the kitchen. He'd turned on the radio, and over the sound of it could be heard the rattle of plates as he prepared himself something to eat. In a minute she knew he would appear with a small tray holding his tea.

Her cousin Alfred had insisted, shortly after the funeral, that Elizabeth buy a television. She hadn't been interested, but Alfred had seen it as a project and, without further reference to Elizabeth, had involved young Jack in choosing and installing one. It stood a little awkwardly in the corner of the room, but, as Elizabeth had to admit, it was a good idea. It served to dispel something of the loneliness they experienced every day and gave Jack an opportunity to discuss the merits of *Robin Hood* and other popular soaps with his schoolmates. On Tuesday and Thursday evenings Elizabeth would make an effort to join him so they could eat their tea together in front of the television and watch *Blue Peter*.

As Jack appeared through the door, Elizabeth straightened in her chair, overcome by a sense of indignation.

'Sorry, Jack,' she said to her son, 'Mr Drew and this gentleman will be leaving soon, but we have to discuss a few things first. Go back to the kitchen and eat your tea. We'll try and be finished by the start of your programme.'

As he left, closing the door rather noisily behind him, she rose from her chair. Then, running her hands through her hair, she confronted the men sitting on the sofa.

She reflected later that night that she had been remarkably composed. The sight of her son had broken sharply through her grief. Whatever the circumstances of her husband's death, she knew without question that he would expect her to create the best life she could for her son. She knew what was said in the next few minutes could affect their lives immeasurably. Staring into the mirror for a moment, she felt her husband's presence.

'All right, Jack,' she thought, 'my love for you faltered, but never ever went away. I will not let you down. I'll try and turn the tables on this unsavoury pair, I'll take command.'

'Who gave you to understand,' she asked, staring directly at Mr Drew, 'that my husband was depressed?'

Not returning her gaze, he replied robustly, 'I'm not at liberty to say, Mrs French, but it was common knowledge. You must have realised yourself. He'd started frequenting The Lion; lots of people remarked on it, because it wasn't like him. He'd come in, hardly speak to anyone, have a couple of drinks, then leave. Fred the barman said he would often try to talk to him, but he made it clear he wanted to be left alone.'

The young man moved uncomfortably on the sofa, but continued with the story. 'It has also come to the company's notice that when a journalist from the *Derby Post* called to see you and your husband, your husband became violent, causing you to pass out,' he concluded dramatically.

Before Elizabeth could reply, Mr Drew added, 'We also understand that your husband was on medication and seeing the doctor.'

'Before you continue with your understandings,' Elizabeth broke into the diatribe, 'let me understand one thing.' She drew breath, uncertain if this was the best line of attack, then continued. 'If your company was in any way able to prove anything, what would they do?'

Sensing a victory, Mr Drew turned to his colleague and then looked up at Elizabeth. 'Please, Mrs French, sit down. We do not want to distress you; in fact my coming with my colleague was intended to discreetly prepare you before the company wrote to you. Because you see, if there is any real doubt as to the cause of death, even after an inquest, the company will decline to pay. But if the situation is handled, how can I say, sensitively, they would undoubtedly agree to some payment, if not the full amount. The problem is that if not handled… delicately, these things can go on for ages and get unpleasant.'

Elizabeth continued to stand. Moving slightly to one side, she grasped the side of her husband's chair for support.

'Now,' she said firmly, 'let me be quite clear. Yes, both my husband and I were deeply upset when we heard of Jean-Baptiste's death. He and his family had sheltered Jack and probably saved his life. Over the years our families have kept in touch, in fact we visited them not long ago. But it was the first time that my husband had seen Jean-Baptiste since the War. Jean-Baptiste painted many portraits of his family and friends, he was an artist. His world was very different to ours, and if, I repeat, *if* he did paint Jack, it was totally without Jack's involvement or permission.'

She raised her hand to prevent them interrupting, then raising her voice a little she continued.

'If you or the Three Counties dare to try to make anything of this, let me state very clearly that I will take you to court for slander. I will not let you sully my husband's name. I will personally make public your allegations in every newspaper in the country. Tomorrow I will phone your Regional Office to inform them of my intentions. I will also contact the *Derby Post* to discuss what right they have to stir up such a dirty little plot.'

Mr Drew started to protest, but Elizabeth advanced towards him, and bending down a little, she looked directly into his eyes. 'Understand, Mr Drew, I will implicate you. Over the years my husband and I have welcomed you into our home and you can't help having seen…' her voice faltered, caught with emotion, 'what a happy family we were. Our lives, young Jack's and mine, have been devastated. We are coping with a tragedy that you can't imagine.'

Both men rose to go, but Elizabeth barred their way. 'Two more things,' she cried. 'I know the barman in The Lion, we have known him for years, and I do not think for one moment that he would suggest Jack had committed suicide. Secondly, that journalist lied. I did not faint when he called. He was extremely rude, and I had every right to be upset and Jack to be angry. Now,' she said, opening the sitting room door, 'never come to my house again. Please leave. If you have one ounce of compassion between you, you will leave us alone. If I discover that you have said anything indiscreet about me or my husband, I repeat, I will sue you.'

Neither man replied, waiting silently as she struggled to open the stiff front door and usher them out.

Her young son was standing behind her as she closed it after them. He clutched her around the waist, crying, 'Well done, Mum, Dad would have been proud of you.'

It was what she wanted to hear. She sensed he had not heard too much of the dispute, and was relieved when she joined him in the sitting room a few minutes later to see he was already absorbed in *William Tell.*

She walked to the window. In the distance she could see the two men walking down the street. The younger one was much taller than Mr Drew, requiring him to bend awkwardly to converse with his colleague. Even from a distance, she could see the conversation was animated. The young man's arms were flailing about. Then they rounded the bend in the road and disappeared from view.

She remained at the window. In the last few months she had lost all sense of time. She had barely looked along the street, but now in the fading light her heart was caught with how content she and Jack and their young son had been to live here. Two rows of mill cottages faced one another, then a row of more substantial Edwardian terraced houses, of which theirs was one. All the houses, even the cottages, had small front gardens. A few years ago the cobbled road and pavements had been replaced by tarmac and modern flagstones, but it still retained its eclectic charm. Roses climbed up fences and walls, lupins and delphiniums fought for space in the flowerbeds. Their large fuchsia was now in bloom, its red and purple blooms moving gently in the breeze. Jack had said it was a garden escapee, as he hadn't planted it, it had just appeared. It grew very vigorously each year and now it was higher than the fence.

She walked back through the house and into the kitchen. Jack had been replacing all the kitchen units before he died, and two large Formica boards rested against one wall with Jack's toolbox at their base. The new cooker, with its much sought-after eye-level grill, had, Elizabeth acknowledged, hardly been used. She opened the small pantry door. In the past it had bristled with packets, tins and cooking equipment. They had even managed to put the new fridge-freezer below one of the shelves. Now everything looked forlorn, with half-empty packets and a single tin of baked beans, and Elizabeth could even detect an unpleasant smell of over-ripe vegetables.

She reached for her pinafore from the back of the door, realising as she put it on that it too was grubby and stained. For a second she felt deeply ashamed. The radio was playing some mindless tune about someone wanting to be 'Bobby's girl'. The singer kept repeating, 'I want to be Bobby's girl, that's the most important thing to me.'

Suddenly she felt extremely hungry. Returning to the pantry she found a half-used bag of spaghetti. She emptied the contents into a saucepan, added hot water and waited for it to cook. Jack had often done the cooking and to amuse her, he would religiously throw a bit of spaghetti against the wall to see if it was cooked. She never really enjoyed cooking, but when Jack had the time he would make what he described as a 'mean spaghetti bolognese'. But tonight there was no bolognese sauce, so she opened the last tin of baked beans and stirred them into the cooked spaghetti. The whole thing was tasteless, but she added butter, pepper and salt and a bit of the remaining cheese she found in the fridge. Whilst not up to her husband's standards, the meal was very comforting.

The next thing she resolved to do was to clean the kitchen and pantry, even if it took until midnight. A new leaf had to be turned, regardless of Mr Drew and the unfortunate young man who had accompanied him. She knew she hadn't strictly spoken the truth; she hadn't accompanied Jack and their son on the holiday in France, and she had fainted as the journalist was leaving. But she was resolute in formulating a plan that would protect her husband's reputation, which in turn would protect her son.

By Wednesday of the following week, Elizabeth had spoken to the Regional Office on the phone. She had initially asked for an appointment with the Regional Manager, only to be told by a secretary who bordered on being annoyingly condescending that the Regional Manager, Mr Deacon, rarely saw clients, but she would pass the enquiry on. Elizabeth replied that this was not an enquiry but a complaint, and if Mr Deacon deemed her not important enough, she would phone the Head Office immediately. There was a silence and then, 'Hold the line, please.' After a couple of minutes Mr Deacon came on the line.

Elizabeth explained quite calmly the visit she had received from Mr Drew and his colleague, filling in a little of the background on the way, and making it clear that she felt they were mounting a kind of conspiracy against her. Was this the Three Counties' normal procedure, she asked, and had the Regional Manager instigated this investigation? She concluded with the warning she had given the two agents.

Not surprisingly, his replies were very cautious. 'Weasel' words, her father would have called them. 'Thank you for your comments, Mrs French. I will look into your complaint immediately.'

'And will I hear from you?' she asked.

'Definitely,' he replied, 'you have my word, and I apologise for any distress our agents might have caused.'

As she put the phone down, she was shaking. After a minute she found a bottle of sherry they kept in the sideboard. She poured herself a drink and sipped it slowly, knowing that Jack would have found her assertive manner most amusing.

The call to the *Derby Post* met with a similar response. *Who are these women?* Elizabeth asked herself. *Is it part of the job description to shield their bosses from any kind of unpleasantness?* However, she was finally given an appointment to meet Mr Gerard, the editor. She was cautioned that as he was a very busy man, he could only spare fifteen minutes; was that sufficient?

'I will leave that for Mr Gerard to decide,' she replied, delighted that her confidence was strengthening day by day.

Her last call was to Angus, her doctor. She had been tempted to visit him at home as he and his wife were family friends, but it seemed unprofessional. They had both been at the funeral and during the reception afterwards, both he and his wife had offered to help with anything that might make Elizabeth's life easier. Angus and Jack's fathers had attended the local primary school together, and the friendship between the two families had remained strong. After university, Angus had entered and eventually taken over his father's medical practice. It was just as National Service was starting, and despite there being two other partners, it was always busy, and he hadn't been called up. Often, if young Jack was ill or needed an inoculation, they would go as a family.

Elizabeth phoned the surgery. She knew Angus' secretary well, and was not surprised to be told that Dr Barry would fit her in on Friday evening.

With all the telephone calls made and Wednesday being a half day closing in Derby, Elizabeth resolved to spend the rest of the day cleaning her house from top to bottom, filling it with flowers and writing a list to stock up the pantry.

On Thursday she decided to search for a new outfit, something simple but smart that would carry her through the meeting at the *Derby Post*, and possibly an interview with the principal of the teacher training college, if she decided to carry on with her studies.

Derby was beginning to feel prosperous, with new shops springing up throughout the town. Jack had preferred her in classical clothes, but she felt that she needed to look a little less dowdy. She knew that the meeting with the *Derby Post* editor wouldn't be easy, but at least if she was well turned-out, an expression her mother had often used, it would boost her confidence.

She settled on a new fashionable full skirt, matching blouse and cardigan, teamed with a pair of high-heeled court shoes, something she'd never worn before. Admittedly, she had to accept that she felt better sitting down in the shoes than standing up, but they gave her a slight feeling of power as she walked into Mr Gerard's office.

He was a younger version of Alfred Hitchcock, overweight with crumpled clothes and a somewhat well-rehearsed air of weariness. She was aware that for the first few minutes he was hardly listening to her, but as she related her story, he became more engaged, eventually confessing to remembering some of the details that had been brought to his attention a few weeks previously.

'Why are you here, Mrs French?' he finally asked. 'I don't yet see what you want from me.'

'I am here because your young journalist is stirring up trouble that could affect my insurance claim,' she replied. 'But more important than that is my husband's reputation, and whilst I might not be able to prevent you from publishing anything, I want you to know that I will fight you, even if it involves a scandal.'

'Are you threatening us, Mrs French?' he asked.

Elizabeth raised her hands up to her lips, entwining her fingers and closing her eyes as if in silent prayer. She remained like this for a moment, totally lost in her thoughts. Then she opened her eyes and declared abruptly, 'How unkind, you know I haven't the power to threaten you.' She thought for a second, then, regaining her composure, she continued. 'But I am informing you about enquiries, investigations, call them what you will, that have been made by your paper. You possibly don't know the details, but I am fighting for my son. Can you imagine what it would be like for him if there were allegations about his father? Maybe it's tolerated in the upper classes, but it's still a crime. Then there is this sudden, out of the blue suggestion that my husband might have committed suicide. Can you imagine...' She stopped. Her voice was so full of emotion that she was unable to finish her sentence.

'Let me ask one final question, Mrs French. Do you think your husband committed suicide?

'No,' she replied, 'why should he? It's a nightmare. At times I feel out of my depth, but I will fight this, I have to, for our son. Surely you understand?'

Letting her regain her composure, he said, 'I am going to get my secretary to get you a cup of coffee, whilst I go and ask a few questions. Audrey!' he cried, summoning his secretary. 'Please organise a drink for Mrs French, and possibly a couple of those chocolate digestives you hide in your desk.'

Not waiting for her reply, he left the room. Elizabeth watched him through the glass partition as he wound his way to the corner of the big open-plan office. On the way he indicated to several colleagues that they should join him. One she recognised as the young journalist who had visited her.

Audrey arrived with coffee and biscuits, remarking that her boss had to be kept away from the digestives otherwise he would consume the whole packet in one go. Elizabeth observed the turmoil beyond the glass partition with interest. Everyone seemed very animated, apart from a couple of journalists studiously bent over their type-writers. Even at ten-thirty in the morning there was already a haze of cigarette smoke lingering above the organised chaos.

Would I fit into a place like this? she asked herself, attracted by the buzz and the thought that no two days would be the same.

Mr Gerard returned, ambling his way back into the office. Flopping heavily into his chair, he leaned across the desk towards her.

'I've spoken to David, the journalist who called on you. I won't go into the ins and outs, but you have my assurance that we will not be taking any more interest in your husband's death. David is a good journalist and destined for greater things than working on a local newspaper, but he has a lot to learn. I'll clip his wings a little, until it's safe to let him fly.'

Elizabeth waited for him to continue, but instead he rose from his chair, indicating that their meeting was finished. 'Mrs French,' he concluded, grasping her hand, 'you have my deepest condolences.' Then, still holding her hand, he added, 'One last thing: should the Three Counties turn down your claim, and you feel you wish to con-tinue the fight, please let me know. Together, I think we could be a formidable team.'

Elizabeth emerged from the *Derby Post's* office into the sunlight. She saw that it was nearly eleven o'clock, well over her allocated fifteen minutes. Audrey, the secretary, had turned out to be rather charming, commenting on Elizabeth's elegant shoes as she left.

She felt triumphant, but at a loss what to do next. It was market day and the town was busy, but she felt strangely conspicuous. *I'm all dressed up with nowhere to go*, she thought, *with no one to share my triumph.*

As it was too late for coffee and too early for lunch, she resolved to catch the next bus home. She stopped at the bus station kiosk and bought Jack two tubes of Rowntree's wine gums. He had started repeating some of the television jingles, and 'Don't forget the fruit gums, Mum' was one of his favourites. She realised guiltily that since her husband's death she had detached herself from her son's world, but now she knew was the time to be brave and step back in.

As the bus wove its way through the suburbs and out into the coun-tryside in the direction of home, she felt nervous, accepting that her last visit to see Angus that evening would be the hardest. But, if Jack had visited him recently, he might hold the key to the tragedy.

CHAPTER FOURTEEN

*Someone once called this law against
homosexuality the blackmailer's charter.*

– JOHN BARRIE, *VICTIM*

The surgery was on the outskirts of town, but still walking distance from Elizabeth's home. She considered keeping on her new outfit, but she felt more comfortable in slacks and a blouse. Plus the new court shoes were definitely not designed for serious walking. After catching a glimpse of herself in the mirror as she started to leave the house, she returned to her bedroom to put on some lipstick and to wind a blue chiffon scarf around her neck.

In the last week, she had started to claw her way back to some kind of normality, but she was nervous that she could so easily let it slip through her fingers. She had seen that there was something wrong with Jack every day since the phone call from Françoise; everyone could, even young Jack, and yet she had felt powerless to help. She wondered if the pain would ever go away, or remain like a scar that was barely visible but always there.

The surgery waiting room was surprisingly empty.

'People haven't got time to be ill on a Friday night,' remarked Angus as he led her into his office. He sat her down, then pulled up another chair next to her, rather than sitting behind his desk.

'Oh no, Angus,' she pleaded, 'sit behind your desk, please. I want to feel that I am the patient and you are the doctor. I can't explain, but it will make it easier for me.'

He removed the chair and put it back in its place.

'All right,' he replied, 'but remember, if you dissolve into tears, which in your circumstances is perfectly natural, I will find it hard not to leap over the desk and give you a hug.'

'Agreed,' she laughed, remembering how good he always was at lightening a situation. When he had nursed her mother prior to her death, he had always made her smile with his kindly banter.

'Have you any idea why I am here?' Elizabeth finally asked, in an attempt to take charge of the situation.

'Not really,' he replied. 'Tell me, Elizabeth.'

For the second time that day she related the incident when the two agents had called.

'They said that Jack was seeing a doctor. Is that true? If it was, how would they know?' she asked, fighting to control her voice and the approaching tears.

'This is silly,' said Angus, getting up immediately and positioning his chair in front of her again so that their knees touched and he could grasp her hands. 'Yes, Jack did come to see me. Yes, he was upset. In fact he was at his wits' end to know what to do. This is unprofessional of me, but Jack was my friend, Elizabeth, and it was pitiful. He loved you, Elizabeth, you know that. But he wasn't infallible, none of us is. He'd made a mistake, I will be honest. He told me everything and he couldn't see a way out. He asked for my opinion, for my help. But,' he strengthened his grip on Elizabeth's hands, 'I didn't sense for one minute that he was suicidal. You're not the only one in this equation, Elizabeth, there's young Jack as well. He adored him.'

'I know, I know,' she sobbed. 'I wouldn't listen to him, I just turned away. Did he tell you about Jean-Baptiste?' Her grief overwhelmed her again. She thought she had it under control, but here it was again bursting to the surface.

'Listen, Elizabeth,' Angus continued. 'I told him your forgiveness would take time and that he had to be patient. I advised him to take control of the situation a little. Not to be a complete doormat. It wasn't love he was trying to recover; it was also respect.'

Her sobbing reverberated around the room.

'Do you want me to continue?' he ventured.

She nodded, clutching his hands for comfort.

'He told me all about Jean-Baptiste. I feel that was incredibly brave of him. We can't begin to understand the intensity of the situation. Jack knew their whole family could have been slaughtered if he had been discovered. He said that he stopped fearing for his own life very early on. It was their lives he feared for. He said he had, and continued to have nightmares, where the family was dragged into the courtyard by the Germans and shot. We talked honestly about his brief sexual relationship with Jean-Baptiste. I was angry at first that he had been so stupid as to have admitted it to you.'

'He wasn't any good at lying,' she intervened.

'Yes, I realised that. I told him our two fathers had gone to school together and well, like my dad, I went to public school. Boys had crushes, fantasies and sexual relationships. It sounds sordid, but these things happen. Jack was not homosexual, Elizabeth, nor did he want to hurt you. He was kind, sensitive and he loved you. But for a brief moment in his life I believed he loved, desired, whatever, Jean-Baptiste. And ask yourself, is that so terrible? He had saved his life.'

'But why did he allow himself to... do it a second time? I mean, he was on holiday with his son.'

Angus felt exhausted. He was a family doctor, but that didn't always equip him to deal with all the complexities that his daily surgery threw at him. Elizabeth calmed down and accepted a box of tissues. They smelt rather unpleasantly of disinfectant, but she buried her face in them.

'All I know, Elizabeth, is probably the same as you. He stopped in Paris on the way back and went to Jean-Baptiste's apartment. He left young Jack in the car. He told me Jean-Baptiste was fairly drunk, but he, Jack that is, made him understand that he wanted nothing more to do with him. He accused Jean-Baptiste of tricking you both into coming over for a stay, saying he was having an engagement party. Apparently, there was a very unsavoury character there at Jean-Baptiste's apartment that afternoon, another artist, he thought. They were both drunk. He felt everything was getting out of hand, and he was worried about young Jack being on his own. He was sure Jean-Baptiste's sister – what is her name?'

'Françoise,' Elizabeth replied.

'Well, that when Françoise initially phoned to tell you about his death just before Christmas, it was a kind of coded message for him to keep a low profile. The French police did contact him, but as he wasn't in the country at the time of Jean-Baptiste's death they lost interest.'

'Yes,' she admitted, 'I knew that, but it doesn't answer the question why he...' As usual she sought for the right words. 'Why was he unfaithful to me for a second time? It's so sordid, Angus, I never in a million years thought anything like this would touch my life. It's a crime, you know that. I'm not a prude and my dad would say it takes all sorts, but not Jack, not my Jack! Sometimes I let my mind... Oh God, Angus, I can't bear it. If he'd been unfaithful with another woman, maybe I could have forgiven him, but this, it feels dirty, and the thought of young Jack finding out...'

'You are right, Elizabeth, it's a crime, but I don't think we are talking like for like here. And I also think that eventually the law will change. As a doctor I'm privy to various things and I know that there's a report being published soon that will recommend greater leniency. It will undoubtedly cause a fuss, but since the War things are changing, becoming more tolerant, I hope. But, Elizabeth, I can hand on heart say I do not think Jack was homosexual. He was just for a brief moment in his life consumed by a passion, and, my dear, you have to accept that. Don't carry the guilt around with you that you reacted wrongly, most women would have done exactly the same. You are human too. He drowned, it was an accident, you lost a husband that you undoubtedly loved and who loved you. For Jack's sake, let it rest there.'

She sat for a moment, in the realisation that Angus was not going to be drawn more on the subject. His receptionist knocked on the closed door, then shouted, 'I'm off now, Dr Barry, I'll leave you to lock up.'

As they heard her leave, the surgery felt eerily quiet, before Elizabeth broke the silence by asking, 'But how did the insurance agent know he'd been to see you?'

'Well, it did occur to me that what's his name, your insurance agent? Drew, something like that? He's a regular at the pub, Jack once pointed him out to me.'

'Yes, Mr Drew, I never liked him, but you know Jack, he was always kind with him.' Then she asked, 'When did you go to the pub with Jack?'

'After he first came to see me,' Angus replied. 'I was rather concerned about his state of mind, so we arranged to have a drink.'

'So you *were* worried about him,' Elizabeth persisted.

'That's not fair, Elizabeth,' he replied. 'Yes, I was concerned. In fact, I suggested that we all make up a foursome and go out for a meal at that new Chinese restaurant that's opened up in Derby, but he didn't want that. He said it was too soon.' His unspoken thoughts of Jack sitting, hands clutched around his beer, exuding a sense of complete hopelessness, now made him feel a fresh sense of unease about Jack's death. 'He was my friend. I cared about him. Don't beat me for that, Elizabeth.'

After a pause, Elizabeth asked, 'What if the insurance company contacts you? Do you think they might? What would you say?'

'All they can do is ask for a record of Jack's health. As it was good, apart from the occasional trouble with his back, that shouldn't be a problem. I didn't prescribe him antidepressants, fortunately.'

This time Elizabeth grabbed his hands. 'But did you offer them to him?' she asked.

Angus didn't reply at first, then renewing his pressure on her hands he replied, 'Well, yes I did. I offered him a course of mild barbiturates, really to help him sleep, but he wouldn't hear of it. And a bit out of order I know, but I suggested he have a cigarette now and then. Certainly helps me when I'm feeling a bit, well, you know, low, or I need to relax. But I stand by what I said earlier. In my opinion he wasn't suicidal. He was depressed, and that can be very debilitating. Now,' he said, 'we are going home. Not your home but our home. We'll pick young Jack up along the way.'

Elizabeth didn't argue but took another tissue in an attempt to tidy up her face. She suddenly felt very weary, but surprisingly calm knowing that Angus was right. If she carried her guilt around like some kind of heavy baggage it would damage not only her, but her relationship with her son. She resolved to try to demonstrate her continuing love for her husband by being the best mother and companion she could be for young Jack.

BELPER, DERBYSHIRE, 1968

Elizabeth was amazed at the clarity of her memories. Just over a decade later, her son was now a man, a man in the same mould as his father. Sometimes the resemblance was so profound it took her breath away. It would not be easy to gracefully release him to another woman. However, she respected his judgement, eager to know about the girl with the Mary Quant umbrella.

The rain had continued overnight, but the wind had subsided. When Jack joined her for breakfast, she teased him again about his girlfriend.

'Come on, Jack. What's her name? Don't be so mysterious.'

He looked up from the local paper he was reading.

'It's Nancy,' he replied, then biting into his toast and sending a flurry of crumbs over the paper, he continued, 'Hey, Mum, look at this, isn't that Mo's brother?'

Elizabeth leaned across the table. 'Well, yes, it must be,' she replied, clearing the crumbs off the paper. 'Singh Raj. Someone told me he was doing well. My word, "Raj Estates" he's calling himself,' she laughed. 'I always got the feeling he was the bright one. Nice photograph, handsome-looking man.'

'Yes, I'm sure he was,' replied Jack, 'he was that bit older than me. I think Mo still helps run the shop. What a laugh, "Raj Estates"!'

They both quickly read the short article about the young local man starting up an estate agency.

'No, I'm impressed,' Elizabeth remarked. 'With all these foreigners arriving, there's a market out there. It must be a nightmare for most of them, dealing with some of the old established firms in Derby.'

Jack nodded and stood up. 'Now I'm off, and you'll be late for school if you're not careful. Can't let the Headmistress set a bad example.'

She was about to speak, but he raised his hand, then bent down to kiss her. 'No more questions about the beautiful Nancy.'

'Understood,' she laughed. 'But it looks as if she might need that umbrella today.'

She followed him into the hall and watched as he donned his father's old flying jacket, which they had found in the shed when they moved. It always comforted her to see him in it, and she enjoyed teasing him that he didn't look as handsome as his father had when wearing it.

She stood in the front doorway as he went outside. His motorbike burst into life, filling the hall for a moment with the smell of petrol.

'Take care,' she shouted, fully aware that her words would never penetrate the noise of his bike.

CHAPTER FIFTEEN

Would you believe in a love at first sight?
Yes, I'm certain that it happens all the time

– THE BEATLES, *'WITH A LITTLE HELP*
FROM MY FRIENDS'

DERBY, 1968

Jack was constantly amazed that his relationship with Nancy had never once faltered from the moment they had met that February. A bitterly cold March had come and gone, but now it was mid-April and the weather was beginning to soften. As they sat, backs against a dry-stone wall, acres of daffodils stretched in front of them, moving in yellow waves. Beyond the mass of yellow nodding heads, a network of fields of all shapes and sizes gave way to the soft dales. But the sky stole the show: a bright blue, it created the perfect backdrop for billowing white clouds, which tumbled back and forth as the wind called the tune.

'There's a poem here, isn't there?' Nancy said. 'Wandering as a cloud, then seeing daffodils, Wordsworth I think?'

'Yes, Dad used to recite it,' Jack replied.

They huddled together, sheltering from the breeze. Nancy turned her head away from the view, nestling her head in Jack's jacket.

'Days like this scare me,' she murmured. 'They are so beautiful. I want to run through the daffodils, hug the sky, bury my face in the clouds, but it's all so fleeting.'

He knew what she meant. He felt it too. Every time he saw her, touched her, smelt her, listened to her voice, he felt privileged, amazed that this extraordinary woman desired him. Even after just a few weeks together, they had become best friends. They had seemingly fallen overnight into a relationship where they felt confident in each other's company, ready to laugh, tease and play together.

'Run through the daffodils,' he taunted her.

She looked at him quizzically for a moment. 'Certainly not, I would trample them.'

'Well, take your shoes off, and dance through them,' Jack suggested, kissing her lightly on the nose.

Thoughtfully she looked down at her shoes. Then, smiling, she removed them, then continued casually with her trousers, jumper, bra and finally her pale pink French silk knickers, leaving only her green beret still pinned firmly on her head.

Standing before him for an instant, her childlike cries of 'Catch me, catch me!' resounded across the landscape.

Jack hesitated, then shedding all his clothes he followed her naked into the field. The sun was warm, but the breeze was cool, and when Jack finally caught her, their bodies tingled as they clung together, falling gently to the ground lost in their lovemaking.

'D.H. Lawrence,' she suggested as they lingered a little longer in the sun.

'Let me guess,' Jack replied, '*Sons and Lovers*? No, of course, *Lady Chatterley's Lover*, but wasn't it daisies rather than daffodils?'

Picking a daffodil head, she delicately fitted it over his penis.

'This will have to do,' she laughed, 'although it does look more like one of those "Flower Fairies" illustrations. So what page of the book did your *Lady Chatterley* fall open at?'

'I remember it was the Penguin edition, which made it feel a bit more respectable,' he replied, 'but I can't remember the page, I think it was Chapter 12. Actually, I found it disappointing after all the fuss. I don't think I ever finished reading it.'

They both experienced a slight feeling of guilt as they walked back, trying to stick to the path of destruction they had created through the flowers. They dressed hurriedly, rubbing each other's arms in an attempt to get warm. When they reached Nancy's flat later that afternoon, she realised she had lost her green beret.

'Why do you wear berets, is it a French thing?' Jack asked as he searched the picnic basket in case it was there.

'I can't hear you,' she replied over the music Jack had put on, 'turn it down a bit.'

'I thought you liked Sergeant Pepper.'

'I do,' she cried, appearing from the kitchenette with a plate of sandwiches held together with little cocktail sticks and topped with either an olive or a cube of pineapple.

'These,' she announced triumphantly, 'are double decker sandwiches. I hope you are impressed. Straight from the pages of *Good Housekeeping*.'

'I thought you didn't like women's magazines?'

'I don't, they intimidate me, but Rosemary gives them to me. Heaven knows why she takes it, because she's probably the most undomesticated person I know. Well, barring me.'

She placed the sandwiches on the coffee table, then returned to the kitchenette to reappear with two large wine glasses.

'These are butterscotch Angel Delight with banana. The only reason I produced these is because it involved no cooking and was headlined as the perfect TV supper.'

'Can I point out,' Jack laughed, 'that we do not have a TV.'

'Thank goodness, it used to rule Rosemary's schedule. If she missed *Emergency Ward 10* or *Z Cars* she would be very grumpy. Admittedly, I did join her sometimes for the Wednesday play. If you miss it, Jack, let's get one.'

The strains of Sergeant Pepper faded as the LP finished.

'But what did you say, something about my beret?'

'I couldn't find it in the picnic basket. I just asked why you wear berets, is it a French thing?'

Nancy inhaled deeply, pondering before answering the question.

'Yes, maybe, but it's more than that. I want to look different. Men on the whole don't like their women to look different. Different often means disturbing. I'm not like most women I come into contact with, I don't see being married as the be all and end all. I admire Agnes and Rosemary. I'm pretty sure they haven't burned their bras – if they have, I haven't noticed,' she laughed, 'but they're not afraid to live their lives without a man in tow.'

'So,' he said, flopping on the sofa, 'you want to be disturbing, possibly a little dangerous, and the beret helps?'

'In a strange way it does. Love me, love my beret,' she laughed. 'Go on, Jack, be honest, your mates find me a little odd.'

He felt at a disadvantage sitting on the sofa, with her standing in front of him.

'I know they find you sexy,' he replied carefully, 'beautiful as well, but I suppose they are in awe of you. I'm sure they're wondering why you've taken up with someone like me.'

Moving to the opposite sofa, she sat down, then prompted him. 'Go on, say it. I know people say I have a past, a reputation.'

He suddenly felt nervous. They had some details of each other's lives, and she had explained about her childhood with Edna and Bill and the appalling circumstances that had led her to eventually taking refuge with the Sloams.

She had been eager to introduce him to Agnes and her friends, although he realised that they had obviously been primed about his age. However, he was used to being in the company of his mother, and found it somewhat amusing that when he mentioned Radio 4, *The Archers* and even the serial *Mrs Dale's Diary*, they instantly warmed to him, and he guiltily had to admit he had them eating out of his hand.

'Come on, Jack,' she continued, curling her hands around a large mug of Earl Grey tea. 'It's time to tell me what you have heard about me.' She was wearing her reading glasses, and the steam from the tea clouded the lenses, forcing her to push them back onto her head.

He laughed, and leaning forward he took her glasses, and cleaned them on the sleeve of his shirt. As he replaced them, he grasped her hand, kissing her fingers playfully.

'Ok,' he said, offering her a double decker sandwich. 'Betty said she had heard you'd had an affair with your boss. But as Brian pointed out that was hardly a sackable offence. And yes, there were some unsavoury stories about the notorious Bill. And of course your friendship with...' he hesitated, then emphasised 'black men, but since you introduced me to Louis and Bartholomew, that's kind of taken the edge off your scandalous relationships.'

She laughed, perching her glasses on the top of her head again. 'But you would like to know more,' she teased.

'Yes, I'll be honest, I'd love to hear why you left Rolls-Royce, but I can hand on heart say that I can't believe anything you tell me would make a difference to how I feel about you.'

He thought for a minute, suddenly feeling more confident. 'You never did properly finish telling me what happened to the Sloams. I mean after Paris, then what? That I would like to know.'

Twirling a strand of her hair, something he noticed she did when she was nervous, she began with a statement.

'You need to know I am not proud of what finally happened between Jacob, Ruth and me. My only defence is that I was young, and frightened of the prospect of a future without them. And ultimately they were right, I did have to stand on my own two feet, although at the time I felt rather like Bambi on ice...'

DUFFIELD, DERBYSHIRE, 1956

Nancy turned the blue airmail letter over in her hands. It felt so fragile, not robust enough to have survived a journey across the Atlantic. This was the second letter she had received since Ruth and Jacob had departed to America. Carol had handed her the first when she had returned to the house in Duffield after shopping in Belper.

It was a year after they had returned from Paris, and in that time Ruth had become increasingly disabled with arthritis. Both of the Sloams' children had now moved to America and had finally persuaded their parents to join them. Nancy had taken it for granted she too would go, but they soon made it clear that this was not the case. Whilst they cherished Nancy they were not prepared to invite her to join them. They had patiently explained that they would now be living with their son, and that for the present she must forge her own life. They would of course write regularly, and even a holiday was mooted.

But Nancy was devastated, immediately caught up in a web of disappointment, anger and fear. Living with the Sloams for nearly four years she had blossomed, embracing all that they had offered. Jacob had once said, when she complained about not having one particular interest that she excelled in, that it was sometimes better to have a little knowledge on a variety of things, rather than an in-depth knowledge on one particular subject. Now she felt her interesting yet calm life was being swept away. She was far more frightened than people imagined, and so she reacted in a way that was completely out of character, rounding on the family and at times begging them to take her with them. Each time they declined she begged them to reconsider, promising she was prepared to live on her own in America, find a job, not be in any way a burden to them. Each time when they refused, she would cry bitterly, flouncing to her room and refusing to join them for meals. Carol tried reasoning with her, but she wouldn't listen.

Eventually Jacob asked her to join him in his study. When she sat down, he explained yet again that neither he and Ruth were particularly well off; they rented the house they now lived in, and their sons were prepared to take care of them in their old age. As a family she knew they were close, and although he had never spoken of it, she must have realised that many of their close relatives had suffered unspeakably during the War.

'I will admit,' he continued, 'Ruth is completely distraught at the thought of leaving you behind. We both are. But our sons and, I believe, their wives are adamant that you remain here. You have become an attractive and accomplished young woman in the past few years, but you might find occasionally that can work against you, particularly where other women are concerned.'

When she started to protest again he silenced her.

'Nancy, you are very dear to both Ruth and me, but you must live your own life. We will not leave you destitute, you know that. But I will not have Ruth upset any more by your behaviour. I care for you deeply, and please try to understand this is not the decision we would have wanted, but we must respect our children's wishes. If you aren't prepared to make this short time we still have left together pleasant, then so be it, but I insist that you show some sensitivity, if not for me then for Ruth's feelings.'

He touched her shoulder lightly before leaving her alone in the room.

She wanted to articulate just how fearful she was at having to embrace the world on her own. But she remained silent, not causing any more fuss but frequently retiring to her room in order to underline her unhappiness.

She knew she was causing everyone distress, but she was still not prepared for the fateful day when she returned home from her trip to Belper to find they had left. Agnes and Carol remained to pick up the pieces.

They explained that Ruth and Jacob had departed that morning, and were on their way to Liverpool where they would board a liner for America the following day. Agnes endeavoured to explain how deeply sad they were to leave her behind, and Carol offered her a letter that Jacob had written.

She had rebuffed Carol, declaring she did not want the letter. Agnes tried to calm her down, but she was adamant. Years later Nancy wished Agnes had confronted her, but instead in her usual conciliatory fashion she had absorbed Nancy's anger, turning it into her own form of guilt.

Carol had no such inhibitions, picking the discarded letter up and slitting the envelope open. She removed a fifty-pound note which she gave to Nancy, calling her an ungrateful young lady. She put the letter on the table, adding, 'I suggest you read it, if not now, save it for another time. I am surprised at you, Nancy, I truly thought you had more compassion. They both loved you like a daughter, but perhaps that was the problem. I know Ruth couldn't bear the thought of saying goodbye to you, that's why Jacob arranged that they leave discreetly whilst you were out.'

Both Agnes and Carol had left her for a while, whilst Carol conjured up a cup of tea in a nearly empty kitchen. When they returned Nancy was crying bitterly. A wisp of smoke hovered in the grate above a tiny pile of ashes. Burning her toy dog Mac in the same grate years before had been a rather pathetic grand gesture, but this, she knew, was a petty reaction to not getting her own way.

This second letter felt more delicate. She peeled it open carefully, paying attention to the opening instructions printed along the sides. Foreboding gripped her heart when she saw Jacob's handwriting. It was not the confident hand she remembered, but a spindly relic of its former self.

Ruth had died peacefully in her sleep. They had regretted not taking her with them, but they had been influenced by their children, Jacob wrote, who thought Nancy needed to create her own life.

However, Ruth had missed her and they were planning to invite her for a holiday. The rest of the letter Nancy found hard to read, but the words 'love', 'friendship' and 'loyalty' made the sentiments Jacob wished to convey crystal clear.

She replied immediately, pouring out as much sorrow and regret as she could cram into the confined space of an airmail letter. Less than a month later, it was returned unopened, together with a further letter from Charles, Ruth and Jacob's son. Charles explained that his father too had died. He said it was impossible to be too sad as his parents' love had survived for over fifty years under at times unspeakable circumstances. He wished Nancy every happiness, enclosing a few photographs of them all together in Paris. In one Nancy was wearing her first beret, a present from Ruth.

At the end of the letter there was a postscript, asking if she had found the box of books his father had left behind for her. He thought Carol might have them. He hoped so, as he thought they would be a suitable legacy in memory of his father.

Carol was delighted when Nancy contacted her by phone. She declared she had always been confident that Nancy would come around and get over her disappointment, but at the time she had been shocked by her behaviour. Yes, she had the box of books Charles had mentioned. She knew of Ruth and Jacob's deaths as Agnes always kept in touch. She insisted that Nancy come to visit, as soon as she could.

When Nancy arrived at Carol's trim little bungalow on the outskirts of Duffield she was warmly greeted. Together they lugged the big cardboard box from behind Carol's sofa in the front room. They were both emotional as they untied the string, with Nancy bursting into tears when they finally opened it to reveal a large piece of paper which read, 'Further Reading for Nancy, my Best Student'.

Some of the books had handwritten notes inside them, brimming with Jacob's observations and humour.

War and Peace: *overlong but worth the effort, read the book before you see the film.* Lady Chatterley's Lover: *not his best, in fact you might want to go to page 154 straight away.* Rebecca: *rather girly, but beautifully written. I suggest you try anything by Daphne du Maurier, you will love them all.* Les Misérables: *very depressing, suggest you wait until you are over thirty.*

The box was a complete balm. She knew that it conveyed all that had been wonderful about those years they had all spent together, and nothing could take that away from her. She felt very humble, and ashamed that after being given the privilege to live with them she had allowed it to end so unhappily.

After the symbolic burning of the first letter which she had never read, both Agnes and Carol had been adamant that she take the fifty pounds, and also gave her the address of a friend of Ruth's who was ready to offer her a room immediately. They had paid for the room for a year, to give Nancy time to decide what she wanted to do. Agnes also explained that in with the destroyed letter had been an introduction to a friend of Jacob's at Rolls-Royce, who would arrange to put her on the secretarial intake which occurred every year. Fortunately, Agnes explained she knew him and would contact him; it was then up to Nancy if she wanted to pursue the opportunity.

Over the following weeks Nancy's pain dulled a little. She contacted Ruth's friend, who was kind but elderly, sharing her house with several cats and two small smelly dogs. When she applied to Rolls-Royce she was immediately accepted as an office girl with a place at the secretarial school. Her skills in both shorthand and typing were already well above average and within a year she was promoted to the typing pool. She began to see Agnes regularly, who eventually suggested that she might be interested in renting a room with a friend of hers, Dr Rosemary Brent.

Rosemary was a handsome woman in her early sixties. She lived on her own, but took in lodgers, renting out three rooms in her sizeable Victorian house. She was a paediatrician at the Children's Hospital, feared but respected by her staff. She let the other two rooms to medical students. On arrival Nancy felt a little intimidated. Inviting her into the kitchen, Rosemary held court and explained the rules of the house. Each lodger had their own cupboard in the kitchen, and the only bathroom was to be kept spotless. The front room was for Rosemary's personal use, although her guests, as she referred to them, could use the small back sitting room where there was a television. If you lost your key you had to pay for a new one, and all telephone calls had to be entered in the book by the phone and paid for later. Rent was to be paid in cash weekly.

'Do you have a boyfriend?' she asked Nancy. 'Believe me, I do not mind, I just like to know. I have had three husbands: the first one I mislaid, the second I divorced, and the third one died. I am not averse to boyfriends, girlfriends staying the occasional night, but I like to be consulted beforehand.'

The reality was that Rosemary broke all the rules, whilst everyone else tried to toe the line.

She was the first to open her guests' cupboards and use whatever she needed urgently at the time. 'I've finished your marmalade, darling,' was a frequent cry. 'I'll get some more, promise.' The bathroom looked like it had been stirred with a spoon when Rosemary had finished with it. The phone book could never be found, as Rosemary invariably used it for taking notes and then put it in her handbag. She could never remember who had paid the rent, causing ill feeling at times when she had been given it on a Friday, only to ask for it again the following day. She lost her key regularly, even the emergency ones under the plant pot near the front door.

However, everyone adored her, including her army of retainers. The elderly cleaning lady had seen her through two marriages and would on occasions proclaim that she could tell you a thing or two about her employer. There was a series of young girls who did the ironing, a window cleaner, a gardener, and an odd job man, who helped himself to his pay from the rent box when Rosemary wasn't about, causing yet more confusion. Judging from the numerous photographs around the place, she was adored by her two children, but they appeared to have the sense to phone frequently and visit rarely.

Nancy was a loner, but found it comforting to be surrounded by this bustling household. Most weeks she would share a glass of wine with Rosemary, or one of the other tenants, but her life was very much her own.

Her secretarial skills were of such a high standard that she rose from the dreaded typing pool to junior secretary within a year. She wasn't vain but acknowledged that her good looks and natural elegance were often seen as a threat by other women of her age. She made friends, but they never became close, apart from Agnes whom she saw regularly. She had the occasional boyfriend, but when the relationship eventually turned to sex, as it inevitably did, she remained compliant for a while then extracted herself from the friendship as gracefully as she could.

All her female colleagues seemed preoccupied with finding a partner, becoming engaged, marrying and producing a family. She couldn't pretend to want to take part in this game, and so over the years she was happy on the whole to be left alone, and not invited to play. She joined evening classes, read prolifically, and went to the cinema at least once a week, as well as visiting the newly opened Playhouse in Nottingham when Rosemary recommended some new playwright who was making a name for him or herself in the late sixties. When she felt she could afford it she would take day trips to various cities, and at least twice a year she would accompany Agnes to London. They shopped, lunched, visited exhibitions and occasionally spent a night so they could go to a show.

Derby had hardly been affected by the War, regardless of the fact that it had one of the largest aeroplane engine factories on its outskirts. Nestling into the Derwent valley, which was often shrouded in mist and fog, it had allegedly made it hard for the German bombers to locate it. Two adjoining factory buildings had been successfully converted to look like a chapel from the air. However, one German pilot had managed to navigate his way to the factory, destroying several workshops and killing six workers, but it was nothing in comparison to the destruction of Coventry less than a hundred miles away.

Not having the benefit of city status, and lacking a university, Derby's culture revolved around its two main employers, Rolls-Royce and the railway. In the sixties many traditional stores closed down, unable to compete with the burgeoning string of new chain stores. The marketplace now had a coffee bar with a jukebox, several new dress shops, and both Italian and Chinese restaurants. Three out of its five cinemas closed down, leaving the Odeon and the Gaumont with long queues outside during the weekends.

Nancy did not feel she came from Derby, even though she had spent most of her life in and around its centre. In the back of her mind was the constant thought that one day she must move. She had no desire to find out if she had French connections, although she did dream that one day she might have the courage to explore the country more and maybe even live there. Her job was demanding, and whilst she felt she was disliked by the Rolls-Royce personnel officer, a tall thin single woman known derisively as the Totem Pole, she quickly rose to a top job as secretary to one of the directors in the legendary Marble Hall.

It was a prestigious position, and she took delight each morning in pushing open the heavy main door to be greeted by a uniformed commissioner sitting at a large wooden reception desk. 'Good morning, Miss Dupray,' plus some other little pleasantry, the weather, a snippet from the morning papers, whether her boss had arrived before her.

Two impressive staircases supported a balcony, from which ran two corridors accommodating the spacious offices of the board of directors and the chairman of the company. Apart from the marble floor and two large marble columns, the rest was panelled in highly polished oak, which emitted a heady odour of beeswax. Even on the hottest days the hall remained cool, its silence only broken by the tip-tap of the secretaries in their high-heeled shoes, or the jovial banter of the directors as they used the staircase.

It had a reputation for being haunted by the pilot depicted in the window, and Nancy confessed to Agnes that she did find his presence unsettling as he gazed down on her. But she unashamedly loved the fact that this was hallowed ground for any employee working for the company. Walking up the staircase every morning gave her a sense of importance. This was the powerhouse, and she was part of it. She accepted that it would be difficult to find such a prestigious position in another firm outside of Derby.

Through the intervening years she had never contacted Edna. Bill, to her relief, had never made an appearance. Occasionally Edna sent her a Christmas card via Agnes, with the same sentiment: *Lots of love, hope to see you soon.* So she was surprised when a card appeared in the middle of June. Then she remembered this was her birthday month.

Her birthday month had been Bill's idea, as there was no record at the Orphanage of her actual birth date. He suggested to Edna that they create a date for her birthday. She remembered being intrigued by the idea. Bill had explained in a mock serious manner, with a wink at Edna, that your birthday was the date you were actually born, and there was usually a celebration and a present. 'That's of course if you have been good all year,' he added. Edna always forgot, but Bill remembered each year, announcing at the beginning of June, 'All right, Nancy, what day are we going to choose?' There would always be a present and a pretty card, and if the weather was good, he would organise a trip somewhere.

Inside the big grubby envelope Edna had sent this time, she found a gaudy floral card. The sentimental verse barely left room for Edna's message: *Happy Birthday Nancy, please come and see me soon. I have something very important to tell you. Lots of love, Edna.* Clipped to the card was a ten-shilling note.

When Nancy explained about the card, which she had placed on the television, Rosemary suggested that Edna might have had a Premium Bond win and be feeling profligate with the winnings. Nancy doubted it. This was unfinished business.

Her fear of Bill had diminished. She was a different person. Edna's house was only a short distance from her office, but she had never been tempted to go back. Now and then she had bumped into old neighbours, but she was reluctant to chat, sensing that they were too. She had been told on one occasion that Bill was working in Germany. Now, as she admired the two birthday cards on the television – Rosemary having dashed out and bought one the following day – she felt a sudden unexpected curiosity about Edna's plight. She couldn't decide whether this was caused by vanity on her part, a wish to boast, 'Look how well I've done,' or a genuine desire to see Edna. She accepted now that the old woman had done her best, and without her natural kindness her childhood could have been a lot worse.

She considered going after work one evening, but that meant turning up in her office clothes. Tailored suit, high heels, hair tamed into a ponytail. She knew she would be conspicuous walking along Carlton Street to Edna's house. Jeans, flat pumps, her favourite weekend gear, were far more appropriate.

As she turned into Carlton Street at the corner near the Carnegie Library, she was surprised how little had changed. The rows of terraced houses still glared at one another through an assortment of cheap lace curtains. Most of the front doors were the same, apart from a couple of mock Georgian ones, with mean little stained-glass lights. Children still played on the streets, although now there were more cars in evidence. But it was the children that exposed the radical difference from the time when she had met her friends under the streetlight on the corner. All the children now, she observed, were from the Caribbean, and most of them seemed to find no discomfort in going shoeless.

Had she been happy here? she pondered. It seemed such a long time ago. She had to accept that it was she who had radically changed, not the children who continued to play carelessly as they had all those years ago. It was just the colour of their skin that was different, various hues of glowing chestnut, topped with curly hair similar to hers apart from its jet-black colour. She had always felt an outsider, her name, her looks, the fact that she was referred to as being 'fostered'.

'What's fostered?' she'd once asked Edna.

'In your case, very little,' she remembered Edna replying. 'I used to get a bob or two for looking after you, but that's just about run out, and there ain't no more from where that come from. Now don't look glum, you ain't going anywhere, we'll manage with a bit of help from our Bill.'

Memories invaded her mind like wasps on the attack. Randomly they inflicted pain. Pain that she had been so careful to avoid over the intervening years. Three little girls stood chatting as she had done all those years ago. And as she walked down the street the image of Bill appeared with uncanny clarity. She knew that she had always struggled to join in with the banter of her friends, but when Bill appeared, walking towards her on the way home from somewhere, she had always run towards him. Usually he'd shouted her name, and together they would hold hands as she walked triumphantly past her friends, knowing that they were envious of the special care he took pride in bestowing on her.

What feelings would she experience now, she wondered, if he walked towards her? Fear, revulsion, pity or a deep underlying sadness that it had all gone so terribly wrong? What would her life be now if she had remained at 18 Carlton Street? There would have been no Agnes or Rosemary, no living with the Sloams, or spending time in Paris. Would she instead be living in one of these terraced houses trying to create a home?

For a moment she couldn't remember exactly where number 18 was, but then she saw the ornamental china Alsatian dog sitting on the window ledge. Bill had won it at the fair years ago. It was Edna's pride and joy, and woe betide any child who went anywhere near it. Once a year, when the lace curtains were washed, Rex – named by Edna – was ceremonially taken to the kitchen sink for a clean. Edna was solely in charge of this operation. One year, at the annual fair, their next-door neighbour's son won a large glass fish. It was green and blue, with bulging eyes and a swirling tail. Edna was outraged that it might upstage Rex and declared it vulgar. The glass fish had gone, but Rex had stood the test of time and remained.

Knocking on the door was unnerving. Did she really want to confront the past? When she had lived there, most of the front doors were left open during the day. She knocked several times, resorting to eventually shouting through the letterbox. She felt a touch resentful that she had made the effort only to find Edna not at home. The street was now empty, as if caught up in the drowsiness of the summer afternoon. All the children had disappeared, leaving just a dilapidated tricycle abandoned on the pavement.

She was determined to draw some kind of conclusion from her visit. Approaching the house next door where the fish had once graced the windowsill, but had now been replaced by a highly coloured vase, she knocked on the door. It was opened almost immediately by a tall black man. Without any form of greeting, he turned and headed down the narrow hall, shouting over his shoulder.

'It's Nancy, isn't it? She's in the garden. She said you might come today.'

The houses were all the same, so she was not surprised by how familiar it all seemed. Even the undertones of mustiness and damp had remained. She followed him through to the kitchen. The woman at the sink did not bother to look up as Nancy negotiated her way past a bike and into the garden. Edna was struggling to get up, aided by her neighbour.

'I told you, Louis, I told she would come.'

Louis seemed unsure what to do, but Edna clutched firmly onto his arm. Nancy knew she would never have recognised her. She was half the size she had been fifteen years ago. In front of her stood a birdlike woman, the thick swollen legs now reduced to two sticks. What had been large capable hands were now alarmingly thin.

'It's cancer,' she said in response to Nancy's look of surprise. 'I knew she'd be shocked,' she said to Louis as he lowered her back into the deck-chair.

'How beautiful you look, Nancy, you must be nearly thirty but you look eighteen. What's that actress called, Audrey Hepburn, like Audrey Hepburn. You're taller of course, and you have prettier hair, but lovely like her, you always were a stunner even as a little girl.'

A child started to cry from the house, followed by the sound of a woman shouting. In response to the cries Louis left, with a promise of a nice cup of tea in a minute.

'Louis, he's wonderful,' said Edna, 'they're just so kind. Beatie is good too, her bark's worse than her bite, but they've all got hearts of gold, including the little ones. I won't hear a word against them. We invite them over here, to do the jobs we don't like, then moan about them. I can tell you, Nancy, they're far more caring than a lot of white people I could mention. They're big into family. They know how to care for old people.'

This tirade of praise seemed to leave Edna tired, and she closed her eyes whilst Nancy found herself a chair. When she regained her strength, blinking into the sunlight, she continued the conversation as if the intervening years were just a blip in their relationship. The tea that Louis brought in two large mugs was weak and sickly sweet.

Josh, his small son, offered an unopened pack of Cadbury's chocolate fingers, then patiently waited whilst Nancy removed the wrapping, accepting two before he ran back into the house. Louis half knelt down between Edna and Nancy. The ground was cracked and dry, showing little evidence of a lawn. A tree afforded a little shade, but the only colour came from several rather defeated-looking lupins, which appeared to be all that was left of a flower border.

'I'm going to leave you two ladies alone,' Louis said, 'girls' talk, I expect. That's what you want.'

He reached across, placing his large black hand lightly over Nancy's. 'You'll stay for supper?' he said. Nancy sensed it was an instruction, not a request.

'Oh yes you must, Nancy, you must. It's lovely food, spicy but really lovely,' declared Edna, 'unless of course you're seeing your boyfriend.'

The word 'boyfriend' hung uncomfortably in the air, and for the first time since she'd arrived Nancy sensed Edna recognised the fragility of their renewed relationship. For a moment Nancy considered her reply, a meeting with a friend, a trip to the cinema, the perfect excuse to avoid staying too long. But then the tedium of her organised life suddenly overwhelmed her. Louis towered above her as she remained seated in her chair. The strong sunlight on his ebony-coloured face accentuated his strong features and twinkling eyes.

'The boyfriend would be welcome too,' he teased, 'providing he's white.'

Laughter exploded from Nancy. 'There is no boyfriend, black or otherwise, and I would love to stay for supper. Thank you.'

For the rest of the afternoon, Nancy and Edna sat cautiously filling in some of the gaps of the previous years. Now and then they would be joined by Josh, who would gently hold Nancy's hand. He helped bridge the gap when their conversation lapsed, whilst still unspoken thoughts clouded the air. She found his warm little hand comforting, turning it over to marvel at its pink palm.

'Like a pussy cat,' she told him seriously, causing him to giggle as she kissed its centre.

Edna dipped in and out of sleep, but awakening finally to the sound of Josh's giggling, she raised her head like a turtle emerging from its shell and suddenly exclaimed, 'Bill's married now, he's got two little girls, twins. They live in Germany. She's German.'

Nancy knew that this had to come. Holding the child's hand was reassuring, and she encouraged him to sit on her knee. 'I'm not interested in Bill,' she replied softly.

'I understand, but he's not all bad, Nancy. He adored you. He was so sorry it happened. He said he would never forgive himself. He's always kept in touch with me. He came back a while ago. He wanted to see you, but I persuaded him not to, said it wasn't fair, you'd built a new life.'

'Why would I want to see him, and why would he want to see me?' exclaimed Nancy.

Josh sensed the change of tone in her voice and slipped from her knee to return to the kitchen.

'He raped me, Edna, he beat me up. I'm not passionate about children, but holding Josh's hand, having him on my knee, brings it home that because of Bill I can't have children of my own. You said "boyfriend" a while ago, but what do I say to them? I was raped and beaten up at sixteen and I can't have children. It would have to be a very special man to want me.'

Edna's body swayed back and forth. 'I'm just so sorry, Nancy, I didn't think he'd really hurt you.'

Nancy rose awkwardly from the deck-chair to kneel in front of Edna. 'What do you mean, Edna, really hurt me? You must have heard me cry out.'

'I just thought, well, I told you I didn't think he'd hurt you.' Her face crumpled. 'I'm so sorry, I've missed you. I lost you both, you know. Bill keeps in touch a bit but it's not the same.'

'Don't be sorry, there's no need, the past is the past.' Nancy clutched Edna's claw-like hand, accepting for the first time how Edna's generation viewed the world differently. It was accepted that men often took a blow at their wives, whether from drink or frustration. A black eye or a bruised leg or arm would go unmentioned in the street where they lived. Nancy knew it was too late to burden Edna with more guilt. If she was to offer friendship it would have to be without malice.

'Edna, we can be friends, I am more than happy if we are, you were good to me when I was a little girl. But not Bill. If you ever try to bring Bill back into my life, or even talk about him, I would not, could not cope with that.'

At that moment Louis carefully manoeuvred himself and a large Formica table into the garden, followed by Josh and a tiny toddling little girl.

'This is Lizzie,' announced Louis, 'she's been asleep for most of the afternoon.'

'So you have two children?' asked Nancy, heading for the kitchen to see if she could help.

'No, three,' corrected Beatie, the woman she had seen at the sink when she had arrived. Nancy was relieved that Beatie seemed to acknowledge her presence and was at least speaking to her. 'One too many,' she continued.

'Oh Beatie, Beatie, don't say that, Amos is a fine little chap.' Louis encircled his wife from behind, kissing the nape of her neck. Without turning she playfully hit him on the head with a wooden spoon.

'One too many,' she replied.

Their supper was delicious, chicken and chickpeas in a spicy sauce. Their lodger Bartholomew joined them, bringing with him bottled beer.

'It's lovely,' said Nancy, 'really delicious.'

'Well, it's not Kitekat,' Beatie replied.

'Oh Bartholomew,' Louis cried, patting his lodger on the back, 'it's all your fault, you should never have told Beatie that people say we eat Kitekat because it's cheap.'

'Not only eat it, but like it,' Beatie added. 'Have you heard that?' she fired at Nancy.

Nancy hesitated. As a virtual teetotaller, the sudden intake of beer was pleasantly taking its effect.

'Yes,' she replied honestly, 'I have heard people say that.' But then, suppressing a giggle, she added, 'It's obviously not true.'

Louis and Bartholomew leapt to their feet, laughing and punching the air.

'Meow, meow,' Louis said to Beatie.

'Beware,' she retorted, 'you will get it on your toast one morning.' Turning to Nancy, she continued, 'It's disgusting, so many people think we are savages. We all went to grammar school, and look at Louis, he's a bus conductor, and Bartholomew works in the Foundry, and before I had Amos I worked as a cleaner at the Nightingale pub. The publican said he wasn't prejudiced but would I be off the premises before they opened at eleven o'clock. We'd always been brought up to believe it was the "mother country". What a joke that was.'

'I don't like the smell of Kitekat,' added Edna, unaware the tone of conversation had changed. 'Nasty stuff, but I suppose cats will eat anything.'

Everyone collapsed into laughter, and, sensing the party spirit, Bartholomew disappeared inside. Then, opening his bedroom window, he shouted, 'Come on you cats, dance!' Calypso music leached into the air.

'It's the first thing he bought over here,' Beatie told Nancy, 'a Dansette record player.'

Edna let them help her through the hole in the hedge back into her own garden. She was unsteady but adamant no one should accompany her.

'I haven't been in her house for ages,' Beatie confessed. 'It's a real mess I think, but she deserves her dignity. She knows we are here if she needs us, and to be honest she's helped me. We hadn't been here long, it was winter time, so every time I went out people were huddled up in their coats, and hardly anyone acknowledged me. If I went into a shop it was as if I didn't exist, I just put my items on the counter, paid, and that was it. Just so different to back home.'

She reached forward and caught hold of Josh as he attempted to run after a stray cat that was crossing the garden.

'Anyway, one afternoon I noticed Edna's milk was still on the step, so I said to Louis I'm going round. I put on my coat and knocked at her door and when she opened it, it was if she was the first person since we had arrived that looked at me without seeing my colour first. I remember she said, "Hello love, come on in. Oh, it's not our usual milkman. He left me an extra pint and I'm not paying for it. I've been meaning to knock on your door, but didn't want you to think I was prying." And from then onwards we've been friends. I can tell you when I got back home, I just cried and cried. I missed my mum and Edna was the first person that showed us any kindness. It's got a bit better now, I think when neighbours saw Edna being friendly they started saying hello and talking to the kids. It's not as bad as it was.'

They could her Edna battling with the door, but before she closed it she shouted, 'Goodnight everyone, and remember, Nancy my luv, we've got a deal, haven't we?'

Bartholomew, sensing his opportunity, swept Nancy into his arms and danced with her around the garden. Louis and Beatie joined them, whilst the two little ones climbed into the deck-chairs. Their tummies full, they were asleep in minutes. At around eleven o'clock Nancy decided she must leave, aware that the last trolley buses usually finished before midnight. Beatie saw her to the door.

'So what's the deal with Edna?' she asked.

'Well, I suppose it's that we can become friends again. I will try and come and see her regularly,' replied Nancy.

'So it's got nothing to do with Bill?'

'You know him?' Nancy asked cautiously.

'Yes, he's been a couple of times. Louis doesn't like him, but Edna says he was like a brother to you, but you fell out and that's why you never visit her.'

'That's not quite true,' Nancy replied, 'but I'll tell you another time.' But then she changed her mind. Aware that if she didn't hurry she would miss her bus, she compressed the story, concluding, 'It's horrible, and perhaps for Edna's sake I shouldn't have told you. But it's a long time ago. I'd like to be friends, Beatie, so it's important to me you know the truth. Edna can embroider it a bit, but believe me, mine is the truth.'

The two women faced one another. Beatie shook her head, then clutched Nancy to her breast. No words were spoken. Nancy turned and ran down the street, thankful she was wearing flat shoes.

She jumped on the bus with an energy that was completely new. Times were changing, she thought, and it felt as if her world was opening up a little, if she was brave enough to allow it.

CHAPTER SIXTEEN

Forgiving you is my gift to you.
Moving on is my gift to myself.

– ANONYMOUS

DERBY, 1964

To everyone's surprise Edna lingered for nearly another two years. During that time Louis, Beatie and the ever hopeful Bartholomew became Nancy's close friends. She became Auntie Nancy to the children, taking pleasure in playing and giving them gifts when she came to visit. But she was equally thankful she could pass these energetic little souls back to their parents when she left.

Within weeks of her first visit she and Beatie had organised Edna, cleaning the house, which included giving Rex his annual wash. Nancy found it uncomfortable at first moving about the house she had been brought up in, and she was surprised how very little evoked warm memories of her life there. It remained cramped and dingy with a pervading odour of gas and mould.

Her bedroom appeared not to have been touched. Even a ghostly brown stain on the mattress from her first period remained, triggering recollections of the past. She had steeled herself into starting to clean the room, until Beatie had taken over, aware of its significance. She could never bring herself to go into Bill's bedroom. After all these years she felt as if his presence was lurking behind the door ready; should she open it, it would release memories that she had tried so hard to obliterate.

As Edna slept in the front room now, Nancy bought new curtains to allow her more privacy. Agnes also became involved, sourcing a new mattress for Edna's bed. Louis disposed of the old one, remarking that it was so alive with bugs it could have possibly walked to the tip of its own accord.

Edna continued to manage her own finances, and whilst constantly complaining about the price of things, she was cajoled into employing a woman from across the road, to come in and give her an 'up and downer' twice a week and take care of most of her washing. Nancy also talked her into paying for two hot meals every week, delivered by the newly formed Meals on Wheels service.

Nancy sometimes tried to analyse why she wanted to help Edna, and even enjoyed it. She concluded at first it made her feel useful. But then she accepted that when she arrived each time and heard Edna shout, 'Nancy, is that you, love?' a kind of compassion of which she hadn't thought she was capable fractured the somewhat self-absorbed existence she had created for herself.

If she could make Edna laugh, or spoil her with a little luxury, it gave her pleasure. She accepted it must be hard for her not to say 'Do you remember when we...' but she never broke her promise by referring to Bill. She only squeezed her hand frequently, saying, 'You're a good girl Nancy, I don't deserve all this fuss.'

Most weekends Nancy visited, and after caring for Edna she and Beatie would go to the cinema, or if it was a Sunday during the summer they would take a picnic to the park. Bartholomew would often join them, bringing one of his numerous girlfriends. Nancy knew that he admired her, but sensed Beatie had possibly cautioned him about her vulnerability. She was grateful, for although she liked him and rejoiced in his good-natured humour and sense of fun, she found him unusual rather than sexually attractive.

Occasionally they would encourage him to sing from his wide repertoire of Jamaican and Evangelist songs, marvelling at his naturally deep melodic voice. When she and Beatie walked out together, as they liked to describe it, they both felt a sense of people's wonder, or sometimes disgust, as they tried to decide how to react to these two beautiful women, one black, one white. On one occasion someone spat at them, and on another a woman called them whores. But upsetting as it was, it only strengthened their resolve to display their friendship for everyone to see.

On one occasion the Rolls-Royce personnel officer called her into her office.

'A delicate subject,' she began, 'but you have been seen talking to two black men outside the main entrance. Apparently you were laughing with them. To my way of thinking this is completely unseemly in your position as secretary to the Chief Engineer. I am only telling you for your own good,' she tapered off, recognising Nancy's amusement rather than discomfort.

Nancy was sorely tempted to reply, 'Jealous, are you?' but crudeness wasn't her style. She restrained herself to thanking the Totem Pole for her observations, but remarking that she felt that who she spoke to was entirely her own business, and she would like to know who had seen her.

When she returned to her office, she quizzed her boss, suspecting his liberal views would match her own. He immediately saw the funny side of it, although he still teased her a little about her friendship with Louis and Bartholomew. The following morning he confessed he had told his wife, who was most indignant, insisting that he challenge the personnel officer on Nancy's behalf. Whilst she had every right to maintain her own prejudices should she wish, this was not the ethos of the company.

A few days later Nancy was to encounter Miss Radcliffe again as she crossed the balcony above the Marble Hall. Her sour face was devoid of any expression, and she looked neither right nor left as they passed. Nancy was left to imagine a possible Hitchcockian moment where she would be thrown over the balcony onto the cold marble floor below. The mystery would remain unsolved, leaving her ghost to join that of the young pilot who reputedly haunted the building.

Bill had returned once to see Edna, but Edna had kept to her side of the agreement, and their paths never crossed. His approach was more subtle, a shirt left behind on a chair, a sausage and bottles of German beer in the fridge, a photograph of his daughters stuck on the wall, a half-eaten Toblerone on the mantelpiece. Like a dog peeing to make his mark, Nancy could sense his presence. But in deference to Edna's poor health, Nancy didn't question her, just gleaned what information she wanted from Louis and Beatie. They said he had normally only stayed two nights. And the last time he had been they saw him taking Edna out in a taxi. However, he had never bothered to call in to see them, and they sensed Edna's relief when he had left.

Edna's death was neither dramatic nor sudden. She was taken to the Royal Infirmary with low blood pressure. A transfusion had helped, but it wasn't the answer and after a few days she faded peacefully away. Rosemary dropped in to see her briefly each day, as the Children's Hospital had been closed and she was now based at the Infirmary. Agnes called in when she could, and her Jamaican family and Nancy took it in turns to be by her bedside whenever possible.

'There's a will,' she told Nancy towards the end. 'Just a little something for you and Bill, there's no real family, but if anyone did crawl out of the woodwork it's all tied up legal like for you and Bill. When the time comes, you'll find Bill's address in my bedside cabinet.'

Nancy did not know how to react; she was astonished that Edna had anything to leave. She had her post office account and pension book, but that amounted to very little. By the time she had formulated a reply Edna was asleep; or feigning sleep, Nancy wasn't quite sure, but no reference was made to it again before she died.

It seemed natural that she should take care of all the funeral arrangements. David Mortimer, her boss, was both sympathetic and helpful, insisting Nancy make use of the office phone, and suggesting she should take a few days off if necessary. For a day she was able to blank out facing up to the fact that she had to contact Bill, but eventually she retrieved his address written on the back of an envelope from Edna's bedside cabinet.

Edna's only involvement in religion as far as Nancy could recall was when she went to the church bazaar in the summer or turned on the radio for carols on Christmas morning. But the local vicar had sprung into action as soon as he had been informed of her death by the neighbour across the road. He offered to administer the service and the burial, even mentioning that the Nightingale pub did a very nice finger buffet if Nancy wanted anything afterwards.

When the arrangements were completed Nancy sent a telegram to Bill. She sincerely hoped he wouldn't come, but felt in the back of her mind he would, if only to sort out the will which the solicitors held. They had already contacted her and arranged an appointment the day after the funeral. They also informed her that they had contacted the executor of the will, a Mr William Dodd.

Bill had been in the background for the past three years. Beatie had always warned Nancy if he was visiting Edna, enabling her to keep out of his way, and he had never made any attempt to contact her. Now she knew she had to face the reality of not only seeing him, but engaging in at least one conversation with him. At times she felt a little ashamed that a part of her wanted to impress him with what she had achieved in the intervening years. *It's nearly fifteen years*, she acknowledged, surprised at how the years had swiftly passed by.

On the night of his attack she had shouted 'You're ugly, you're old,' but now all these years later she realised that he could have only been in his late thirties. As a child growing up she hadn't considered his age. He was the same age as many of her friends' fathers. Edna called him her son, and it had been many years before Nancy had discovered he too had been fostered. She never sensed that Edna was jealous of his affection for her; rather that it provided them both with a shared interest in her care and wellbeing.

The attack she had never erased totally from her memory. It wasn't so much the pain that she had experienced but rather the feeling of helplessness and fear that any man could inflict such damage on a girl who he had cared for and professed to love. He had stripped away part of her life. She had disciplined herself not to dwell on it, particularly the fact that she would never be a mother. But she still inexplicably sensed that she mustn't be too complacent. He could still represent a threat to her.

Funerals were a complete mystery to Nancy as she had never been to one, so she was shocked when the funeral director enquired whether she would be the only relative walking behind the coffin. Relieved that this problem could be resolved before the funeral day, she made it clear that she would already be in church, supported by her friends. Whilst they explained the usual procedure was for the coffin to arrive followed by relatives, she explained that in this case she preferred for personal reasons to be in the church prior to the coffin entering.

She arrived at the church early, taking the front pew with Agnes and Rosemary on either side. Rosemary, Nancy knew, would actually enjoy the whole occasion. To her it would be pure theatre, and if Bill did arrive and cause any problems, she would happily take centre stage to protect her.

The large Victorian church felt colder inside than the mild November weather outside. Refraining from turning around in case she saw Bill, Nancy was nevertheless aware of people arriving in the opposite pew once the coffin had arrived. Louis, Beatie, Bartholomew and several other neighbours stood respectfully in line. Nancy glanced across at Beatie, in a secret acknowledgement that the wreath they had chosen together was perfect. Neither of them liked chrysanthemums and so had chosen a somewhat expensive display of red roses, something they knew Edna liked.

As she averted her gaze for a second to the rest of the congregation, she suddenly found herself looking directly at Bill. He stood alone, dressed in a dark suit and black tie. Stockier, shorter than she remembered him, he still had thick black hair. For a second he held her eyes. Then awkwardly he started to search for a seat. Nobody in the front pews offered to move along, and Nancy had to steel herself not to turn around to see where he eventually sat.

Fear gripped her, and the image of him as he raped her all those years ago sprang with extraordinary clarity into her mind. In a flash it passed, and she felt the reassuring presence of Agnes and Rosemary. They had felt her unease, and were holding her hands.

As the coffin left the church, she, Agnes and Rosemary led the little procession into the weakening afternoon sunlight. At the graveside Bill stood opposite Nancy, but she avoided looking at him, only finally acknowledging him at the pub afterwards.

Rosemary was magnificent at the reception, sailing from one group of neighbours to another, and on one occasion carrying Amos on her hip whilst Beatie battled with a badly-behaved Josh. Eventually she alighted on Bill and, in a voice teetering on the edge of rudeness, she enquired if he was Mr Dodd, and if so her friend Miss Dupray would like a word with him. She commented later that she felt he was obviously a bully, and completely out of his depth when confronted by someone with an air of authority. Floundering for a second, he had replied robustly, 'Yes, I am Bill Dodd, but what's it to you?'

Without waiting for him to finish, Rosemary exclaimed, 'Well, isn't that wonderful, come this way and I will facilitate the meeting.'

Bill stood his ground. 'I don't need you facilitating anything,' he retorted.

Rosemary stopped, turning back slowly for maximum effect. For a minute, she said later, she experienced a sense of fear, as his eyes had reduced to mere pinpricks, and the pulse on his thick neck started to thump dramatically. Calmly she continued, 'I think you do, Mr Dodd. Under the circumstances Miss Dupray does not wish to see you alone, and she has asked me to chaperone any meeting that might be necessary.'

At that moment Nancy stepped forward.

'Thank you, Rosemary,' she said, squeezing her hand. 'All I have to say, Bill, is that tomorrow we have a meeting at the solicitor's. Edna left a will, and I understand you are the executor. I gather we are both also beneficiaries.'

The room, which a minute ago had been full of the sound of eating, drinking and moderately jolly chatter, now fell silent as Nancy and Bill faced one another.

'I need to talk to you, Nancy,' he exclaimed loudly.

'Fine,' she replied, aware that all eyes were on her. 'I agree to talk, providing Rosemary is present. She's a doctor, member of the council and a newly appointed magistrate. We can have complete confidence in her discretion.'

He looked confused, then, sensing defeat, he left the pub, murmuring to Nancy as he walked past her, 'So, I'll see you tomorrow then.'

She arrived at the solicitor's ten minutes late, to ensure she wasn't closeted in a waiting room with Bill. Rosemary had offered to accompany her, but she felt she would be perfectly secure at the solicitor's. The secretary's office was less than half the size of her own, she noted with some satisfaction, but conceded that this was compensated for by its high Georgian windows which overlooked an old churchyard. One whole wall was filled with books, and their smell evoked bittersweet memories of Professor Sloam in his study. There was even a faint odour of pipe smoke.

She felt comfortable in these surroundings. She had met one of the partners, a Mr Bennett, at a soirée Rosemary had held after she had been elected a magistrate. This gave her confidence as she shook his hand, before she took her seat beside Bill. He didn't rise but just acknowledged her presence with a nod. The nod spoke oceans, and without any more niceties Nancy learned to her amazement that Edna had owned her house, and that the will stipulated that together with its contents it was left in equal measure to her and Bill.

'It was a surprise to me as well.' Bill spoke for the first time. 'I went to see her nearly a year ago, and that's when she told me, apparently her husband had been a builder and she inherited it when he died. I never knew anything about him either. She'd written a will herself years ago, but she said she wanted it proper, I mean legal,' he corrected himself.

'So what does this mean?' Nancy asked Mr Bennett.

'Well,' the solicitor replied, 'It's very simple. You and Mr Dodd own 18 Carlton Street and all its contents. There is also a post office account, but I suspect that amounts to very little. Mrs Blore had an insurance policy which will cover the funeral expenses. When the house is sold and the estate settled we will pay equal halves into your bank accounts. It will not amount to a great deal.'

Bill interrupted. 'Hold on a minute, I have a couple of options. Those houses are worth nothing as you say, not at the moment, but there's plenty of coloureds looking for rooms. It wouldn't be a problem to rent at least three rooms out, maybe even more the way they live.'

Nancy raised her hand as if to halt him, but he continued, 'Hang on a minute Nancy, given a chance I'd have said this yesterday, but your hoity-toity friend stopped me.'

Addressing the solicitor, she explained, 'He means Rosemary, she acted as a kind of chaperone yesterday at the funeral.'

The pulse in Bill's neck began to visibly throb as he turned to Nancy, declaring, 'What do you want a bloody chaperone for? You're a big girl now. Don't think I'm frightened by the likes of her. All I wanted to suggest is that you – we rent it out, or that you go and live in the house. You obviously like the neighbours judging by the do at the pub. If you took care of it, paid the rates and so on, I wouldn't expect anything out of it, and then in a few years we could sell it for probably a lot more than we could get now. It would be close to work for you, ideal, you could do it up a bit, I'd be ok about helping with that.'

'Well, it's an idea, Mr Dodd,' put in the solicitor, 'and we would be happy to facilitate it for you, but this is a private discussion which you need to have with Miss Dupray.'

Bill appeared to have forgotten his presence sitting across the desk, and ignoring him, he asked, 'What do you think, Nancy? Of course this lot would facilitate it for us, charging a bloody fortune is what he means. What do you think?'

With an audible intake of breath Nancy considered her reply. The first words that came to mind were the polite response normal for these occasions, commencing with 'I'm sorry Bill but...' Then she thought, *why should I apologise to this man?* She sensed Mr Bennett was disturbed, so she smiled gently at him, then addressing Bill, she spoke firmly.

'I am not prepared to rent or live in Edna's house. As you say I am good friends with the neighbours, something I hope will continue. But I want the house sold, whatever it fetches. I will be grateful to Edna for leaving a share of it to me, but then as far as I am concerned the matter is closed.'

'But what if I decide I don't want to sell it, what then?' Bill rose, addressing Mr Bennett. 'I have every right, haven't I?' he demanded.

'You have the right to contest anything,' Mr Bennett replied, 'but the will clearly stated that the house was to be sold and you and Miss Dupray would receive equal shares. You could, as I said, contest that, but as you suggested earlier it could cost you a sizeable sum in legal fees.'

'You're all the bloody same,' shouted Bill. Then, flinging the office door open, he cried, 'Well, sell the bloody place, Nancy, if that's what you want.' Then he addressed the solicitor. 'And I'll expect a cheque from you when it's done.'

When later she recounted the whole episode to Rosemary, she said she'd felt admiration for Mr Bennett, who replied calmly, if somewhat recklessly, 'Minus our fees, of course, Mr Dodd.'

Bill left in a flurry, knocking a framed photograph off the desk of the secretary who sat timidly watching the proceedings. Nancy felt icy cold. The memories of that night when she was sixteen came flooding back again, as they had at the funeral. She started to shake, which prompted Mr Bennett to slip a coat around her, exclaiming to his secretary to make a cup of tea for Miss Dupray with plenty of sugar.

'He's dangerous, Miss Dupray,' he remarked. 'For the first time in my office I felt physically threatened. I imagine there is quite a story behind all of this?'

'There is, there is,' Nancy admitted.

'I'll have a word with Dr Brent, with your permission,' he continued. 'I think a word in the right quarters might help. Well, at least he lives in Germany, which is one thing on our side. I suggest that we put the house on the market immediately.'

When she returned to her office that afternoon, Mary, the temporary secretary from the typing pool, informed her rather shyly that she had taken a message from a man who wouldn't leave his name. Flicking earnestly through her shorthand book, she carefully read the message he had left.

"'Tell Nancy she is more beautiful than ever. Tell her it's not over, it never will be. Edna…'" She stumbled. 'I'm sorry, I think he said Edna, I'm sorry – "Edna warned her." I'm sorry, Miss Dupray, I asked his name twice, but he just put the phone down.'

Nancy liked Mary, who stood in for her occasionally. She often saw Mary's father's name and photograph in the local paper, announcing that Councillor Gerald Blunt had yet again pulled off some advantageous deal for the town. Rosemary knew him and said he was a rather pompous wide boy, but then Rosemary was at times a little intolerant, Nancy had discovered. In any case, Nancy found his daughter Mary both charming and efficient.

She put her arm around her. 'Don't worry, you've coped very well. He's an unpleasant man, a nightmare part of my past,' she laughed.

But to her relief the nightmare did appear to be over. Bill disappeared. The house was sold quickly, enabling Nancy to rent a flat of her own, using Edna's money to tailor it to her liking. She knew that this was possibly the time to move away from Derby. She had held no real affection for it in the past, but it now began to feel like home. Her small circle of friends had become her family, and she felt secure knowing that if Bill did ever return they would be there to defend her.

CHAPTER SEVENTEEN

Strong men tremble when they hear it
They've got cause enough to fear it
Much blacker than they smear it
Nobody mentions my name!

– 'SIKES', FROM *OLIVER!*

DERBY, 1966

It was nearly two years before he did return. A Sunday, Nancy's least favourite day of the week. Sundays always seemed to be endlessly waiting to be filled, reminding her that she was alone. She spent the morning reading the Sunday papers, but with the realisation that the seductive Sunday supplements, which now accompanied most papers, only served to heighten her feeling of loneliness. Their endless articles on food, designer furniture, fashion and the latest exhibitions made each of the pages spring out, demanding to be discussed and shared with a partner.

She considered having a television, but dreaded the thought of becoming addicted to it. Agnes had taught her to knit, and whilst the patterns came from fashionable designers, she felt that knitting on your own was possibly the first step on the road to spinsterhood. She took pride in her reputation amongst her friends, that her style was seen as a little avant-garde. Occasionally, she would join some of the other secretaries at the lunchtime gatherings, where you could get coffee, sandwiches and join in an impromptu disco if someone had remembered to set it up.

She happily accepted her boss David Mortimer's constant reminders that he couldn't contemplate being without her. She knew she was an excellent secretary, always just one step ahead of the game, always anticipating his requirements. But something was missing from her life. She admired Beatie, leaving her home thousands of miles away to start a new life. Women were now coming into the forefront of business throughout the country, but the many she admired – Laura Ashley, Vivienne Westwood – all had a man in the background to share the dream.

Feeling melancholy, she gazed out of the window, and as she did so the streetlight across the road came on, illuminating Bill standing beneath it. He saw her and waved, then turned and walked away.

A torrent of fear swept over her, leaving her breathless. Her first instinct was to phone Rosemary, but she stopped when she realised that it would shatter the aura of normality that had been created by two years of peace. What could Rosemary actually do? No crime had been committed. She drew the curtains, shutting out the twilight, and poured herself a glass of wine.

But in the end it was Rosemary she turned to. Beatie had contacted her the following day to say Louis had seen Bill working in one of the shops in the Foundry. After some discreet enquiries he discovered that Bill had been appointed as supervisor in the casting shop. He hadn't been able to discover if his wife and family had accompanied him. Beatie assured her that they would try and find out as much as they could, and Louis and Bartholomew wanted her to know if there was any 'funny business' she should contact them.

Her flat was very close to the cathedral in the centre of Derby. Parking was already causing a problem and between five and six o'clock there was always a fair amount of activity as people returned home, so she felt confident when she returned from work at around that time that there would be plenty of people about if Bill did try to accost her. However, this didn't stop her peering through her curtains before she went to bed, and on several occasions he was just standing under the lamp, not even looking up at her window. Unsure of what to do, she was relieved that over the following weekend he did not make an appearance.

But then on the Monday, as she went to unlock her door, he came from behind and gently pushed her into her flat. She attempted to scream, but fear stifled her ability to cry out. Then, realising he was unsure of himself as he lowered his body heavily into a chair, bending forwards and holding his head in his hands, she regained her composure, and allowed him to speak.

'Christ, Nancy,' he exclaimed, straightening up so he could look at her. 'It's fifteen years since what happened. You never let me explain.'

Nancy sat down in the chair opposite, but her silence seemed to provoke him to continue.

'I loved you, I took care of you as a little girl, you were my everything. I wanted to give you everything. I wanted to give you the earth, to take care of you. You never understood. I was drunk that night. I was angry and jealous. I couldn't believe that pimply youth meant more to you than me. Do you understand, Nancy? It haunts me nearly every day of my life.'

Nancy sensed she was walking on a tightrope. How she reacted in the next few minutes could tip the balance of her life.

She spoke calmly, trying to avoid any trace of resentment in her reply. 'Yes, Bill, I do understand, at the time I thought of you as my big brother, because that's how it had always been. But what happened was wrong, drunk or not, Bill, it was not right.' She rose from her chair. 'But as you say it was fifteen years ago. I have put it behind me, as should you.'

There was silence, then she added, 'Can I offer you a cup of tea?'

He looked startled, as if he half wanted the torrent of abuse he had expected.

She walked towards the kitchenette, but instead of following her he just raised his voice so she could hear him whilst she made the tea.

'I've divorced the German bitch, she went off with a fellow Kraut taking the two German sausages with her. Mind you I'm sending money for the twins, it's not their fault, bless 'em. You're still on your own, Nancy. I could offer you the earth. I'm not short of money. I reckon I could make you happy. A nice little house with your own car.'

He remained silent for a minute, then continued, raising his voice further so she could hear him above the sound of the electric kettle coming to the boil.

'I wouldn't expect sex or anything. If we married eventually that might come later, but it definitely wouldn't be part of the deal. We could go abroad a bit for holidays, Nancy. To Spain, Italy… my God, you'd look fantastic in a bikini on one of those beaches. What's that place in France, St Tropez? You'd outdo Brigitte Bardot any day.'

'Thank you,' she replied, placing the tea in front of him.

'You are beautiful Nancy, right from a little girl you had style and class. Think about it, Nancy, you could do worse.'

She wanted to cry out, '"Could do worse"? I think not, Bill, I'm damaged goods, something you and Edna will always refuse to accept. I don't want to be your obsession.' But she calmed herself, knowing her only objective at this stage was to get him out of her flat of his own volition.

He took a drink of tea. 'What's this?' he exclaimed, half spitting the contents back into the mug.

'Sorry,' said Nancy, 'it's Earl Grey, it's all I have.'

Sensing he was on the back foot, she was unnerved by the way he quickly regained his composure. Rising from his chair, he sniffed the tea suspiciously again.

'Where would you want to move to?' Nancy enquired, endeavouring to feign interest in his proposal.

Again he looked deflated, as if her reaction sucked the energy from his body. 'I've been offered a job in Norfolk, part of the firm I used to work for in Germany. But if it didn't suit you that wouldn't be a problem.'

Nancy sipped her tea, drawing warmth through her hands as she gripped the mug tightly.

'I would want to continue to work,' she said.

'Of course, of course. I know you're a career girl, not a problem. I wouldn't want you home all day, we'd get someone to do the housework. I know there wouldn't be kids but...' For the first time his voice held a sense of enthusiasm. 'We could perhaps have a dog, or a cat. You used to like cats, and do you remember Mac?'

She didn't reply. All these years later she still carried his two button eyes around in her purse.

'Let me think about it, Bill,' she responded. 'I will be honest, I have been thinking about a change. But I have my evening class to go to now. Why don't you phone me at the office tomorrow?'

His body sagged, as if the stuffing had been punched out of it. 'Where's the evening class? I thought we might go for a meal.'

'Leave it until tomorrow,' she replied.

He clumsily rose from the chair. 'This isn't easy, Nancy, but you know it's what Edna would have wanted. She was good to us. Do you remember Mac?' he asked again.

'I remember everything, Bill. Mac dropped to bits,' she lied, 'but I kept his two button eyes.'

'Give it a whirl, Nancy,' he implored as he approached the door. 'You've never married, that's always given me hope. The blokes at Rolls-Royce call you the Ice Queen.' He stopped, uncertain of how to finish the sentence.

Nancy laughed in surprise. 'I didn't know that.'

He was now through the door and on the landing. As he started to descend the stairs, she added, 'Bill, promise me you won't hang around outside, please, it's unnerving when I see you through the window.'

'Ok,' he replied. 'I just wanted to let you know I was back.'

She closed the door. She was overcome with a huge feeling of relief, and also a realisation that this man who she had once adored was alarmingly childlike.

'She runs circles around you, Bill,' Edna would taunt him, and she unwittingly did. Showing off her school work, reading out loud, often winning when they played a board game with Edna on winter nights. She had run happily into his arms whenever he came home from work, or back from a trip. As she became older, he had always respected her privacy, being careful not to come into the kitchen when she was washing herself at the sink, always knocking on her bedroom door before coming in to sit on her bed for a chat. When the first televisions arrived in the shops, he was one of the first people in the street to buy one, so she could watch *Muffin the Mule*, *Robin Hood*, *Wagon Train*. They were constantly singing the title songs together.

As she stood now with her back against her front door, fear turned into a newfound realisation about the past. Bill had nurtured her, believing that she blossomed solely for him. She wanted to run down the stairs, stop him, saying that she would forgive him, that she understood, but begging him to leave her alone and let her live in peace, so they could both get on with their separate lives. But she had read too many crimes of passion, too many novels where obsession dominated and destroyed people's lives. She knew she was in danger, and she knew it was naïve to think she could deal with it on her own.

The police station was on the other side of town, but it was close to Reginald Road School where she attended her evening class each week. Normally she walked, but as she was aware that Bill could easily be following her, catching the bus seemed the best option.

Her own experience of visiting a police station was only courtesy of the television. Edna had loved *Dixon of Dock Green* and Rosemary was a fan of *Z Cars*. The Reginald Road police station was a combination of both. Its façade had all the reassuring attributes of a Dock Green station with a large lantern above the impressive doorway, but two police cars parked outside gave it an air of modernity.

She felt a little apprehensive as she pushed the heavy door open. The smell of the reception evoked memories of her school days, a mixture of overcooked food and disinfectant. Sitting hunched in one corner beneath a sign saying 'Strictly no smoking' was an old man wearing a stained raincoat and tweed cap. He was either oblivious to the sign or reacting to it defiantly by taking long drags on his cigarette, allowing the ash fall directly onto the blue and white tiled floor.

PC Watts, the middle-aged constable behind the desk, was on the phone. He indicated to Nancy that he would be a minute and she should sit down, rolling his eyes a couple of times to show the person on the end was going on a bit. Finally, replacing the receiver, he leaned over the wooden counter and, speaking in a mildly ironic tone, addressed the old man.

'Albert, you know you're not supposed to smoke here. Now be off with you.'

Not replying immediately, Albert ground the stub of his cigarette into the floor, then Nancy thought she caught the mumbled words, 'Then fucking arrest me.'

The constable laughed, then turning his attention towards Nancy, he remarked, 'Mr Albert here wants a cell for the night.'

Nancy stood up; she felt suddenly quite weak. Then, to the obvious surprise of PC Watts, she replied, 'That's what I think I could do with.'

'What, a cell for the night? Come on, luv, not sure one of our cells would suit a smart young lady like yourself.'

Resting one arm on the counter for support, she described a little of the history of her and Bill, and the evening's encounter in the flat.

'He seems obsessed by me,' she explained. 'If you could caution him, warn him off, that might help.'

PC Watts remained silent for a while, filling in all the relevant details on an official document. 'Now let me get this straight,' he said. 'He hasn't actually threatened you, or been violent?'

'Apart from pushing me into the flat uninvited,' Nancy corrected him, 'and standing in the road looking through my window, that feels pretty threatening.'

'Yes, I understand, but there's nothing we can call him in for, it's just your word against his, I'm afraid. Now, if I understand you right, you also said that, just to get rid of him, you gave him the impression that you were taking his offer of marriage seriously?'

Nancy felt an intense weariness take over. She remembered Agnes talking about cases of violence against women she came across in her profession, and her frustration that a battered wife was often just dismissed by the police as a 'domestic', with very little done to protect her from further abuse.

'I suggest,' PC Watts continued, starting to conclude the exchange, 'that you tell him honestly how you feel, best with someone else present, and then hopefully he will back off. I'm afraid without any actual real signs of violence, there's not a lot we can do, my dear.'

The old man in the corner rasped and coughed, shattering the atmosphere. When he became silent Nancy started relating what she had feared to explain in the first place. 'Bill raped and attacked me when I was sixteen. It must still be on the police records. I was hospitalised and although the police were involved Bill left the country and I didn't continue to press charges.'

She was immediately aware that PC Watts' attitude changed. Strangely, she thought, he seemed less friendly, asking her to sit down whilst he had a word with the officer in charge. As she sat down on one of the wooden benches, the old man got up. He cleared his throat then aimed a gobbet of spit towards the reception counter, before hobbling out of the door.

After a few minutes PC Watts returned and, after dealing with an angry woman who had come to report the noise made by her neighbours, he escorted Nancy into a small room and asked her to wait. The duty officer, she was told, would be with her shortly. The room was windowless and devoid of any kind of comfort or distraction, just a table and four chairs.

PC Watts brought her a cup of tea, but it was nearly an hour later and she was about to leave when two officers, one male, one female, entered the room. The female officer introduced herself as the duty officer for the night, and her colleague PC Smith would be taking notes. Without apologising for the delay, she explained in a perfunctory tone that having talked to PC Watts and read through his notes, she agreed with him that at this stage there was very little they could do to help her.

'But he raped me,' Nancy insisted. 'I feel under threat, not only that he might rape me again, but he is capable of causing me further bodily harm.'

'Miss Dupray, what allegedly happened fifteen years ago is of course very distressing. We have checked our records and couldn't find anything. As you chose not to press charges there is very little we can do.'

Nancy felt a wave of hostility, a feeling that in some bizarre way she was being looked on as the guilty party. For a second she had been relieved when a female officer had entered the room, but her relief was short-lived as it was immediately clear that the duty officer would not be extending any gender sympathy. She appeared to have striven to strip herself of any kind of femininity; her immaculate crisp blouse and uniform acted like a barrier between them. Her colleague PC Smith remained silent, but Nancy knew that he was running his eyes over her from top to toe. At one point he looked briefly towards her, extending a smile that could have been interpreted as sympathy or lust, she would never know.

'I repeat,' the duty officer continued, 'I suggest you take PC Watts' advice and do not get too hysterical.'

'I am not hysterical!' protested Nancy, but before she could finish the young woman bent forward across the table.

'That's not what I understand, Miss Dupray,' she replied somewhat triumphantly. 'PC Watts mentioned here in his notes that when you first arrived you suggested that you felt the need of a cell for the night. I personally feel that has the ring of hysteria about it.'

It was useless, Nancy knew. To leave quietly would be the only way she could retain a degree of dignity. She rose and, refusing to sign the notes, walked purposefully back into the reception. Ignoring the cheery goodbye extended by PC Watts, she pulled the heavy door open and descended into the street. It was dark, but she knew the area well and made straight for the nearest telephone box. The idea of returning to her flat offered no comfort. As she dialled Rosemary's number she peered through the glass, searching for any sign of Bill lurking in the shadows.

Rosemary always responded well to emergencies, and without demanding details over the phone, she appeared with her car at the phone box within minutes. Bundling Nancy inside, she offered the comfort, sound advice, humour and sanctuary that Nancy needed. Rosemary's circle of friends was impressive, and her position as a magistrate gave her access to the Chief Constable.

'I'll explain to him tomorrow,' she told Nancy, 'that if you are attacked, raped, murdered, whatever grisly fate that might be bestowed on you by Bill, I for one will hold the Derbyshire Police Force responsible.'

Together they went immediately to Nancy's flat, where she collected enough clothes to last her for at least a week.

As expected, Bill phoned her at her office. His voice gave no indication that he was aware of her movements the previous night. She had thought out quite clearly in advance what she was going to say. She explained that she did to some extent understand how he felt about her, and as a child she had been grateful for his care and attention. However, never under any circumstances had she, or would she consider living with him. Without waiting for a response, she informed him of the steps she had taken the night before.

Rosemary never did explain what she had said to the Chief Constable, but when Nancy eventually returned to her flat, a local bobby or a police car was often to be seen patrolling her street.

Louis and Bartholomew kept her informed about Bill's whereabouts. He had remained in Derby, working at the Foundry. Nancy found his presence unnerving, but after a few uneventful months her confidence returned. Even so, each night she instinctively looked out of the window into the street below just to make doubly sure he was not watching her again.

She was for the first time conscious of how good she felt. Lucky, she thought, to be young and healthy, and to have an interesting job and a circle of dear friends. She loved the autumn, even though at times she felt it was achingly sad reminding her of pre-Raphaelite paintings of autumn leaves. As she arrived at work and entered the Marble Hall, she took extra delight in the clicking of her high heels on the floor. She was normally the first to arrive, but as she climbed the stairs David leaned over the banister, indicating that he would like her to come immediately into his office.

She could sense from the tone of his voice he wasn't his normal self, and when he asked her to sit down, she could see he was upset.

'Nancy, something rather horrible has happened. It's something that affects us both, but hopefully we can successfully handle it together.' He shifted uncomfortably in his chair, then leaning towards her he continued, 'When your foster mother died – I think it was Edna, wasn't it? Well, you told me a little about the rather unsavoury character who had been at one time like a brother to you. He was called Bill, if I remember? Just before the weekend, my wife had a phone call from a man. He didn't leave a name, but I think you will probably say it was Bill.'

'She had a call from Bill?' Nancy straightened in her chair. 'A call from Bill? Why, how would he know how to contact Katie? I don't understand.'

'All he said was that he thought it right that he should inform Katie – he used her name, which really upset her, I can tell you – that you and I were having an affair. That it had been going on a long time. That you had a reputation with married men, and you were also partial, and these were his words, to a "bit of black", and you were not opposed to taking a bob or two for favours given. Katie was completely stunned, and had the sense to say, "This is ludicrous, why should you tell me?" He apparently replied he was fond of you. That he thought you had fallen into bad hands. He concluded with "I don't want it to end in tears," and put the phone down.'

'Oh, how terrible for Katie,' Nancy cried. 'But it's crazy, she knows that it's not true. And yes, of course it's Bill.' She started to relate her recent dealings with him. 'The police warned him off, I'm sure, but to be honest I wondered when – no, I feared he would raise his ugly head again. I am so, so sorry, David, please tell Katie how sorry I am, what an awful experience for her. I'll contact the police immediately.

Do you think Katie would mind speaking to them? What did he think he might achieve?'

As she tried to continue to express her revulsion at what had occurred, she sensed that David wasn't really listening.

'Nancy, look,' he began. 'I am sure Katie doesn't believe him, but he has sown a seed of doubt in her mind. She's always liked you, but I think like a lot of women she's slightly in awe of you. You perhaps don't realise, or perhaps you do, I don't know, but a lot of my colleagues tease me about having such a beautiful, super-efficient secretary.'

Nancy felt unsure where this was taking them, but she remained silent, apart from whispering, 'This is so terrible.'

'I mean, we both know that there has never been a hint of anything between us. But now Katie has doubts and nothing is going to change the way she feels. I spent the whole weekend trying to make her see how stupid, even libellous, the whole situation is, but she wants me to find another secretary. It's my way, she says, of proving to her that there is nothing in this.'

'But what about me?' cried Nancy. 'Is anyone thinking about me? I've worked hard to achieve working for you. Come on, David, surely Katie doesn't believe there is anything going on between us? I mean, I find that totally insulting, just because I have some very good Jamaican friends, why should that mean, well…' She hesitated, trying to find the words. 'That I don't have any morals. I honestly thought you and Katie were more intelligent than that.'

'It's got nothing to do with your Jamaican friends, Nancy. I too find that insulting, you know we both supported you when our over-eagle-eyed personnel officer inferred – well, I'm not quite sure what she meant to infer, but whatever it was, it was, how do they say, out of order.'

They spent the next hour arguing back and forth, but David always came back to the point that his marriage was at stake, and he wasn't prepared to take the risk, even though Nancy had asked to have the opportunity to speak to Katie and explain her situation.

Tears did not come easily to Nancy, but on this occasion she was wracked by a deep sobbing. 'This is wrong, David, you know it is. How can you do this to me? I've always been loyal to you,' she cried out in frustration.

To her horror, he picked up the phone and before she had time to protest Nancy heard him say, 'Miss Radcliffe, could you join us, please? Yes, immediately, thank you.'

Nancy leapt out of her chair. 'No, David, no, that's so unfair. Aren't you prepared to stand up for me?'

'On this occasion, no,' he replied. 'Not if my marriage is at stake. I'll do anything I can do to help. It's hard, I know, but your personal problems have regrettably...' He sought for words. 'Well, they have affected our working relationship.'

'Don't be so pompous,' she retorted as the door opened.

It was obvious when Miss Radcliffe arrived that she had been briefed already. Her face bore an ill-disguised look of triumph as she instructed Nancy to pull herself together, suggesting she should take the rest of the day off.

'I have arranged for Mary Blunt to act as your replacement. She is developing into a very efficient secretary and, as the daughter of one of our leading councillors, I am sure she can be relied on to be discreet.'

Nancy felt rage grip her body. 'I will not take the day off,' she declared. 'This is totally unfair. You should be defending me, not treating me as if...' Words failed her. She strode past the Totem Pole and into her adjoining office, where Mary was sitting at her desk.

'Please leave, Mary,' she commanded.

'Stay where you are, Mary,' Miss Radcliffe countered, shouting from the inner office.

But Mary had already timidly gathered up her papers, to allow Nancy quickly to sit back on her chair. The younger girl looked confused and stood to one side as David and Miss Radcliffe swept by her and into Nancy's office.

Gathering her composure by straightening items on her desk, Nancy finally looked up. 'You will have to forcibly remove me. I am not prepared to leave. As yet I do not know my rights, but I will find out immediately. Regrettably, it's obvious that I cannot ask my Personnel Officer.'

Miss Radcliffe advanced towards her, but David restrained her. 'Please leave us,' he instructed her, 'and you too, Mary.'

'I have to protest,' Miss Radcliffe cried, 'this is a personnel matter. Miss Dupray is acting in a very undignified manner.'

'I asked you to go, and Mary,' David replied. 'This all has to be resolved in a much calmer manner. As Personnel Officer you should realise that.'

When they left, he moved closer to Nancy's desk.

'I am sorry, Nancy, this is being handled in a very unfortunate fashion. Continue with your work, and I assure you that no one will disturb you, or lock you out when you go for lunch. This needs more consideration.'

The day dragged on, with no one approaching her, but it gave her time to gather her thoughts. This time she was resolved not to turn to any of her friends. They had done enough. To ask more, she decided, might endanger relationships that were precious to her. As she sat pondering her fate, a plan began to formulate in her mind. A frisson of excitement swept through her.

The following morning she was not surprised that David was waiting for her, together with one of the directors.

'John is going to sit in with us whilst we chat, Nancy, I hope that's OK with you?'

John was one of Nancy's favourite directors. Over the years they had built up a warm relationship. She knew many details of his five grandchildren, numerous dogs and passion for cars.

'This is terrible, Nancy, a truly awful state of affairs. David has shared the whole story with me, and whilst I feel Katie's response is unfair, I do feel she is digging her heels in and another solution has to be found. Let's sit down and discuss some options, shall we?'

He moved his chair, indicating David should do the same so that they could sit in an informal group rather than across a desk. Nancy smiled at him, relieved that here was someone she respected and could trust.

'David and I have talked formally to Miss Radcliffe, and we have her assurance that if you return to the typing pool she will make every effort to find a similar position for you with one of the directors or chief engineers. If it isn't possible immediately, she could move you to Sinfin; not as prestigious, I accept, but with obviously the same salary and conditions.' He raised his hand sharply as Nancy began to reply. 'Let me finish, or perhaps you would like to continue, David?'

'I've also talked to our financial director,' David continued, 'and another option is that we could offer you a form of redundancy. If you left now, the company would offer you half a year's salary together with personal letters of reference from John and myself. Neither offer, I agree, is particularly pleasant, but your Bill has got us all with our backs against the wall. John and I have discussed it, and going to the police is another option, but we have no proof he even made the call. It's your decision, Nancy. In a year's time hopefully this will all be forgotten. You are a rising star. If you stayed with the company, I can guarantee you'd soon find your way back here in the Marble Hall.'

Nancy hesitated. She could hear the rattle of the tea trolley progressing slowly from office to office. Both men, she felt, looked slightly smug, as if they had in their usual masculine way rescued everyone from a difficult situation, and within a short time their lives would be back to normal.

She felt betrayed by John. She looked around the room, accepting that this had become a substitute for a real home. She had helped David to choose the two paintings on the wall when the office had been redecorated. On a side table she would often fill a vase with flowers. She frequently bought magazines to put on the coffee table for guests waiting to see her boss, and one of her best tailored jackets hung on a coat hanger with two silk scarves, ready to boost her confidence if she had to attend a last-minute meeting.

She breathed in sharply, considering for the final time the decision she had taken the previous night. *What have I to lose?* she thought.

Rosemary, she knew, would have approved. She became a little tense, realising that this must be the performance of her life. Then, looking at both men to engage their attention, she began.

'Firstly,' she replied, 'he is not my Bill. I find that totally insulting. You might be interested to know that Bill attacked me when I was sixteen.' She paused and watched them take this in. When no response was forthcoming, she added, 'Since then I have worked hard, so hard, to build a life for myself, even though I have had to cope with his obsessive behaviour. And I am not sure what you mean by his having your backs against the wall. We all know what he's saying is a lie, so why don't we just ignore it, or report him to the police?' She drew a deep breath to steady herself, then continued. 'But putting that aside, David, I am going to be completely upfront with you. This is now your decision, not mine, and you might perhaps prefer if John didn't remain for what I am about to say.'

David looked mystified, raising his eyebrow a little as he glanced at John.

The tea trolley stopped outside the door. Nancy stood up and accepted the tray of coffee and biscuits, asking for an extra cup for John. As she poured the coffee, she was aware that their air of superiority had diminished a little.

'I reject the offer of a position in the typing pool. I know full well, as both of you do if you are honest, that Miss Radcliffe would not strive in any way to find me another suitable place. In fact just the opposite.' This time she was one to raise her hand for silence from both of them. 'Please let me have my say, I am already tired and hurt and disappointed that you should be telling me what is best for me, whilst it is blatantly obvious it is what is best for you, David.' Neither man spoke as she continued. 'This afternoon I have an appointment with the Union. They already feel I am being treated unfairly and they will take up the fight. Their immediate response was, "If they're not careful they could have another Ford Dagenham on their hands. It's power to the woman now." Well, may I add, sitting opposite you both, I sincerely hope he is correct. However much Rolls-Royce likes to present itself as a modern, democratic firm, there is still a lot of inequality, and if I have *my* back to the wall, I will be more than happy to help expose it.' Finding herself breathless she paused dramatically, knowing she had the ace card still up her sleeve.

'But there is an alternative. I accept your offer of so-called redundancy, but on my conditions, which are: I want a whole year's gross salary, together with the glowing references you have so kindly offered me. However, if you reject that, I will fight with the Union's support, but I will also expose you, David.'

'Expose me? What in heaven's name do you mean, Nancy?'

She had always liked David, but now she savoured the moment before replying. 'I presume you do not want your affair with your wife's best friend Wendy Rudd to be exposed, and that's why you so readily agreed to my dismissal. A mess like this would eventually turn up your misdemeanours, I'm sure.'

'That's a lie!' he roared, jumping from his chair. 'A downright lie, and you know it.'

Nancy again gathered her composure. 'Please sit down,' she said. 'I feel threatened by your hysteria. I have been a good, efficient and loyal secretary. But do you think I didn't notice your assignations in the office and the expense claims for dinners for two while you were away on business? Given that I have been placed in this position, I will go directly to your wife and Mr Rudd. Now it's time for you to decide.'

'You bitch,' David cried, 'you selfish, scheming little bitch!'

'Enough!' shouted John. 'How dare you use such language? If this is true, you are a complete scoundrel. I have known Nancy for many years, David, and I have never known her to gossip or to be in the slightest bit vindictive, which makes a refreshing difference to many of the personnel on the premises.'

By three o'clock she had two cheques in her hand, one for half a year's gross salary from Rolls-Royce, and the other for the same amount from David's own bank account. John gave them to her with the letters of reference.

'Miss Radcliffe will be sending you various forms you have to sign, but it's over, Nancy, and I am deeply sorry. Incidentally, she doesn't know any of the more unsavoury details of all this. David is worried you could try to blackmail him later, but I assured him that would not be the case. I am right in vouching for you, aren't I, Nancy? This is very unorthodox, but I have staked my reputation that there will be no repercussions. I'm happy to think I'm retiring soon. I feel I can never extend the hand of friendship to David again, and I sincerely hope that Katie doesn't learn the truth.'

'Of course, John,' Nancy replied, 'and thank you. On Monday I walked into work truly happy and content, and today I leave with my world in tatters. I am deeply sad, but I've survived in the past, and I will again.' She stepped towards him, and was pleased he responded by hugging her gently.

DERBY, 1968

Jack blew out one of the sputtering candles that Nancy had lit as she told her story.

'My God, Nancy, that's an incredible – well, it is a saga. I'm proud of you.'

Nancy laughed. 'Thank you. It was pretty shocking. As I left the building I met the Union guy on his way to see me. I didn't explain fully, but said I had accepted redundancy. He was really upset, obviously longing for a fight. I think he rightly thought I'd let the side down, but believe me, I was just too weary to want to battle with them all, and have my private life examined.'

'God, I'm not surprised, what complete bastards. You know the Totem Pole's leaving, don't you? Betty told me.'

'But,' she continued, 'there is a happy ending, although I'm not so sure sagas can have happy endings. As I walked down Nightingale Road, I passed Cowlishaw's Pie Shop and I spotted an advertisement in the window, saying they urgently required an assistant, no experience necessary. I don't know why, but I just walked in. They said can you type, do accounts, that kind of thing? I said I had just been sacked from Rolls-Royce and then I burst into tears. A couple of hours later, after several sausage rolls, at least three of those sickly coconut cakes with a cherry on top, plus a gallon of tea, I'd more or less told them my life story. I started the following day, and after a week I realised it was the best job I'd ever had. And can you imagine how I took pleasure in the revenge that the Chief Engineer's secretary could now be seen serving in the local pie shop? It was a challenge but rewarding. I hadn't realised how boring Rolls-Royce had been. All engine specifications, technical reports, I hadn't a clue about. The only real excitement had been when the test beds were running and you got a report about how many dead chickens had been thrown into the blades before they stopped.'

Jack was laughing now, more out of relief now he knew the whole story. 'Well I never, so you became Sweeney Todd's assistant?'

'Yes, and there were at least two people I would have happily turned into pies.'

He gathered her into his arms. 'I sense, Nancy Dupray, you fancy yourself as an entrepreneur like Mary Quant, only your empire would be pies? Whatever, Nancy, I admire you, you are very special. But of course, like all these powerful women, you need a very special man supporting you, and like any knight in shining armour, burning and slashing a path for you to enable you to succeed.' He held her close. 'May I somewhat arrogantly suggest, Miss Nancy Dupray, that I am that very special man? Marry me. I may be young, incredibly handsome, but I also have my head screwed on, and did I forget to add that I happen to be hopelessly in love with you?'

She continued laughing, throwing her head back so her hair reached her waist.

'A very pretty speech,' she retorted, 'but I haven't even met your mother yet. A little soon, I think, to start talking about marriage.'

'But you will meet Mum next week at Brian and Betty's wedding. You will be the perfect escort for the best man. I will proudly introduce you to my mother. She's special too, you'll see. We could even announce our engagement.'

'You're completely mad,' she cried, 'one thing at a time.'

Releasing herself from his embrace, she walked towards the kitchen, but not before glancing briefly through the window to the street below. Bill had not tried to contact her or linger outside her flat for months, but she knew it was only a matter of time. She knew that to involve Jack in this conflict with Bill was dangerous and unfair. But she accepted that she too was in love, a heady feeling that she had never experienced before. She tried to hide it from Jack, but she couldn't hide it from herself.

CHAPTER EIGHTEEN

England swings like the pendulums do
Swinging chicks and swinging Ty-Phoo
Pour out a cup of it and you'll agree,
Ty-Phoo's Britain's swingiest tea

– ADVERT, TY-PHOO TEA

DERBY, 1968

Betty had wanted the wedding in the afternoon because of her morning sickness, but her father had insisted it was in the morning to accommodate lunch for close family and friends and then a dance and a buffet at a local pub for a larger group of guests in the evening. After some fierce discussion Brian had persuaded Betty that he and Jack would wear morning suits and top hats. He also organised a vintage Rolls-Royce to take Betty and her dad to the church, and then afterwards to the reception. He justified the expense to Jack by explaining that hopefully you only got married once and therefore it was worth making it memorable.

As Jack stood next to Brian in the church waiting for Betty to arrive, his thoughts were full of Nancy. Each time he saw her he was startled by his emotions. The feelings of desire and pride to be in her company never seemed to diminish. He was confident of her love, but troubled by how fragile their relationship was, in the light of the age difference, her past, and Bill. Losing her was unthinkable, but he knew that to retain her was not going to be easy. Frequently she was gay, funny and immensely loving, but when he touched on their future she would become withdrawn, refusing to discuss long term plans. 'Live for the moment,' she would say, 'whatever the future holds we will always have the memories of our time together.'

The organ started to play. Betty had refused to have 'Here Comes the Bride', so the congregation were a little hesitant in rising to an unfamiliar overture. Jack turned round swiftly as he sensed a second of confusion, but was reassured when he saw Betty gliding down the aisle on the arm of her father. Beneath the veil he could see her face was composed and radiant. All the worries of babies, bridesmaids' dresses, morning suits and guest lists seemed to have evaporated, just leaving a beautiful bride approaching the man she loved.

The ancient church, smelling musty in spite of the sun shining through its stained-glass windows, the music, the ritual of the service, all only served to move Jack's emotions as the congregation stood to welcome the bride. Thoughts of Nancy disappeared as he now assumed his role as best man.

When the bride and groom left the church, he escorted Mary, Betty's chief bridesmaid, followed by a bevy of five others, all shapes and sizes as Brian was to remark later. As they burst into the spring sunshine, he spotted Nancy standing alone. She looked out of place, elegant in a pale blue silk suit, its box jacket complemented by a small pillbox hat of navy to match her gloves, shoes and handbag. The photographer was herding everyone into position for a group photo, but Jack escaped for a second and, running towards her, swept her dramatically off her feet. When they had laughingly embraced, he pulled her over towards his mother who was standing with a group of Betty's relatives.

As he approached, he knew they were all startled. He relished in anticipating the moment when he would announce that 'this is Nancy, my girlfriend'. The photographer had been delayed as the largest bridesmaid, an ample girl called Lucy, was struggling with a broken bra strap.

'I knew I should have gone for a double D,' she cried, to the huge amusement of the guests. Brian would always think that this was possibly the best photograph of the wedding, as he, together with a group of bridesmaids, tried to come to Lucy's aid. Fortunately Betty's mum had a safety pin, which, after a fair amount of struggling accompanied by amusing comments from Brian's friends, finally saved the day.

Jack's mother had been looking forward to meeting the mysterious Nancy, but now she felt unsure of herself. This beautiful and indisputably sophisticated young woman was not at all what she had been expecting. Betty had told her that Jack was seeing someone older than him, and she had sensed that Brian was always a little guarded when he spoke of Nancy, always referring to her as the 'beautiful Nancy'. However, this first meeting was a shock. Her age wasn't reflected in her looks, just in her composure.

'I'm sorry, Nancy, I know very little about you, Jack's been very secretive,' she confessed, 'but it's lovely to meet you. Where do you come from, are you a Derby girl?'

Jack had insisted that Nancy attend the wedding even though she had protested that she hardly knew anyone. But the invitation was to both of them, so once the decision was made that she would accept, she felt it necessary to prepare her replies to questions that either Jack's mother or other guests might ask.

So, in reply to Elizabeth, Nancy feigned a little laugh. 'I really don't know where I come from. I am an orphan, then was adopted when I was very young. I lived and grew up just outside Derby and then moved to Duffield.' She proceeded to give Elizabeth a summary of her working life. 'You're a teacher, aren't you?' she eventually asked, confident she had supplied enough information to satisfy Elizabeth.

Just as Elizabeth was about to reply, Jack interrupted, 'Quick, Nancy, I've asked the photographer to take a photograph of us together. Sorry, Mum, we'll catch up soon.'

Elizabeth was immensely proud of her son. When the insurance company had finally paid out the full amount after her husband's death, she and young Jack had taken joint decisions on how to shape their lives. Once they had decided to leave their old house, Jack had been enthusiastic in helping to decide where they might live. When they moved to a large 1930s mock-Tudor semidetached house in a leafy suburb, Jack had immediately taken charge of the garden and the allotment, despite his young age.

However, his pride and joy became the garage. It stood separately at the side of the house, with impressive doors and the same mock-Tudor detail on the roof. To Elizabeth's amusement he spent hours researching a suitable car for her, and was completely overjoyed when she decided on a brand new Mini. Her driving instructor would often let Jack accompany them when she had lessons, which resulted in Jack learning to do a three-point turn on their drive before she did.

She had come to terms with the pain of her husband's death, accepting that it would never go away. What gave her comfort was her son's company and their shared interests, which acted as a distraction from her grief. She decided that to retain his love, she must allow him to have his own privacy, encouraging him to be the master of his own destiny. When he decided not to go to university but to take up an engineering apprenticeship, she deliberately didn't interfere, hiding her disappointment as best as she could.

She had returned to her teacher training within a few months of her husband's death, qualifying as a primary school teacher within the year. By the time Jack was in his late teens, she was headmistress of the school. She adored the job and was both loved and respected by her staff, the pupils and their parents.

She had a wide circle of friends, but never once felt the need to find another partner. She accepted that her sexuality had died with her husband. She knew she was slightly out of step with the times, dressing for comfort rather than the current fashion. Jack had liked her in classical clothes, and whilst she did attempt to liven her wardrobe up occasionally, it was usually because there was a demand for a new outfit for a family event, or Christmas. Her one concession to modernity was her Mini, but secretly she admitted that was to appeal to young Jack.

Now her son stood before the wedding guests, making a speech that was well prepared, funny in parts, and, to her relief, not smutty.

He had started off rather nervously, but after a couple of minutes she realised he was starting to relish the opportunity to speak about Brian, his closest friend.

Occasionally he would look towards Nancy, and for the first time Elizabeth felt a pang of jealousy. She had taken for granted that Jack's girlfriend would have been in the mould of Betty or Mary, a local girl who possibly worked at Rolls-Royce, some young woman that she would have felt at ease with. But Nancy was unquestionably different.

Later, at the reception, Elizabeth sat at one of the empty tables, watching the couples on the dancefloor. The music stopped for a moment and one of the younger guests quickly changed the record for The Rolling Stones' 'I Can't Get No Satisfaction', which immediately dispersed most of the more mature guests.

Elizabeth noticed Nancy picking her way across the dance floor, possibly in search of the toilet, or 'powder room' as Elizabeth was amused to discover it had been renamed. To her delight, a few seconds later Jack joined her.

'Not dancing, Mum?' he teased her, but quickly continued with the question she was expecting. 'So what do you think of Nancy, then?'

'She's lovely, Jack,' she replied honestly. 'Not quite what I was expecting, older, more sophisticated than, well, you know, the young ladies around here. But it's obvious that you both care for one another. But I suggest you take your time, Jack. You're young, there's no rush.'

Before replying, he gently took Elizabeth's hand. 'I've decided to move in with her, Mum. Trust me and please don't fight me.'

'I've never fought you, Jack, you know that. But what will people say? You're not even engaged.'

He continued to hold her hand. 'I know, Mum, I know, but times are changing. Betty's already pregnant, but who cares? If you love someone you want to be with them, don't you?'

Get a grip, thought Elizabeth, *you mustn't feel that the bottom has fallen out of your world; it just feels that way at the moment. Jack's bound to go his own way. He's right, when you love someone it changes everything. Whatever, he'll probably get married soon and you have to accept that. You wouldn't want it any other way,* she concluded.

Jack had never thought about being married. To some extent he had always taken on the role of the man of the house, although as he grew older he realised that this had become something of an illusion nurtured by his mother to compensate for the loss of her husband.

He and Nancy acted like any other couple, dividing the shopping, planning the weekends, discussing their days. Nancy would regale him with stories from the pie shop. She was obviously happy there, delighting in helping them expand, but fighting a battle about the quality of the ingredients and the fast-paced changes in the eating habits of the British public.

Pies were out and tarts and quiches were in, she would declare. At her own request, Doug Cowlishaw had sent her and Jack on a trip down to London to the new Habitat shop, to get ideas for the interior décor of the second shop he and his wife Moira were planning to open in the newly proposed shopping centre in Derby. They came back with bags full of kitchen equipment, but Nancy accepted that it was always going to be an uphill battle persuading Doug to modernise his business, and she had to concede that Derby certainly wasn't moving as fast as London.

But she and Jack were bursting with ideas and smartened up her little kitchen, swiftly creating a home together. On Nancy's insistence, Jack visited his mother once a week, often staying the night. Their relationship was different, but Elizabeth accepted that it would be unwise to criticise and was simply relieved that Jack came home each week.

He had explained a little more about Nancy's circumstances and Elizabeth was pleasantly surprised by their circle of friends, even though she feared that they might be seen as 'living in sin', as some of her relatives liked to describe it. Sometimes, after he and Nancy had been working at the allotment, they would call in with vegetables and flowers. Neither woman found it too easy to be relaxed in each other's company, but she was grateful for Nancy's obvious sensitivity in avoiding creating a rift between her and her son.

Jack had also explained that Nancy would not trap him by getting pregnant as she was unable to have children. This saddened her, but gave her some hope that the relationship would eventually fizzle out. She refused to comment on Jack's choice of a partner. To the question frequently posed by friends and relatives, 'Is he still going out with that woman?' her dignified response became, 'If you mean Nancy, yes he is, and he seems very happy, which means I am happy too.'

She knew that if they continued to live together, she must break down the barriers and publicly acknowledge Nancy as part of the family, but she felt it was all too soon.

Part Two

CHAPTER NINETEEN

*Sometimes it's not just the dogs
that need rescuing.*

– BATTERSEA DOGS' HOME

ALLESTREE, DERBYSHIRE, 2014

Jack finally left the hospital after signing for a small package containing Nancy's clothes. The nurse had suggested that they could give them to the undertakers so Nancy could be buried in them rather than the hospital gown, but Jack decided that Nancy probably would have chosen the white gown, as he agreed with Josh that it did make her look rather angelic.

When he reached Nancy's house he was relieved to see Nimble in the garden. He was lying under a bush, which gave him shade, but more importantly, a good vantage point to see what was going on in the street. He barked when he saw Jack, wagging his tail in recognition of a familiar face. Brian and Betty were also there, talking to Nancy's neighbours across the fence. Over the years, Betty had become pleasantly plump and Brian, despite playing cricket during the season, had developed a sizeable paunch.

'How did you find out?' Jack asked. 'I tried to phone, but I guessed you were away on holiday.'

'We got your text,' explained Betty, 'but Mary phoned us this morning to tell us that Nancy had died. She was very upset, Jack, she said you had attacked her.'

'She was bloody rude,' added Brian, striding across so he could put a reassuring arm around his friend's shoulder. 'She gave Betty a right dressing down, about us being friendly with Nancy behind her back. Then your Sheila phoned and said she couldn't contact you. She sounded worried, and then Trevor her god-awful husband came on the line. He said if we were going to see you, to tell you he wanted an urgent word with you about your attack on his mother-in-law. Arrogant sod. I told him I'd known you since you were eight years old and you hadn't a violent bone in your body. He didn't reply, just repeated would I kindly tell you if we saw you. Mary is staying with them. I mean, "would I kindly", what bloody arrogance.'

Jack was about to reply, but Brian quickly drew breath and continued, 'He'll persuade Mary to leave you, Jack. He's a scheming bastard. He's frustrated because he's managed to convince Mary that you should sell up and move in with them to some poncy house in Duffield. The fact that you said "no way" is like declaring all-out war with him. You having a go at Mary is just the bloody excuse he needs. I'd like to tell him a thing or two.'

Jack reached out, gently hugging Brian for a brief moment. 'Thanks for your faith in me,' he murmured. 'Mary said some truly unforgivable things about Nancy only a few minutes after the hospital had phoned to say she'd died. I admit I was bloody angry and told her in no uncertain terms I was disgusted by her. She stepped back in surprise and fell over the coffee table. I tried to help her up, but she'd have none of it. She might have had a few bruises, but when I left she was in the garden.'

'Brian, calm down,' Betty intervened as the next-door neighbours started to retire tactfully through their front door. Then, turning to Jack, she gave him the hug he so sorely needed. 'It's a shock, Jack, but she was happy at the end. She found you and she found Nimble.'

ALLESTREE, DERBYSHIRE, 2011

When they finally met again, Nancy was to tell Jack that Nimble had saved her life. Just when she was ready to give up, he had wandered in and lovingly changed everything around her. She was sixty-four when her partner Seamus had died. Devastated as she was, she had to acknowledge that they had experienced more than twenty blissful years together. After his death, she had continued working part-time for another five years, and then suddenly age seemed to descend on her.

The inevitable signs of getting older had been cause for amusement with Seamus, but on her own, the constant searching for glasses, the back pain and then eventually a hip replacement were daunting to face alone. Their relationship had always had to be discreet, and consequently when Seamus died she only had a small circle of friends to fall back on. Then, as they retired, died or left the area, she had to acknowledge that, as she had no family, her world was diminishing rapidly. Even in her late seventies, she continued to drive, but after the hip operation, she felt nervous and reluctantly sold her car.

Having lived with a doctor for so many years, she knew that Seamus would have had very little patience with her depression. His philosophy would have been to get out there. But she had done voluntary work, charity shops, evening classes, even aqua classes for the 'seniors' as they tactfully called themselves.

She would often sit at Seamus' desk, drawing comfort from the photographs of his children and, she had to admit, a very flattering portrait of her taken by a professional photographer, as well as one of her and Jack taken at Brian and Betty's wedding all those years ago. Seamus said that she looked like Jackie Kennedy, and Jack had no right to look so handsome.

Seamus also kept a picture of his wife, but in the top drawer of his desk. She looked so young and frail, as if a puff of wind would blow her away. But she was still alive. Her children had put her in a nursing home after Seamus' death, something he had always avoided.

Most days Nancy now spent wearily in a kind of inertia, only bothering to eat when she became really hungry. But this came abruptly to an end when she received a letter announcing that the lease on her house was coming to an end, and she would be obliged to vacate the property by the end of the year. It stated, in officious terms, that the lease would not be offered for renewal as the property was deemed in need of renovation. Something of the fire had gone out of her, but she phoned the agent immediately.

'Will you be turning me out on the street?' she demanded.

'Unlikely,' was the reply. But they did point out that they had already sent two letters previously explaining the situation. Somewhat deflated, Nancy had to admit that she had received them, and had chosen to ignore them. Later that afternoon a young man from the estate agents arrived. Surprisingly, she thought, he was quite sympathetic, suggesting that they find a house for her to rent or to buy. When she remonstrated about the sheer effort of moving, he explained that it was no problem to employ a firm to do all the packing. 'And I mean all,' he emphasised, 'right down to your last pair of shoes. They organise everything.'

'If I go quietly,' Nancy said knowingly.

'Well,' the young man paused as he accepted another cup of tea, 'I'm sure you don't want to be evicted, Miss Dupray, but that would be the bottom line.'

For a moment her humour returned as she pictured herself as a bag lady on the pavement outside.

'If you help me, I'll go quietly, but I think I might decide to return home and move back to Derby.'

'Not a problem, not a problem,' he declared immediately, factoring the details into his mobile phone. 'Yes, actually we have a branch in Derby. You need to tell me where you would like to go and approximately how much you want to spend. Am I right in presuming that you want to buy?'

Nancy looked towards the photo of her and Jack. 'I honestly don't know where I want to go exactly or even how much I can afford, but…'

'See it as an adventure, Miss Dupray. We'll help in every way. Raj Estates are renowned for their attention to detail, and customer satisfaction.'

When he left, leaving a strong odour of aftershave behind him, Nancy tried to analyse why she had suddenly said she wanted to return home. She had never really thought of Derby as 'home'. So why back there? Both good and bad memories flooded back. Most of the good ones had been kept alive during her life with Seamus. He'd always encouraged her to talk about her friends, sensing, she guessed, what a monumental decision it had been for her to leave it all behind. He treated Bill as a friend, something she had found vaguely disturbing at first, and whilst shocked when after Bill's death she had confessed the truth, he was his usual compassionate self and not judgmental. Several times he had offered to take her back to Derby.

'You need closure on it, Nancy,' he would say. 'After all these years I doubt if anybody's going to be downright nasty to you. Heaven knows, you were brave. Anyway, I wouldn't mind meeting Jack, see if there's any competition.'

She knew that it wasn't that simple, but maybe he had been right. Deep down she needed closure, and the thought of living in Duffield seemed rather attractive. She'd been happy there all those years ago and it wouldn't feel too unfamiliar, even though she guessed it had changed over the intervening years.

She slept soundly that night after spending the evening sorting out her finances. She suddenly felt excited, and when the phone rang over breakfast, she was able to tell the 'nice young man' that she would like something in the Duffield area. His constant 'no probs' were beginning to get a bit tedious.

The house she found was not in Duffield, but in a village three miles away. Duffield had proved too expensive, but its neighbouring village Allestree had inched its boundaries along the Derwent River towards Duffield so that the two locations had virtually merged into one. It was a two-bedroomed semi-detached house built just after the War. Its only redeeming feature, Nancy thought, was its close proximity to the park. In fact, if she stood in the corner of the bay window at the front, she could see one of the entrances, with its ornate Victorian gates and the sign that announced the opening hours.

The house had the air of being unloved for many years. Nancy had always thought of herself as resilient, but now for the first time, she felt daunted by her situation. A woman of eighty, completely on her own, buying a rundown property in an area that had dramatically changed over the years.

Courageously, and not without humour, she demanded that she needed proof that the elderly central heating system worked, and that the one toilet did flush properly, as it had seemed a little reluctant when she tried it. After some financial negotiations, and insisting that at least the central heating system was overhauled and all the rooms were painted before taking occupancy, she signed the contract.

Nancy moved into her new home on a wet afternoon at the end of October. She had spent the previous few weeks surrounded by large plastic bags into which she had emptied much of her previous life. She contacted her neighbours and few remaining acquaintances, inviting them to a 'help yourself' coffee morning. In her front room she piled all her unwanted *objets d'art*, kitchen and garden equipment, as well as many of her books, in the hope they would find a new home. At midday she declared the coffee morning over, and a firm of clearance men arrived to take away all that was left. Sadly, she realised that two of her large framed film posters had disappeared without her noticing, but as her heart was so heavy, it hardly seemed to matter.

The agents were true to their word and arranged a removal firm to pack and label all the remaining items. She stayed in a guest house near to the park the night before she took up residence in her new home. She was pleasantly surprised that the central heating was working, its radiators emitting a heavy smell of paint. The decorator, whom she had only spoken to on the phone, had suggested that he could do a very reasonable job if she chose white for the woodwork and magnolia for the walls. Magnolia, he reassured her, went with everything. She accepted glumly that colour had gone out of her life and magnolia was a suitable choice, although she knew that Seamus would have hated it.

So the house was clean and the kindly Polish removal men, despite speaking little English between them, were enthusiastically placing boxes and furniture where Nancy indicated. Having mislaid the kettle, they gallantly shared their thermos of tea. Then accepting a generous tip, they headed back to Norwich, leaving Nancy standing at the window watching their lorry depart.

Returning to the kitchen, she rummaged through the packing boxes marked 'kitchen' and finally found the kettle. A further search revealed a box of Earl Grey tea and half a packet of digestive biscuits. Preparing herself for a little break from all the activity of the day, she plugged in the kettle. There was a sharp bang and all the lights went out.

It was late afternoon but already getting dark. Fumbling her way from one room to another, she lowered herself into an armchair. Comforted by its familiarity, she fell into a deep sleep.

When she awoke she was cold, with no electricity and no central heating, but after a battle with a box of matches, a saucepan and the gas cooker, she was at least able to make a cup of tea.

The removal men had kindly assembled her bed and placed the box labelled 'linen' nearby. Unable to find her nightclothes, she opted for her blouse and knickers. Piling duvets and pillows onto the bed she created herself a nest. Seamus had once remarked that there was some-thing of the sloven in her as she loved to eat and drink in bed. Agreeing, she had explained that it was a hangover from when she and Jack had shared a flat. It was always hard to heat, and they often went to bed with their supper rather than huddle around the electric fire. As she finished the packet of digestive biscuits, she remembered she had eaten her first takeaway pizza in bed with Jack, accompanied by an Italian Chianti in a straw covered bottle. When she had been disposing of some of her possessions before the move, she had come across the empty Chianti bottle, a half-burnt candle still remaining in its neck.

She pondered as to why the memory of Jack kept returning so viv-idly, jostling in her mind with memories of Seamus. Lying in this strange room watching the shadows cast by the lights of the occasional passing car, she was overwhelmed with weariness. In a maudlin way she contemplated that to die peacefully this evening, warm and cosy in her nest, pleasantly full of digestive biscuits and tea, would not be a bad way to go. What remained of her life was neatly organised into boxes. She could imagine the ladies in the charity shop sorting everything out. Her photographs would be thrown away, not unkindly of course, but who would want them? Who would recognise the faces and the life that had gone with them? Would anyone take joy looking at the rather mean-looking black and white photographs she had taken in Paris all those years ago? She had agonised about throwing them away, when she had packed, but they still remained precious, even the business card at the bottom of the box from the young man who had said he was taking photographs of beautiful women. Whilst they remained in their shoebox, a little of her past life still clung to her, to dip into or hold onto before she died. But she was sure the cashmere coat that Seamus had given her for her sixtieth birthday would find a place in the charity shop window, together with the Crown Derby tea service that the removal men had packed so carefully. It was raining outside and without any bedroom curtains it seemed to noisily invade the room. For a moment her situation frightened her, but eventually she drifted into a troubled sleep.

She woke in the morning with the rain still dashing against the window. Hearing a car start, she was able to catch a glimpse of her neighbours, a young couple. They glanced up at her window before getting into their car, obviously on their way to work. Thankfully the phone was working and by mid-morning she was able to call an electrician. After explaining her situation and twice dropping her age into the conversation, she was able to arrange for him to come that afternoon. Within minutes he had repaired the fuse, pronounced the whole system a death trap, and warned her to have only one appliance on at a time. By the following week, Nancy had paid out a serious sum of money, but the house was now rewired and a replacement toilet graced the bathroom.

It felt like climbing up a mountain. Unopened packing cases still filled up most of the rooms. Windows stood begging to be dressed. She acknowledged this was a self-inflicted disarray, but she didn't have the energy to confront it.

Her neighbours on the other side were also young, leaving early in the morning and returning well after dark. They had called in once to say a cheery hello, but that was all. An elderly man with a Jack Russell dog walked by twice a day and, realising he was a man of habit, Nancy was able to be in her front garden at the appointed time. He introduced himself as Ray, from number forty-two, and was more than happy to chat and advise on dustbin men, shops, buses and so on.

'You should come down to the park, it's lovely, and you can even get a cup of tea at the weekends if you go into the rose garden. Patch loves it. You're not supposed to let dogs off the lead, but I do. There's nobody about much at this time of year.'

'I will sometime,' Nancy assured him, knowing that everything, positioning lamps, considering where to hang pictures, unpacking another box, was an effort that brought her no comfort. Her body felt heavy and stiff, with the constant niggle of arthritis in her joints. Reading was becoming increasingly difficult with failing eyesight, and whilst she had taken to wearing her glasses around her neck, she often couldn't find them in the morning. She had never been a huge fan of television, but once the electrician had got it to work at last that was a comfort.

It was a bright November afternoon. The weather man on the television had enthusiastically declared that it was unusually mild for the time of year. Nancy couldn't help but agree. The large overgrown holly bush in her small front garden looked sleek and glossy in the afternoon sun. She remembered Jack saying that a heavy crop of red berries meant a bleak winter. During their brief time together, they regularly spent time at his allotment where there were holly bushes, a variegated one with green striped leaves and one that flowered in the spring and bore abundant berries in the winter.

Jack had inherited his father's passion for gardening. At first, she remembered, he had been embarrassed to admit that he took his allotment very seriously, cultivating soft fruits, vegetables and flowers for his mother. After his father had died, Elizabeth had apparently expected them to dispense with the allotment, but he had been adamant that they keep it. He said he felt close to his father when he was working on his little plot and that the smell and the contents of the garden shed acted as something of a balm to his grief. Several times he and Nancy had made love in that shed, Jack declaring that probably his mother and father had done the same.

Nancy knew nothing of gardening, as Edna's only outdoor space had been a yard full of dustbins, prams and unruly children. Jack had taught her the importance of always having seasonal flowers and vegetables. She learned a little about cultivating lettuce and tomatoes. However, her greatest triumph was growing several sunflowers from seed.

As the memories invaded her mind, she suddenly felt ashamed that she hadn't taken a visit to the park, even though Ray and Patch had invited her several times. She looked at the clock; it was nearly three o'clock, with just enough sunshine left to aid her first excursion. Donning her cashmere winter coat and a pair of sensible shoes, she ventured forth, but not before turning back to find her walking stick, something she despised but that had become essential after her hip operation. Ray was already there and she could see Patch playing with another dog.

'He's found a friend,' explained Ray, 'but it's a bit strange, he was here yesterday and no sign of an owner.'

'He looks like something out of a Dulux advert,' remarked Nancy.

They both sat together on the bench, happy to bask in the remaining sunshine. Patch continued to run around while Scruffy, as Ray called the stray dog, came and sat patiently next to them.

'He's got no collar and no registration tattoo in his ear,' said Ray. 'I reckon someone's abandoned him.'

Nancy had no real interest in dogs. Seamus had a black Labrador when she first met him. It sat rather triumphantly in the back of his car when he did his rounds, but it was a family pet and so never invaded their private space. When it died, she felt that, on reflection, she had been a little mean in not encouraging him to have another, but at the time she felt their life hardly needed any more complication.

'I'll phone the RSPCA, I think,' Ray remarked, as the dog placed its paw on his knee appealing for attention with its big brown eyes.

'What is it?' asked Nancy, 'I mean what type?'

'It's either an Old English sheepdog or a Bearded Collie. Nice dog, whatever it is, it's very gentle.' The dog, sensing Nancy's interest, transferred its attention to her, resting its head on her knee and emitting a deep sigh.

'You've made a friend there,' chuckled Ray.

Nancy stroked the dog's head, conscious of the comforting warmth of its body as it pressed against her legs.

'They said it's going to turn very cold tonight,' she said, engaging Ray in a subject she knew he liked. Nancy had soon learned after they met that Ray prided himself on predicting not only the weather, but the state of the nation. His forecasts on both topics were usually gloomy, but uncannily accurate most of the time.

The sun had slowly faded, leaving a sharp nip in the air. Ray hailed Patch, insisting he sit before he attached his lead. The other dog watched with interest, then proceeded to follow them as they headed home.

'Go on, be gone with you,' Ray shouted. 'Go on, off you go.'

'But what will happen to him?' Nancy asked. 'It's going to be a cold night.'

'I'll phone the RSPCA,' Ray replied. 'Don't worry, he'll be fine.'

The dog continued following them, but at a distance. Then, finally sitting down in the middle of the pavement for a few seconds, it eventually stood up and turned and headed in the opposite direction.

Nancy felt the fresh air had done her good, and for the first time since she had moved in, she found the energy to prepare a proper cooked supper, rather than continuing with her constant diet of cake or biscuits.

She loathed sitting in the lounge, as she still hadn't put any curtains at the bay window and was aware that the television must illuminate her room to anyone outside. Retiring to bed early in the anticipation of reading a book, she glanced out of the window. The road was partially lit by a streetlight and, on the opposite pavement, there sat the dog, looking up at her bedroom window. *How in heaven did he know where I live?* she thought, amazed that he had the sense to sit on the opposite pavement so he could be clearly seen.

'Shoo,' she shouted, gesturing sharply. She closed the curtains and then arranged herself in bed, juggling a cup of coffee, a book and her glasses. She had recently found that she was reverting back to books that she had read many years ago, having never thrown away any that Jacob had bequeathed to her. The stories remained the same, of course, but her experience of life, thirty or forty years since, often brought with it a different understanding to many of the books she had read in her youth.

She became engrossed for a while, enjoying the warmth of her electric blanket that she had rediscovered in one of the removal boxes. But her thoughts kept reverting back to the dog. Finally, she left the comfort of her bed and looked out of the window again. He had gone. She felt relieved, but in a way saddened. Where, she thought, was he sheltering for the night?

In the morning she was not surprised to see that it had snowed. A light covering enhanced her view of the park, transforming the harshness of winter into something much softer.

Her central heating was working well, and she happily accepted that that she was beginning to feel at home. In Norfolk the milkman had still called, but Ray had explained that here this service had finished many years ago, so she had to stock up from the supermarket. At least the Sunday papers were still delivered, but far too big to be pushed through the letter box; instead she had suggested that the paperboy left them in a plastic bag on the doorstep.

As she opened the front door, the bag fell into the hall – closely followed by the dog. He looked cold and wet and weary, his coat in a tangled mess. He walked stiffly, and then sat down, obviously anticipating a harsh rebuke. But, as Nancy explained afterwards, it was like love at first sight. Not being used to dogs, she was completely at a loss what to offer him. Water? Milk, tea? He settled for water first and then warm milky tea. They shared toast and two boiled eggs. He had perfect manners and although he was obviously hungry, he made no attempt to gulp his food down, accepting the egg soldiers in a gentle, well behaved fashion.

She phoned Ray, but then remembered that he went to his daughters' on a Sunday, so she and the dog settled down to a leisurely day spent mostly in front of the fire. As he dried out, the smell that pervaded the house was decidedly doggy, but Nancy felt it was rather comforting. At least another living thing was sharing her space. Contrary to Ray's predictions, he made no attempt to chew anything or to sit on the furniture. He just seemed to take pleasure in following her about or sitting at her side or on her feet. Nancy reflected that it was a long time since she had felt so amused. He appeared to listen patiently to her comments, and always rewarded a kind word with a wag of his tail. When he scratched at the door, she nervously let him out again, impressed by his toilet training, peeing against the fence and pooing at the bottom of the garden.

That night he remained in the hall for a couple of hours, and then quietly joined her at the side of the bed. When she awoke, they rose together, carefully negotiating the stairs, and after he had completed his toilet, they shared a cup of tea. Opening a packet of digestive biscuits, she broke them into bite sized pieces, adding a little fried bacon and a whole fried egg. She speedily learned that it was easier for him to eat from a large bowl than from a plate. A vague memory of Seamus buying dog biscuits came winging back. When Ray arrived after he had picked up her phone message, he had already contacted the RSPCA. They had promised to pick the dog up if it didn't snow too much that afternoon.

But it did snow, and it was Wednesday before Fred from the RSP-CA arrived, apologising profusely for the delay caused by the bad weather. However, in those two days Nancy and the dog had bonded, making it difficult for Fred to get him in the van.

'Not unusual,' Fred remarked. 'Come on, boy,' he pleaded. Then, sensing it was useless, he lifted the dog expertly and carried him to the van in his arms. As the doors closed, the dog looked back at Nancy with eyes that reflected her own feeling of loss.

'What will happen to him?' she asked. 'Could I keep him?'

'He'll be fine. We'll check him out and if it gets nearer to Christmas and nobody has claimed him he'll go to the Bearded Collie refuge near Ilkeston. The lady who runs it is brilliant. She's as mad as a hatter, but loves dogs. She always manages to find them good homes. I would think he's about eight, and you can sense he's been well looked after. They're very easy dogs to find a home for as they are so appealing. They are always quite wise and very nimble, and you should see them jump and run. Phone us in a couple of days if you want and we can tell you what's happening to him. You never know, his owners might turn up, although it's strange they haven't reported him missing by now.'

This is crazy, Nancy thought as she closed the door. *What do I want with a dog? I can barely look after myself, but the house seems soulless again.* Not even the three Christmas cards gracing the window ledge could disperse her feeling of loss.

Although she was far from patient, she let two days pass before phoning to enquire about the dog. Fred wasn't there, but a young man explained that he had been traced. His owners had emigrated leaving him with a young couple who had subsequently split up. 'A very common story,' the young man explained. 'Couples split up and neither wants to take responsibility for the dog. The young woman said he had just run away, but that's unlikely as it's over sixty miles away. No, I guess he'd been abandoned, anyway, happy ending, he went off to the Bearded Collie Refuge. Rita, the Bearded Collie lady, is wonderful; she'll make sure he gets a good home.'

'How do I contact her?' Nancy asked. 'May I have her number please? If he's not happy, I'll have him.' Her voice cracked. 'Sorry,' she said, but couldn't continue.

The young man hesitated. 'Fred's back now, I'll have a word with him.' She sensed the young man putting his hand across the phone whilst he explained the situation to Fred.

CHAPTER NINETEEN

When Fred came on the phone, Nancy didn't allow him to speak, but declared immediately, 'I know you will think I am a silly old woman, possibly too old to care for a dog, but believe me, I could do it. Fred, I know it's a lot to ask, but I'd like to have him.'

'Good to hear from you, Miss Dupray,' Fred replied. 'It's a bit out of order, you understand, but I'll enquire. I'll speak to Rita and phone you back.'

He hung up and Nancy moved towards the kitchen. A cup of tea would while away the time, she thought, accepting that it would be unlikely Fred would contact Rita immediately. But the phone rang within minutes.

'Rita Bishop here. I understand you found the Bearded Collie and you've decided you could give him a home. You've never had a dog before, and you are over seventy?'

'Yes,' replied Nancy, somewhat surprised by Rita's interrogation.

'Why do you want a dog, Miss Dupray?' Rita asked, ignoring the niceties that usually accompanied a telephone conversation.

Nancy thought hard, hesitating for a second. 'Because I know I could make him happy. It wouldn't be the liveliest of relationships, but I felt that he is getting on a bit, like me. I'm lonely, but it's more than that. I honestly think he would be happy sharing my home. In fact, we would make it our home. Does that make sense?'

'Completely,' said Rita. 'I'll be with you in about two hours if that suits you. He can come to you on trial if you agree. It will help me out over Christmas and by the New Year you should both know whether it's a marriage made in heaven.'

Rita and dog arrived by the early evening, but Rita refused to stay for long as it was continuing to snow. She explained a few ground rules, gave Nancy a large bag of dog food, and, to Nancy's intense relief, seemed totally unfazed by her inexperience in caring for a dog.

'It's not rocket science,' she counselled Nancy. 'Be kind, but be the boss, that's all you have to remember. Any problems, just phone. Oh, and if you can afford it, I'd get someone to give him a good grooming occasionally. It's a back-breaking job if you're not used to it.'

The dog moved towards Nancy, then sat at her side, as if he too was listening to the lecture.

'We are probably about the same age,' Rita remarked, 'the wrong side of seventy I would guess, but hey, we're not dead yet, and if you're like me, not ready to die, far too much to do. The RSPCA are a bit tricky about dogs going to people of a 'certain age' but well, let's see how you get on. He seems very pleased to see you.'

Nancy rested her hand on the dog's head. 'I think he likes me,' she replied as she felt him lean more heavily against her legs.

'Well, have a good Christmas, and not too much pudding for the dog. We'll get together in the New Year over a bottle of your choosing.'

With that Rita Bishop left, cursing her small white van as it reluctantly coughed itself into life.

Nancy phoned her neighbour Ray immediately. 'I've got the dog,' she explained.

'Crazy,' he replied. 'Now don't you try taking him out in the snow, he might be nimble but you're not. I'll pick him up every morning whilst the weather is bad, and he can come with Patch and me. Does anyone know his name?'

'No,' she replied, 'but I've just thought, I'm going to call him Nimble.'

'Well, not a bad name for a dog,' Ray agreed, 'but let's make sure we don't end up calling you Tumble! Be careful you don't trip over him, especially going down the stairs.'

That night she slept more soundly than she had done for years, only woken by Nimble nudging her arm as she lay in bed. Over the next few days, her motivation came flooding back. New curtains were chosen from a catalogue, boxes unpacked, and a small Christmas tree purchased, complete with lights and decorations. Nimble was consulted on most of these decisions, as Mac her toy dog had been when she was a young girl so many years before. *Ray's right,* she thought. *I am crazy, but happily crazy.*

CHAPTER TWENTY

And there's a hand my trusty friend!
And give me a hand o' thine!
And we'll take a right good-will draught,
for auld lang syne.

– ROBERT BURNS, 'AULD LANG SYNE'

A few days later the weather turned mild again. With the pavements free from snow, Nancy and Nimble ventured the walk to Allestree village. Ray had assured her that she could take the bus most of the way back if it proved too much for her. The village lacked a big supermarket, but the local Co-op had survived, plus a row of rather upmarket shops and a Post Office. The walk was something of a revelation as several people stopped to chat when they saw Nimble, and a mother with a toddler asked if her son could stroke him. Nancy agreed, slightly worried that Nimble would bark at the small child, but on his lead, with Nancy by his side, he just sat, graciously accepting the attention.

Ray had suggested that she stop at the Methodist Hall where she could buy a coffee and cake. However, in the run-up to Christmas, the hall was offering not only coffee and mince pies, but Christmas lunch with all the trimmings. Having worked in a care home for so many years, the smell of a boil-in-the-bag turkey and overcooked Brussels sprouts came as no surprise, but nonetheless she and Nimble ventured inside.

The hall was quite joyous, Nancy thought, strewn as it was with old-fashioned garlands and a large overdressed Christmas tree twinkling in the corner. All the tables sported jam jars full of holly plus place settings with festive paper serviettes and Christmas crackers. She hesitated at the door, daunted by the room full of unfamiliar faces. A tall thin woman approached her, dressed in a twinset and pearls. She had the air of someone used to being listened to.

'Sorry, no dogs allowed,' she announced. 'You can leave him outside, but you can't bring him in.'

'I quite understand,' Nancy replied. Sadly admitting to herself that she had actually been looking forward to the boil-in-the-bag turkey with all the trimmings, she added, 'I'm afraid I wouldn't dream of leaving him outside.'

As she turned to go, a man several years younger than her shouted, 'Hold on a minute Joan, we don't turn people away, this is Christmas. Sit over here, love,' he instructed Nancy, 'here in the corner. What's his name?' he asked, bending down to stroke Nimble.

'Nimble,' Nancy replied.

'Well, Nimble,' the man replied, 'you can sit under the table.'

Joan gave them a withering look and returned to the kitchen with something of a flurry. Nancy sat down reluctantly. 'I don't want to cause a problem. I understand that rules are rules.'

'Rules, in my opinion, should occasionally be broken,' he replied, 'especially at Christmas. I'm Brian, by the way, and that's Joan. She's something on the local council, used to be a teacher, a complete nightmare. I'd like to say "but she has a heart of gold" but that would be untrue,' he added, laughing. 'Now, we can offer you a turkey dinner or the vegetarian option, followed by Christmas pudding or a mince pie and then, in my opinion the best bit, a piece of local Stilton and some Jacob's Cream Crackers. If you really want to push the boat out, there's wine too. My wife is in charge of the cooking, ably assisted by me and a team of enthusiastic ladies of varying ages and skills.'

The turkey dinner was as expected, but the Christmas pudding and the Stilton made up for it. Between waiting on most of the tables,

Brian returned to chat, establishing that Nancy had just moved into the area that she had left forty years ago.

'We're just around the corner. My wife Betty has lived in Allestree all of her life. Sorry,' he started to say. Then he sat down at the table. 'What did you say your name was?'

But before she could reply, he reached over and took her hand. 'It's Nancy, isn't it, Nancy Dupray, Jack's Nancy?'

For a second she froze. When the realisation hit her that it was Brian sitting opposite her, she replied, 'How did you know it was me?'

'It's the hair and the beret. I said to Betty in the kitchen, I'm sure it's Nancy. Now you sit here and we'll join you for a coffee in a minute, or would you prefer tea?'

'Tea please,' she whispered, 'Earl Grey if you have it.'

As she sat alone waiting for their arrival, she felt withdrawn from the jollity going on around her. Each table, which an hour ago had been laid so pristinely, was now a muddle of pulled crackers, remnants of mince pies and screwed up napkins. Nearly everyone was wearing a paper hat, apart from several festive souls who looked resplendent in red felt Father Christmas hats or reindeer horns. It was such a long time ago, she felt nervous to confront the past. She was sure her sudden disappearance all those years before had caused many people confusion and pain, and she was equally sure that to have to confront it again would cause her distress. Why was she here, she questioned herself? Seamus had said she needed closure, but she wasn't sure she was ready for it so soon.

She got up from her chair, aware that it could be possible to leave discreetly amongst the festive confusion. But Nimble was slow to respond, leisurely stretching himself as he emerged from under the table. She could see Brian returning, followed by a plump woman in an apron who she recognised at once as Betty.

'Now don't you run off,' Brian cried.

Betty now stood in front of her. 'My God, it is Nancy, the beautiful Nancy Dupray.' As the two women hugged one another, Brian encircled them both in his arms. 'We have a photograph of you and Jack at our wedding over forty years ago. It used to be on the sideboard.' Betty's voice trailed off, leaving the words 'used to be' hanging in the air.

'I have the same one,' replied Nancy.

'You looked like Jackie Kennedy,' Brian intervened.

Nancy laughed. 'That's what Seamus used to say. He used to tease me that I only put it on the desk so as to show off my Jackie Kennedy hat and my handsome boyfriend.'

They all sat down, including Nimble who appeared quite content to return under the table.

'Was Seamus your husband?' Betty asked. 'We did hear that Bill died many years ago.'

'Bill died twenty-five years ago and Seamus was, well, we never married, but we lived partly together for many years. He was a doctor. He died about ten years ago.'

'Come on, ladies,' Brian declared, 'if you're going to reminisce, I suggest our place this evening over gin and tonics. Although I bet you're still into wine, Nancy? You were the first person I knew who ordered a glass of wine in a pub.'

Nimble stretched, wagging his tail as he sensed conviviality in the air.

'What's his name?' Brian asked. 'Did you say Nimble, as in "Jack be Nimble"?'

'Well, yes I did,' Nancy replied. 'I'm not really sure if I ever thought about it, but it's kind of appropriate,' she laughed, 'Jack be Nimble.'

After lunch at the Methodist Hall, they had driven Nancy and Nimble home, insisting Brian pick her up that evening so that they could all have supper together. The house was on the other side of the park to hers, with views of the river. Nimble was also invited but would have to stay in the utility room, Betty explained, as she was allergic to dog hair. However, Nancy was touched to see that Betty had put a blanket and a bowl of water down for him when they arrived that evening.

'Can he have a biscuit?' she asked Nancy. 'I don't want him to feel left out.'

This was the Betty that Nancy remembered from all those years before. They hadn't been close friends, but Nancy had liked her, actually thinking at the time that she could have done better than Brian. But Jack was always loyal to Brian, although on occasions remarking that he sometimes felt uncomfortable with his conservative leanings.

When Nancy was finally installed in their lounge, Betty announced, 'Now we're going to eat on our knees Nancy, I hope that's all right. Brian will wheel in the hostess trolley,' she laughed as he made a face at her.

'The hostess with the mostest,' he remarked, negotiating his way from the kitchen to the sitting room with an elegant metal trolley laden with food. 'Please, girls,' he added, 'if I hear anyone mention diets, I'm off. It's Christmas, time for a bit of cheer. Now what can I get you to drink, Nancy? I do know a bit more about wine now, so there's a nice Chablis in the fridge, but I thought we'd start with a glass of champagne to celebrate your return.'

He hesitated, letting Betty continue, 'It's good to see you, Nancy, really good.' Overcome with emotion, Nancy fought back the tears. Sensing her distress, Brian cracked open the champagne.

'So, what's the toast?' he asked, passing Betty and Nancy a glass each.

Nancy's voice broke for a moment. 'How's Jack?' she whispered. Betty reached across, then shuffling from her chair, she knelt next to her. Gently grasping her hands, she replied, 'He's fine, Nancy. Fine, healthy, maybe not as happy as we would like to see him, but fine.'

'I don't want to get in touch, Betty,' Nancy replied. 'It's most embarrassing I know, but it's just good to know he's OK.'

'Well, if you ever want to catch a glimpse of him, Mary sends him shopping at Dennison's every Saturday morning whilst she has her hair done,' Brian told her somewhat triumphantly. 'Ten thirty on the dot, he's always there.'

'Enough,' Betty stopped her husband in his tracks. 'He's fine, Nancy,' she repeated.

Nancy allowed the tears to fall, but felt a massive sense of relief as she accepted that this was the reason she had returned. She had fought, trying to smother her feelings for Jack, but it had never truly worked. Seamus had understood, as she had understood his uncompromising love for his wife. Betty encircled Nancy in her arms whilst Brian joined them, putting a hand on each of their shoulders as they remained in silence for a few seconds. He broke the spell as he heaved Betty back onto her feet.

'Come on, ladies, drink that champagne and let's have some food, and, if you're up to it, Nancy, start to fill us in about the last forty years. Look, Betty's found that photograph of you at our wedding.'

'It's a lovely photograph,' Betty remarked. 'I can remember feeling a bit jealous when I saw you looking so elegant.'

'But you looked wonderful,' Nancy replied, 'I can remember feeling quite jealous when I saw you. Not only did you look radiant, but you had no complications in your life like Jack and I.'

'This is the best one,' intervened Brian, thrusting another photograph in front of them, 'Lucy with her snapped bra strap. If those breasts had burst free, what a sight for sore eyes that would have been!'

'Lucy, of course, I'd forgotten her,' remarked Nancy. 'She worked in the typing pool with Mary, didn't she?'

'Yes, that's right,' replied Betty, 'she married Stan. Do you remember Stan? Always the life and soul of the party. They had five kids. As the years went on she put on a lot of weight, but a lovely woman. She died a couple of years ago, the big C, very tragic. We see Stan occasionally, always with a grandchild in hand, he's a grand bloke.'

'And you, Betty,' Nancy enquired, 'how many children do you both have? I remember your little girl being born. In fact, didn't you bring her along to that Christmas party Jack and I gave?'

Betty took Nancy's hand. 'We don't have any children, Nancy. Our baby Alice died when she was only eighteen months old, just after you disappeared. We tried for more, but none came along. Things would be different now, there's a lot they can do, but in those days you just accepted it. But we do have seven nieces and nephews, and our god-daughter Sheila.'

'That's Jack's daughter,' Brian added. 'We're kept very busy, I can tell you.'

'Betty, I am so sorry.' She remained holding Betty's hand but reached out to take Brian's too. 'I'm so sorry. You were the perfect parents. But you are obviously the perfect auntie and uncle.'

'I remember that party that you and Jack gave, don't you, Betty?' Brian remarked as he passed Nancy another mince pie from the hostess trolley.

'I certainly do,' laughed Betty, 'you looked amazing and Jack's mum was there with, what was she called, your friend, Rosemary? I remember feeling how sophisticated it all was. The swinging sixties had finally hit Derby. And do you know it was the first time I'd met any Jamaicans. All that nonsense of you having black gentlemen friends. They were so wonderful, genuinely kind, made such a fuss of our Alice. Changed our opinions, Brian, didn't it? Enoch Powell with his, what was it called, "Rivers of Blood" speech, nasty piece of work he was.'

'It was the perfect party,' replied Nancy. 'I wonder what happened to Louis and Beatie, and all their children, and yes of course Bartholomew. It's all so many years ago. Jack and I had such fun getting it all organised.'

DERBY, 1968

Nancy had confessed to Jack that she hated Christmas, telling him about Edna's half-hearted attempts at turkey dinners. But as Christmas approached, they threw themselves into decorating the flat, creating an alternative Christmas tree out of a large branch sprayed silver and decorated with lights and baubles. Nancy covered every available space with holly from the allotment and different-sized white candles in an assortment of glass containers.

They decided impulsively on a party three days before Christmas, inviting all their friends, both agreeing that there would be none of Jack's relatives but definitely Elizabeth. Doug and his wife brought

mince pies from the pie shop. Rosemary brought plates of sophisticated nibbles; Louis, Beatie and Bartholomew provided ingredients
for a Jamaican punch, which consisted mainly of rum; and Betty and
Brian arrived with the much-admired baby Alice, who slept peacefully in the Moses basket that Jack and Nancy had bought her in London.
Jack was delighted that despite all the rumours about him and Nancy,
all the work colleagues they had invited arrived with their girlfriends.

As he ducked and dived, talking to everyone, sorting the music and
ensuring that his mother was comfortable talking to Agnes, he found
it hard not to keep looking at Nancy. Wearing a simple black cocktail
dress, black high-heeled shoes, bright red stockings and a black beret
decorated with holly and mistletoe, she was the complete belle of the
ball. She was like a genie that had been let out of a bottle, and for
the first time he felt she was completely relaxed. They served the hot
mince pies at ten o'clock and insisted that everyone sang carols.

Once the last guest had left, Jack swept Nancy into his arms. 'Marry
me, Nancy, it can only get better.'

'You're drunk, Jack French,' she cried, 'but maybe, maybe.'

They sat curled up on the sofa, finishing off some of the leftover
food and discussing what a magical evening it had been. Far better
than they had ever thought.

Nancy disentangled herself from a now sleeping Jack and rose to
draw the curtains. As she looked down, she saw an all too familiar
figure standing in the shadows.

Christmas and the rest of December passed peacefully, unlike the
New Year, which roared in with storms and bitingly cold winds. As
they coped with frozen pipes in their none too warm flat, Jack regaled
Nancy with renditions of 'I've got my love to keep me warm' and 'In
the bleak midwinter', belting the words particularly loudly when he
came to 'Earth stood hard as iron, water like a stone'. Regardless of
being clad in numerous sweaters and the need for copious hot water bottles, he was deeply happy taking care of Nancy. As February
approached the weather softened, and with it, he believed, came the
promise of a bright new future.

As the only apprentice at Rolls-Royce who could speak reasonable French, he had been asked to visit the large aircraft factory in Toulouse to discuss an exchange of apprentices. Personally, he hadn't thought it a very sensible idea, as the language was a big barrier. But he had been delighted to accept the invitation, which would also give him the opportunity to explore the city and absorb some of the atmosphere. Sitting in the cafés next to the river, watching the sun turn the stonework from grey to a rosy hue, he allowed himself to dream that perhaps he and Nancy could live here.

On his return, Nancy had seemed a little distant, even when he had given her the carefully chosen bra and French knickers he had brought her as a present. Eventually he had asked, 'So Nancy, what's the matter?'

She remained aloof for a moment, appearing not to understand.

'For God's sake Nancy, what's up?' He never liked to confront her as the difference in their ages made him feel a little on the back foot, no matter how many times she assured him she felt totally secure in his company.

She approached him, wriggling into his arms and brushing her face against his sports jacket.

'You smell delicious,' she said, 'tweedy, and oh so much my Jack.' Tears filled her eyes as she lifted her face to his and whispered, 'It's Bill, he's back. He's been back since the party, he was there that night after everyone had gone. I looked out of the window and he was there. Since then he's been there several times.'

'Why didn't you tell me?' Jack demanded. 'Because you felt I wasn't man enough to handle it? Thanks, Nancy, very flattering.'

'Don't, Jack, you know that's not true. I don't say it very often, because I know what it entails.' She hesitated, then savoured the words, 'I love you.' She turned away from him but continued to speak. 'I've never loved anyone before. Well, maybe Mac. And I burnt him on the fire at the Sloams', if you remember.' She laughed a little.

'And you don't want me to go the same way?' he replied, turning her sharply around so he could look into her eyes.

'In a way that's it, Jack, yes. He's dangerous, and it would be foolish to think otherwise.'

'Nancy, he's not very bright. He's a brute and Brian's dad says he's been in all kinds of trouble. We need to speak to Rosemary and Agnes, they'll know what to do. I agree that the police are pretty useless, but to be fair, their hands are tied. There is never any real evidence.'

'But there is this time,' Nancy interrupted, taking an envelope from the mantelpiece. 'This arrived yesterday, a Valentine's card, but look.' She held up a small piece of fabric. 'It's part of a dress he bought me when I was about ten. It was my favourite dress for ages until I grew out of it.'

'But is it his handwriting in the card?' Jack asked.

'I've no idea,' she replied. 'I thought of taking it to the police. What do you think?'

For a moment she panicked as Jack silently examined the scrap of material. *Does he need these kinds of problems at his age?* she thought. *He's bound to tire of it all.*

Jack looked up, oblivious to her distress. 'I'm going to talk to Brian. Mum's always said he's more streetwise than I am. Perhaps Rosemary too. Nancy,' he repeated, 'this is a shared problem and we face it together, agreed?'

'But why should you have all this?'

'More insults,' he replied. 'Because I love you and I am totally realistic as to what that means. I'm convinced that if we were married, that would be an end to it. Now come on, there are two more presents, and some chocolate and coffee and a large smelly cheese in my bag.' He walked to the window and drew the curtains, but not before glimpsing a figure in the shadows.

'He's not there, is he?' she asked.

'No,' Jack lied, as he watched the shadowy figure retreat down the road. 'He's not there; and if he was, what harm could he do to us?'

* * *

Brian was standing over him when he finally regained consciousness in the hospital. He only remembered the stifling fear of losing control, the split-second realisation that his brakes had failed. Then nothing, until he heard Brian's voice.

'You're going to be all right, Jack. Bits and pieces broken, but you're ok.'

He felt the trolley move and was aware that he was being wheeled down a corridor. Brian was walking next to him.

'They're going to patch you up, mate, you'll be as right as rain.'

The sign saying 'Operating Theatre' hovered briefly above him. The next time he woke, his mother was standing by his bed with Brian.

'You're ok, Jack, your brakes failed. You sailed across the red lights at the bottom of Queen's Road. Bit of tricky driving, that,' added Brian. 'You missed a lorry and a couple of pedestrians, and ended up hitting a wall. Bike's a bit of a mess.'

'Oh stop it, Brian, he's ok,' cried Elizabeth. 'You're alive, Jack, and lucky to be alive. Your leg is fractured, you've injured your shoulder, but the surgeons say you will mend.'

As she spoke, Nancy walked towards his bed. She didn't acknowledge anyone, but just stood looking at Jack, both hands pressed against her lips.

'I've checked the bike,' Brian continued, 'and the brakes have been tampered with. It's a clever bit of work, Jack, they appear frayed but... I know you had the bike MOT'd when was it, a couple of weeks ago? It's with the police now.'

Nancy knew that without a shadow of a doubt the culprit was Bill. Only the hushed voices of other visitors in the ward penetrated the silence that now surrounded Jack's bed. The realisation that both she and Jack were at the mercy of Bill's obsession caused her to grip the end of his bed in order to steady herself. She felt utterly alone, knowing she had unwittingly exposed Jack to unthinkable danger. A danger that she feared his youth and love for her would prevent him from acknowledging.

Seeing Nancy's distress, Brian put his arm around her. 'Come on, luv, come and sit next to this young man, he's in need of your loving care. Give him a cuddle. Well, maybe not, could be painful,' he laughed, in an attempt to lighten the situation.

'We must go.' Elizabeth rose and then kissed her son awkwardly, trying to avoid the drip and bandages that encompassed him. Then she turned and, kissing Nancy briefly, she held her eyes for a moment and said, 'Take care of him, please, he's all I have.'

Gathering up Brian, she turned at the exit to wave goodbye to her son, but he and Nancy were entwined and oblivious to her farewell. She felt a spasm run through her whole body, not of jealousy but helplessness. She had known only a little about Bill until today, when Brian had filled in some of the gaps. If the rumours were true, her son was in danger, but she had no option but to stand aside.

In many ways she admired Jack's passion for Nancy. She remembered the deep emotion she and her husband had experienced when they first acknowledged their love for one another. Those memories had sustained her through the years, even now making her blush when she recalled their delight with each other's bodies once they had relinquished their inhibitions. How sad it had ended; how bittersweet life could be. As they walked down the hospital corridor she felt Brian take her arm, and as she inclined towards him, tears flooded down her cheeks.

Jack healed remarkably fast. He insisted on returning to the flat rather than convalescing at his mother's, and whilst his relationship with Nancy remained loving, something of the carefree abandonment of the previous year had been lost.

When he returned to work and the day-to-day routine they had previously established was resumed, he felt less anxious, but he knew that he couldn't let this uncertainty continue. The police had examined the bike and agreed with Brian that it was possible that the brakes had been tampered with. However, they didn't appear to take his and Brian's concerns about Bill seriously. Nancy had spoken to Rosemary, who promised to lobby the Chief Constable, and an uneasy amnesty was established.

Jack had stopped using the word 'if' and now adopted 'when' during his discussions with Nancy about their future. He'd been invited by the Toulouse aircraft factory to spend a further two weeks devising the proposed apprentice exchange. Nancy had insisted that she was perfectly happy to stay in her flat whilst he was away, even though both Agnes and Rosemary had offered her a bed. At Brian's suggestion they had had a phone installed, and if Bill was seen loitering outside, Nancy had agreed to phone the police immediately.

CHAPTER TWENTY-ONE

*Do you like me more than you don't like me or
do you not like me more than you do?*

– SHELAGH DELANEY, *A TASTE OF HONEY*

ALLESTREE, DERBYSHIRE, 2011

Brian bent forward to fill Nancy's glass. 'My God, Nancy, it seems such a long time ago, but at the same time like yesterday. Don't you agree, Betty?'

'Yes, but wasn't that accident just before you disappeared, Nancy? I can't tell you how shocked everyone was, do you remember, Brian? And of course, Jack, well, he was devastated.'

Nancy clutched her glass. Then, taking a sip, she raised her eyes to meet those of Brian and Betty.

'I can't imagine, all these years later, how I had the strength to leave. I just blanked out the pain I realised I would be causing. All I knew was that I had to be focused. I only accepted later how scared I was, but I had to protect Jack, that's all that mattered.' For a moment no one spoke, until she continued, 'But tell me, tell me truthfully, please, how did Jack react? I never knew whether he hated me, or finally understood.'

DERBY, 1970

When Jack left for Toulouse the second time, he was confident that on his return he and Nancy would quietly get married and move away from Derbyshire, leaving behind the nightmare of Bill. He and Nancy both spoke a little French, and he had already started making overtures to his personnel officer about the possibility of his remaining with the aeroplane factory in Toulouse to oversee the apprentice exchange scheme. This was his third visit and he knew that he had begun to establish a good relationship with his French colleagues.

On his return he headed straight from the airport to Nancy's flat. He usually travelled light, but on this occasion he had bought Nancy a selection of gifts, including a pair of calf-length leather boots. He'd seen them at the last minute in the duty-free shop, and nearly missed the flight sorting out the right size. Two other packages contained lingerie, and a third chocolate and perfume for both Nancy and his mother. His hands were so full he clumsily rang the bell, rather than use his key. Nancy had known roughly the time he would be arriving, and he had been slightly surprised she hadn't been there to meet him. He waited impatiently for her to open the door, enjoying the fact that he was laden down with gifts.

When she didn't reply, he rang again, then finally, placing everything on the floor, he searched for his key. As he opened the door, he was surprised by how cold it felt. Then the realisation hit him. The flat was completely empty. Nothing remained apart from a large pile of magazines and a box containing his own clothes and belongings.

He wanted to sit down, but there were no chairs. He leaned against the wall in search of comfort, then, sliding to the ground, he buried his head in his hands and cried out for Nancy. His sobs wracked his body. He wanted to scream, to try and make sense of something that felt completely senseless.

Before long his distress turned to panic. Where was she? Had Bill hurt her? Was she even dead? He found the phone and made a series of calls, starting with his mother. She, Rosemary, Agnes and Brian were all equally shocked. Yes, they had all seen her recently, but no one had any inkling where she might be.

Finally, he left, leaving his luggage and gifts inside the flat. Unable to cope with buses, he took a taxi to the pie shop. It was Saturday afternoon, and only one customer was contemplating the depleted selection of cakes left on the shelves. When Doug's wife saw him, she immediately called her husband to take over. Then, putting her hand on Jack's arm, she led him into their own rooms at the back of the shop.

'She's ok, Jack, don't look like that, she's ok. She's not hurt or anything. She came in here nearly a week ago and said she was handing in her notice – leaving.'

'Leaving for where?' Jack mumbled in response.

'Not for where, Jack,' Doug replied, entering the room, 'but who with.'

'What do you mean?'

'It's hard, Jack, but she said she and Bill were going to get married. That they were moving directly to Germany. I tried to question her, we both did, but all she could talk about was how guilty she felt about leaving us in the lurch. She point blank refused to take the wages we owed her. We both kept on saying but what about Jack, but she seemed so remote, she just said, "It's for the best, he'll get over it." But yes, she was upset.'

Doug's wife picked up the story. 'I can tell you we were both really worried, so we contacted Bill on the Monday at the Foundry. It was lunchtime and he was having a kind of leaving do with his mates. He invited Doug along, I had to get back to the shop.'

'We went to the Nightingale pub,' Doug continued, 'quite a crowd of us. Bill seemed very cheery, his mates had clubbed together to buy him a stainless steel beer mug. You know the kind of thing, something you never use. There was a little speech and congratulations to him and his bride-to-be, and his new job, which sounded impressive. He wasn't ashamed to tell everyone how much he and Nancy would have over there.'

The bell rang and Doug hastily returned to serve in the shop.

'But Nancy wasn't there?' asked Jack.

'Yes, she was,' Moira continued, 'as Doug was leaving she arrived. You know what Doug's like, he adored Nancy. No, let's be honest, he really fancied her, but then so did lots of men. But he said she looked fine, she kissed him and told him she would definitely get in touch at some stage. She said she and Bill were destined for one another.'

Jack gripped the back of a chair. 'You know Bill raped her when she was only sixteen? After that she could never have kids of her own.'

'I know, I know, Jack, but sometimes destiny takes a funny turn. Nancy's a big girl, not far off my age. To be fair I don't think for a minute she didn't care for you deeply, but perhaps she was sensible enough to realise it wouldn't work out.'

'Crap, crap, crap,' Jack shouted. 'I'm sorry but that's absolute crap. He's a thug, he's bullied her, scared the shit out of her. Christ, how am I going to find her before it's too late?'

'Moira's right,' Doug said, re-entering the room. 'I did have a word with him, and he said – and I kind of believed him – that it was Nancy who had proposed marriage to him. He said he wasn't badly off and could take care of her. Maybe she saw what side her bread was buttered, she liked nice things.'

'Fuck you, Doug!' Jack yelled, his voice exploding into the room. 'Fuck you, Nancy wasn't like that!'

He left the shop, pushing past several customers waiting patiently to be served. He ran down the street, not clear where he was running to. As he turned the corner he saw Bartholomew approaching.

'She's gone,' he shouted, 'She's gone!'

'What do you mean, man, who's gone?'

'Nancy's gone, she's gone.' Jack's body weakened and he fell into Bartholomew's arms. Bartholomew held him, enfolding him in his arms. Then, rocking him gently like a child, he chanted in his rich Caribbean voice, 'Jack be nimble, Jack be quick, Jack jump over the candlestick. I'm not surprised she's gone, man, not surprised. She is something truly special, but I kind of guessed she'd go.'

'But why, but why? And with Bill!' Jack sobbed.

'Because it wasn't quite right, you know that, Jack, deep down. We all kind of knew that; Bill's a bad one, but…' He didn't finish, but heaved Jack back into a standing position.

'Now, I am going to take you to my place, and we are going to have a little drink.'

Jack was about to protest, but weariness flooded his body. Resting on Bartholomew, he allowed him to walk him to his flat. It smelt warmly of spices. A large ginger cat immediately sat on his knee, and after two large tumblers of rich brown rum Jack fell mercifully into a deep sleep.

Leaving the flat, but not before instructing the cat to 'take care of Jack', Bartholomew jogged down the street to the telephone box to call Elizabeth.

She sounded distressed but relieved Jack was safe. 'I've been searching for him. Thank god he's with you.'

'I'll need some help getting him home,' Bartholomew laughed, 'I've knocked him out with rum. Come in about an hour, and we'll pour him into your car.' His kindly laughter acted as a balm to Elizabeth's fears that she might be the catalyst that had provoked Nancy's sudden departure.

Jack could not remember his mother and Bartholomew getting him home, although Bartholomew's rhyme kept recurring in his dreams. 'Jack be nimble, Jack be quick, Jack jump over the candlestick.' He dimly remembered something about if you did 'jump over the candlestick' there was good luck on the other side.

He sought out Bill's colleagues at the Foundry and they only endorsed the story that he had returned to the factory in Frankfurt where he had worked on and off since the fifties. He took a flight to Germany within the week, but with no German and nothing much to go on, the journey had been depressingly fruitless. He managed to trace Bill's ex-wife, but she was unhelpful, virtually showing him the door. The factory manager knew of him, but the personnel officer was reluctant to proffer any information on his whereabouts, suggesting that as the company had other branches all over Germany, he might write to Head Office.

On his return, Jack was called into the Chief Engineer's office and given a warning that if he didn't return to work in a proper manner, he stood the chance of being dismissed. He felt numb. Each day it was a challenge to get out of bed. He wrote to the Head Office in Germany, but there was no reply. Rosemary, Agnes, all his friends cautiously offered help, but they agreed that she must have left of her own accord, and they too felt a degree of hurt and rejection.

ALLESTREE, DERBYSHIRE, 2011

Something of the Christmas cheer had gone out of the room as Betty had related Jack's reaction to Nancy's departure. On occasions Brian interjected, but was tempered by his wife, Nancy realised, to avoid causing her any offence.

'So understandably you all thought I was a selfish bitch. I guessed that, perhaps that's what I wanted you all to think.'

'No, Nancy,' Betty replied, 'some might have thought that, perhaps even Brian,' she added, smiling at her husband. 'But honestly we were all genuinely worried. Bill was a brute. We all knew that. What we did try to do was care for Jack as best we could. So, your turn, my luv. What did happen?'

DERBY, 1970

Shortly after Jack's departure for Toulouse, Nancy had a call from Elizabeth inviting her for coffee at the Kardomah café in Derby. Nancy had no illusions about the invitation. She knew it would be to talk about Jack. In a way she experienced a feeling of relief; her own anxiety troubled her constantly.

Elizabeth looked at her watch. Nancy was late, but then she saw her walking swiftly down the hill towards the café. Her appearance was one of total simplicity; a beige trench coat, a pencil skirt, knee-length boots and her extraordinary hair tied back under a brown beret. As she entered the crowded café, Elizabeth was aware that several people looked at Nancy with obvious admiration. She apologised for being late, explaining that she had been delayed by the crowds standing outside the Derbyshire Building Society. There were rumours it had crashed, and angry shareholders were holding a protest meeting.

They ordered coffee and Elizabeth pressed Nancy to try one of the cinnamon teacakes. 'Jack used to love them,' she remarked.

'He still does,' Nancy replied softly, 'and am I right in thinking it's Jack we're here to talk about?'

There was a long pause as people jostled between the tables.

'I want you to consider leaving him, Nancy. Believe me, I have no doubt how much you care for him, and I have no doubts about his feeling for you. But,' she took a sip of her coffee, 'can you understand? I feel it will end in disaster. Jack told me the history of Bill and the appalling tragedy of why you can't have children.'

She hesitated again, giving Nancy the opportunity to reply, but she remained silent. 'He's so young, Nancy. When you see him with Betty and Brian's Alice, you can see that he'd make a great father. And, will Bill ever...'

'Ever what?' Nancy spoke for the first time.

'Ever leave you alone?'

'I don't know, Elizabeth, I don't know.'

'I know it's wrong to ask you this, Nancy, but I feel so helpless. I keep asking myself what my husband Jack would have said.'

'And what do you think he would have said?' Nancy asked quietly.

Elizabeth pushed her teacake to one side. 'I don't honestly think he would have disapproved of your relationship. In fact, I know he would have admired you. But then, Nancy, he's not here to protect you both. I'm deeply sorry to have to suggest you part. I know I run the risk of Jack never forgiving me, but...' She stopped speaking, and the two women remained silent as the bustle of the café continued round them.

At last Nancy spoke, her voice barely audible above the noise. 'This is the first time I've been truly happy, Elizabeth. Well, perhaps that's not entirely true. As a young child growing up, Bill did everything in his power to make me happy. He protected me and loved me, but then it all went wrong and the legacy of that now threatens our lives.

I have no doubts whatever that Bill tried to injure Jack on his bike. Jack's solution is for us to marry, leave the country, and I want that too, but something tells me that running away is not the answer. God forbid, it might actually be the most dangerous thing to do. I agonise over it every day. When I wake every morning it's the first thought in my mind.' They fell silent again.

'What does Rosemary think?' enquired Elizabeth. 'I respect her opinion.'

Nancy hesitated and then replied honestly, 'I don't really know, but I think Rosemary imagines Jack is too young for me. I am concerned at times. I worry that Brian and Louis might take things into their own hands if Bill makes another move, but Jack has a very level head. He once told me when we first met that you described him as an "old soul". You're right, Elizabeth, he is, and that's why I love him so deeply.' Tears filled Nancy's eyes and she struggled to find a handkerchief in her bag.

'Let's go,' said Elizabeth. 'We can find somewhere more private. I'll get the bill.' She rose from the table and went in search of a waitress.

When she had settled the bill and returned to the table, Nancy had gone. Only her damp handkerchief remained beside the uneaten teacake.

Nancy walked as if she were in a trance, picking her way through the lunchtime crowds until she reached the library. She'd spent so much time there over the years; reading, borrowing books, avoiding odd-looking characters who used it as she was now, as a sanctuary against whatever problems they might have.

Two leather armchairs remained in a corner opposite a picture by Joseph Wright. One chair was already occupied but the other was vacant. She sank into it, finding refuge within its sturdy arms. She gradually regained her composure, comforted by the warmth of the interior and the familiar smell of old and new books.

Since Jack's accident she had constantly considered her options in preventing a tragedy. The risk of anything happening to him was unthinkable. He was so young; wise, yes, but also vulnerable. She had always known she had no right to put his life at risk. Dramatic as it sounded, she accepted Bill would always be a threat. If she disappeared, would they both try and find her? Or should she – could she bear to submit to Bill? It seemed unthinkable, but maybe it was the only way out.

Out of sheer exhaustion she dozed for a while, until a member of staff enquired if she was feeling unwell. Startled, she realised she must have been there for longer than she had imagined, and needed to return to work.

As she hurriedly left the library, she still felt utterly exhausted. She had no plan, and had made no decision, but as she stepped into the afternoon light, there stood Bill.

His surprise at seeing her was only equal to her horror at seeing him. For a second she thought she was going to faint, but he steadied her with his arm. She remained motionless, and then she inhaled deeply, clearing her head, allowing those previously unthinkable thoughts to merge into the only possible answer to her dilemma.

'I need to talk to you urgently. You offered me marriage once, do you remember?' she cried, in a voice verging on the hysterical. 'Do you remember?'

Still holding her arm, he replied softly, 'Of course I do.'

'Well, I accept, do you understand? I accept, providing you never ever go anywhere near Jack again.' She felt him release her arm. 'This isn't love,' she continued, 'Well, not love for you, do you understand? Do you understand?' she cried, her voice now loud enough to raise interest from passers-by.

'I do understand, Nancy, you have my promise, and believe me, I will make you happy.'

CHAPTER TWENTY-TWO

---

*The love of gardening is a seed
once sown that never dies.*

– GERTRUDE JEKYLL

NORWICH, 1970

As Nancy boarded the train for Norfolk ten days later, she accepted that she was leaving behind a web of deception. She had been shocked by Bill's compliance to all her demands. She sensed his fear that if he made one wrong move, she would destroy his fantasy. He never mentioned Jack, and although she had made her motives very clear, he avoided commenting on her decision.

In fact, a silence consumed them, only broken when the logistics of the situation demanded they speak to one another. Bill cleared her flat in less than a week, and at her request, all but a few possessions were to be put into storage. The storage company was given details of their supposedly new address in Germany where Bill had worked over the years. He handed in his notice at the Foundry, explaining he was returning to Germany, leaving a false address where he could be contacted if anyone wanted him. He invited a small gathering of workmates for a drink prior to his departure in order to announce his new job and his forthcoming marriage to, as he described her, his childhood sweetheart Nancy.

Nancy returned to work, fighting great waves of sadness as she endeavoured to leave everything in good order. Each evening she visited her friends in turn; Agnes, Rosemary, Carol, Louis and Beatie, Bartholomew, and Brian and Betty. Unbeknown to them, she took her leave over a cup of coffee or tea or a glass of wine, and deposited a small gift on a window ledge or table as she left. She felt that no one was suspicious; maybe a little curious at her unexpected visit, but as Jack was away, they imagined she was simply lonely.

Leaving Doug and Moira Cowlishaw was the hardest, as she felt she was abandoning them just as the business was expanding. They had started to rely on her judgement, but she knew at the same time that Moira was a little wary of her husband's huge admiration for her, and there had been occasions when she sensed that if she had given him any encouragement, things would soon have got out of hand.

So it was with Moira that she had her final conversation, explaining how deeply upset she was to leave them so suddenly. But she had decided that her decision to marry Bill and to move to Germany was the best for everyone. Moira was appalled, telling her she was a complete fool. But Nancy could detect that despite her genuine response, she was possibly relieved that her own life would now remain intact.

She considered visiting Elizabeth, but that was an indulgence she dared not allow herself. Elizabeth would have to deal with Jack's loss, and the less she knew about her departure the better.

As she boarded the train, the sound of her phone ringing as she finally left her flat still resounded in her ears, swirling around her head like the snatch of music that remains long after first being heard. It was a persistent ring, imploring her to answer, but she had resisted, knowing it could only be Jack calling from France.

Bill met her at Norwich station, and they drove in relative silence to a village a few miles out of town. She had never considered what the intervening twenty years had brought to him. He had spoken briefly of his life in Germany, of his twin girls, and of his divorce. The only other information she had gleaned was when Bartholomew, who worked at the Foundry too, occasionally mentioned him. Apparently Bill had progressed to being foreman, and then manager of a department within the factory.

The firm he was now working for in Norwich, he now explained to Nancy, had been trying to persuade him to join them for some time.

'Company car,' he said as he opened the door to let her in. 'They can't seem to do enough for me. You wait until you see the house they've rented for us. All part of the deal.'

She resented the word 'us'; it implied so much. She felt as if she was on a tightrope, one false move and she could tumble down. The sinister thought was that no one knew where she was, and apart from Jack, hardly anyone would want to find her.

The Cowlishaws would certainly not be slow in coming forward to explain to anyone who cared to listen why she had left. Would Agnes and Rosemary pursue her? But then why should they? Sadly, she accepted that they were mature enough to read all the signs correctly, and possibly respect her for the decision she had taken. She guessed they would have talked to not only Jack but also Elizabeth. She knew the hardest thing would be not to contact Beatie; they had become such intimate friends. *Whatever*, she reflected wearily, *the dice have been cast*.

Bill sensed her discomfort. 'Relax, Nancy, it's going to be fine. You'll love the house.' He rested his hand on hers. 'And don't you worry, honest, all I want to do is to see you smile, like you did all those years ago. Perhaps we could have our own live Mac?'

'And call him Bullseye?' she had replied bitterly, uncertain whether he would get the reference.

But she knew that she had to meet him halfway at some stage if she was to avoid disaster. They pulled into the village and turned into a small estate of pre-war houses. Each one had a mock-Tudor façade, similar to Jack's mother's house, and a large front garden. Theirs was at the end of a cul-de-sac, and whilst the front garden was spacious, it looked somewhat neglected. The house, however, was clean, warm and well-furnished.

'It's three bedrooms and a box room,' Bill explained. 'The central heating's only just been put in. The owners are away for two years. What do you think, Nancy? Come and look at the kitchen, it's quite modern. It's quite posh, don't you think? There's even a shower in the bathroom and one of those newfangled things, we had one in Germany, a bidet I think they call them.'

Nancy wandered about. She felt an intense claustrophobia, which only started to subside as she became in tune with the house, feeling in a strange way that it understood her plight and was endeavouring to protect and welcome her. It was posh, as Bill had observed, if posh meant lots of highly polished reproduction furniture and overstuffed sofas, but sadly not elegant like the Sloams' house in Duffield.

'It's fine, Bill,' she eventually replied. 'A bit big for two people.'

'Now I'm going to put the kettle on,' he said. 'I've bought Earl Grey. You go and choose your bedroom. I'm happy to go anywhere, even the box room. You choose first.'

She turned and looked at him for the first time since he had picked her up at the station. He was, she guessed, in his fifties, but he looked older, forlorn even. For a second her heart went out to him. 'Thanks, Bill. Believe me, I'll do my best if you leave me for a while to...' Her voice trailed off.

'You take all the time in the world, Nancy. I promise you will have nothing to fear from me, ever. Do you understand? Ever,' he repeated.

'And Jack?' she questioned, daring to break this newfound intimacy.

'Goes without saying,' he replied. 'I understand Mary Blunt is waiting in the sidelines for Jack. He'll be fine, Nancy.'

She felt he wanted to continue, but turning, she climbed the carpeted stairs and left him in the hall. Then she walked from bedroom to bedroom, finally deciding that the second-largest bedroom, overlooking the back garden, was the one she would choose.

Sitting on the bed, she was aware of a totally new emotion sweeping through her body. Jealousy was something she had never experienced, but the vision of Jack holding and caressing another woman shocked her intensely.

She conjured up his presence, feeling his young, strong body against hers. The earthy smell of his sweat after they had made love. The joy of trivial conversation as they caressed each other. These precious intimate experiences she had now brutally banished from her life. She was shocked that in the rush to escape from the dilemma, she hadn't realised that the thought of Jack rekindling these emotions with someone else would torment her for perhaps the rest of her life.

Bill appeared at the door. A cup of tea was balanced on a tray with a plate of biscuits, and in his other hand he carried her one of her suitcases.

'I knew you'd choose this room,' he said, 'because of the garden. Check out that top drawer in the bedside table, a little present. We'll eat later if you want, these biscuits will keep you going.'

He placed the tray on the ornate dressing table, then left the room, closing the door behind him. She pulled open the drawer of the bedside table as instructed. It revealed the gift, roughly wrapped in tissue paper. As she unfolded the layers, she discovered a soft white toy dog. Unlike Mac it was professionally made and had embroidered black eyes and nose, together with a soft pink collar. She placed it on the bed and for a while just looked at it, examining its shape, not so dissimilar from her childhood toy. Then as the light from outside faded, she unpacked her small suitcase, which Bill had placed outside her door. Donning the underwear Jack had brought her back from France, she slid into bed. She hugged the toy dog close to her heart.

Bill left her completely alone. Each weekday morning he would rise at seven, take breakfast and leave a cup of tea outside her bedroom door, then go to work. Often he returned as late as seven. There were no shops near the close, so he bought boxes of food every few days. They ate together in the evening, after which Nancy would retire to bed. She had insisted on bringing all her books and Bill supplied a daily newspaper.

Years later she accepted that this period was probably her long-overdue nervous breakdown. From being found wandering in the Orphanage, to the savage attack by Bill, to the Sloams departing, she had balanced each trauma precariously one on top of another, like a pile of children's bricks. Finally, they had come crashing down, leaving her overcome with fatigue, not knowing how to start building them up again.

At first she had felt so depressed that she avoided even going outside. She avoided all contact with the neighbours. She imagined that she must have appeared somewhat of a curiosity, living with a much older man in a house that was far too big for the two of them.

But eventually the garden beckoned her with an invitation to prepare it for winter. She found a healthy supply of garden tools in the shed, as well as gardening manuals. Bulbs saved from previous years rested dormant in shallow wooden boxes. Her gardening skills were at first very limited. Her only experience had been with Jack at his allotment. Undeterred, she tackled the lawn, the borders and an abundance of rose trees and shrubs, becoming more confident. At the bottom of the garden behind the shed and a rather dilapidated greenhouse, she found a large area that had been abandoned. Blackberry bushes fought with nettles, thistles and a patch that had been used for garden refuse. In amongst this chaos were several fruit trees, revealing that it had once been a well-cared for orchard.

Bill had repeatedly told her that there was no need for her to find a job. 'You just relax,' he would say, 'you've worked all your life, take it easy for a time, we aren't hard up.'

And besides, she didn't want to work. The idea of creating a new life was abhorrent to her, but she accepted she needed a project, and the garden became her lifeline. By late afternoon, after working all day, she was exhausted.

When it rained, she read through all the gardening manuals Bill had bought her. At the weekend he would drive her into Norwich, leaving her to browse and shop. Occasionally they would go to the cinema. On Sunday their routine extended to a lunchtime meal at a local pub close to the Broads. Bill liked to watch the boats, happily assisting anyone who needed help. Nancy would walk along the towpath watching the wildlife. On her return, Bill would often introduce her to the people he had been chatting to, enjoying their surprise, she knew, when he announced, 'This is my wife, Nancy.'

'I'd like it if we did get married, Nancy,' he said occasionally, 'but no rush, your call as I promised.'

While she gardened, she devised a plan. It kept her sane and alleviated some of the pain. In a year or maybe two, she would leave Bill. Hopefully by that time Jack would have embraced life without her. She had a little money so it would be no problem to disappear again, perhaps to France. If Bill did try to follow her, at least she would be alone and without complications.

She was immensely relieved that Bill did not pressure her to get married. In fact, she felt that the pent-up sexual desire he had once felt for her had now somewhat diminished. Occasionally at night she experienced a kind of nervousness as she heard him go to his room, but she had resolved that if he demanded sex, she would not fight him. They had struck a kind of deal and she would stick to it for as long as she felt she could.

As winter set in and the days grew shorter, she spent less time in the garden. Bill had suggested that they go to a hotel for Christmas, but by mid-December she had developed an all-consuming bout of flu that kept her bedridden over the Christmas period. Bill was as attentive as she would allow him to be, but she was relieved when he returned to work.

She accepted that she had become a recluse, and whilst Bill made no demands on her, not even questioning her daily routine, she felt that she had somehow become a prisoner in the house. Once in a while, someone knocked on the door, but she never answered, even though it must have been obvious that she was at home. She ate very little, denying herself food as a kind of self-inflicted penance.

Towards the end of January, the weather turned mild and she ventured into the garden. Her spirits revived a little when she saw the bulbs she had planted were pushing their way through the ground, and a carpet of snowdrops had miraculously erupted amongst the apple trees. She opened the door to the garden shed and there, leaning against the wall, was a bicycle. Tied to the handlebars was a Christmas tag with the message, *Happy Christmas Nancy – love Bill xxx*

Inevitably, she had a sense of anger whenever Bill offered an act of kindness. She found it hard to react with any warmth to his often clumsy attempts to please her. But the bike immediately evoked a feeling of joy. It was obviously brand new, a kind of retro old-fashioned Raleigh with a basket. Instead of the normal black, it was painted in two-tone dark red and cream. Not really dressed for the occasion, she nevertheless wheeled it out into the cul-de-sac, aware there were probably several pairs of eyes watching her.

She remembered it had been Bill who had taught her to ride a bike. She must have been about eleven years old. She remembered him holding onto the back of the seat as she started off, then releasing his grip once she started to pedal, running alongside her crying, 'Keep going, Nancy, keep going.' When they returned home, he would regale Edna with stories about how his little prodigy was doing, although in truth it had taken her a few weeks to learn. Later, when she had lived with the Sloams in Paris, she had often borrowed a bike from one of the students at the university. *But you never forget*, she thought as she sailed down the road and out of the cul-de-sac, realising at the same time that she had left the kettle on the hob and the house unlocked.

But she was free. The rush of cold air filled her lungs, forcing her to cry out as she inhaled noisily. She cycled around the small estate, aware that she probably only had fifteen minutes before the kettle ran dry. But it was enough, and by the time she had returned to the house, she had planned her first excursion. When Bill arrived home, he found the bike in the hall.

'I was nervous it would get stolen from the shed,' she explained.

'So you like it?' he enquired eagerly. 'It's brand new. I've checked it out so you should have no problems with it.'

'Not even with the brakes?' she replied sharply.

She had never asked him if he had tampered with Jack's bike, knowing that if she did, the reply would only put a bigger barrier between them. He hesitated for a few seconds, then turned and walked silently into the kitchen. She followed him, and as he filled the kettle at the sink she continued, 'It's a very fine bike, Bill, thank you. I know I'll enjoy riding it.'

He remained silent, but she sensed that as she left the room he might have been crying.

Bizarrely, Nancy felt that this was a life-changing moment. She cycled every day, often battling against extreme weather conditions. She bought maps of the local area and kitted herself out in warm waterproof clothing. When she felt a glimmer of joy return, she would don one of her many berets, pulling it firmly but unfashionably over her ears as an act of defiance against her previous life.

When she returned home, she was ravenously hungry and was happy to accept Bill's offer of a fish and chip supper. Since they had left Derby, she and Bill had rarely engaged each other in long conversations. She knew he was nervous of trying to discuss any kind of future together, but now she felt a kind of masochistic pleasure as she offered up nuggets of her day's adventures on her bike. His gratitude was palpable, she thought, similar to a dog gazing up at its owner when spoken to kindly.

He would often arrive home with a small gift, a thermos flask, or a pair of hand-knitted gloves or socks. She felt her strength returning, but it was a new kind of strength, one that demanded she stop wasting her life and embrace a future that could eventually be of her own choosing.

Jack's presence had begun to fade. She acknowledged with sadness that he must have started to embrace life without her. She took comfort in thinking that their passion would remain with her, and told herself that she would cherish the memories, grateful that, no matter how briefly, she had experienced a relationship that was so special.

Bill offered her the local paper each night, and by chance she saw a vacancy at a residential care home that she had passed only the day before on her bike.

She often became completely lost while she was out cycling and had to turn to her maps to plan her route home. However, after a few weeks of intensive exploring she began to get a real feel of the area, the landscape and its moods. She and Jack had loved Derbyshire, but now she began a love affair with Norfolk, charmed by its meandering Broads and close proximity to the sea. She would often alight at one of the impressive churches that had been built by one of the rich wool merchants, and huddle in the porch eating her sandwiches. The churches were often unlocked and while she loved to explore inside, she found it was always slightly warmer in the porch.

As she cycled further inland one day, the landscape became more undulating, and when she mounted a steep hill, she saw what appeared to be a stately home in the valley. It was nestled at the bottom of a long drive which descended steeply to the front of the house. Directly in front of the house was a large courtyard where several cars were parked, then a small lake surrounded on two sides by weeping willows that dipped their swaying branches like elegant fingers into the sparkling water. To the other side she could see formal gardens that finished as the land rose, giving way to fields of sheep. The winter sunshine cast soft shadows from the skeletal trees, where Nancy spotted patches of snowdrops and the occasional winter primrose. The gates to the drive were open and a large sign announced that this was Montgomery Residential Care Home for the Severely Disabled.

As she dismounted from her bike, she could see a small group of people walking towards the lake. One was in a wheelchair pushed by a nurse. The others were clad in a mish-mash of warm, brightly-coloured clothing. They formed an ungainly procession as they trailed behind the wheelchair. Each one, Nancy could see, had some kind of disability. As she watched, one of the older girls broke into an awkward run, and on reaching the lake threw a handful of bread from a bag into the water. Immediately a group of ducks charged swiftly towards them, followed by two equally fast swans. She could see that everyone was now laughing and throwing more food into the lake.

Enchanted, she stood watching, unaware that she was blocking the drive. Startled by an approaching car, she moved to one side. As it passed slowly by her, the driver sounded his horn, waving at her and to the excited little crowd that were now awaiting his arrival. When the car stopped, he stepped out, accompanied by a large black dog. Then, indicating her presence at the top of the drive, he encouraged everyone to wave. One young man removed his scarf so that he could be seen more clearly. She returned their waves, propping her bike against the hedge so that she could use both arms. When they finally stopped and drifted back towards the house, the man in the car turned and gave her a final salute as he followed them to the entrance.

The incident, rather than lightening her mood, made her feel strangely depressed as she cycled home. More than depressed, she decided, more a feeling of shame that she had become so self-obsessed, so uncaring. Whatever her thoughts about Edna, she had always been a genuinely caring person. She had also discovered that Bill would put himself out to help anyone, despite his rough reputation. Regardless of his divorce, she knew that he still sent money for his daughters. She didn't usually venture into his bedroom, but one morning she had gone in to turn off the radio he had left on and was surprised to see how many photographs of the twins he had on his chest of drawers. Sometimes a letter would arrive with a German postmark, but he had never invited her to share its contents.

She remembered that Jack, Brian and their entire crowd were constantly involved in helping each other out, creating a natural camaraderie, from which she had remained aloof. It was only at Cowlishaw's Pie Shop that she wanted to get actively involved in helping in a purely unselfish way. Agnes, Rosemary and Louis all gave of themselves unsparingly. But what, she thought, had she given in return? Jack had once said her style, her *joie de vivre*, enhanced a room as soon as she walked into it. But she acknowledged as she rode slowly home that that was not enough, and she had the capacity to do better.

The job advertisement in the local paper said that the Montgomery Residential Care Home was looking for an assistant to the manager. The job required first-class secretarial skills together with the ability to help in the day-to-day running of the home and its activities. Previous experience in residential care would be helpful but not essential. Please write in full stating experience etcetera. She wrote her letter immediately, and two weeks later she received an invitation to attend an initial interview.

She spent the two days beforehand in the library researching the home. In the local newspaper archive, she waded through articles about it from the past ten years. They mostly covered local fundraising activities, one of which, she discovered, was a coffin race down the drive. The local Round Table built makeshift coffins and mounted them on a kind of chassis with wheels. Then, dressed as undertakers or skeletons, they raced them down the drive. After reading several articles she discovered that the trick was not to overshoot into the lake, but judging by the photographs, this was difficult to accomplish. However, surprisingly enough, no one seemed to have been seriously hurt and she could imagine that Jack and Brian would have been serious contenders, given the chance.

She was reluctant to tell Bill that she was applying for a job, but after he discovered her reading about the home, she explained.

'I'm not surprised,' he told her, 'a bright person like you needs something more than this. If you work out there you'll need a car. Don't worry, we'll sort it.'

Her interview was just before midday, and the only local bus that stopped there was first thing in the morning. Nevertheless she refused Bill's offer to take a morning off work and take her, instead deciding that she would cycle, arrive early and have time to smarten herself up. She chose the twinset and pearls look, with the added bit of glamour of a cream blouse. On arrival she changed from pumps into high-heeled court shoes and swept her hair as best she could into a ponytail. Her only make up was a little mascara and the dull red lipstick she always used. She was nervous, as she knew her appearance often worked against her, alienating her from some women, whilst having the reverse effect on some men.

The room showed signs of a hurried lunch, with plates and coffee cups piled up on a table together with a platter of leftover sandwiches. On the other side of a long table sat two women and two men. The elder of the two women rose to greet her, announcing kindly that she was Joan Bishop, the manager, and that the job she had applied for was to be her assistant. Nancy warmed to her immediately. She appeared to be in her mid-fifties; large but not overweight, she created an air of confidence. Her no-nonsense approach and obvious capability were in direct contrast to the female personnel officer, who appeared timid and out of her depth. Joan waited for the personnel officer to take the lead, but when it appeared she was uncertain of her role, Joan herself introduced the other two male members of the panel.

'Miss Dupray, this is Dr Seamus Ferguson, our doctor in attendance at the Home.' He was a similar age to the manager, and rising immediately, he offered her his hand. She vaguely thought she recognised him. He then in turn introduced the fourth member as the Chairman of the Board of Governors, who remained seated but offered his hand across the table. As she stretched somewhat uncomfortably to grasp it, she was aware of a strong smell of mothballs pervading from his tweed suit.

Later Seamus was to tell her that she had done an inspiring interview. She had obviously done her research and had an impressive work pedigree. She was also the only candidate who was articulate enough to express why they actually wanted the job.

Nancy explained that she had left her previous employment to move to Norwich and was about to be married. The Chair of Governors immediately asked if she had been married before, and if she had any children. Slightly shocked, she replied that this was her first marriage, and that regrettably she was unable to have children. Caught in a moment of slight confusion, she was about to add more when the manager assured her that this wouldn't be necessary. 'In fact,' she added, turning to both the personnel officer and the Chair of Governors, 'I don't think we are officially allowed to ask those types of questions.'

Seamus and Joan were keen to make her understand that whilst working as an assistant, she would be in daily contact with residents who were often very unwell, both physically and mentally. Nancy knew her reply was sincere. She wanted more than a nine-to-five job. Without the prospect of a family, she wanted to become involved in something where she could work in an environment that would call on all her existing skills and allow her to develop others, and become a member of what she had gleaned from her research was a very happy community.

During the interview Nancy had been aware that the Chair of Governors was not on her side. Whilst she was convinced that she had performed well, she had felt it had been an uphill battle. As she started to take her leave, she felt deeply saddened that it was extremely unlikely that she would return.

When she had shaken hands with everyone, Seamus suddenly exclaimed, 'Aren't you the girl on the bike? About three weeks ago at the top of the drive?'

Laughing, she admitted she was, and now casting discretion to the wind she added, 'And I came on my bike today.'

'Not in those shoes, surely?' Joan asked.

'Good God, you must be hungry,' Seamus added, 'We've kept you over the lunch hour. Here, take some sandwiches. I recommend the egg and cress, a bit squashed but still delicious.'

Joan was laughing, and Nancy sensed that these two had a special relationship that she would have enjoyed sharing. Seamus insisted on wrapping a selection of sandwiches in several paper serviettes balanced on a paper plate.

'Have a picnic,' he suggested. 'If you go into the garden it's out of the wind, and often catches the sun. You'd be welcome to sit in the main hall, but you would undoubtedly be pestered by our delightful guests, some of whom would not be averse to helping themselves to your sandwiches.'

A week later a letter dropped through her door and to her amazement and immense excitement it offered her the position. She discovered later that despite the Chair of Governors' opposition, Seamus actually wielded the most power in the Home. Whilst he was not resident, he divided his time between his own practice and the Home. He was hugely popular with both patients and staff, and well-respected by the rest of the Board. Joan told her eventually that he had said he would resign unless they offered her at least a trial, overruling all further objection.

Amazed by her success, Nancy spent the rest of the day saddened by the fact that she had no one to share her good news with. At midday, Joan Bishop phoned to congratulate her, explaining that the three-month trial was only a formality, but she had forgotten to mention that they required a third reference. Again, she said, just a formality, a reference from someone who had known her personally for a number of years and could vouch for her character.

'Maybe a doctor, or a family friend? Quite honestly,' Joan admitted, 'I hardly see the point, but certain members of the Board are sticklers for detail and...' but the rest of the sentence was left unfinished, as if she felt that at this stage discretion was called for. Nancy agreed to arrange for a reference and then they settled a starting date in ten days' time.

She sat by the phone, silently contemplating problems she hadn't realised existed before the phone rang. She had explained that she had come to Norfolk to get married, but the implication of that statement hadn't really sunk in. Secondly, who could she ask for a reference? Even after her mysterious departure she knew that Agnes or Rosemary would help her, even Doug's wife. But it was less than a year since she had taken the decision to cut herself off from everyone and that decision had been to protect Jack. She felt, after all the turmoil, it was too early to risk it all for the sake of a reference.

Then she thought of Elizabeth. Would she help? She hadn't known her for that long, but surely she would bend the rules just a little. She continued to sit by the phone, and then eventually she called directory enquiries. Gathering her thoughts, she dialled the number to the primary school where Elizabeth was headmistress. As she expected, Elizabeth wasn't available, so she arranged to phone back rather than leave her number, although she did leave her name. When she did phone back, shortly before four o'clock, Elizabeth answered the phone.

'Where are you?' was her first question. 'Are you in England? Are you all right, Nancy? I have been so worried, genuinely, I have been so worried. Jack was distraught, I felt so guilty. Where are you?'

'I stayed in England. We never went to Germany. But let me explain why I am phoning. Rest assured it's not going to cause any problems.'

Elizabeth remained silent while Nancy explained about her new job. She didn't mention Bill, but did stress that she wanted her whereabouts to remain a complete secret. When Elizabeth started to question her, she silenced her abruptly and simply repeated her request for a reference, giving Elizabeth the address to send it. Elizabeth didn't hesitate to agree. They could both sense that their conversation was drawing to a close, and yet there seemed an ocean of things they wanted to say.

'Are you all right, Nancy? Please tell me. Believe me, I do care.'

'I know you care, Elizabeth,' Nancy replied, 'and I am fine. It hasn't been easy, but hopefully this job will make a difference. Please, I am trusting you not to reveal to anyone where I am living.'

'And Bill?' added Elizabeth. 'What of Bill? I never believed you married him.'

'I didn't,' replied Nancy, 'but I intend to. And what of Jack? How is Jack?'

She had promised herself she wouldn't ask, but the words just tumbled out. She could hear Elizabeth's intake of breath.

'He's ok now, Nancy. In fact he and Mary have just announced their engagement. I feel it's rather too soon.' Again she took a deep breath, but before she started to speak again, Nancy bridged the gap by thanking her. Then, without waiting for her to continue, she gently put down the phone.

Jack, she thought, *Mary's not the one, give it time.* She sensed a feeling of inertia sweep through her body. She was powerless to help him. No matter how painful, they had to forge their own separate lives.

CHAPTER TWENTY-THREE

You better shape up, 'cause I need a man
And my heart is set on you

– 'YOU'RE THE ONE THAT I WANT', FROM *GREASE*

Nancy and Bill were married just a month after she started working at the Home. She had explained to Bill formally that for her credibility at the Home she needed to get married. She had anticipated that he might be angry at her seemingly cold approach to something he had expressed longing for. On the one hand she felt a little safer than before, since at least a small group of people knew she existed. If he turned on her, she would leave, feeling reasonably confident that her job didn't depend on her getting married. Yet she was still nervous; she had never allowed herself to forget that she was on thin ice, and the memory of him punching her in the face before raping her all those years ago remained like an indelible ink stain in her mind. Fortunately, he never appeared to drink at home, and she never sensed he returned home drunk.

Thankfully, his reaction was just the opposite to what she had feared.

'Nancy, my love, you have made me the happiest man alive. You'll see, I'll make a loving husband for you. I know you thought I was old once, but I was young, stupid – no, wicked, I know. You'll see, you won't regret it. Now you tell me what you want. Shame Edna's not with us, she'd have been proud.'

She wanted to reply, 'But what about Jack? You weren't young or stupid then,' but she held her counsel. This whole exercise had been to protect him, and she didn't want to risk endangering him again so soon.

'You make the arrangements, Bill, I'm so busy. Something simple, and then perhaps a few days away. I've never been to Brighton, might be nice.'

'Anything you want, darling,' he replied, tossing the word into the air for the first time. 'Anything you want, darling, you just have to ask.'

After that he continued to call her 'darling' and she decided that it was a very small concession for her not to object.

She adored her position at the Home and she happily embraced all aspects of it, feeling that at last she had an alternative home, a family and a purpose. There were thirty-five residents, but the Home also served as a day centre for local communities, so there was a constant flow of people passing through. She had never come into contact with mental and physical disabilities before, but with the help of Joan and the rest of the staff she soon learned the best ways to understand the needs of the residents. Seamus always displayed great compassion, mixed with a droll sense of humour, when tending his patients.

The day before Nancy's wedding, Joan arranged a tea party for the residents and staff. Seamus made a short speech, after which he presented her with a large multicoloured crocheted bag made by the handicraft group. As he passed it over, he whispered in her ear, 'They want you to use it on the day, but I've explained that it might not go with your dress.'

'It will be my bouquet,' she replied, to his obvious surprise.

She was conscious that it appeared rather strange that she had not invited anyone to the wedding and would only take a long weekend for the honeymoon. Bill had wanted her to invite some of her work colleagues, but she had argued that after only a month it was too soon to single out special friends. He seemed to accept the fact that she wasn't interested in the details. Deliberately, all she knew was that the ceremony would be at the registry office in Norwich, followed by a small buffet reception at the Grand Hotel afterwards for a few of his friends.

It was April, but apart from a few showers the weather was fine. On the morning of the wedding, Bill placed a bouquet of white roses on her breakfast tray together with a card that said, 'to my precious Nancy, all my love Bill'. She dressed in the same outfit she had worn to Brian and Betty's wedding. For a moment, when she stood calmly in front of the mirror, she saw Jack by her side. Fighting back the tears, she grabbed the crocheted bag and then descended the stairs to find Bill waiting at the bottom. With him was his best man David, a workmate.

'David's going to drive us,' he explained, and through the window she saw David's blue Ford Capri decked with white ribbons. The journey to the registry office seemed surreal, conducted in virtual silence. Nancy watched many of the Saturday morning shoppers acknowledge their wedding car with warm smiles, which she found it impossible to respond to, leaving it to Bill to give a cheery wave. When David helped her out of the car she thanked him, fully aware that her body language must have left him wondering about the true circumstances behind their wedding.

As they approached the registry office, a newly married couple was descending the steps, surrounded by wedding guests all jostling to throw confetti and congratulate the bride and groom. Nancy stopped. She knew she could just turn and walk away; it didn't have to be this way. Then she felt Bill's arm gently helping her forwards, and she allowed herself to be led into the registrar's office. Letting the words and responses flow over her, she tried to convince herself that the ceremony meant nothing; she was only doing it to protect Jack.

On leaving the office, Bill enquired why she was juggling the large crocheted bag with her bouquet.

'It's to bring me luck,' she replied, 'like a horseshoe.'

Years later she was to find the one photograph that David had taken of them as they walked down the steps of the registry office. The highly coloured crocheted bag dominated the picture, as if protesting against their ill-starred union.

In the afternoon they travelled to Brighton, where Bill had booked them into a large Edwardian hotel. Their room was on the front and had a large bay window from which they could see the sea. It was dusk when they arrived, but the streetlights illuminated the crashing waves and the seagulls soaring above the turbulent sea.

They ate dinner in a crowded dining room served by an army of waiters. She felt sad that Bill was obviously not at ease, and gently helped him with ordering the wine. They hardly spoke, apart from Bill's clumsy attempts to tell her how beautiful she looked.

She had resigned herself quite calmly to the fact that this was the night that Bill would take his conjugal rights, and had resolved that she would try to comply as best she could. But now the reality struck home. If she resisted, would he attack her as he had done all those years ago? How long was she really prepared to submit to this power he had already established over her?

She slipped into bed first, aware that she was a little drunk. Then, as Bill appeared from the bathroom, she wanted to laugh when she saw his striped pyjamas. He'd buttoned up the jacket, but it strained against his stomach and the white cord of his trousers swung from side to side as he walked.

Everything was awkward, his kisses, his fondling of her body, but the worst was his constant murmurings of love and desire. Eventually he heaved himself on top of her, parting her legs, and then struggling with his pyjama cord, he gripped his penis and thrust it between her legs. She braced herself, ready for the final penetration, but he fumbled and sweated, cursing and swearing, until he finally rolled off her and onto his side. She remained still and silent until finally she heard his breathing become more even, and she was aware that he was asleep.

Her relief was palpable. She rose and stretched, feeling every muscle relax as she washed herself in the bathroom. Then, pouring herself a glass of water, she drew back the curtains slightly and watched the sea change colour as turbulent clouds swept across the full moon.

In the morning she arose and dressed early. Leaving him in bed, she went out and walked along the front. It was cold and the wind whipped her face. A few people were walking their dogs, but apart from that the whole seafront was deserted. On the way back she felt exhilarated by the wind behind her, pushing her along. As she approached the hotel she saw Bill sitting at a table in the window of the hotel dining room. When he saw her, he waved, and she saw relief spread across his face. As she entered the hotel, a waiter took her coat and led her to Bill's table.

'Here you are, sir,' he reported, 'I've found your bride. Are you in for the full English, Madam? Bacon, eggs, mushrooms and sausage or a kipper if you'd prefer it?'

She returned Bill's anxious smile. 'The full English and a pot of coffee please,' she replied.

They spent a peaceful day exploring Brighton and, while that night they shared a bed, it was the last time they ever slept together. On their return their routine reverted to normal. Bill was sometimes absent until late in the evening. Nancy suspected he might have a companion, but she finally felt that he was no threat to her.

When she explained the relationship to Seamus years later, he had startled her by saying how very poignant he felt it was that Bill had desired her for all those years but then been unable to make love to her. 'A complete blessing for you, Nancy, I accept that, but sad for Bill.'

She had been shocked at the time, but then accepted that for right or wrong, she had made a deal to protect Jack, and she could only be thankful that when Bill's dreams hadn't quite materialised the way he'd hoped, he had continued to keep his side of the bargain and treated her with love and respect.

Nancy realised that she was an enigma as she drove around Norwich in her bright yellow Citroën 2CV that Bill had so lovingly bought her. He had admitted that he thought it the worst possible choice of a car, and it did prove to be a complete nightmare. Nancy even nicknamed it Cauchemar. But she loved it with a fierce passion, enjoying the notoriety of driving around with the top down, her hair streaming in an unruly mess of curls behind her.

Surprisingly, after her marriage to Bill, her life fell into shape for the first time. She felt her circumstances were intensely personal, but acknowledged that the quizzical glances she received from neighbours, work colleagues and strangers whenever she appeared in public with Bill gave her a frisson of satisfaction. She was young, disturbingly attractive and intelligent, with a natural elegance that suggested good breeding, and yet she was married to a man much older than her who displayed none of these characteristics.

NORWICH, 1975

Nancy felt that Bill was relieved to have slipped into middle age. He'd become overweight and spent most of his leisure hours in front of the television or with his workmates at the pub. Occasionally they would go to the cinema together or shopping at the weekend, but that was the full extent of their relationship.

Although they shared the close proximity of living in a house together, she no longer experienced any fears when he was around. Only once had she been jolted into the reality of the situation again, when she left the cinema late one night with a young nurse she had made friends with. As they edged through the crowds to get to the car park, she saw Bill in the shadows. She guessed he was searching the crowds to catch a glimpse of her. A dull fear had swept through her body and she tried to push it to the back of her mind, but without success, and it haunted her mind for many months.

What now surprised her was that she had no desire to escape. Her life was fulfilling, and she wasn't bogged down with what she saw as the minutiae of domestic life. Her sexuality was on hold as far as she was concerned. She accepted that admiring glances were essential to her wellbeing, and enough to satisfy her femininity.

His biggest pleasure, she knew, was when she shared her day with him over a meal in the evening, or when she invited him to the Home to help with some of the charity events. Bill was a favourite with all the residents, who enjoyed his working-class banter and genuine kindness, and he showed a natural affinity with their disabilities. For several years he took on the role of Santa Claus at the Christmas Fayre.

On one occasion as Nancy and Joan looked out of their office window, watching Bill help Seamus and a couple of inmates erect the summer marquee, Joan commented quietly, 'That Bill of yours is as strong as an ox, Nancy. God knows what we'd do without him. But,' she continued, 'but we do all wonder, my dear, why you married him.' She paused, waiting for Nancy to respond. When nothing was forthcoming, she put her arm around Nancy and murmured, 'I'm sorry, Nancy, that was out of order. Bill's a lovely bloke, it's just that we all sometimes wonder. You know what people are, me included.'

'I married him to save my life, Joan,' Nancy quietly replied, turning her head to meet Joan's gaze. 'One day I will tell you the story, but the time's not right, not yet, for his sake as well as mine.'

Bill had spent the whole evening helping with the marquee and all the paraphernalia of the Fayre. Afterwards, he, Nancy, Seamus, Joan and a couple of the nurses had all gone for a final drink at the pub in the village. Seamus had left quite early as although he had a full-time housekeeper taking care of his wife, he'd explained to Nancy that she just loved to sit quietly with him before bedtime. On occasions she could be quite lucid and talk about the past.

Bill had bought a round of drinks and insisted that Seamus accept a large bag of pork scratchings for Bess, his black Labrador, who appeared rather depressed that she was leaving the gathering so soon.

'Why doesn't he put her in a home?' Joan remarked.

'What, the dog?' Bill had retorted.

'No,' Joan had explained as they all laughed, 'his wife. It's hopeless. It's a degenerative disease that started after she had their little girl. A great shame, he's a remarkable man.'

'Bloody right, Joan,' Bill replied, 'bloody right, he's a real gent.'

Nancy turned away, always slightly embarrassed by Bill's enthusiastic comments. But as she did, she was aware that Bill was slumping forward. His head abruptly hit the table, knocking over his beer. Both the nurses flung themselves into action, laying him down and pumping his chest. Nancy ran into the lane to see Seamus' car disappearing over the brow of the hill. She screamed, but it was too late. When she returned to the pub, Bill was dead.

In the aftermath, she experienced such intensely violent emotion that she had to divorce herself from work and friends for a while, until she came to terms with what she could only describe as a huge weight being lifted from her shoulders.

She explained later to Seamus that the day Bill died, she had felt her youth had finally drawn to a conclusion and the woman in her broke free, scattering the past behind her. Those who knew her thought that she was suffering from intense grief, but it was not grief. It was a deep guilty secret joy.

As they had had no real common ground, she was unsure of whether he had left a will. But not surprisingly she couldn't find anything. What startled her was how little he had in his bedroom. Photographs of his daughters, a photograph of their wedding, and a bedside drawer full of bits and bobs. Even his wardrobe was only half-full, and his chest of drawers held just a motley selection of underwear, socks and sweaters. All his life seemed to fit into one black plastic dustbin liner.

She wrote to his daughters immediately, finding an address on the back of an envelope. Inside was a brief letter, written in German. It had never occurred to her that he spoke German, but then it had never occurred to her to want to know anything about his life.

After the funeral Joan had asked her if she had heard from his daughters, as it was obvious they had made no attempt to attend or send a wreath.

'He didn't have much to do with them,' Nancy had replied. 'He never even talked about them.'

'But I thought Eva had just had a baby? And what's the other one, Heidi, he told me she was a nurse.'

'Bill told you… When did he tell you? He never spoke about his daughters.'

304

'Sorry, Nancy, but he did. He occasionally showed photographs to Seamus and me, and I think some of the patients too. I sensed he was proud of them. I thought… oh, I'm sorry, but I thought you knew.'

Her first reaction was to be angry. Later, though, she told Seamus, she just felt ashamed, humbled, deeply sorry that she hadn't been compassionate enough to just enquire, even once, about his family. A sense of guilt often engulfed her as memories resurfaced of when she was a child and he a young man. How his kindness had protected her from the harsh reality of her situation.

When the revelation had sunk in, she turned to Joan, saying, 'Now's the time.' Briefly, she told her story, asking her to share it with Seamus too.

'Both Seamus and I sensed there was something. Seamus was about to tease you when Bill told us about his granddaughter. You know Seamus, the glamorous granny line. But I told him not to, and he agreed that it might not go down too well. You poor dear, you mustn't blame yourself in any way. You were remarkably brave, and he was happy just to be in your presence, anyone could see that. It's a terrible story, but I'll be honest, we'll miss him. At the end of his life he was able to bring a bit of happiness into many of our patients' lives. Plus he was possibly one of the best Father Christmases we've ever had. Let the past slip away, Nancy, don't make the mistake of carrying it around like heavy baggage.'

She acknowledged that Joan was right, and eventually found comfort when she organised a headstone for his grave. It read:

In loving memory of William Dodd
From Nancy Dupray and Montgomery Residential Home

CHAPTER TWENTY-FOUR

Oh! What a tangled web we weave
When first we practise to deceive!

– SIR WALTER SCOTT, *MARMION*

ALLESTREE, DERBYSHIRE, 2011

Relating her story to Betty and Brian had been easier than she thought. It was a huge relief to have finally been able to put the record straight.

She was now warm and cosy in bed, with the copious nightdress Betty had lent her wrapped around her body.

'It's flannelette,' Betty had told her, 'you can't beat it.'

'We're Darby and Joan,' Brian had added, 'both in our winter flannelette night attire. I did suggest Betty buy some babydoll ones but it didn't go down too well.'

They had insisted that she stay the night. With Nimble snoring at the foot of the bed, Nancy felt a sense of wellbeing that she hadn't experienced since Seamus had been alive.

Unlike Bill's funeral where just a handful of people were in attendance, Seamus' funeral drew hundreds, so much so that it was managed like an event, with organised car parking and speakers relaying the service to those standing outside. With Bill she had been supported by a circle of friends endeavouring to help her cope with a grief she didn't feel, but at Seamus' funeral she stood alone, squashed into a corner at the back of the church. Only a small circle of friends had known that she had been his partner for over twenty years, and for the sake of his family even they continued the pretence of not publicly acknowledging Nancy and Seamus' relationship.

As she drifted into sleep, her dreams rested on her life with Seamus. She had known, possibly even before Bill's death, that she found Seamus attractive. She adored his sense of the ridiculous and his ability to engulf everyone with his Irish charm, although his serious side was equally attractive. He regularly discussed his patients, helping her to understand the causes of their disabilities and how best to make their lives more fulfilled. She loved the way he would sometimes jokingly seek her out, prefixing his words with a 'Miss Nancy'. 'Miss Nancy, you are looking particularly beautiful this morning,' or 'Miss Nancy, please don't flash those green eyes at me, it's not good for a man of my age,' or, getting Joan to endorse his comments, 'Now Joan, don't you think Nancy's shoes are the chicest things you have ever seen?'

She in turn would often engage him in quite heated discussions about the latest book she was reading or film she had seen. After Bill's death she had been obliged to leave their rented house, and, under Joan and Seamus' guidance, she was able to lease a house in the centre of Norwich, and even to find a lodger whose rent helped to top up the shortfall in her finances. But it was Joan who inadvertently drew them together. It was a Friday morning, and Seamus phoned to say he would be late as he had a problem and wouldn't be able to do his rounds until eleven o'clock.

At lunchtime Joan had explained to Nancy that Seamus' dog had died. 'It was old age. She was fifteen, but still a shock, they were constant companions. I've just seen Seamus sitting in the garden round the back. It's freezing cold out there. Be a luv and go and see if you can cheer him up and get him to come inside, we don't want any more deaths.'

Nancy remembered putting on her coat and taking an extra coat and scarf for Seamus. As she silently approached him, he had been holding his head in his hands, and his shoulders were shaking gently. As he became aware of her presence, he looked up and blew his nose, wiping away the tears that clung to his face.

'It's only a bloody dog, I know, but she was my constant companion. She was forever faithful, always pleased to see me. In a strange way she shared my life totally.'

Nancy hesitated, unsure of how to respond, before placing the coat over his shoulders. She wrapped the scarf around his neck and finally reached for his hand. Immediately he lifted it to his lips and gently kissed it. They sat silently for a moment, and then as he turned his head towards her, she reached out. Taking his head in both her hands, she kissed him softly on the lips. For a second he didn't respond, then a sense of pent-up emotion engulfed them both, and they embraced with a passion and a love that remained the foundation of their relationship for the next twenty years.

When their relationship finally began, they set down ground rules. Seamus would never contemplate leaving his wife. He loved her dearly and Nancy accepted this without question. For a while his wife had been admitted into a psychiatric hospital, but despite a constant cocktail of drugs, her condition remained unstable. At home, Seamus explained, she was content living in her own world, occasionally engaging in the lives of her children when they returned home. The children had accepted her growing dissociation and saw their mother as 'special'. So instead of institutionalising her, Seamus juggled a series of carers and housekeepers, and as the children grew older they also took on some of the responsibility for their mother's care. They both agreed that the children should be kept unaware of their father's new relationship. They would share their lives, but as discreetly as possible.

Her life with Seamus had been different, but they had also created a home together. He usually spent at least two nights during the week with her and, when the children were not at home, all of the weekends. In the autumn they always took a holiday, usually to a city such as Paris or Berlin where they became Dr and Mrs Seamus O'Connor.

It had been a happy twenty years, Nancy reflected. Although she never came into contact with Seamus' children, she shared their successes and failures with him. At Christmas she helped decide on their presents and stocking fillers, and on their birthdays she agonised with their father over what present would be suitable.

Several of Seamus' closest friends were privy to their relationship and as the years wore on, Nancy was automatically included in invitations to dinner and trips to the theatre. Joan was the most supportive, and when she retired, Nancy was appointed as manager of the Home.

Her life for the first time took on a normality that she had never thought possible. Her job was demanding but her life with Seamus gave her the energy to embrace, enjoy and revel in its challenges.

Nancy woke the next morning to the sound of cups being rattled in the kitchen. Nimble had disappeared and within minutes Brian knocked at her bedroom door.

'Are you decent?' he asked, 'I'm coming in with a cup of tea. Nimble's outside peeing in the snow. The garden's fenced, he can't go anywhere.'

'Wonderful, tea in bed. Seamus was a great one for tea in bed, although it was usually me who made it,' declared Nancy.

'Sensible man,' replied Brian, 'but I have a problem that Betty will not attempt to get out of bed without at least two cups of tea.' He placed the tray beside the bed. 'Enjoy, and don't think about getting up until you smell the bacon cooking for breakfast.'

Nancy glanced around the room. Photographs of nieces and nephews hung on the walls. A selection of china owls sat on a shelf and Brian's cricket trophies filled a cabinet beside the fitted cupboards. The floral lined curtains matched the bedspread and a dainty dressing table groaned with toiletries. Betty had provided her with a towelling dressing gown together with a charming selection of towels and face cloths.

The smell of bacon wafted into Nancy's room, but as she donned the dressing gown Betty opened her door. Juggling a cup of tea in her hand she sat down on the side of the bed.

'I can't be doing with mugs,' she laughed, 'me mum always liked porcelain and so do I. Sit down, Nancy luv, I just want five minutes with you before Brian starts bossing us about. Did you sleep well?'

'Perfect,' she replied, joining Betty on the bed.

'It's just… Nancy, forgive me and if you feel I'm prying just stop me, but Bill… did he continue to… well, abuse you?'

'If you mean sex, surprisingly no. Was I scared of him? At first a little, but I had to protect Jack. It seems crazy now, but there seemed no one to turn to. Yes, I could have asked Rosemary and Agnes to help but that wouldn't necessarily have protected Jack. Elizabeth asked me to leave, and that's what I did.'

'My God, I didn't know that till yesterday, Nancy, and nor did Brian. Jack was beside himself. I feared for him at one stage. Brian and I pushed Mary onto him, I don't mind admitting.'

'Breakfast in five minutes, ladies,' Brian shouted up the stairs, 'ready or not.'

Nancy laughed. 'He's so lovely.'

'Well, he has his moments, but yes, he has a good heart. I keep telling him he's like a bottle of wine, he improves with age.'

'I didn't know Jack had gone to Germany looking for me. Times have changed, the police were hopeless. I was a "domestic" in their eyes, I don't think that would be the case now. I can still remember carrying around this overwhelming fear in the pit of my stomach that something was going to happen to Jack. I really did believe, and still do, that Bill was capable of murder. I'm still ashamed to say what a relief it was when he died.'

Betty placed her cup and saucer on the bedside cabinet. 'I'm not so sure, Nancy. Yes, times have changed, but it's taken a long time, and you still hear of women being stalked. What about that case in Belgium where some bloke kept a young woman in a cellar for years? Bill could have done that to you, nobody would have known. I'm not what you would call a feminist really, not the strident kind, but men still have the upper hand a lot of the time.'

'You're right,' Nancy replied. 'Things have changed but not enough. I saw a lot of cases in my work, Betty, you'd be shocked. Mental cruelty as well, which can be as terrifying as physical.'

'If you girls are not down in two minutes I'm going to eat all the bacon,' Brian shouted.

They both burst out laughing, and descended the stairs carefully carrying their cups and saucers.

The table was laid to perfection with china cups and saucers, linen serviettes and a formidable selection of cut-glass jars of jams and marmalades. Brian stood at the cooker brandishing a metal spatula. 'Right, get ready for the full English.'

'We've just been chatting about Bill. Nancy was brave, Brian, truly brave; I was saying even though times have changed women can still be at risk.'

'Not just young women,' Brian replied. 'Have you told her about Stan's grandson? Lovely lad, he's gay, and about a week ago he and his partner were accosted by a gang of thugs, and he ended up in hospital for a day. Yes, things have changed since we were young and mostly for the better, but there's still a way to go. Now, two sausages or one Nancy?'

'This is just so perfect,' exclaimed Nancy, 'a real treat. I'm sorry I'm not dressed. It makes me think of Seamus actually, he loved breakfast. He said that for him it was the best meal of the day.'

'So was he the love of your life?' Betty asked.

Nancy sat down. 'Well, yes,' she replied, 'but Jack second and Nimble definitely third.'

When Brian ran Nancy and Nimble home later that day, Nancy felt that the house welcomed them back in a way she hadn't experienced before. It felt like home, or at least a place where she knew she could now live with confidence. Both Brian and Betty had expressed a sincere desire to remain friends. Brian had volunteered to put up a couple of much-needed shelves in her kitchen. They were going to visit relatives over Christmas but insisted that on their return they would pop round straight away to see her.

'You must come to the Methodist Church,' Betty had suggested. 'It doesn't matter, luv, if you're of their persuasion or not. It's about people supporting one another. They have a little evening social gathering once a month, and during the summer we have a couple of bus trips out to places. There are jumble sales and fundraising, that sort of thing. We've even got one or two young members with kids, which is lovely.'

After Brian had dropped her off, Nancy placed the Dennison's carrier bag they had given her on the kitchen table. Betty had persuaded her to take home some of the leftover buffet food from the night before. There was also a Christmas card and a small gift labelled 'not to be opened until Christmas Day, love Betty and Brian' at the bottom of the bag. Even though she had assured them that she would be fine, they were concerned that she would be on her own over the festivities.

'You must decide what you really want for Christmas,' Brian had advised, 'then go out and buy it for yourself. What about a coffee machine? You said how much you liked ours. Crazy really, all those stupid capsules, but lovely coffee. If I had ever thought years ago I'd own a coffee machine and had the stuff delivered to my door, well!'

He tailed off as Betty took a gentle swipe at his head, remarking, 'Let Nancy decide what she would like for Christmas. You and your coffee machine, you've become addicted.'

What do I want? she thought when she returned home and switched on the electric kettle for a cup of tea. Nimble nudged her, edging her towards the bag of mince pies on the table. Then sitting down, he looked at her, communicating with his big brown eyes that a mince pie might be a good idea.

She bent down to ruffle the untidy mess of hair on his head. 'You might be right, Nimble,' she said out loud, a habit she had dropped into since he had arrived in her life, 'you might be right. What I would really like for Christmas is just a glimpse of Jack.' He wagged his tail in response to her voice, partly, she felt, in agreement, and partly with an eye still on the mince pies.

It was Thursday, so still two more days before Christmas on the Sunday. Betty had joked that Jack always went to Dennison's on a Saturday morning at ten thirty while Mary had her hair done.

'She doesn't even give him a list,' Betty had explained.

'Just moans when he gets it wrong,' Brian had added.

They had been careful not to say too much about Jack, but they had hinted that he wasn't totally happy.

'He lives for his grandson Tom, virtually brought him up,' Brian explained. 'Grand lad, done well at university. All a bit of a scandal when Sheila got pregnant when she was only sixteen. She was doing all right until that awful Trevor came on the scene.'

'That's not fair,' Betty had retorted, silencing Brian with a look. 'That's a story for another day.'

So, Nancy thought as she poured herself a cup of tea and finally broke a mince pie in half so she could share it with Nimble. *Would I dare go to Dennison's this Saturday, and good heavens, would I recognise him?*

A wisp of excitement ran through her body and she knew immediately that the decision had been made. Brian and Betty had said they were shopping on Friday and so there was no fear of bumping into them. Her neighbour Ray had already advised her about buses, and she knew that she could catch one to the supermarket from the bottom of the road. It would even take Nimble for fifty pence. Nimble was perfectly happy to get on the bus, especially as nearly everyone admired him. Nancy felt he was a great comfort pressed against her knee.

'Not sure I could do this without you, Nimble,' she whispered.

The bus was twenty minutes late, so it was past ten thirty when she edged her way into an overcrowded supermarket. An elderly but lively shop assistant whose name badge announced that he was called Charlie had shown her where to tie Nimble up and had offered to keep an eye on him.

She was daunted by the crowds, and although it appeared jolly, with Christmas songs playing in the background and assistants wandering around dressed as pixies and handing out sweets, beneath the turmoil there was also a sense of panic as earnest shoppers piled their trolleys with mountains of produce. *Crazy,* she thought, half relieved and half amused, *I'd never spot Jack in all this lot.*

But she did, after just a few minutes, at the bottom of the first aisle. It was the fruit and vegetable aisle, packed with shoppers agonising over what to choose to last them over the Christmas period.

Jack was dressed in green corduroy trousers, walking boots, a black woollen coat and a sensible patterned tweed scarf around his neck. The thick hair she remembered was now mostly grey, cut in the inevitable short back and sides. The waves were gone, and his face bore the signs of age, but he was still tall, upright, and surprisingly how she remembered him at twenty-two, or at least how she thought she remembered him at twenty-two. She wasn't a hundred percent sure, and it was difficult to get a good look amid the crowds. She waited a while, then, spotting a gap, she moved in next to him, joining him in a thorough examination of some locally grown parsnips.

Making room for her he observed, 'I'm not sure these are local, they look a bit too white for me.'

'Do you grow parsnips?' she enquired, selecting a few and putting them in a bag.

'Well, yes,' he replied, 'but it's not been a good year, too much rain. I prefer my spaggy ones to these, more taste.' He leaned towards her, smiling. 'Pick the little ones,' he instructed, 'they're always the sweetest.' He carried on examining the vegetables, now turning his attention to the cauliflowers.

'It's Jack, isn't it?' she asked, realising instantly that she had broken the pledge to herself that she wouldn't make herself known to him.

When he replied, 'Yes,' she could tell he was embarrassed by not knowing who she was.

'I'm Nancy,' she replied. For a second she felt faint, as if the whole supermarket was whirling around her. Even the sound of Christmas music and constant announcements over the tannoy had disappeared. 'Nancy Dupray,' she repeated. 'I'm sorry; I didn't expect you to recognise me.'

But that wasn't true. Deep down she had hoped he would. She had dressed with care in her cashmere coat, red beret and scarf, hoping that would trigger the memory. He didn't answer straight away, just looked at her, even avoiding the hand she held out for him to shake. Eventually he took it and, shaking it, remarked, 'I'm sorry, it's a long time ago.'

'You haven't changed,' she replied cheerfully, 'I recognised you almost straight away.'

Crowds of people were now encroaching on their monopoly of the parsnips and cauliflowers, and Nancy stepped aside to let them through.

'I should have recognised the beret,' he remarked, and with that he manoeuvred his trolley through the crowds and disappeared out of view.

Well, she thought, *what did I expect?* Her mood had changed, and for a while she walked aimlessly around the supermarket, resenting the festive atmosphere. The supermarket tannoy was constantly telling the customers of special offers, always adding, 'Another good reason for shopping at Dennison's.' 'Fresh salmon, oysters and prawns all at our fish counter, reduced and ready to go,' it announced, 'and with every purchase a free lemon – another good reason for shopping at Dennison's.'

The thick Derbyshire accent that delivered the announcement suddenly made Nancy laugh. *Right,* she thought, *I'm going to have fresh salmon, oysters, prawns and a free lemon. I'll buy two bottles of champagne, one for Nimble and me, and one for Betty and Brian for when they get back.* By the time she had collected Nimble and reached the bus, her shopping bag was more than full of seasonal cheer.

Jack found it difficult to concentrate while trying to coordinate the rest of his Christmas shop. Nancy Dupray! He wouldn't have recognised her apart from that hair, and of course the beret. Bit of a cheek to come up to him like that. If he was sixty-five she must be nearing eighty. Where had she sprung from? He knew he looked good for his age, or that's what people told him. Anyway, she'd recognised him. For a second he was amused. How bizarre. But then a long-forgotten anger welled up inside him. *Bloody cheek*, he thought. But the lid had come off the can of worms, he realised, and he found it hard to regain his composure and continue fulfilling his Christmas list.

Although he allowed a few friends to commiserate with him about doing the weekly shop, he actually found that he quite enjoyed it.

They obviously didn't believe him, but it was true. For many years during his childhood he and his mother had shopped together.

They would drive to the shops together and she always allowed him to advise her on parking, where they were going to shop and what they were going to buy. Inevitably they ended up in one of the new coffee shops, where he was rewarded with a toasted teacake and a glass of fizzy orange. His mother took no real pleasure in cooking, so a lot of their weekly shopping involved packets of lemon meringue pie mixes, Heinz soups, tins of beans, spaghetti rings and Mr Kipling cupcakes.

He knew that Mary would be annoyed if he arrived late to pick her up, but suddenly that didn't seem so important. He'd married Mary on the rebound, after his youthful relationship with Nancy. Now perhaps it was time to revisit those decisions, for better or worse, before embarking on difficult choices that he knew had to be made for his and Mary's future.

As he finally loaded his shopping into the back of the car, it started to snow. A light dusting of white flakes settled on his jacket. Better snow than rain, he thought. After nearly a week of torrential rain, the river Derwent was about to burst its banks. As he drove to pick up Mary some of the roads still had flood warnings. Since his father had drowned in the fifties there had been several attempts to tame the river, but it still flooded on occasions, although not so dramatically as in his father's day. It had robbed him of his father, but Jack still loved the river, knowing great stretches intimately. The mills along its banks were once the source of great innovation and prosperity in the area. Many had now closed or been turned into outlet shops or tourist attractions, but they remained proud, rising majestically along the river.

Before his grandson Tom could even walk, he would carry him on his shoulders for miles along the towpaths, eventually reaching the start of the Peak District. They would stop to watch the wildlife, and as Tom became older, they would take a small fishing net along to catch tiny fish or frogspawn. In later years they would climb some of the great outcrops, walking long distances that involved nights spent under canvas or at a hostel. This was the private life that he and Tom created, in the absence of Tom's own father, who had left the sixteen-year-old Sheila before the baby was even born. Jack had spoken to their family doctor, who agreed to Sheila having an abortion, but at the last minute Sheila changed her mind, hoping, Jack always thought, that her young lover would return. He never did, of course, leaving Mary to blame Jack for not handling the situation successfully.

Mary had never been particularly maternal, always happy to pass her daughter over to anyone who would care for her. Sheila, whilst loving her baby son, found it hard at sixteen to abandon her young friends. After a few months she returned to work, putting Tom in one of the first nurseries. They remained living at home, but it wasn't without its difficulties, so everyone was relieved when Sheila started going out with a cashier at one of the local banks. He was ten years older than her, divorced, with a young child he rarely saw. He came from a large family but to Mary's dismay lived on a local council estate just outside Belper. Nonetheless, when he proposed to Sheila, Jack and his mother gave them the deposit for a house and the dream wedding Sheila wanted.

Jack had to admit that his new son-in-law was ambitious, bright enough to spot any chance of promotion, and committed enough to study the necessary exams that would aid his career. However, his only outside interest was football, which usually resulted in a prolonged session of drinking in the local pub with his friends.

Jack suspected very early on in the relationship that Sheila was not as happy as he would have wished, and Tom seemed to have shrunk into a world of his own. Mary, on the other hand, got on well with Trevor, pointing out that you would never have guessed that he came from a council estate. To Jack's embarrassment she would flirt with him, accepting his heavy-handed compliments and laughing at his crude suggestive jokes. Jack realised almost immediately that he disliked his son-in-law as much as he had disliked Mary's father so many years before. They resembled each other, both arrogant, with a complete disregard for other people's needs.

He became worried when Tom became more withdrawn. When he confronted Sheila, she admitted that her son and Trevor hadn't hit it off. For one thing Tom had no interest in football, she explained, something that really rankled with her husband. Tom loved to read and to draw, but most of all he wanted to be with his grandad, sharing the world they had created together. The result was that Tom began spending every weekend with his grandparents. Jack would meet his grandson on Friday afternoon from school and deliver him back there on Monday morning. Mary had sided with Trevor, making it clear that she thought Jack spoilt his grandson.

But Jack stood his ground, and Mary eventually capitulated and helped to make up a room for Tom. Jack was happy to see that they began to become close, often cuddling up together on the sofa to watch an episode of *EastEnders* or *Coronation Street*. Mary also used to bring the catalogues home from the department store where she now worked, and together she and Tom would go through the illustrations for the latest fashions.

Nevertheless he was without doubt Jack's boy, refusing at ten to call him Grandad anymore. Sheila and Mary had tried to explain it sounded disrespectful to call his grandad just Jack, but he had argued that Jack didn't look like a grandad, he looked like a Jack. The outcome was that, for many years, Jack it was, a name which was accepted by his friends as possibly a substitute for Dad.

Mary sat inside the hairdressers waiting for Jack. She felt aggrieved that her shampoo and set had been done by one of the younger girls. Mavis the manager had apologised, but explained that she was booked to do a wedding: the bride, the bride's mother and five bridesmaids. But she had been doing Mary's hair for over twenty years, and Mary felt that she should honour her appointment regardless. The whole salon seemed to be in a huge jolly turmoil, completely taken over by the wedding party. Regular customers sat waiting patiently, eating mince pies and drinking Mavis' home-made mulled wine. The whole place was steamy and festive, apart from Mary, who sat silently flicking through a magazine.

Jack didn't normally come in, but on this occasion he had been given instructions by Mary to buy a large box of chocolates for the girls and a bottle of brandy for Mavis. He emerged through the door covered in snow, bearing the gifts, to be greeted by a shout of joy from Mavis.

'Look girls, Father Christmas! Let's make use of the mistletoe.'

Abandoning the rather startled bride's mother, she ran over to Jack and kissed him warmly on the cheek.

'Where's the mistletoe?' he cried.

'Over here,' replied Mavis, repositioning him under a pathetic sprig of mistletoe hung from the lightbulb. She winked at her colleagues, crying, 'Now let's do it properly,' and then kissed Jack firmly on the lips. Her body felt hot and sweaty against his, and for a second he felt his sexuality start to rise, but the overwhelming smell of peroxide that always accompanied Mavis rescued him from any potentially embarrassing situation.

'I'd be happy to find you in my stocking any day,' Mavis cried, to the delight of all her customers. Jack felt near to tears. Here was warmth, simple pleasures and a precious camaraderie that you couldn't fault, even though half the Christmas garlands were falling down and the lights on the bottom half of the Christmas tree had broken.

Without glancing at Mary, he stretched up and released the mistletoe from the light bulb, then systematically went round all Mavis' ladies, kissing them on the cheek. When he reached the bride, who sat uncomfortably on a stool dressed in tight jeans and a sweater, and sporting an elaborate hairdo and veil, he stopped to stand back and admire her.

'Well, I can't kiss the bride before the wedding,' he ventured.

'You certainly can,' she said, slipping off the stool and capturing him in a feisty embrace. 'At least you're sober,' she cried, 'I doubt whether Craig will be when we get to the kissing stage.'

The whole salon erupted in laughter, but as he turned to face them all, he saw Mary had left, leaving the chocolates and the brandy on a chair. Wishing them all a merry Christmas, he headed for the door, but not before Mavis whispered in his ear, 'Sorry Jack, afraid you might have got a black mark because you're a bit late, and Mary's already a bit miffed because I didn't do her hair. Although she's been telling us about this fabulous new house you're going to buy. She said it's Georgian, very posh. Get you, Jack French,' she concluded affectionately.

He didn't reply, but squeezed her arm and departed swiftly.

Mary sat in their car, conspicuously festering over whether to instigate a row or to remain completely silent. As he approached the car, Jack slipped a little on the snow. He didn't fall, but as he gathered his balance, he sensed by the way Mary looked at him for an instant through the passenger window that she had wanted to reach out and steady him.

Sadly, he realised that as usual she was sitting rigid in her seat, choosing to inflict pain as she regularly did through her ability to maintain a silence that only she would choose to break.

As they drove without speaking from the hairdressers, the sound of Mavis' parting shot about a new house rang in his ears.

'So, what have you been telling Mavis?' he finally asked. 'Something about us buying a Georgian house?'

Mary turned, and to his surprise a smile spread across her face.

'Yes, it's so exciting. Trevor phoned just after you dropped me off. The house he wanted us all to buy, well, they reduced the price yesterday. He reckons, that is the estate agent reckons, if we act quickly it's ours. An architect friend of Trevor's has done him a favour and already been round to have a look at it. He says the stable on the side is perfect for us. Like a bungalow, we can have a large bedroom, en-suite bathroom, a big kitchen and lounge, even a utility room. Sheila's really excited. You have to take your hat off to Trevor, Jack, he's got his head screwed on.'

Jack remained silent. Mary's outburst had steamed up the inside of the car, and he was finding it difficult to negotiate the combination of heavy traffic and the snow that had developed from a flurry into a storm.

'Well, go on, say something,' Mary implored, 'I know you weren't keen to start with, but well, it's a chance in a lifetime.'

'Let's discuss it at Sheila's,' he replied, 'I need to concentrate on this weather. If it freezes tonight it will be a nightmare.'

When they arrived, Trevor met them at the door. 'Heard the good news, Jack?' he started. 'I think it's time for a drink.'

Their house was situated on a new estate in what was called an executive cul-de-sac. Five years ago it had become Sheila and Trevor's dream house, fitted out from top to toe in luxury carpets, overblown curtains and a mixture of reproduction furniture, which in Jack's opinion shouted bad taste. He still mourned the fact that Mary had insisted on disposing of most of his mother's antique furniture when she died.

Trevor led them all into the dining room where his granddaughter Tracy was pouring some Prosecco into champagne flutes. She stopped and kissed her grandparents, exclaiming, 'Oh, it's just so exciting. I can't wait to tell the girls at school. Dad says if things work out I might even be able to go to the High School for my GCSEs.'

'So the deal is…' Trevor started.

'No, Trevor,' Jack interjected, 'there is no deal and there never will be. I made it clear months ago that I will not sell our house to move in with you and Sheila.'

Both Trevor and Mary started to speak, but Jack silenced them by continuing over the top of their protests.

'Yes, I agree it's a lovely house, but early Victorian, Trevor, not Georgian, no matter what the estate agent says. I am not sure how much you would want from Mary and me, but together with the conversion to the stable I don't think it would leave us with much change. Secondly if Mary and I had to go into a home eventually, we'd have nothing to sell to pay the fees, unless we had an agreement that we could turn you out if needs be.'

Sheila started to speak. 'Dad, how could you say that? We'd always take care of you.'

'Well, I'm not so sure that you'd be able to, love. But the third thing is, what's in it for Mary and me? You'd live in the big house and we'd live in a one-bedroomed granny house next door? Mary, do you really want that? May I remind you that you moved me into a separate bedroom a few years ago? You didn't ask me, didn't even give me a reason, you just did it. But you are not doing this without me stating my position. Yes, the house has a beautiful garden full of outstanding trees, but I have a garden and an allotment that goes back to my great-grandfather.'

'There,' shouted Mary, 'I told you, stubborn as an ox, never cared for what I wanted ever. You selfish old man.'

'I'm nowhere near seventy yet,' replied Jack, 'the same age as Mick Jagger – no, in fact I think I'm a few years younger, but whatever, I don't feel old yet and I don't want to live in a bloody granny flat.'

Tracy was starting to cry, but Jack continued, 'There is of course another solution: we separate, Mary, and sell up. There should be enough for you to help purchase the property without me, and with four bedrooms, you might not need to do the conversion. That's not what I want, believe me, but I will not be pushed into something I know would undoubtedly end in disaster.'

There was complete silence. Mary suddenly looked forlorn. Lowering herself into a chair, she said to Jack's surprise, 'I'll need to think about it.'

The silence continued. Eventually Jack said, 'I'm not staying for lunch, Sheila, not the right time, luv, but thank you. I'll be late tonight, Mary, there's a double showing at the cinema this evening.' He stopped. 'In fact why don't you come? It's Fred Astaire and Ginger Rogers, and then that Australian film, *Strictly Ballroom*. I could pick you up around seven?'

She looked up, shaking her head, and then reached for the glass of prosecco. As he passed Trevor to reach the front door, his mobile phone bleeped with a text message. He read it in the car.

Under NO circumstances move in with that wanker. Happy Christmas. Love, Tom.

The snow had stopped but the roads remained dangerously slippery. All traffic had come virtually to a standstill. As Jack crawled along in a trail of cars, he reflected on his life with Mary. He accepted he too had faults, but he knew that he had genuinely tried to make her happy. And yet after the first few years she had refused to let him, and he had never been able to fully understand why.

CHAPTER TWENTY-FIVE

Mary, Mary, quite contrary.
How does your garden grow?

– NURSERY RHYME

DERBY, 1951

Mary had apparently met Jack when they were both five. Her father Gerald was judging the 'best kept rabbit' competition at a local fête, and Jack's long-eared rabbit had won. She remembered neither Jack nor his rabbit, but did recall her father taking her around on his shoulders, introducing her to everyone as 'my little Princess'. She even vaguely remembered her dress, a fancy organza affair with several lines of smocking. Even at five she sensed her father was an important figure in the community, and to be on his shoulders above the crowd was an experience to be relished, even though she detested the smell of the Brylcreem which he used to slick back his thick black hair.

Each year was a constant round of functions, to which her father, as one of the town councillors, was invited. It wasn't obligatory to attend, but she knew from an early age that her father enjoyed his status. Her mother seemed totally indifferent to these occasions; her only contribution was attiring Mary in a selection of stylish clothes, which she purchased from Daisy Montague's stylish shop in the Strand, one of Derby's more elegant streets.

As an only child with very few close friends, Mary was approaching her teens before she realised that her family was somewhat different to other people's. Her parents led completely separate lives; even the house seemed to be divided into separate zones. Her father occupied the back bedroom, her mother the front, while she had the small box room. The large bathroom was shared, but she never remembered ever seeing her parents occupy it together.

The front room was her mother's territory, dominated by a large television, a highly patterned Axminster carpet that fought somewhat violently with the densely-patterned embossed wallpaper, and several toby jugs, to which her mother admitted to being partial. Her father occupied the dining room, converting it into an office, but with the added comfort of a large sofa and his own television. The kitchen was small, and only used for quick breakfasts and heating tins of soup and pre-cooked meals.

As a child, Mary would often find comfort by sitting in the hall on the last step of the highly polished wooden staircase. Here at least her parents would pass, answer the phone and acknowledge her presence if they had to squeeze past her to climb the stairs. If she was alone, as she often was, she would watch the light from the coloured glass in the front door cast shadows on the walls. But the finial on the newel post gave her the greatest comfort: a carved pug's head. He was very ugly, but he was her friend in a household that lacked warmth. On occasions she would stretch up and stroke his head, unsure why she was crying, but confident that he understood.

She couldn't remember a time when her mother did not work. From an early age there was always a stream of women, some kindly, some not, who were given the task of taking care of her whilst her mother worked at the biscuit factory on the other side of the town. Her father always vaguely suggested that Freda was something in administration, but Mary knew this to be untrue, that like her mother's colleagues who they sometimes met at the weekend in Derby, Freda's job was packing biscuits off a conveyor belt.

She never felt truly comfortable with her mother's friends, finding their cheerful, sometimes loud camaraderie embarrassing, and was thankful they never came to her home. The idea of the neighbours catching a glimpse of Freda with some of the less than smart women she worked with filled Mary with horror. Freda made no attempt to engage with her neighbours, calling them a 'stuck-up lot', and when as a family they had occasionally been invited by one of them for a drink, Freda always refused to go.

'If we go, we'll have to have them back. You go, Councillor Blunt, you're a dab hand at that kind of thing.'

And invariably Gerald would go, taking Mary with him, and announcing in a hushed but dramatic tone, 'Freda's not well again, I'm afraid, so I've brought my little Princess along instead. I hope you don't mind.' Mary used to sense, in spite of all the fuss, that they did mind, but nevertheless she would be obliged to spend the next hour sitting uncomfortably listening to her father regale the gathering with his new plans for some innovative improvement in Derby.

When she reached the age of ten she received her own key, and to her relief was able to let herself into the house and prepare her own tea. Normally, she would rush through her homework so she could spend the rest of the evening watching the television. The two highlights of her life were accompanying her father to an event, and joining her mother on a Saturday morning to meet friends for a coffee at the newly opened Kardomah café in Derby, followed by a trip to the cinema if the film was deemed suitable.

She soon became aware that her father viewed the possibility of her failing the eleven-plus as inconceivable. When she plucked up the courage to tell him she was unsure if she would pass, he brushed it aside.

'Nonsense, Mary, I'm sure you will pass. The headmistress Miss Naylor and I are extremely good friends, and rest assured that can make a difference if there is a problem. Trust me, Princess, I have already marked her card.'

When the letter arrived saying she had failed but was invited to attend the new secondary modern, her father had flown into a rage. His florid face looked on the point of exploding as he left the house, reversing his elderly but highly polished Daimler off the drive at an undignified speed.

At primary school, she was somewhat comforted by Lily, who had also failed. Lily had been her very special friend, since they had both joined the primary school together. For two years they had enjoyed a very happy friendship. Lily had two elder brothers, a cat, a dog, two hamsters and a loving mother and father who welcomed Mary into their home on any occasion. Mary would sit on the bottom stair, and often fantasise with Pug what it would be liked to have a life like Lily. To come home to a mummy who had your tea ready and was preparing your daddy's dinner so you could all sit down together and talk about what you had been doing at school. Lily's dad always insisted in escorting her home if she stayed later than six o'clock, often accompanied by Lily and her brothers. Their homes were nearly in sight of one another, but if it was getting late her escorts could be relied on to make sure she arrived home safely. Mary worried that she must invite Lily to her house sometimes, but her mother was never there, and she could sense Lily's parents did not like to leave their daughter with one of Mary's carers.

However, during the summer holidays her father was often at home, and Lily started to become a regular visitor. She and Mary constructed a tent in the garden made from an upturned wooden clothes horse covered with a sheet. Gerald found his daughter several old blankets for the floor, and odd bits and bobs from the kitchen to create a little home. Dolls were given special beds, and even Lily's cat paid them the occasional visit. Mary was delighted her father was taking an interest in their little fantasy, even providing fizzy drinks, crisps and biscuits.

The weather during the holidays had been constantly hot, enabling the girls to play together every day. Lily would arrive after lunch. Mary would have the tent all tidy, trying to provide an additional little luxury before Lily's arrival. Her father would either be in his office or sitting in a deck-chair reading a paper and watching them play. Mary was supremely happy.

One afternoon after Lily had arrived, Mary decided that she would add the final touch by spraying the inside of the tent with her mother's perfume. Not telling Lily, she ran upstairs into her mother's room. She only rarely ventured in, as it was always a horrible jumble of clothes, shoes and half-used make-up. The curtains were always drawn and the whole room smelt deeply of cigarette smoke. But Mary quickly found her mother's bottle of Blue Grass perfume. It came in an elegant bottle with a spray top that Mary was allowed to use if they were going out to the cinema. Standing over the dressing table, she also selected a few items of make-up, a half-used powder compact, a lipstick without a top and a black eyebrow pencil. Running excitedly into her own bedroom she removed a small mirror from the wall, then scampered quickly downstairs, past Pug and back into the garden. Her father remained in his deck-chair, his newspaper now covering his face, but there was no sign of Lily.

'Where's Lily?' Mary cried, searching the tent and the rest of the garden.

Her father removed his paper. 'She's run off,' he explained, 'gone home.'

'But why?' cried Mary.

'I've no idea,' he replied, 'she just up and went.' He replaced the paper over his face. 'Now there's a good girl, you carry on playing, she'll be back I'm sure.'

Mary waited, but she felt a hollow fear inside her stomach. Why had Lily left so suddenly without telling her? She knew instinctively that something was wrong. She woke her father, shaking his knee violently.

'Why did Lily go home?' she cried.

He rose, and turning on her he shouted, 'For goodness' sake, Mary, I've no idea, perhaps you were unkind to her. Now tidy up all this tent mess, it's going to rain.'

As her father went into the house, she left the garden and ran down the road until she reached Lily's house. The family were in the garden, and Lily half hid behind her mother as she heard Mary approach. Lily's mother disentangled herself from her daughter and, gently bending down to speak to Mary, she said, 'Darling, go back home. Lily doesn't want to play at the moment, she's not feeling too well. There's a good girl.'

But Mary pulled herself free. Running up to her friend, she cried, 'I've got some of Mum's perfume. We can spray the tent, it will be lovely.'

'No, Mary,' Lily's mother replied severely, 'not this time, now go home please.' With that she took Mary to the gate. 'You go, I'll watch you until you get home.'

That night, as Mary lay crying into her pillow, she heard angry voices coming from the front garden. Peering out of the window she saw her own father and Lily's father in a heated argument. Her own father was shouting, 'Completely ridiculous. How dare you, a man in my position. I suggest you keep your daughter away from my Mary, lying little madam.'

The two men were of similar height, and for a minute they sized one another up as if preparing to fight. Then Lily's father grasped her father by the throat and spoke quietly into his face. Releasing him after a second, he turned away, but not before kicking her father's car which was parked on the drive.

Later that night she heard her parents arguing, but in the morning all appeared normal. Her mother went to work and her father made promises about the wonderful few days they were going to have at the seaside. When she returned to school, Lily was friendly but very quiet with her, preferring to spend time with another group of girls.

In the end Mary asked, 'Why don't you want to be friends, Lily? What did I do?'

'Nothing,' Lily had replied. 'Mum and Dad said you can come to our house any time you like, but I mustn't come to yours. Perhaps it's best if we aren't friends for a while.'

But five years later, when Lily heard that Mary had also failed her eleven-plus, she had put her arms around her, insisting they renew their friendship at the secondary modern.

When Mary arrived for the first day at the grammar school, she was under no illusion that she was there under false pretences, and deeply sad that she wouldn't be sharing school life with Lily. After the letter had arrived, her father seemed to be constantly on the phone talking to various 'big-wigs', as her mother called them. Miss Naylor called several times and from what Mary could understand there had been a mistake, coupled with the fact that, as her father had stated, she had been very ill on the day of the exam. But happily there now appeared to be a place, as some of the pupils had turned their offers down because of the price of the uniform and equipment needed. Her mother also told her that Gerald had agreed to supply all the wood for the new sports hall. Her mother normally never commented on her husband's business affairs, apart from pointing out that whilst he looked down on her job at the biscuit factory it paid many of the bills he chose to ignore.

'I can't see his step-brothers agreeing to cough up for free timber for a sports hall. They hardly acknowledge his existence at the best of times; and I'm not bloody surprised the way he prances about doing his councillor this, councillor that twaddle.'

'You don't love him, Mum, do you?' Mary had surprised herself by asking the question, as emotions were not something ever discussed between the three of them.

Her mother remained still for a moment, a cigarette poised between two fingers. Then she ground it into the ash tray. 'Better the devil you know than the devil you don't,' she replied.

Mary ventured another question, one that had been troubling her for a long while. 'Do you love me, Mum?'

Freda lit up another cigarette, taking a deep drag on it before expertly exhaling the smoke above her head. 'Of course I do. What a question. If I didn't love you I'd have gone years ago. Now try and do well at the Grammar. On Saturday we've got to get that uniform sorted out. I fail to understand why you need six pairs of green knickers and a raincoat as well as a blazer.'

'We could get second-hand,' Mary suggested, genuinely wanting to help.

'Well not second-hand knickers,' her mother laughed. 'No, Mary, you'll have all new.'

A further cloud of smoke drifted above her mother. As Mary approached to hug her, Freda reached for the kettle.

'No nonsense now,' she said, avoiding the embrace. 'You'll have all new, Mary, and you'll have it with my love. Now let's have a cup of tea and a biscuit and catch up with the end of *Coronation Street*.'

Regardless of the fact that each year Mary was usually near the bottom of her form, she enjoyed the grammar school. Her father never tired of telling anyone with the patience to listen that she was a bright girl, and that they were lucky to have her there. He would then continue by adding that he had thought long and hard about a private school, but that his own experience of it hadn't been that satisfactory, plus he didn't fancy parting with his little Princess.

He was constantly obsessed by who Mary was making friends with, pointing out to her that it was important she mixed with the right kind of girls. She was savvy enough to realise he meant those with money, and that she only needed to casually mention a family he was in awe of to elicit a rather embarrassing response.

'Freda, Mary's been invited to Josh Martin's daughter's birthday party next weekend. Has she anything suitable to wear? Probably worth a visit to Daisy Montague's, we don't want her letting the side down.'

Freda would invariably reply with a measured response. 'Whose side are we talking about, Gerald? She has a wardrobe full of dresses, none of them paid for by you, I might add.'

The conversation would end abruptly in stalemate, neither of them seemingly wanting to confront the reality of their relationship.

Since Freda had been appointed manageress of the assembly line at the biscuit factory, she spent even less time at home, and Gerald would often not return from his functions until the early hours of the morning, or at all. Freda never commented, and the only time Mary asked him why he hadn't returned home one night, he had lightly passed the matter off with an explanation that he had had a little too much to drink, so had stayed with a friend.

'A man in my position can't afford to be done over by the police for drink driving, even if I am on very good terms with the Chief Constable. Not worth taking the chance.'

To Mary's great joy, Lily passed her thirteen-plus and joined her at the grammar school. They picked up their friendship immediately. Homework was now often shared at Lily's house, and as they grew older they were allowed to go shopping or to the cinema together. Most Monday nights, Lily's family would ask her to join them eating their tea in front of the television whilst they all watched *Jukebox Jury*, everyone competing to guess the next hit record. During the winter she would often stay the night, sleeping on a mattress on the floor next to Lily's bed. Mary had only once started to ask Lily about what had happened in the garden many years before, but Lily had stopped her abruptly.

'Please, Mary,' she had begged, 'it's not important, for both our sakes don't ask. Mum and Dad are happy we are friends, let's leave it at that.'

But the unspoken rule remained that Lily never visited Mary's home. Her parents never commented on their renewed friendship, apart from Freda occasionally remarking how lucky Mary was to have a friend like Lily, and insisting Mary kept the family supplied with an assortment of biscuits.

At sixteen they both left school with a respectable number of O-levels. Lily wanted to be a vet and secured a job as an assistant nurse to a local practice. Mary felt she had no choice; her father insisted that she apply to Rolls-Royce. He explained that he knew Miss Radcliffe, the personnel officer, who he was confident would accept Mary with welcoming arms.

Mary felt intimidated by the vastness of the several sites that Rolls-Royce occupied. For the first time she became aware of what an integral part it was of the town she lived in.

'You either work at the Celanese, the railway, Combustion or Rolls-Royce,' her father had told her, 'and believe me Rolls-Royce is the *crème de la crème* for young ladies like you. A fine place to find a husband.'

Six other girls from the grammar school had made the grade, and all seemed delighted that the typing pool was adjacent to some of the larger drawing offices. Miss Radcliffe, true to her father's word, had singled her out, and she was soon appointed as office girl in B Block, one of the largest offices for both draughtsmen and production engineers. She found the first few weeks terrifying, a round of delivering mail, collating complicated engineers' specifications, and running messages for the more senior draughtsmen.

The noise of the factory leached everywhere, as did the acidic smell from the Foundry, which perversely clung to your clothes even when you had returned home. Before eight in the morning the surrounding streets were alive with hundreds of employees, walking, cycling, parking their cars, all heading for their particular site where fast-moving queues lined up to clock in. After eight o'clock the streets fell abruptly silent, apart from the last stragglers' footsteps as they hurried to avoid the penalty for clocking in too late. Even the changing seasons found it hard to break through the permanent greyness of the area. Sad clumps of weeds jockeyed for position in the few places where the sun was able to penetrate the narrow streets. And when the late autumn pea-soupers descended, the area became a confusing maze, only penetrable by those who knew it well.

The only relief for Mary was that for a day and half a week she attended the Rolls-Royce secretarial school, which was housed in new prefabricated buildings a short way from the factory, and had the luxury of a stretch of grass where students could sit during their break if the weather was fine.

Apart from Lily's brothers, she had had very little contact with young men of her age. Her initial timidness earned her the nickname of Squeak, but as the months moved on, she became more confident and accepted that the majority of the banter from her male colleagues was meant good-naturedly. The only cloud on the horizon was when she had to walk through the factory, where the presence of a young woman gave rise to shouts, whistles and in Mary's opinion some very unseemly comments. Most of her female colleagues seemed to actually relish the situation, endlessly discussing their foray onto the factory floor as if it was some kind of triumph that they had accomplished unscathed.

333

However, Miss Radcliffe constantly praised her for her competence, and she began to feel for the first time that it would be possible to escape from the drabness of her home. After a few months she was asked out on her first date. Stan, the young man in question, invited her to the new Locarno Dance Hall in the centre of town, where they would join up with other colleagues from the drawing office. Stan was far from her dream boyfriend. He was not only short and stocky, but had the reputation of being a little uncouth, coupled with a strong local accent. But he had asked her out very politely on several occasions, assuring her, although she sensed somewhat ironically, that he would deem it a privilege if she accepted his invitation.

As others from her group of friends would be going, she fell in with the plan that they were to meet outside the main entrance to the dance hall. Caught up in the excitement of her first date, she purchased a bright blue taffeta dress from a new chain store on the high street. As it was Friday night her mother was out, but her father promised to take her into town. Accepting his offer, she was also determined that he drop her off around the corner from the Locarno, as she felt that the embarrassment of emerging from his Daimler would not be a good way to start an evening out with Stan and his friends.

Immediately after work she had gone to the hairdressers, allowing her fine blonde hair to be teased into an abundance of curls on the top of her head. Now in front of her dressing table she applied her make-up carefully, not wanting to resemble Freda, who had a fairly heavy hand when it came to eyeliner and lipstick. Her father never usually came into her bedroom, but he suddenly appeared smiling at her reflection in the mirror.

'My little Princess,' he remarked, 'pretty as a picture.' With that he pressed himself against her, and as she looked at his reflection, he added, 'You'll never feel another like that, I bet, young lady?' For a second she had no idea what he was talking about, until he moved to one side, revealing in the reflection his erect penis emerging from his trousers.

She remained still, repulsed. She thought immediately of Lily. Anger consumed her, but also fear.

'Now come on, Mary,' he continued, 'only a bit of fun. Nothing to be afraid of, all very natural, you know.'

Her fear subsided. What remained was disgust that this pathetic man was her father. Deep down, even from an early age, she had known he was worthless. She rose and, picking up her bag and coat, she brushed by him without looking into his face. She walked slowly down the stairs, touching Pug as she passed, before opening the door and leaving the house.

At the bus stop she started shaking uncontrollably, but regained her composure when the bus finally arrived.

It was her first visit to the Locarno, and it felt surreal as she walked carefully down its wide staircase onto the dance floor. It was early and only a few brave souls were dancing, but as the night wore on, the alcoves with their brightly-coloured curving plastic sofas started to fill up, and the dance floor became a mass of gyrating bodies under a revolving disco ball that rained drops of light on to their faces.

Her first big night out started to become a blur as she accepted as many Babychams in their coy little glasses as Stan was prepared to offer. At least she felt safe with him, sensing he was amused but not judgemental as she abandoned herself to the music and the drink. Unaware that her much-anticipated night out had become a sordid nightmare, Stan carefully protected her from the heaving masses of the Friday night revellers.

Walking with the rest of the crowd to the bus station afterwards, she was able to avoid any kind of embraces Stan might have been contemplating, as the effort of keeping her upright was his main priority. He had offered to accompany her home, but as it was the last bus that evening, she had refused, gathering her dignity in order to thank him for a lovely night out.

On the bus home she was violently sick, to the horror of both the driver and all the passengers. Her father's car was not on the drive, and her mother had gone to bed. Her dress was ruined; a mixture of drink and vomit had destroyed the taffeta. The following day when her mother was out, she burnt the whole outfit in the garden, and to her relief it was several days before her father returned home. Nothing was said, and life continued as before, but the menace of his presence constantly haunted her.

Finally she contacted Lily. They met in the local pub and Lily was full of stories of her life at the vet's. One of the young vets had already asked her out a couple of times, and she confided that she was seriously attracted to him. Eventually Mary plucked up courage to divert Lily's chatter and say, 'I know, Lily, or I think I do, why you ran away all that time ago. I remember your dad coming round and there was…' She stopped as Lily took her hand.

'Don't, don't say any more, Mary, please. But if your dad is trying anything on with you, you must get out. Do you understand me? Just get out. My parents have been constantly worried about you. Dad told me years later he always felt guilty he had never gone to the police. But they were genuinely pleased when you came back into our lives, and they could half keep an eye on you. Mum could never understand how your family works.'

'I'm not surprised. In fact, you know, Lily, it didn't work, still doesn't.'

Lily took her hand and confided, 'Mum once tried to have a word with your mum, but she said it was impossible, there was no common ground. I'm telling you, Mary, your dad's got a bad reputation. He might flounce around as a councillor but there are very few people who have any respect for him.'

She hesitated a little to check on Mary's reaction, then, taking a sip of her drink, she continued.

'I was lucky, I was so scared but without realising why, and fortunate enough to be able to tell my parents. He didn't hurt me, just frightened me. But do you know, the memory of it has never left me. Who knows whether Mum and Dad were right to turn a blind eye? But Mary, you mustn't let him ruin your life.'

Mary glanced nervously around the pub, then, sensing that above the noise she would be safe to continue talking, she grasped Lily's other hand.

'It's ok, he has never tried to seriously abuse me. He's a coward and I think he's frightened of me now he's exposed himself.' She choked on the word, and they both laughed. 'Well, you know what I mean, Lily. Mum's useless, all she wants is an easy life. Your family gave me something very special. At least I learned through you all what normal family life should be like. Tell your mum, please, Lily, and your dad if you think it's right, say thank you from me.'

The conversation flagged, and although they saw one another occasionally after that, their friendship faded. When Mary saw an announcement of Lily's engagement to her vet in the local paper, she sent a card of congratulation, but Lily never replied.

Life for Mary now became a routine, the same kind of routine she had observed her mother adhering to for most of her life. Neither of her parents had ever tried to create a home. It was just a place to stay when they were not at work. For Mary work was a welcome escape, a place where she felt she had a purpose. She attended two evening classes a week. Friday and Saturday evenings were spent with friends, and Sunday she lounged about most of the time in her bedroom, only rising to join her mother for yet another ready-cooked meal, before settling down to watch television. She considered herself lucky that Freda continued to pay for a cleaner to come in once a week, which including doing the bulk of her washing and ironing, enabling her to avoid any household responsibilities.

Stan asked her out a couple more times, but she knew the incident with her father had damaged her. Whilst she tried to return Stan's less than sophisticated attempts at passion, she just felt awkward. She longed to have a boyfriend different to Stan, someone she admired and respected; the knight in shining armour who would take her away from this nightmare she was forced to call home.

Unbeknown to Jack, he was the young man she aspired to. After two years she had progressed to becoming a junior secretary to one of the senior engineers, whose office overlooked the huge area where Jack and his colleagues plied their skills at designing aeroplane engines. In Mary's eyes Jack was very special, tall, good-looking but with a gentle, almost self-effacing manner. Her friend Betty described him as 'a bit of an intellectual'.

'His mother is the headmistress of a primary school,' she told Mary. 'He's lovely, really kind and considerate, not as lively as my Brian, but a real gentleman.'

The possibility of catching Jack's eye, having a brief chat, joining him and some of his mates in the canteen at lunchtime, became the highlight of Mary's day. And whilst she knew that Betty had already fixed him up with someone, she hoped that there might be a chance he would one day notice her.

When she changed her hairstyle, abandoning her French pleat for a more contemporary look, Jack had noticed, taking time to pay her a compliment on how nice she looked. The compliment sustained her for many weeks, resulting in her spending most of her wages on buying yet another outfit in the hope of eliciting further words of praise. When she heard from Betty he had finished with his girlfriend, her spirits had risen, only to have them dashed by the inevitable scandal that broke when Jack started a relationship with 'the older woman', Nancy.

Nancy had left Rolls-Royce under a cloud of unsavoury rumours. Mary had hardly known her, as the secretaries residing in the Marble Hall liked to remain a set apart from the rest of the female staff. When Nancy did appear occasionally, Mary was in awe of her elegance. She was undoubtedly beautiful, but in a disturbingly understated way. Betty had known her briefly and said that she found her a little distant but with 'no side to her', always ready to help out, unlike some of the 'stuck-up girls' she often encountered from the Marble Hall.

On the day Nancy had left, Mary had been asked to stand in for her. It was an awkward situation, but Mary had been impressed with how calmly Nancy seemed to handle the whole episode, even leaving her desk and papers in order. The general gossip was that she had been having an affair with her boss, coupled with the fact she was often seen in the company of two black men who lived in the area. Whatever the reason, Mary was deeply shocked when Betty informed her that Nancy and Jack were an item.

'She must be at least twelve or more years older than Jack,' Betty had protested. 'Brian has tried warning him off, but he won't have any of it, he's totally infatuated. I've promised Brian I'll try and have a word with him. I can't believe his mother would approve.'

But Betty and Brian's life abruptly changed with an unexpected baby on the way, and it wasn't until their wedding that Mary saw Nancy again. She had been invited to be chief bridesmaid. Jack was best man so he would, she knew, be expected to escort her during all the formal proceedings. As she anticipated, he performed his duties perfectly, not only taking care of her and the other bridesmaids, but complimenting them on the pale yellow dresses Betty had chosen for them all.

However, when she and Jack walked down the aisle together, it was obvious that he was searching the crowds for a glimpse of Nancy. During the reception Jack asked Mary to dance, as he did all the bridesmaids, so whilst enjoying for a brief moment being in his arms, it did little to satisfy her dreams.

But when nearly two years later Betty announced that Nancy had suddenly and mysteriously disappeared, Mary felt there might be a glimmer of hope. Here at last was the opportunity she had been waiting for to make a bid for Jack's affections.

CHAPTER TWENTY-SIX

*Becoming a city having been a borough was a
great step forward. It tells everybody in the
country that this is an area of importance.*

– DERBY COUNCILLOR, QUEEN'S SILVER JUBILEE

DERBY, 1971

For weeks, even months after Nancy's disappearance, Jack would wake in the middle of the night, his body listless, his mind grappling constantly with how or why she could have left him. He allowed himself to create different scenarios, some with happy endings, some not. Each morning he would pray that the pain would subside, only to find that it continued to linger, constantly invading his thoughts.

On Friday nights he would meet Brian in the pub. Betty had won the argument and now there was a group of girls who joined them, mainly from Rolls-Royce. Ignoring Jack's sullenness, all his mates treated him with sensitivity, as if he was someone recovering from a long illness.

'Just leave him alone,' Brian would say, but at the same time encouraging Mary to talk to him. As she was neither pushy nor loud, he felt relaxed in her presence. Their friendship slowly flourished, and he began to pick her up on his motorbike each Friday night. Her father would often rush out to greet him, or, to Jack's horror, invite him in for a drink, where he would be cornered for half an hour listening to Gerald relate how his influence on the Derby Town Council was helping to shape the town in preparation for it being finally being acknowledged as a city.

'We'll see the Queen here one day,' he would proclaim to Jack. 'You mark my words, and after that a university, and yours truly will – well, I don't mind if I do say it – yours truly will have helped push it through. I like to think of myself as a man of vision, isn't that right, Mary?'

Jack was vaguely aware that Mary hardly ever spoke or replied to her father, just concentrated on skilfully judging the best time she could extract them from the little pantomime.

Jack loathed him from the moment they met, but took advantage of the fact that when he returned home with Mary, her father's car was never on the drive. With Freda always in bed, Mary would turn on the electric fire, and they would make love in front of it. He felt a strange power; he didn't love her, or even like her that much, but he used her to satisfy his needs, constantly thinking of Nancy as he thrust his body on hers. She obligingly made the right noises, but he guessed she was often faking. He justified his actions by reassuring himself that she completely adored him and seemed perfectly happy with their imperfect relationship. He felt constantly that the Jack he used to be hovered above him, looking down on the Jack he had become. He felt guilty, but powerless to improve the situation.

As their relationship grew and Mary became more demanding, they would go out at the weekend on Jack's bike. Unlike Nancy, he knew she was nervous, which tempted him to drive recklessly. He could feel her body grow tense, but she never complained. He found her conversation painfully mundane, a mixture of Rolls-Royce gossip and timid opinions on other people's lives. He knew she wasn't that different to most of the girls in the group. It was just that Nancy had been so special, she had unwittingly educated herself, absorbing like a sponge a rich eclectic set of interests.

Betty was realistic to see the gulf between him and Mary, exclaiming on one occasion, 'What you are looking for, Jack, is a more glamorous version of your mother.'

'What, like Oedipus?' he'd replied.

'Probably,' laughed Betty, 'but there you go again, smart answer. Give the girl a chance.'

He started to try, but if he left it longer than a few days before speaking to her, she would either corner him at work, or make some excuse to phone him at home. Eventually, with a further trip to Toulouse looming, he told her as gently as possible that he thought it would be for the best if they had a break in their relationship. She had cried, clinging to him so that, eventually aroused, they had made love again in front of the electric fire.

When he left, they had kissed gently, but not without him whispering, 'Honestly, Mary, it is for the best. I need time to get over Nancy. I've been a complete bastard towards you, and you deserve a lot better.'

It was the first time he had mentioned Nancy to Mary, but now he felt relieved that at last he had expressed his true emotions. He knew he had taken advantage of her, but on Brian's strict instructions he had always taken precautions when they made love, something he had never had to do with Nancy.

When he returned from Toulouse, Mary continued to join the group on a Friday night. They would laugh and chat together, but Jack made it obvious that he did not want to renew their relationship.

The draughtsmen were not expected to take private telephone calls, but nearly three months later his mother rang, asking to speak with him. Mary's father was in her office and apparently making a huge fuss that his daughter was in hospital, dangerously ill.

'Jack, he says Mary is pregnant. There are complications. It's life threatening and they're operating immediately. Her father didn't know she was pregnant and naturally he's laying the blame at your door.'

'But Mum…' He hesitated before speaking, in order to check that no one could hear him. 'I always took precautions, always,' he continued.

'Well, Jack, Councillor Blunt says it's your baby, and Mary apparently hasn't denied that. He insists you left her in the lurch. I've told him in no uncertain terms that I did not think for one moment that is true. Is that right, Jack?' she continued. 'Tell me it's not true.'

'Come off it, Mum, of course it's not true. I had no idea she was pregnant, we split up nearly four months ago. But we remained friends, she never said anything.'

'I think you should go to the hospital, Jack, Mary's a nice girl. Do you want me to join you?'

'Good God no, Mum, I'll sort it out. Accidents happen I know, but honestly... I'm surprised. Is her mother there?'

Elizabeth gently laughed. 'Apparently not, Freda doesn't like hospitals. However, I have just said to our dear Councillor that if it was my daughter and her life was in danger, I'd be there whether I liked hospitals or not.' With that she firmly put down the phone.

When Jack arrived at the hospital Gerald was already there. 'I ought to give you a bloody good hiding,' he started, 'my little Princess.'

Jack felt a rush of indignation, but ignored Gerald's comments and went straight to the reception desk.

'She's lost a lot of blood,' he was told, 'but the doctor says she will be fine.'

'And the baby?' Jack enquired.

The nurse smiled, reaching her hand across the desk to touch Jack's. 'Now, young man, let me explain. An ectopic pregnancy is when the egg starts to develop in the fallopian tube and never enters the womb. Mary's young and she should have no problems in recovering and hopefully having a successful pregnancy next time.'

'Can I see her?' Jack asked.

'I'm not sure she'll want to,' Gerald intervened, 'bloody nightmare.' Jack ignored him, sensing the nurse was sympathetic to his request.

'No one is going to see Mary until I've spoken to her and also to the doctor. I suggest you gentlemen sit down, and behave in a civilised manner, remember this is a hospital.'

The two men sat uncomfortably in the waiting room, with Gerald still continuing to bluster about how shocked he was.

JACK BE NIMBLE

'Hope you'll do the right thing by her, and you know what the right thing is, young man. Marriage, that's what I expect.'

Jack remained silent, aware that if he did speak it would quickly degenerate into an unpleasant argument.

Gerald was about to speak again, when a new nurse approached.

'Now, who is Mr French?' she enquired.

Jack rose. 'I'm Jack French.'

'Oh good,' she replied. 'Well, Mary says she would like to see you, and the doctor says you can have just five minutes.'

As they walked down the corridor Jack felt somewhat exposed.

'I haven't got anything for her,' he said, 'not even flowers.'

'Not a problem,' the nurse replied. 'I have a strong feeling all she wants is a big kiss. Such a rotten thing to happen. What we ladies have to go through,' she laughed.

Mary was lying flat on the bed. As he bent over to kiss her, she reached up and touched his face. 'I'm sorry, Jack, you weren't supposed to know.'

'You should have told me. Were you going to keep it, or were you going to…' The word 'abortion' stuck in Jack's mouth.

'I wanted to keep it,' she whispered. 'I knew it was over between us, but I wanted to keep it. I asked Dad not to tell you, but of course he wouldn't listen.' Tears filled her eyes and she clutched Jack's hand, drawing it towards her face. 'We'd always been so careful. I was so surprised, but I did know I couldn't get rid of it. I didn't even tell Betty. You mustn't feel guilty, if Dad had kept his mouth shut nobody would be the wiser.'

Jack kissed her gently. 'We'll see,' he said. 'I'll be back tomorrow. Now what would you like, flowers or chocolates or both?'

'Both,' she replied, blowing him a kiss as he left the room.

They were engaged within a month. Her father continued to put pressure on him, and Mary needed little convincing that they could create a happy life together. 'Go for it,' Brian had advised. Jack's mother was now more cautious, insisting that whatever his decision she would support him.

Each day he considered how he could possibly escape without appearing the complete cad, but eventually he allowed himself to be caught up in a flurry of wedding plans. As soon as Mary had the engagement ring on her finger, Gerald placed an announcement in the local paper, and arranged for a photographer to take an engagement picture for the county magazine.

Freda appeared to take very little interest, although she did engage Daisy Montague to help Mary with her dress. Both Mary and her father had made it clear that they did not want any of her work friends from the biscuit factory at the wedding. 'You know what they're like, Mum,' Mary had explained, 'a bit loud.'

'They will come to the church whether you like it or not,' Freda had replied. 'They have known you since you were a little girl and been very kind to you over the years. I bet they are already organising a collection for a present. I'm surprised at you, Mary, don't get like your father, a bloody snob.'

But nothing could upset Mary, not even Freda's gibes. Soon she knew she would escape, never to return to this sordid household. She had Jack, and even if her conscience pricked her occasionally, she was convinced that it was all for the best.

As he stood next to Brian at the altar, waiting for Mary to process down the aisle, Jack battled with thoughts of Nancy. Anger still consumed him. Why had she gone? Had she felt he wasn't man enough to take care of her, protect them both from Bill?

The organ started to play. He had virtually let Mary make all the plans for their wedding, but now as he heard 'Here Comes the Bride' he wished he had insisted on something less familiar. He turned and saw Mary, and strangely it felt like the first time. For a second his heart lurched, and his eyes filled with tears. She looked beautiful, delicate and completely radiant. The lace bodice of her dress fitted tightly, emphasising the multi-layered skirt that swept elegantly to the floor. Her long veil was trimmed with lace and held in her hair by a small spray of white roses. Her bouquet was of sweet peas that reflected the soft colours of her three bridesmaids' dresses.

As she left her father's arm, he whispered, 'You look beautiful.'

Thoughts of Nancy did not return. Rather, he felt a sudden humbling realisation that this fragile young woman was now about to do him the honour of becoming his wife. He felt shame, but also relief that he was at peace with himself. He truly wanted to make Mary happy.

Her father had organised a lavish reception at the most expensive hotel in Derby. Most of the city councillors and their wives were there, making up for the fact that apart from one of his half-brothers and his wife, there were no other relatives from Mary's side.

Gerald, true to form, made a long pompous speech, which happily Mary and Jack were able to laugh about on the train down to London in the evening. Brian as best man exercised a fair amount of restraint, but Freda became very tipsy even before the meal started, losing her hat on one occasion and then replacing it at a jaunty angle for the rest of the day.

Elizabeth, also true to form, remained quietly subdued in the background, her thoughts resting with her late husband. She hoped he would have approved. She felt she had tried her best, and when her son presented her with a bouquet 'to the best mum in the world', she allowed herself to shed a few tears.

Jack and Mary spent their honeymoon in Paris. Jack hired a Lambretta and they scooted about visiting all the tourist sites. Mary remained constantly radiant, eliciting admiring glances as she walked with Jack by her side. Jack bought her her first sunglasses and a Chanel silk scarf to wear around her head when she was on the scooter.

After the miscarriage their lovemaking had been restrained, but now they were able to explore each other with a passion that hadn't been there in the past. The spectre of Nancy began to fade, as did Mary's memories of her father's abuse, and her brief relationship with Stan.

Elizabeth decided to sell her house. She and Jack had been happy there, but it was too big and she sensed it was time to move on. She bought a bungalow close to her school, and with some of her capital released she was able to give Jack and Mary a deposit for a house.

Jack had wanted to buy a cottage in one of the surrounding villages, but Mary favoured a brand-new house, sensing possibly that a country cottage was a leftover dream from Nancy.

They moved in four months after the wedding, and Jack had to admit it was fun planning the decor, putting up cupboards and for the first time creating his own garden. At Mary's request he sold his motorbike and bought a second-hand sports car. Mary had wanted a Sprite, but Jack persuaded her that a more robust Triumph TR2 was far more chic. Brian described them as the 'golden couple'. With the top down on their car, Mary wearing her sunglasses and scarf, they felt happy and prosperous.

Jack saw his mother regularly, always managing to call in at least one evening a week. If they had time they would also stop by during the weekends, especially if Elizabeth was offering a Sunday lunch. It was clear, Jack soon discovered, that Mary had no wish to see her own parents. When he suggested they should pay a visit, Mary was reluctant, and if she could be persuaded it was only for a few minutes, hardly time for a cup of tea. Gerald was rarely at home, and Freda was usually watching the television, surrounded by cigarette smoke. Jack secretly wondered how she kept her job down, as even the simple task of boiling a kettle seemed to pose her a challenge.

He also learned very quickly that Mary did not even wish to discuss her parents. If he made the slightest ironic comment about them, or enquired into her childhood, Mary would not be drawn into a discussion, often making the excuse, 'I know you don't like them, so why go on about them?'

This would be followed by a sullen silence that he found it difficult to adjust to. Guiltily he would frequently regale Brian, Betty and his mother with the state of affairs at Mary's home. But it did come as a shock when, eight months after their wedding, his mother informed him that she had just received a phone call from the manager of the hotel that had hosted their reception. The manager had apologised profusely, but had explained to Elizabeth that Councillor Blunt had not settled his bill for the wedding reception.

They had written to him on several occasions, but with no response, and their accountant was now insisting it was sent to the small claims court. He hoped by phoning Elizabeth they might be able to prevent an embarrassing court case.

Later Elizabeth explained to Jack that the manager had seemed genuinely upset. Jack was shocked, but unable to decide the best way to tackle the situation. Both he and his mother felt that Mary should not be involved, as she had just announced that she was pregnant.

'Leave it with me,' Elizabeth had counselled Jack, 'let's see if we can handle this without any unpleasantness.'

The following day she phoned Gerald's office. He was out, his secretary informed her, but she would ask him to call back as soon as he came in. After a few days without any response Elizabeth phoned again, only to be told by the secretary that she had relayed the message but would do so again. After two more days, phoning the long-suffering secretary again, she asked for the number of the City Council so she could find out the best way to contact Councillor Blunt.

Within an hour, she was summoned from a lesson by her own secretary informing her that Councillor Blunt was on the phone and wished to speak to her urgently.

She explained to Jack later that day that she felt the whole conversation was incredibly bizarre. Gerald did not apologise, but just blustered on about how busy he was now that he had been appointed to the Planning Committee, and he was sure that she understood. He was at pains to make it clear that he thought the manager of the hotel should be hauled up by Head Office for daring to contact Elizabeth, and that they obviously did not know he had a 'special relationship' with the manager.

'What does that mean?' Elizabeth asked.

'It means, dear lady, that you have no need to worry, no need at all.'

Jack said she should have left it there, but she guessed Gerald was lying, so she phoned the hotel a few weeks later to check if the account had been settled. The manager revealed that sadly it had been put into the small claims court. The case would take a few weeks, but he dreaded to think what the local press would make of it. He acknowledged that he had accepted Gerald's help whenever he wanted an extended licence for a special event, but that was fairly common practice, something his predecessor had always done too. He had offered Gerald a favourable price for the reception, but had become a little anxious when Gerald kept increasing his demands. When after several reminders the money had not appeared, they had no other option but to hand it over to the courts.

'It's put my job in jeopardy,' he confessed to Elizabeth. 'It's surprising, when…'

'The shit hits the fan?' Elizabeth surprised herself by completing his sentence.

'Exactly,' he said, relieved that she was sympathetic. 'Yes, everyone looks away.'

Elizabeth sent a cheque immediately. She phoned Gerald, explaining that whilst she was appalled at his behaviour, she had settled the debt in an effort to avert a scandal that would be distressing to both her son and his daughter. She made it clear that she expected him both to honour the offer he had made to the hotel, and to send a cheque to her immediately.

'How kind, dear lady,' he replied. 'Never fear, it will be sorted out very shortly. I appreciate your understanding.'

For the second time Elizabeth felt she had been put on the back foot. She was tempted to say more, but for the sake of Jack and Mary she kept quiet.

Jack was appalled. 'You will never see a penny of it again!'

But within a week a cheque arrived for just fifty pounds, with an accompanying letter stating that this was in part payment. However, it didn't say in part payment of what. Over the next few years Gerald slipped her the occasional envelope with cash enclosed, or even a cheque for a small amount. But when he died nearly one thousand pounds still remained outstanding.

Mary's pregnancy went smoothly, although the sudden death of Brian and Betty's little girl did cast a shadow over the birth of Sheila.

Alice had suffered a cot death, which made it all the more tragic for Brian and Betty as they kept blaming themselves.

Jack was completely overwhelmed by his daughter's birth. He had not been allowed into the delivery room, but had to sit anxiously in the waiting room with several other prospective fathers. Frequently, you could hear a distant but unnerving cry from one of the mothers in labour, so it was an enormous relief when a midwife arrived to inform him that his wife had given birth to a baby girl, and that they were both doing well.

Everyone was overjoyed, including Freda, who bravely managed to visit Mary in hospital once whilst she remained in hospital for the statutory ten days. She complained bitterly that she wasn't allowed to smoke even in the corridor, and only stayed a few minutes, but not before presenting Mary with a dainty baby dress from Daisy Montague's boutique.

'It smells of smoke,' Mary complained when she left.

But Elizabeth had tactfully replaced it in its tissue paper, offering to take it home and carefully wash it. Elizabeth liked Freda, sensing her life with her husband was not easy. Despite their having little in common, she respected Freda's ability to hold down a responsible job, together with the fact that she knew Freda admired her son, and given the opportunity would make a fuss of him.

Betty returned to work, and in spite of the tragedy of losing Alice, she and Brian accepted the invitation to be godparents to Sheila. Jack realised how painful it must be for them, but as his mother pointed out, they had big hearts and Betty was a natural mother. The unspoken words 'unlike Mary' hung in the air, but it had soon become obvious that, whilst loving her child, Mary found the day-to-day tasks of looking after her something of a chore.

Sheila was four when Gerald died. It was a mystery: his car was found in a ditch on the outskirts of Belper early one Monday morning. No other car was involved, and there were no witnesses. The coroner's report revealed that he was not under the influence of alcohol, but that it had been a heart attack.

The local paper ran a full-page spread, detailing his tireless work for the council. However, the church was only half full at the funeral. His half-brothers were in attendance, but not their wives. Jack organised a reception at a small hotel close to the church. He was relieved for Mary and Freda that most people in the congregation did take the trouble to come to the reception. Brian and Betty had taken care of Sheila during the service and brought her along to what Brian described as the 'bun fight' afterwards. Jack was proud to see how his daughter charmed everyone, completely stealing the show, telling everyone seriously that her grandad had gone to heaven like her grandma Elizabeth's cat.

Jack had only met Gerald's half-brother Charles briefly once before, at his and Mary's wedding. He was pleased to see him at the reception. Walking over to him with Sheila in his arms, he introduced himself again. Charles was polite, offering his condolences to the family, whilst engaging in a game of peekaboo with Sheila.

'I am now the proud grandfather of eight grandchildren. The eldest in his twenties, the youngest nine years old. One of the compensations of getting old, I feel.' He hesitated before gently taking Jack's arm. 'Now Jack, I need to have a word with you. Well, more than a word, more a discussion. Now isn't the right time, but would it be possible for you to call into my office one day next week? If Mary wishes to join you, or even Freda, that's perfectly fine, but I have to say that in my opinion this matter is best discussed man to man.'

'That sounds a little ominous,' Jack replied, placing a wriggling Sheila on the ground.

'I am afraid it is, Jack,' Charles replied, 'but leave it for next week. I'd rather you come to the office as all the papers are there.'

'I could actually come tomorrow morning,' Jack replied. 'I took a few days off to help Mary. Freda is acting increasingly strangely, and certainly can't return to work at the moment. She insists that there is no will, and as far as Mary and I can see there is very little paperwork to do with his affairs in his office at home. I was going to contact you, as I presumed he kept everything at work.'

'What did he say?' Mary demanded as Charles took his leave. 'He thinks he's something special, always been so mean to my father and mum. When I was small we were always invited at Christmas and Easter, but it suddenly stopped. Mum hates them all.'

'Well, he seemed charming,' Jack replied, 'and if you remember they were very generous when we got married, and when Sheila was born. Let's see, Mary, he wants me to go to his office. I've said I'll go tomorrow. You are of course invited if you want to come, even Freda, but somehow I don't think that would be a good idea.'

He put a protective arm around Mary, sensing that tomorrow would reveal unsavoury things about her father.

'I don't want to go, Jack,' she said. 'You sort it, please.'

'I will, I will,' he replied, 'now go and pile me a plate. Oh, and a cup of tea. At my dad's funeral Mum let me eat more than my fair share of pork pies.'

He sensed Mary's mood lighten as she grabbed her daughter's hand and invited her to help select a plateful of food for Daddy.

* * *

As Jack drove home from Charles' office the following day, he felt exhausted, accepting that telling Mary what he had learned was not going to be easy. He was aware that his marriage could be permanently damaged if he handled the situation poorly. At the florist he stopped off to buy a large bunch of flowers for Mary, and a small cactus with a bright orange flower for Sheila.

Sheila greeted him at the door. Mary was ironing in the front room whilst watching the television.

'I thought Sheila was going to school,' Jack asked as he presented Sheila with the cactus.

'She didn't want to go,' Mary replied, 'and I didn't see any reason to force her, she's only six.'

Jack wanted to launch into the pros and cons of whether it was a good idea to give in to a six-year-old's whims, but he knew this was not the right time. He offered Mary the flowers, saying, 'These are for you, darling, with my love. It's going to be a tough time in the next few weeks, maybe even months, but you must be clear we are in this together.'

She barely acknowledged the flowers, placing them on the ironing board, then unplugged the iron and sat down. Jack turned off the television, and reaching for Mary's hand he related all that Charles had told him.

'Your father was heavily in debt when he died, Mary. You know he worked for Charles and his other half-brother. Well, it sounds as if they've been rather careless and naïve in not paying more attention to what he was doing, but Charles has been going over the accounts and found that – this isn't easy for me to say, Mary – he was defrauding them enormously. Selling their stock for cash. Borrowing money against your house, which they owned. All in the name of their firm. And now he's died, all sorts of people are contacting Charles and his brother to inquire about loans, contracts, investments – things Charles knew nothing about. It's put their whole business in jeopardy. It'll have to go to lawyers, and the police too.'

He decided to omit mentioning the money still owed to his mother.

'They're going to have to sell your family home to recover some revenue. We'll need to help Freda find somewhere to live. I'm sorry, Mary, Charles seemed to think they won't be able to prevent a scandal, and he wanted us to be prepared.'

Mary remained silent throughout the saga, and at times Jack's mind wandered, bizarrely thinking about the flowers on the ironing board and how they should be put in water. When he had concluded, he reached again for her hand, which she had withdrawn half way through his diatribe. At last she responded, and her voice held a tone he had not heard before.

'You believe all this, don't you? You hated my father from the minute you met him. Do you know, he never said a word against his half-brothers? He only spoke highly of them to everyone.'

'That's because he was a snob, Mary. You are right, it would be dishonest of me to say I liked him, but that didn't stop me loving you. Let's be honest, you never wanted to see your parents. I feel sorry for Charles and his brother. Yes, they have been foolish, but they tried to do the decent thing. The decent thing mainly with you in mind, Mary. You and I will survive, but we have to think about Freda. She is a bit strange at the moment. I can't see her going back to work, can you?'

Mary didn't reply.

'What do you think, Mary? Maybe a retirement home would be the best solution. Somewhere convenient for us to visit and take her out.'

Mary got up and took the flowers into the kitchen. When she returned, she plugged in the iron and continued to press clothes from the ironing basket.

'Say something, Mary?' Jack pleaded.

'What is there to say?' she replied. 'The papers are full of what my father has done for the town, but his own family haven't a good word for him. I'm sure my father thought the house was his, part of his inheritance. Perhaps it's us who should be going to the solicitors. But oh no, you believe everything they say. We might as well go to Mum's this afternoon, break the bad news. God knows how she'll react.'

Jack picked Sheila up, and taking her into the kitchen he started to prepare lunch, but not before putting the flowers in water.

When they arrived at Freda's it was late afternoon. Elizabeth was there too, having just dropped by to check if Freda was all right. She explained to Mary that she thought Freda should see a doctor, as she had a suspicion she might have had a mild stroke. On the table was a large chocolate cake that a neighbour had left earlier, together with several packets of biscuits sent by Freda's colleagues from the factory. Freda was still in her dressing gown. She looked unkempt and Elizabeth was holding her hand when they entered the room.

'Hope you don't mind, Mary,' she said, looking up, 'but I've contacted the medical centre. The receptionist is going to phone back with an appointment for your mum. She's not good, are you, my dear?' she said softly to Freda.

Sheila broke the awkward silence by running to greet her grandma.

'Daddy's bought me a cactus,' she cried, 'it's all prickly. He said I can keep it in my bedroom. It doesn't need much water.'

Jack knelt in front of Freda.

'Are you ok, love?'

She looked up, smiling, then replied, 'I'm ok, Jack, just a bit tired, your mum's very kind. You know, I'd like a cup of tea, Mary, go and put the kettle on. There's some biscuits on the shelf.'

But at that moment the doorbell rang. Elizabeth went to answer it. When she came back, she was accompanied by a young woman holding the hand of a girl of about ten or eleven years old.

'This is…' Elizabeth hesitated.

'I'm Nora Clifford,' the young woman announced as she entered the room. To Elizabeth she seemed a very presentable young woman, possibly in her early thirties. Her demeanour was confident, as if she had rehearsed what she was about to say. Looking around the room, she approached Mary. Then she let go of the child's hand and moved to one side. 'This is Grace,' she said, 'this is your half-sister, Mary.'

Jack told Brian later that if at that moment the ground could have swallowed him up he would have been eternally grateful.

'I'm sorry,' she continued quietly, 'I know this is perhaps a shock, but I think your mum knew. Gerald, well, I mean, your dad and I were, well, I suppose you could say were partners for many years, ever since I was quite young. He was with me the night before he died. I am sure there were other women, he was quite the ladies' man. But he and I were on and off, if you'll pardon the expression, for many years. Grace is eleven, and to be fair to him he did his best to take care of us, providing I fell in with his requirements.'

'Stop!' Elizabeth interjected. 'There are two children in this room and Mrs Blunt is not well.'

'I understand, I really do,' exclaimed Nora. 'I'm sorry, it's just the word on the street.' She looked directly at Freda. 'There are a lot of people queuing up for money owed to them by Gerald. A friend of his called me, he'd known about us for years. Nice bloke, we always kept everything very quiet about Grace, but he must have guessed. He said, get down there, Nora, state your claim before it's too late. Now I'm not greedy, but Grace has just passed her eleven-plus.'

As she spoke, Jack turned and saw Grace standing directly in front of the chocolate cake. She seemed oblivious to what was being said around her.

'Would you like a piece of cake?' Jack asked. She did not reply, but just nodded, watching him carefully as he cut her a large slice. She held it in her hands, but to his surprise started eating it the wrong way round, nibbling it from the back towards its point. Crumbs dropped on the floor, but her concentration was so intense she didn't notice.

'All I want is a bit of help putting Grace through grammar school. She was top of her year for the whole county. Can you believe that? They have already offered her a place. Gerald knew it was a bit difficult, but he was proud of her, I think, he said Mary had gone to the same school.'

Freda started to laugh, a high-pitched laugh that made Sheila cry. Elizabeth started to comfort her, but Mary screamed, 'Get out! Get out, you filthy woman, and take your little bastard with you. I don't believe a word you've said.'

Jack reached towards her.

'Don't touch me!' she shouted. 'Just get that little bastard and her slut of a mother out of here.' She approached Nora as if she was going to strike her. 'Don't you ever come near us again.'

Grace remained still, with her back to the proceedings, continuing to nibble at the cake. Sheila tried to bury her head in her mother's skirt.

'Stop, stop!' begged Elizabeth, but Nora had already grabbed her daughter's hand and was heading for the front door.

Jack followed her. 'Please, Mrs Clifford – Miss Clifford,' he corrected himself.

'Don't you fret,' she replied, 'you'll never hear from me again. I'm not sure that wife of yours isn't a bastard too. He once told me he had never married Freda. He called it a relationship of convenience. He was a bastard too at times, but he had a loveless marriage. Don't you worry, you'll never hear from Grace and me again.'

Jack followed them to the bus stop, trying to excuse his wife's behaviour. But Nora would have none of it. There were two other people waiting for the bus, but as it approached, Jack drew Grace back so they would be last to get on. Holding her by the shoulders he looked into her face.

'Grace, you remember you have to go to the grammar school. That's the most important thing in your life.' Nora looked down, letting him continue. 'Do you understand, Grace?' he asked.

She barely raised her head, but nodded, then slipped the last tiny piece of the chocolate cake into her mouth.

Jack turned away as they got on the bus. Walking quickly, he was able to catch a glimpse of Grace as the bus passed. As she gazed out of the window, she looked directly into his eyes and smiled.

CHAPTER TWENTY-SEVEN

Do you cry out in your sleep, all my failings exposed?
Get a taste in my mouth, as desperation takes hold

– JOY DIVISION, 'LOVE WILL TEAR US APART'

DERBY, 2012

The end of January was never, in Jack's opinion, a particularly good time of year. With the Christmas excess over, the shops were full of tired-looking Christmas items stacked unimaginatively on shelves that announced everything was a bargain. His allotment showed little sign of springing to life, apart from a cluster of early snowdrops under the holly tree. The weather continued to be cold and grey.

As he entered the supermarket for his regular Saturday morning shop, he avoided the Christmas bargains, and headed for the fruit and vegetables, stopping for a while to look along the stand that housed the spring bulbs. Dark purple tulips, striped cream parrot tulips, red dwarf ones with their tips tinged with orange. He could never resist them, even though he knew that buying them loose from the market was the cheaper option. And did he need more spring bulbs? No, he reasoned, but he reached for two packets of plain white tulip bulbs anyway. He smiled inwardly. *This is my treat*, he thought.

Often when planting something, he would instil it with a name or a memory. Tulips were usually for his mother, sweet peas were for Mary, and Brussels sprouts always made him think of his father. Contemplating that he was getting a little crazier by the minute, he rounded the corner and spotted Nancy. He was immediately aware that given the opportunity she would have avoided him, but he strode towards her, seizing his opportunity. She still had the ability to look slightly out of the ordinary. She wore a plain navy coat, but around her neck she had tied a long multicoloured woollen scarf with enormous pom-poms.

'You look very cosy, Nancy,' Jack remarked. 'Happy New Year, and I'm so sorry for my rudeness when we last met. I can tell you, Betty really sorted me out when I saw her and Brian over Christmas. It was just such a shock seeing you again.'

Nancy laughed, tears filling her eyes. 'No need to apologise, Jack, being accosted by a seventy something ex-girlfriend, I can imagine it was something of a surprise. Happy New Year to you!' she exclaimed, removing her woolly glove and offering him her hand.

'Have you time for a coffee?' Jack asked. 'As usual I'm on a tight schedule, but I can be finished in twenty minutes. We could meet at the coffee bar.'

Again Nancy laughed. 'It's a date, but if you're there first can you get a table near the window, please, so I can keep an eye on Nimble?' Jack looked puzzled. 'Nimble is my dog,' she explained. 'I think you've already met him, I saw you once stroking him.'

'Do you mean that shaggy...' Jack searched for a more suitable word.

'Scruffy is the word you're looking for,' Nancy chuckled.

'No,' Jack countered, 'he's lovely, a really friendly chap. I didn't realise he was yours. Tell me about him in a minute. See you in the café.'

The coffee was awful – Jack described it as sludge – but the heated mince pies were good. Their conversation was easy. It didn't touch on long-hidden emotions but remained tender and light. Nancy talked mostly about Seamus, and her move back to Derbyshire. Jack spoke of his daughter Sheila and grandson Tom, who had just started university. Half an hour swept by. Eventually Jack carried Nancy's bags to the bus stop, introducing himself again to Nimble.

'Let's do this again, Nancy. It's been good to catch up.'

'Agreed,' Nancy replied, 'but next time the coffee is on me.'

She cried all the way home, her tears dropping onto Nimble's head, which rested gently on her lap. She searched in vain for a handkerchief or a tissue, but found none, resorting in the end to using her glove to dry her face. She continued to cry even after arriving home and struggling to make a cup of tea. Jack was still Jack, she thought.

Slowly her emotions subsided and she and Nimble shared a packet of half price shortbread biscuits in front of the fire. How wonderful, she contemplated, her love for Jack had never faded; it had just been carefully stored away, waiting to be revisited.

Yes, she was a woman of more than a certain age, but thank goodness she could still remember, not just the pain, but the joy that had engulfed them for that short period all those years ago. Given more time, she thought they might have talked about the past, but it hardly mattered now. What did matter was that after all those years they could sit comfortably across a table and enjoy each other's company again. She had been delighted by how much they had laughed, sharing the absurdity of bumping into each other after so many years.

She resolved that she would wait a few more weeks before shopping on a Saturday again. Wonderful as it had been, she hardly wanted Jack to feel he was being stalked. The thought made her laugh out loud, which in turn made Nimble wake up. He rose, stretched, then rested his head on her knee and wagged his tail.

At the end of February Nancy and Nimble caught the bus to the supermarket. All the windows were steamed up, and Nancy and a rather moist Nimble had to wedge themselves into the area reserved for pushchairs. But happily there was the usual camaraderie, with only one young woman remarking that Nimble smelt a bit 'pongy'.

At the supermarket Charlie spotted Nancy, greeting her in his usual friendly fashion and making a fuss of Nimble. 'I'd love a dog like him, you know. Best dog in the world, aren't you, Nimble? So well-behaved, sits there patiently even though kids come up and stroke him. Never heard him bark.'

'I sometimes think he's wiser than I am,' Nancy replied.

As she entered the supermarket, she spotted Jack immediately. He was standing chatting to a young couple, whose toddler was attempting to climb out of his child seat on the shopping trolley.

She wanted to go over and join them, but decided her relationship with Jack was not well-established enough to permit her invading his space. Better to wait, she thought, until he continued his shopping alone.

The supermarket was crammed with hordes of damp shoppers vying with each other to reach items off the shelves. Nancy had lost all sight of Jack, but she selected her shopping and joined one of the long queues at the checkout. When she and Jack had last met, they had both found the dreadful coffee in the café amusing, and in her handbag she had a leaflet advertising a rather smart new coffee machine, for which one had to use their '*premier cru*' coffee capsules. She had purchased one as a gift for herself at Christmas and felt ashamed to admit she was now a convert.

As she stood waiting in the tedious queue, she glanced out of the window to check on Nimble. Her heart lurched. Nimble's space was empty. She could see one other little terrier, and a large Labrador, but no sign of Nimble. An overwhelming panic gripped her. Leaving her trolley, she pushed through the queue and past the cashier.

'You can't go that way, madam,' someone cried, but she failed to notice.

Rushing outside, she was buffeted for a second by the wind and rain, but she regained her balance and headed for the spot where she had left Nimble. He was nowhere to be seen. Charlie had obviously retreated inside to shelter from the pouring rain.

'Nimble, Nimble!' she cried, running into the car park to search between the lines of cars. Several times she bumped into shoppers with their trolleys.

'Have you seen a dog?' she cried. 'A shaggy dog, like the one in the Dulux advert.' A few kindly souls stopped in response to her distress, but most people were fighting to avoid remaining in the rain for too long. She half ran back into the supermarket, grabbing an assistant.

'Where's Charlie, please? He usually looks after my dog.'

'He's on his break, luv,' the young assistant replied. 'Didn't know he was an official dog watcher. He'll be back in a minute.'

Nancy pushed through the crowds, running as best as she could up and down the aisles. When she eventually spotted Jack, he was reaching for a bottle of wine.

'Jack!' she cried. 'Jack, I've lost Nimble, somebody must have stolen him!' She broke into heavy sobs as she leaned heavily on his laden trolley. 'Help me, Jack, please help me. He's all I've got. Charlie usually looks after him, but he's on his break. Oh Jack, he's gone.'

For a moment Jack felt embarrassed, as curious shoppers turned, hearing Nancy's heartfelt plea for help.

'Wait a minute, Nancy,' he comforted her, 'let me pay for my shopping and then of course I'll help you look for him. He's probably not far.'

'But there's no time!' Nancy retorted. 'I've been round the car park, he always comes when I call. His lead has gone, someone must have taken him.'

At that moment Charlie appeared, followed by the young assistant.

'David here says you've lost Nimble. He was there when I left. Bloody kids I expect…' He didn't finish his sentence, in deference to Nancy's gentle sobbing. Looking meaningfully at Jack, he suggested that he would take care of Jack's shopping whilst he and Nancy went in search of Nimble.

'Please, Jack,' Nancy added through her tears, 'I couldn't thank you enough.'

It was still raining, a cold relentless rain driven horizontally at times by the wind. They drove around the car park, with Nancy shouting Nimble's name though the open window. The supermarket was on the edge of the town, and the heavy traffic made it difficult to comb the surrounding area. Between shouting Nimble's name, Nancy continued to sob.

'I'll get out and walk,' she said eventually. 'Perhaps the police could help?'

'You are not getting out and walking anywhere in weather like this,' Jack replied. 'Now for goodness' sake calm down and think sensibly.'

'He's all I've got, Jack,' she whispered. 'You can't understand, without him I think I might have just given up.'

'Of course I understand,' Jack replied severely, 'don't you think I haven't felt the same way? To lose someone you love? Don't tell me I don't understand. Come on, let's get back to the supermarket. I'm late for Mary already, but we'll sort something out.' He reached over and grasped her hand, and raising it to his lips he gently kissed it. 'Come on, Nancy, you're made of sterner stuff. We'll find him.'

Eventually they made it back to the Dennison's car park and found a place to park. Jack held Nancy's arm as they wove their way through the crowds of shoppers. At the front entrance, standing under the Dennison's sign, was Charlie – with Nimble next to him.

Even Jack felt like crying.

Together they all hugged one another, with Nimble wagging his tail furiously.

'He just appeared out of nowhere,' Charlie explained. 'I reckon some kid nicked him, then chickened out before he got home, or was sent back by his parents. He's amazing, Nancy, he even negotiated the automatic doors. One of the assistants found him trotting between jams and cereals. He was obviously looking for you. I've paid for your shopping, Jack, it's in the trolley. You better get off to sort Mary out; we'll settle up later. She'll not take kindly to you being late on a day like this,' he added with a wink.

Nancy looked forlorn and wet, but Jack was happy to take charge.

'Charlie, can you take care of Nancy, please? Put her in a taxi to take her home. You must know a sympathetic one that will take a wet dog? Nancy, I'll call around your place later this afternoon. What number Park Place is it?'

'Fifty-six,' she replied weakly, 'nearly opposite the park gates.'

'Right, have the kettle on about half three. Now listen carefully,' he addressed Nimble, 'you take care of Nancy. I suggest you see that she has a hot bath.'

Shaking Charlie's hand, and pecking Nancy on the cheek, he left hurriedly, knowing he would have to appease Mary with a few more white lies.

He reached Nancy's a little before three thirty.

Opening her front door, Nancy exclaimed, 'You said half three! I've only just got out of the bath.'

She wore a long pale blue woollen dressing gown, with a soft fluffy collar. Her hair was the usual mass of unruly curls, slightly wet from her bath. Nimble stood beside her, his coat still moist from the rain.

'Excuse us both,' she laughed as Jack entered the hall. 'We are both a bit bedraggled. Don't they say that dogs and their owners are apt to look alike?'

Jack ruffled Nimble's coat. 'Well, yes, I have to admit there is a kind of resemblance, but at least you smell nicer than Nimble.'

'Give me a few minutes whilst I get dressed,' she said, leading Jack into the front room. 'The fire is on.'

In the bay window stood Seamus's desk, and in front of it an old leather office chair. Jack examined the selection of photographs, deeply touched to see the one of him and Nancy at Brian and Betty's wedding. There were several others, mostly of Nancy and Seamus on holiday, and a single black and white photograph of Seamus with his dog.

'He fell for me, just after his dog Bess died,' Nancy said as she entered the room. 'He said he met me on the rebound.'

'He looks a lovely man,' Jack offered. 'I can see he had a twinkle in his eye.'

'You would have liked him, Jack. He was a kind, compassionate man and a very fine doctor. There were literally hundreds at his funeral.'

'I guess he knew about me, judging from the photograph of us.'

'Of course,' replied Nancy, 'he would often tease me about my young boyfriend. In a way it was easy for us. I accepted he continued to love his wife, he accepted that I had made an agonising decision in leaving you.'

There was a pause in their conversation. Then she said, 'Do you notice an elephant in the room?'

'I do,' replied Jack. 'You make us a cup of tea, and then shall we see if we can get rid of it?'

'I doubt it will go through the door,' Nancy warned.

'Rubbish,' replied Jack. 'We can always set Nimble onto it.'

For the rest of the day they sat talking in front of the fire. Nancy made Jack a sandwich when she realised he hadn't had lunch. As the light faded, they started to piece together the jigsaw of the intervening forty years.

'Betty told me my mother had given you a reference in order to help you get the job in the care home. She never told me, Nancy. It wasn't until she was dying that she said quite unexpectedly, "Have you seen Nancy?" She was really poorly at the end, and a little delirious, so when she mentioned your name I'm afraid I didn't respond.'

Nancy took a deep breath. She remembered so vividly the day that she and Elizabeth had sat in the café whilst Jack was in France. She had promised never to reveal that Elizabeth had asked her to leave him. *But*, she thought, *does it really matter now?*

'Your mother loved you above all else,' she started, 'and although I only knew her for a short time I knew and respected that it was a healthy love. She wanted the best for you. She could so easily have been clingy after your father died. But she avoided that by building a life for herself, allowing you to grow independently. But after the accident, she felt that like any mother she needed to fight for you. Bill was dangerous, there was no question of that, and I would have reacted the same way.'

'What do you mean exactly?' Jack asked.

Nancy pulled herself awkwardly from her chair. 'Time for a sherry,' she said. 'I used to tell myself I liked dry sherry, it seemed rather chic, but actually I love it as sweet as it comes. Try this,' she said, passing him a glass, 'it's a Sanderson's vintage, Seamus's favourite.' Then she reached for a box of matches off the desk and started to light a selection of candles in an assortment of differently shaped candlesticks, some modern, some old and worn.

After Christmas she had persuaded her decorator that magnolia actually made her feel depressed, and she and Nimble had decided they preferred a soft green paint for the walls and a light grey for the woodwork. He had been reluctant, but when the job was done, he had complimented her on the result and helped her to hang her numerous pictures. The bill had been enormous, but she hadn't cared, explaining to Nimble that they might as well spend it whilst they could enjoy it.

'Do you remember all those candles we bought at Habitat that time in London? I go to Ikea now, they're a lot cheaper, but to me they are a necessity. Seamus used to say it's hard to have a row in candlelight.'

She sat down again, balancing her glass carefully on a small table. 'Now, where was I? Yes, telling you about your lovely mother. We had one thing in common, Jack, you know, we both loved you. Betty probably told you that Bill kept to his word. He never molested me. He was kind and as loving as I would allow, providing I remained faithful to him; I knew I was safe. He offered me a kind of clean canvas, then watched lovingly whilst I coloured it in with new friends, a job which I adored, a home of sorts.'

She reached out to take another sip from her sherry, then continued.

'But when he died, I didn't grieve. I felt it was a release for both of us. He'd kept his side of the bargain, and I'd kept mine. I know I could have been kinder to him as he got older, but I think just having me close brought him comfort.'

Jack refilled their glasses. The light had completely faded, and he switched on a small table lamp, relighting one of the candles that had spluttered and gone out.

'I'm not surprised, Nancy. I think I always suspected that Mum had warned you off. I just went to pieces after you left. Mary pulled me back from the brink. How old was I, twenty-four? In the back of my mind I always thought I would make one last attempt to find you, but then Mary and I decided to make a go of it, and the rest is history.'

They both remained silent, until Nancy reached over and touched Jack's hand. 'The elephant's stuck halfway through the door. Betty and Brian told me all about the scandal over Mary's dad. I never knew him, although I do vaguely remember people talking about him. I kind of had the impression he was a rather benevolent person, but obviously not. But what happened to Grace?'

'Well, I expect Betty told you that Mum and I settled some money on her that allowed her to go to grammar school. Mary never knew, still doesn't. Her mother went off to America shortly after the scandal, so she continued to live with her grandma. Her aunt and uncle were very supportive. She did fantastically well at the Grammar, and even secured a place at Oxford. It was in the local paper. I am sure Mary must have seen it, but we never talked about it. As far as Mary was concerned she was "that little bastard".

'Yes, Betty did mention it, but what really happened to Grace? Betty kind of suggested something more?'

Jack laughed. 'Cheeky buggers, they probably told you about when they bumped into us in Brighton.' He paused. 'It's a long story.'

'We have the time,' replied Nancy, 'but only if you want to take it.'

DERBY, 1982

Grace had contacted him for the very first time shortly after the announcement of her Oxford offer in the local paper. His secretary at Rolls-Royce had said that a young lady called Grace had asked to speak to him. Jack was relieved, as he hadn't decided what to do after he'd spotted the article in the paper. His mother was delighted, insisting she had always felt that Grace would do well regardless of her rather unfortunate background. He was sure that Mary had seen both the article and the photograph of Grace, but she certainly didn't mention it.

When he took the call, he pictured the little girl with the long brown hair eating the chocolate cake. But the voice revealed something different, young but confident. She immediately expressed her gratitude for the yearly legacy. Her grandmother had told her about it when her mother had left for America. Whilst the family were proud, they felt it was her right and that they should accept the money as it would help her education. She continued by saying that what was more important for her was the memory of Jack telling her she must go to the grammar school, that it was the most important thing in her life.

'Those words never left me. Even when my mother took off, nothing seemed to matter but to do exactly what you said.'

'I wish I had that effect on more people,' Jack laughed over the phone.

'Apart from saying thank you, I wanted to tell you that I have also been awarded a small scholarship, so it isn't necessary to continue with the allowance. My aunt and uncle have always been very kind, so there is no need for it any more. I am just so grateful, we all are.'

An alarm started up in the building, making it nearly impossible for Jack to hear Grace over the phone.

'Sorry, Grace,' he shouted, 'the fire alarm has just gone off. I doubt there's any real problem, but we have to vacate the building. Have you time to meet up?'

People were rushing around, some shouting to Jack to hurry.

'Saturday morning,' he shouted, 'the Kardomah. Eleven o'clock?'

'Fine,' she replied, 'see you then.'

He walked down the stairs slowly, realising that it was only a false alarm. He felt rather moved by hearing Grace's voice. She sounded charming, and he slightly regretted that he hadn't chosen a trendier place for their rendezvous. However, realistically, he accepted he was already a grandad, so perhaps it had been the right choice after all.

On the Saturday morning he was late, but nevertheless decided to take his Triumph TR2. Mary had grown to hate it, and he had eventually bought a more suitable family car, but he loved his TR2 even though it was somewhat temperamental at times. The morning air was damp and the car acted like an arthritic pensioner. At twenty past eleven he limped into Derby, but to his relief found a parking space opposite the coffee shop. He leapt out of the car and, paying very little attention to the traffic, ran across the road and into the Kardomah. Most of the tables were full, but he spotted Grace by the window. She stood up, waving and indicating the empty chair.

Before he could apologise she blurted out, 'Your car is fab, British racing green, I love it.'

'Thank you, Grace,' he replied, 'but she's also a nightmare at times. Sorry for being late. Have you been waiting long?'

'Well, yes,' she replied honestly. 'I was nervous, so I arrived about forty minutes ago. The waitress over there, the peroxide blonde who looks like a pale imitation of Dusty Springfield, has been giving me some very ominous looks. Can you order now, please? I'll have another coffee.'

'And something to eat?' Jack enquired.

'Well, yes,' she replied, 'but this is on me. Now I'm not nervous any more, I'll have a toasted teacake.'

'Why were you nervous?' Jack asked whilst summoning the Dusty Springfield lookalike.

'Well, wouldn't you be?' she came back strongly. 'I've been a kind of kept woman since I was eleven, banished from your house and called a bastard, and apart from the miraculous five hundred a year which we happily accepted, you have never contacted me. I do know your mother has made enquiries about me, but that's all. I didn't even remember what you looked like.'

'Young, handsome,' he joked, 'not easily forgotten.'

She laughed. 'At least you have a sexy car.'

'A TR2, sexy? I never thought of that, but on reflection I do think she is lovely, and I suppose I love her.'

'Does your wife love her?' Grace asked, cutting through their good humour like a knife through butter.

'No, not really, but Sheila my daughter does, providing it's a nice day and we have the top down.'

They talked for an hour, and Jack was slightly in awe of her sophistication. She had already spent a term at Oxford and it sounded rather daunting. Within the first few weeks she had become a member of a debating society, plus contributing to an arts magazine. With some amusement in her voice she assured him his investment had been well spent.

They had become oblivious of the bustle around them, but to appease Dusty they ordered another round of teacakes, and finally Jack passed over the present he and his mother had bought Grace: a large leather satchel.

'Mum says it will fit in the basket of your bike. She's convinced everyone rides around Oxford on bikes. I hope you haven't one already. And please don't argue about the money. We both want you to continue to accept it until you graduate. After that we'll let you fly solo.'

'But what about my half-sister Mary? Your wife? Doesn't she have a say?'

'I have no idea,' replied Jack, 'we've never discussed it since you left the house, eating, if I remember correctly, a large piece of chocolate cake.'

'Oh my God, I remember that. Gosh, what a gauche little thing I was, wasn't I?'

'Perhaps,' Jack replied, 'but you have made up for it since.'

For a moment he felt a wisp of sexuality encircle them. As he looked across the table, he realised what a very attractive woman she had developed into. She wore jeans, a polo-necked jumper and a short woollen jacket. Her dark eyes were enhanced with a little mascara, but that was all the make-up she wore, apart from a trace of pale red lipstick. But what really took his eye were her beautiful hands, long fingers with each nail carefully painted the same hue as her lipstick.

Seeing him glance at them, she remarked, 'Gran says my hands show I do very little housework. Which is true I suppose. So thank you for the offer of the money. If it does continue, would you mind if some of it went to pay for a cleaner for Gran? I worry when I'm away that she's not coping that well.'

'The money is yours,' Jack replied. 'We have never questioned how you spend it.'

'Can we meet again, Jack?' she asked as they were about to leave.

'Of course,' he replied. 'I want to hear all about those shimmering towers. Phone me at work next time you're home. Let's meet then.'

Over the next three years Grace would telephone Jack whenever she was back in Derby. The formula was usually the same: Jack would pick her up in his TR2, then they would decide where to go.

It was unspoken, but they were both aware that it was wise to use a certain amount of discretion, so it was usually a country pub, or a restaurant in Nottingham. On one occasion they met in London for the day when Grace was doing some research at the British Library and Jack had a Union meeting. Their friendship blossomed; they both enjoyed each other's company, and frequently found that they had shared interests.

Jack was intrigued to know why she had decided to study law, and was charmed to discover that in the sixth form she had read a book by Maya Angelou that had inspired her. He delighted in the challenge of keeping up with her, as she constantly used him as a sounding board whilst she formulated her opinions in a rapidly changing Thatcherite Britain. Her aura was with him constantly, providing a barrier against his home life of Mary's increasing indifference and even the birth of his grandson. Grace was the only person he could truly share his innermost feelings with. He felt she was wise well beyond her years.

As her studies progressed, she told Jack that she intended to specialise in women's rights. A conversation with Grace, he acknowledged, was in a different league to a conversation with Mary, or even, sadly, his daughter Sheila. It was more like being with Nancy, he realised. He accepted that he found her enormously attractive and felt flattered that she wanted to spend time with him. An unspoken agreement that up until Grace's graduation had protected them from the consequences of drawing too close finally dissolved when she completed her final year.

Jack wasn't surprised when she graduated with a First, just immensely proud that she had achieved her goal. All the graduates were allowed two guests to the ceremony, and he had presumed that Grace's grandmother and aunt would be there. But her grandma did not want to go, feeling the journey would be too difficult, and her aunt and uncle had already booked a holiday for that week.

'It's down to you,' Grace had told him on the telephone. 'If you don't come, I'll be the only one there without someone to clap for them.'

He accepted immediately, knowing full well he wouldn't tell Mary. However, they did consider inviting Elizabeth, but as Jack pointed out, if Mary ever found out, it would have been wrong to have implicated his mother.

Oxford buzzed, with hundreds of graduates, their well-wishers and parents filling every inch of the town. Jack sat next to an elderly couple who were in the audience to witness their grandson's graduation. When he reached the front of the procession, they clapped vigorously, completely overcome with emotion, as did Jack when Grace appeared.

After the ceremony everyone streamed out into the courtyard, a mélange of mortarboarded students, friends and relatives all trying to meet up in groups to take photographs. He saw Grace in the distance talking to a group of students. Catching a glimpse of him, she managed to manoeuvre her way through the crowds, then, dragging him back to her friends, she announced, 'This is Jack,' followed by a pregnant pause. 'What are you, Jack?' she laughed. 'How do I describe you?'

'Tricky,' he retorted. 'How about confidant and best friend?'

Her laughter subsided. 'Yes,' she replied, 'definitely my best friend.'

They had dinner with several other graduates and their parents, then headed at Grace's request to a party on the outskirts of the city. Jack had booked himself into a bed and breakfast. When he warned them that he might be late, they had given him a key.

Grace had changed out of her graduation subfusc, and was now wearing a red pleated miniskirt, white blouse and matching red cardigan; perfectly demure, Jack had thought, until he spotted the sheer black stockings and the high-heeled shoes. Over dinner she had removed her cardigan, and for the party she removed the blouse, leaving just a black strappy top.

'Any more to come off?' he enquired admiringly.

'That depends on you, Jack,' she replied, pulling him into a lively crowd of dancers.

He was surprised he didn't feel old amongst these young people, just a little more mature, but he was envious of their confidence. He had never wanted to go to university, but now as he danced with Grace, he considered that perhaps he had made a mistake. All the chief engineers at Rolls-Royce had university backgrounds, and his lack of a degree was, he accepted, beginning to work against him.

Grace remarked while they searched for the remains of the buffet that these kinds of parties were usually pretty boring after the first couple of hours. She filled their glasses from a large punchbowl, warning Jack that it was called 'Oxford Firewater' and not to be underestimated. Several young men asked her to dance, but she laughingly dismissed them, leaning heavily on Jack in what he felt was a delightfully tipsy demeanour.

As they drove to her flat, he was aware that he too was a little drunk. The flat was on the first floor, and she insisted on taking off her shoes, explaining that wobbly legs and high-heeled shoes were not a good combination.

This was the first time he had seen where she lived, although he understood she shared it with two other girls.

'I meant to tidy up,' she confessed, 'but there just wasn't time.'

'It doesn't matter,' he replied, 'I'm not stopping.'

'That's a pity,' she whispered, kissing him gently until he responded, encircling her in his arms and pressing his body deeply against hers. He started to speak, but she silenced him with a kiss that seemed to last for an eternity.

In the morning when he woke, she had disappeared from the bed they had shared. She appeared minutes later bearing a tray with two mugs of coffee. She was completely naked.

'Don't look like that, Jack,' she exclaimed, manoeuvring the tray onto the crowded dressing table. 'I seduced you. There's no question of that. If you're going to go around with a long guilty face, I might be tempted to throw this coffee over you.'

'Come on, Grace, I don't remember fighting too hard against your seductive powers.'

'Too right,' she replied, 'and anyway once I'd got you up here this lady wasn't for turning.' She sat cross-legged on the bed and encircled her hands around one of the coffee mugs.

He reached across, and taking the cup he took a sip. 'So this was kind of planned?'

'Not kind of planned, Jack. It was planned. Come on, you know it's been bubbling under the surface for years. You'll be pleased I lost my virginity with this in mind. What did our Right Honourable Maggie say the other day? "I am extraordinarily patient, providing I get my own way."'

'You have beautiful breasts, you know,' he said, reaching out to touch her nipples.

'I know I have,' she replied, taking the cup back. After replacing it on the dressing table, she slipped back into bed with him. 'But if the next question is going to be "was it worth it?", the answer is yes, but I hope you agree we both need more practice.'

The affair lasted five years. Grace continued to study for a Master's at Oxford, and then took up her first internship with a firm of solicitors in Milton Keynes. The distances made it difficult to see each other regularly, which Jack thought afterwards had protected them from prying eyes. Now in charge of the apprenticeship scheme for draughtsmen, he was often expected to be away from home, and when Grace moved to Milton Keynes he would even undertake the journey both ways in an evening just so they could share some time together.

On the surface their relationship remained uncomplicated, continuing to be the best of friends as well as lovers. They both accepted that to discuss the future would be unwise. Grace was forging ahead with her career, and Jack had not only his work, but other outside interests, the most important of which was to care for Tom. Mary seemed content, caught up in her world at the department store, where she had finally been appointed as head of the women's department.

There was a minor wake-up call when they accidentally bumped into Betty and Brian in Brighton. He and Grace were walking along the front holding hands, sharing an ice-cream. As they happily fought for the next bite, he spotted Betty and Brian, also hand in hand, walking towards them. Brian started to approach them, but Betty had restrained him. The front was crowded, so it was without too much embarrassment that they were able to pass without stopping to chat. Brian surprisingly never referred to the incident, possibly, Jack always thought, on Betty's instruction, but it had brought him face to face with the fact that he was in a relationship that would eventually have to be resolved. He was anxious that he was jeopardising Grace's chances of a normal, uncomplicated life.

Grace's grandmother had died, and unbeknown to Jack, Grace had applied for a position with a firm of solicitors in Edinburgh. When she received the letter of acceptance, she phoned Jack, briefly explaining that she needed to talk to him urgently. He had been expecting this for a long while, knowing that eventually their relationship would come to an end. He had felt culpable for a long while. He had helped pay for her education and then at the end of it bedded her. What would people think, what would his mother think? He knew his reputation was that of a 'nice young man' – not so young now, but someone who did the right thing.

When they met in her flat in Milton Keynes, Jack was convinced she was about to tell him that their relationship was over, or that someone else had come on the scene. But instead she began by saying, 'Jack, will you marry me?'

He stared for a moment, unsure if he had heard correctly.

'I want you to get a divorce,' Grace continued into the silence. 'I want you to come with me to Edinburgh. I have a wonderful opportunity with this firm. You can get away from your mundane life, find another job. I am sure there are plenty of opportunities for engineers in Scotland, or go for something you have always wanted to do – gardening, cinema. I know it would be hard to leave Tom, but believe me I'd welcome him into our life with open arms. I'm not brilliant with kids, and at the moment I have no desire to have any of my own, but Tom would be different.' She drew breath, and before Jack could reply she continued. 'Age hasn't the slightest thing to do with all of this, so don't start saying it matters. Statistically slightly older men marrying a younger woman have more of a chance of a successful marriage than couples who are the same age. I don't want your answer now. I want you to think about it. I love you, and I want to be with you for the rest of my life. I've felt this way since you cut me that enormous slice of chocolate cake.'

She insisted that they didn't discuss the matter there and then, and he left shortly afterwards. He was astounded, and struggled to concentrate on the journey back up the M1. When he arrived home, he wished desperately for someone he could talk to. His mother, Brian or even Sheila, but it was impossible. It would be cowardly to involve them in a decision that only he could make.

They met in Leeds the following week. Grace had been invited to the Leeds partners of the firm she was to work for. Jack had business in Sheffield and had offered to meet Grace for an early dinner, then run her back to Milton Keynes. He wasn't too familiar with the city, so they had arranged to meet at a street near the Town Hall.

It was dusk, and crowds of people were heading home. In the sky he could see a massive flock of what looked like starlings zig-zagging across the sky. One minute they appeared to disappear, the next minute they would return in even greater numbers. It was so spectacular that people stopped to stare, pointing them out to other passers-by, so eventually the crowds on the pavement became a hazard to those who were seriously trying to get home quickly.

He saw Grace from a distance. She stopped to look at the birds, then left the pavement to walk on the road and avoid the crowds. He considered how she had changed in the last few years. Her thick dark hair was cut in a short bob, and she wore a navy suit teamed with a loose trench coat. Her handbag looked expensive, together with her black briefcase and red leather gloves.

'Did you see the birds?' she exclaimed as she lowered herself into the car. 'Look, they're still there. I've never seen anything like it.'

Jack bent over to kiss her. 'How did it go?' he asked.

'Brilliantly,' she replied. 'One of their partners is a woman, and she was just so welcoming. A really good experience.'

'I thought Scottish law was different to English?' Jack asked.

'It is,' she replied, 'but they want me to concentrate on European law. Human rights, that kind of thing. It's going to be tough, I know. They already expect a lot from me, but Jack, it's a dream job.' She turned towards him. 'So,' she said, 'what have you decided, yes or no?' She looked away again, staring out of the window as if nervous of his reply.

'It's not as simple as that, Grace,' he replied.

'It is,' she countered.

He imagined for a moment that she had anticipated his reply and was about to leave the car. He reached across. 'Look at me, Grace, don't turn away. It has to be no,' he said, gripping her hand. 'But let me have my say. Firstly, our age does make a difference. You are ready to fly. In five years' time I fear you would find our relationship a burden. In a way you have become obsessed by me.'

'That's not true!' she cried. 'How could you say that? That's so unfair.'

'Well, not obsessed,' he conceded, 'but when I told that beautiful, vulnerable little girl to get to the grammar school despite all the problems, you have admitted many times, it kept you going. Kept you focussed. Secondly,' he continued before she could interrupt, 'you said my life was mundane and in your eyes you are probably right. But that's because yours is just taking off. Mine is mundane, but there is a lot I like about it and love.'

'You mean Tom?'

'Yes, Tom, Sheila, my mum and – well, I don't know if I truly love Mary, but I feel responsible for her. I love my cinema, the choir.'

'Don't forget the allotment,' she added.

'You don't doubt my love, Grace, I've never felt like this before. Well, maybe all those years ago with Nancy. But if love is all about just taking, that's not my kind of love, and not yours either, I think.'

'I hear what you're saying,' she replied, 'but I disagree. Love is about being brave, not being cowardly. Yes, I think I'll fly, but I wanted you to fly with me.' She opened the car door. Looking up, she said, 'The birds have gone.' Then, without looking back, she walked away down the street.

Jack sat watching her go, agonising that all he wanted in life was walking away from him. He could have held on to her for a while longer, he knew, but in that time he would have altered the lives of the loved ones around him, and possibly ruined hers.

After a while he started the car, then drove slowly along the road, turning left towards the signs indicating the motorway. In the shadows of one of the shop entrances, he failed to see her standing looking out for his car.

CHAPTER TWENTY-EIGHT

Thanks for the times
That you've given me

– LIONEL RICHIE, 'THREE TIMES A LADY'

DERBY, 2012

The memories flooded back as Jack sat with Nancy. It had been so long since he had allowed himself to think about Grace. For a moment he found it difficult to regain his composure.

'You've never seen her since then?' Nancy enquired gently.

'No, and at times I feel ashamed. She was right, I was a coward, but then I'm glad we never actually hurt anyone. I am sure she is happy, successful no doubt. Who knows, maybe kids as well. I have been tempted to find out, but I think that would be even more cowardly, or maybe I just don't want to be hurt.'

'I just feel – I know this sounds stupid,' Nancy whispered, 'but to me it's such a tender story. Thank goodness for a brief while you experienced true happiness. Call me romantic, Jack, but you deserved Grace, as she deserved you.'

Nimble moved from in front of the fire.

'He wants to go out,' Nancy explained.

'And look at the time!' Jack jumped up. 'I'm already late at the Regal. We have two showings tonight. Why don't you come, Nancy? Can you be ready in five minutes? I'll see to Nimble.'

'It's a date,' she replied, pulling herself out of the chair.

The rain had subsided a little, but the cinema was far from full. Jack had worked part-time at the cinema for many years, even before his retirement. The couple who owned it had invested time, money and their complete enthusiasm in bringing the old Regal to life again. Thankfully now their investment was paying off, and it had developed into one of Belper's most popular venues. Nancy had a prime seat, with a small table, and a large glass of wine. It was after eleven when she and Jack left but they were still able to buy fish and chips on the way back.

When he finally arrived home, Mary had left him a plate of sandwiches and a mug ready for him to make a cup of instant coffee. He'd rather expected her to have stayed at Sheila's for the night, but the likelihood was that Trevor had run her home.

He was supremely happy that Nancy had had such a good time. There were things he knew he could do to help her. Walk Nimble, sort out her garden, and generally be around if she needed help. She might appear a little frail, but she was still vibrant, full of life, the same Nancy he thought he had lost.

Mary never mentioned the argument over the house, and it was only through Sheila that he found out Trevor hadn't given up on it.

'I'm surprised your mum didn't go for my divorce option,' he had suggested good-humouredly to his daughter over the phone.

'That's unkind, Dad,' she replied. 'You're a great one for taking the easy option, aren't you? Mum's unhappy, ever since they made her redundant. Think about it. She's got nothing going on in her life. You've got the Regal, your cinema club, the choir, the allotment. What's she got? She'll not even drive anymore.'

Jack sat down as he guessed the conversation was going to last for some time.

'Honestly, Sheila,' he continued, 'you know I've tried. If I suggest she joins me at the cinema, or even going away for a weekend, she's not interested. All she seems to want to do is stay at home and occasionally see you or Betty. She's put on loads of weight. The supermarket list swings from mountains of low-calorie meals to, well, just the opposite.'

Sheila laughed; she too had put on weight over the years. 'It's not easy, Dad, you're naturally slim.'

'Rubbish,' he replied, 'I'm active; I mean, loads of women your mum's age go to the gym, I even have a friend in her eighties who walks her dog every day.'

'She is depressed, Dad. Did you know she takes Valium?' Sheila added.

'No, I didn't,' Jack replied, genuinely shocked. 'So you think I should have sold up, and let us move in with you and Trevor?'

'You'll be surprised to know, Dad, I was relieved when you stood your ground. I admit I'm a coward too where Trevor is concerned. Once he gets something in his mind it's difficult even to have an opinion, and of course he always gets our Tracy on his side. He's still on the case. He might get another promotion, but even then we'd be struggling, but he will not give in, well, not yet anyway. I drove Mum back the other night because he's a bit iffy with her at the moment. He thinks she should raise the riot act with you.'

Jack fell silent for a second. 'Tom agrees with me, you know,' he explained. 'He even texted me the other day, with a "Don't do it".'

'Don't talk about Tom,' Sheila laughed, 'you know he hates Trevor and adores you. He thinks the sun shines out of your bottom.'

'Well, it's nice that someone does,' Jack laughed in return.

He heard a car stop outside the house.

'Got to go, darling,' he said, 'Betty's just dropping your mum off. You're right, I need to do something. Bye, love.'

He opened the front door, taking Mary's shopping and waving to Betty as she turned the car around and drove off.

'So what have you bought?' he asked, injecting a good measure of enthusiasm into his voice.

Mary headed for the kitchen and sat down. 'I got a few things from Marks and Spencer, Betty had some vouchers for twenty percent off.'

'Let me see?' said Jack, maintaining the enthusiasm in his voice.

'I'd rather have a cup of tea,' she replied, 'it's exhausting, all that walking. I don't know how Betty does it in those high heels.'

'Cup of tea, coming up. And Mary, I've decided, no ifs or buts, we should go away for a little break, just the two of us. Anywhere you like, Paris, London, wherever you say. We can afford it and we aren't getting any younger. And a good hotel, one of these boutique jobs you see advertised.'

Mary accepted the tea, then, reaching for a chocolate digestive from the biscuit tin, she replied hesitantly, 'I've already booked to go away at Easter. That friend of Betty's, Evelyn, the one whose husband died suddenly – well, she and her friend were booked to go on a cruise to Norway. Her friend can't go now, so she asked if I was interested. It's at Easter and you're always busy at the Regal with kids' films, so I said yes.'

'Now, let me get this straight,' Jack said slowly. 'You've booked to go on a cruise to Norway, somewhere you probably have guessed I would love to go. You've booked to go on your own, without even asking or telling me?'

'I'm not on my own,' replied Mary, reaching for another biscuit. 'I said I'm going with Evelyn. Come on, Jack, you always do what you want. It's expensive, but as you just said we can afford it.'

'But wouldn't you rather go with me?' Jack finally asked.

Mary stood up, gathering her shopping. 'What do you think?' she replied, leaving the room.

As he sat finishing his tea, he heard her close the bedroom door. It was choir practice in the village tonight; nothing religious, just a group of people generally his age who just enjoyed singing together. Lester, the leader, was one of those natural musicians who had the ability to coordinate them well enough, so each year they were just about good enough to give a couple of concerts, usually in the pub. The money they raised in the hat at the door was usually donated to the Alzheimer's Society – the joke being that was if anyone could remember to send it. It was a mixed group, both men and women, often husbands and wives.

He looked at his watch. Did he really want to go, could he face the warmth and camaraderie that drew people there every week? Mary had never been, not even to one of the concerts. Tom and his girl-friend usually made the effort. Tom often joined in for the last song, his arm around his grandad, belting out the last number. *Next time,* he thought, reaching for his coat, *I'll live dangerously and invite Nancy, she'd love it.*

Easter was bright but bitterly cold, the daffodils bending their heads bravely against the wind. At this time of year, working on his allot-ment, Jack thought of his parents. His mother had always supported his father's passion for gardening, and he was glad that he had kept it going since his father's death. His mother had died a few years ago, as elegantly and peacefully as she had led her life. It was a virulent cancer, so her death was mercifully fast.

Nevertheless, Jack felt she should have had many more years left to enjoy her retirement. They had always kept to the promise they had made when he was a boy, to keep the memory of his father alive. It was completely natural between the two of them. As Tom became older, he also spoke of his great-grandad as if he had known him. He would occasionally ask about his death, relishing, typically for a young boy, in the story of the Derwent flooding.

As he battled with the cold, struggling to dig over part of his vege-table plot, his mobile phone rang.

'It's Nancy,' she shouted as if he was a long way away. 'Nimble and I would like to invite you for lunch on Easter Sunday. I know Mary's away, so perhaps you have a window available,' she joked. 'Betty and Brian have already accepted my invitation and I've booked a table at The Peacock at Rowsley. They don't allow dogs in the restaurant, but apparently Nimble can sit in the hall if I attach his lead to a hook.'

'Hold on a minute,' Jack replied, 'let me get out of the wind, I'm at the allotment.'

As he closed the shed door behind him Nancy continued. 'Are you in the shed?'

'Yes, and it's bloody cold.'

'I remember at times it was very hot,' Nancy laughed.

'Well that's very naughty of you, Nancy,' Jack replied, remembering how it had been one of their favourite places to make love.

'Is that knothole in the plank still there?' she asked.

'Yes, it's still there,' he said, walking towards it. He bent and looked through it, vividly remembering how he and Nancy would make love against the wall, and he would use the hole to check if anyone was around.

'I'm surprised the shed is still standing,' she giggled. 'Now, enough of this risqué talk. My invitation, are you going to accept?'

'Well, thank you, Nancy. We have a children's film showing in the afternoon, but they'll have to do without me for once. I accept with pleasure.'

They exchanged Easter eggs at Nancy's front door, then headed for the Derbyshire hills. Nancy was wearing a deep green beret with a small artificial daffodil attached to it. Nimble sported a yellow ribbon tied to his collar.

'The advantage of getting old is you can be as silly as you like,' Nancy commented, 'although I do promise to take my beret off during lunch.'

'You'll do no such thing,' replied Jack, 'you look wonderful, a little eccentric, but that's always been your style.'

The lunch was delicious, and Nimble seemed very content lying in the hall by the fire. Betty confessed she felt a little anxious about Mary.

'You mean she might cut up rough if she knows Jack is having an affair with Nancy?' Brian asked.

'Don't be outrageous, Brian!' chipped in Nancy. 'I think Jack can do a darn sight better than an old woman with a dodgy hip, ex-girlfriend or not.'

Betty was driving so Brian was allowed to enjoy the wine, which in turn allowed him to get a little maudlin. He proposed a series of toasts. To Jack's mum and dad, his own mother, Nancy's Seamus and finally his baby daughter.

'We buy her an egg every year,' he confessed, 'then Betty and I sit and eat it together.'

Betty reached across the table, holding his hand gently. 'Now stop it,' she said. 'I realised I've bought over a dozen Easter eggs this year for family and friends. You only seem to have turned your back for a minute in our family and there's another niece or nephew on the way.'

They were the last to leave the restaurant, with Jack and Nancy deciding to head for the hills so they could walk the ever patient Nimble before it became dark. They stopped at the top of one of the hills near to Thorpe Cloud. As Nimble raced ahead the wind caught Nancy's beret and sent it pirouetting down the hill and into the valley. She screamed with surprise.

'Well, I hope the sheep find it, and rather than eat it one of them wears it. It's pure wool, the very first beret I owned. A present from the Sloams when I was in Paris.'

'I'll run down and see if I can find it,' Jack offered. 'You stay here.'

'No, no, Jack,' Nancy laughed, 'things come to an end eventually, don't they? If it's a joyous end like that, who's to complain? People often say there are no compensations in getting old, but I don't agree. The big compensation is that you're lucky enough to have got there, and even luckier if you can rejoice in memories from the past.'

She stood for a second looking at the view, then Jack encircled her in his arms and gently kissed her eyes and face. She relaxed her body against him.

'Do you remember Bartholomew?' he whispered.

'Yes, I remember him,' she replied.

'When you disappeared, he was the first to find me. I was totally distraught. He got me drunk on rum and kept singing to me. Jack be nimble, Jack be quick, Jack jump over the candlestick.'

'I remember him singing that too, to the little ones,' Nancy added. 'He used to say if you jumped over the candlestick without getting burned you would find luck on the other side. He was a lovely man.' She disentangled herself from Jack's hold. 'I wonder what happened to him. I always thought he was into voodoo, but in a nice way.'

They walked slowly back to the car holding hands, followed by a somewhat disappointed Nimble who had anticipated a longer walk.

'Did you call Nimble after the rhyme?' Jack asked.

'Kind of,' replied Nancy. 'The RSPCA guy said he was nimble, and yes, I have to admit, I thought of the rhyme and you. Just be happy I didn't call him Jack.'

CHAPTER TWENTY-NINE

Not standing by graves
Say her name in conversation
At tables where glasses are raised
Say her name where you live
In the company of friends.

– IMTIAZ DHARKER, 'SAY HER NAME'

DERBY, 2014

Throughout the next two years they saw each other regularly. Nancy sometimes came to the allotment with Nimble, or Jack would pick her up to go to the cinema.

In late summer they picked a basket of raspberries together, helped by Tom. He'd just come down from university and was surprised to see Nancy sitting in a deckchair, Nimble at her side. Jack wasn't surprised that they hit it off immediately; Tom was studying forestry and landscape gardening, and as usual Nancy was full of questions. Jack sensed she was slowing down, as she often needed assistance getting out of her chair, but she remained lively, chatting to Tom over a cup of tea, before catching the bus home.

'So one of your old girlfriends?' Tom had joked to his grandfather.

'Yes, a good bit older than me, but she was very beautiful in her day.'

'You can see that even now,' Tom remarked, 'you cheeky old thing. I bet I can guess what you got up to in the potting shed.'

'And you would be right, young man,' Jack replied. 'It's a family tradition; I believe it goes back to your great-grandfather's time. I trust you will uphold it.'

As the summer drew to an end, the weather men continued to remind people that the temperatures being recorded were amongst the highest on record, and there was a total ban on hosepipes. Even Dennison's had issued smart shorts and t-shirts for all its assistants brave enough to wear them. Charlie had told Jack that his wife had laughed so much when she saw him in the shorts that he felt obliged to wear lightweight slacks instead.

But a few days after Nancy's death the weather broke, with spectacular storms sweeping the country. After Nancy's death and the fight with Mary, Jack had taken refuge with Brian and Betty. They offered him a bed and their garden shed for Nimble. They all sensed Nimble was looking for Nancy, so eventually he was allowed to share Jack's bedroom at night despite Betty's allergy.

The first job was to arrange Nancy's funeral. Betty's Methodist friends, who had happily accepted Nancy into their fold, offered to take care of everything, even the service. Jack accepted their offer, but made up his mind that Nancy's funeral would take place at the little 16th-century church near to his allotment. They had on occasions walked to it and, many years ago, signed their names in the visitors' book.

'Did you know she wanted to be cremated,' Betty had asked him, 'and her ashes to be sprinkled near to Seamus's?'

'But I think we should erect a little stone in her memory in the churchyard,' Jack had insisted, 'somewhere for Nimble and me to visit.'

'There's a will,' Betty had announced. 'I know because she made it just after Easter, she was adamant about going to the same solicitor's in Derby she had used years ago. Brian and I are the executors. We've spoken to the partners and we all need to go in for the reading as soon as possible. Brian has already written an announcement for the *Norfolk Post* and our local rag.'

'Do you think she knew she was dying?' Jack asked. 'I thought it was just the heatwave that was slowing her down.'

'Who knows, Jack,' Betty replied. 'I just know she was very content. You better ask Nimble, she confided everything to him.'

The solicitor was kind but brief. 'Nancy has asked that her house be sold. There are five bequests: three to Seamus's children, one for Brian and Betty, and one for Jack. And the deceased asked me to write a few brief comments which she wished me to share with you.

'*To Seamus's children, all my love, your father was a wonderful man who gave me much happiness. To Brian and Betty, have fun. To my dear friend, Jack with all my love. Please find happiness and take care of Nimble. I leave you all my remaining worldly wealth. In time, please give Tom £1000. I thought him a fine young man.*'

Jack wept. It was so unexpected. All he could say at first was, 'We must give her a good send-off.'

'The very best,' replied Brian, putting his arm around him. 'Don't they say you have to be buried with ham? So best quality ham it will be, and a bit of foie gras if the Methodist ladies can get their act together. Nancy knew about the good things in life.'

'And champagne,' Jack added, rising from his chair and offering his hand to the solicitor.

On the way back from the solicitor's they discussed the arrangements, searching for ways that they could make it special. Jack had arranged via Sheila that Mary would be out and he could stop and pick up some things from their house. Sheila had said her mother was very upset, and she herself was shocked at the allegation that her father had hit her mother.

As Brian pulled up outside the house, Betty flung the door of the car open.

'What's that police car doing there?' she cried, running towards it. 'Is there anything wrong?'

A young policeman came from around the back of Jack's house, followed by a policewoman.

'It's all right, madam,' he said, 'nothing to worry about. We are just looking for Mr Jack French.'

'I'm Jack French,' Jack volunteered. 'Is everything all right? It's not Tom, my grandson, is it?'

'No, no, sir, we just want a word with you, a delicate matter. Better if we go inside, if it's ok with you.'

'Can I come with him?' Brian said.

'You can, sir, it's entirely up to Mr French.'

Jack led them into the front room, whilst Betty walked off towards the police car, having recognised the driver.

'Now at this stage, Mr French, this is just a conversation, not even a caution. We just want a few facts. Your wife has contacted us saying that you attacked her three days ago, and she is frightened to return home.'

'That's bloody ludicrous!' interjected Brian.

'Sir,' the officer responded, 'perhaps it's best if you leave us. We are not arresting Mr French, we just want a few facts. His side of the story, so to speak.'

Brian hesitated, but Jack nodded in agreement with the police.

'You go, Brian,' he insisted.

Brian nodded reluctantly. 'I'll be outside with Betty, ready to put the kettle on.'

The police informed Jack that Mary had reported that she had been feeling faint after his alleged attack and the doctor thought it was possibly caused by the fight. She also had bruises down her left side and pain in her arm.

Jack methodically explained the whole incident, even pointing to the crack which remained in the kitchen door.

'I pushed her away, and I accept the fact that when she did fall it probably caused bruises. I offered to help her up a couple of times, but she refused. When I went upstairs to collect some things, she was standing in the garden.'

'So the argument started after your wife informed you that your ex-girlfriend had died?' the officer asked cautiously.

'My ex-girlfriend as you call her was eighty, her name was Nancy Dupray, and yes, Mary's response to her death was, well, I would describe it as harsh. I admit I should not have acted so angrily but I can hand on heart say I have never hit my wife.'

'Well, that's as it may be,' the officer replied, 'but your wife says she is frightened to come home.'

'Is she pressing charges?' asked Jack.

'Well, not at the moment, sir.' He looked at his notes. 'I understand she's living with your daughter and your son-in-law, Mr Trevor Phillips. I understand he advised her to call us.'

Jack gave a hollow laugh. 'Please tell my wife, or I can tell her, but you can assure her that within an hour I will have left this house and I do not intend to return. If you need to contact me I will be staying with friends.'

The officer took down the necessary details.

'Do you want anything more from me?' Jack asked.

The officers left, admiring the roses on the way out. Brian looked ready to explode.

'It was PC Roberts driving the car,' he explained to Jack, 'been a mate of mine for years. Of course he couldn't comment, but my God, I didn't half put him right.'

'You certainly did,' Betty replied, 'the way you talked about Jack, you'd think he was going to be beatified.'

'It's fucking Trevor, isn't it?' Brian demanded, ignoring Betty.

'Well,' replied Jack, 'if you remember since a few days ago I am a man of not insubstantial means. Mary can sell the house, she can have half of my pension, she'll then be able to give Trevor the leg up he wants.'

'Disaster,' shouted Betty, already organising a cup of tea. 'It will be a disaster if Mary moves in with them.'

'He'll want to negotiate for more than half,' Brian added.

'Then I'll let it go to court,' Jack replied. 'He won't want that. I'm not ungenerous, but I have a feeling I could be called on to pick up the pieces, and to protect Mary I'm not going to agree to more.'

The discussion continued for the rest of the afternoon, as Jack packed his belongings into both of their cars.

Jack contemplated whether it was seemly to describe a funeral as a success, but Nancy's funeral, he thought, certainly deserved to receive that accolade. Everything had been perfect. The late September sun had warmed even the interior of the church. The trees were just starting to be tinged with autumn colours. Crisp acorns and chestnuts crunched underfoot, and a gentle rain of leaves fell intermittently to the ground.

As he walked behind the coffin, acknowledging faces both known and unknown, he thought, *you have a fine turnout today, Nancy, and however strange it might seem, we have eventually managed to go down the aisle together.*

After finding that the Co-operative undertakers only offered flowers and coffins from a catalogue, he had visited the most exclusive undertakers in town. They had no problem with interpreting his requests. He wanted it simple, but chic. A wreath of just lilies, white roses and ivy, with a similar display at the front of the church. An order of service which bore the portrait of Nancy that Seamus had commissioned. A short but careful resumé of her life, and on the final page a sketch of Nimble done by a friend from the Methodist Church. He found the local vicar very sympathetic and keen to understand the true nature of Nancy's life. During his address he referred to Jack, saying that he had described Nancy as like a diamond with many shining facets.

Jack and Nimble alone accompanied the coffin to the crematorium, then returned to the Methodist Hall to mingle with all those that had attended the funeral. Several people from Norwich, mainly former employees of the Residential Home, had taken the trouble to make the journey, and to Jack's surprise a tall youngish man introduced himself as Seamus's son. He explained that he and his twin brother had only met Nancy once, a few years after his father died. His godparents had always known about the relationship and had always spoken very affectionately of Nancy. Eventually he and his brother and sister had visited her. He explained they were immediately charmed by her, and also amazed when they walked into her house that it still bore the marks of their father.

'We realised,' he explained to Jack, 'that we as a family owed Nancy an immense amount of gratitude. She and our father were obviously very happy together, but they were discreet enough never to let the dilemma of their relationship affect our lives.'

Their mother was still alive, aged ninety-four, continuing to live peacefully in a care home in Norwich. When the solicitor had contacted them about the will, he said they all felt rather humbled that Nancy had remembered them. He asked Jack if they might have any photographs he might find of Nancy and their father together.

But the big surprise of the day was when the elderly Bartholomew appeared. Josh had told him about Nancy's death after meeting Jack at the hospital, and he had seen the announcement of the funeral in the local paper. Jack, Betty and Brian were delighted to see him.

'We loved her from the moment we saw her,' he explained to them all in his rich dark voice. 'That first evening we all danced together. If ever we met on the street, she would kiss me – in those days a brave thing for a young white woman to do. She loved music, any kind so long as it had a good rhythm, she would say. Now listen, man, I would like to sing for her now. Do you think these kind folks would let me do that?'

Jack silenced the chatter and clinking tea cups, and Bartholomew stood in the centre of the room.

'My friends,' he announced, 'this is for Nancy, may her spirit rest in peace.'

His rich voice filled the room. A melodic evangelist song that sent shivers down the spine. When he finished there was silence. Then everyone clapped as Jack and Brian embraced him, for a moment all of them transported back to their youth.

Tom hadn't been able to attend, but he sent a long email to his grandad imploring him to just get away and not allow himself to be caught up in any of the family disputes, selling and buying of houses, sorting out probate, and so on. *It can all be done for you by other people*, he wrote. *You have the money, pay people to sort it out. Just go*, he advised, *it's the kindest way out at the moment.*

Betty and Brian agreed. 'Go to France,' they suggested. 'You might be able to find out more about your dad, if that's what you want.'

Part Three

CHAPTER THIRTY

It is late at night and someone across the way
is playing "La Vie en Rose". It is the French
way of saying, I'm looking at the world through
rose-coloured glasses, and it says everything
I feel. I've learned so many things … not just
how to make vichyssoise or calf's head with
sauce vinaigrette, but a much more important
recipe. I have learned how to live.

– AUDREY HEPBURN, *SABRINA*

BURGUNDY, FRANCE, 2015

Jack woke with a start. He'd dozed off whilst soaking up the October sunshine, which had accompanied him ever since he left England the previous week. Nimble was under the table avoiding the heat. Without being asked, the waiter had left him a plastic bowl of water. He had ignored it at first, but as Jack stirred, the dog rose, stretched and lapped from the bowl.

The café was crowded, its long low windows thrown open. Many of its clientele stepped through the open window rather than use the door. It overlooked a small market square, with several roads converging onto it. On the right, steep steps from the road led to a small area lined with trees and an area for playing boules. Before stopping for coffee, he and Nimble had walked along the cobbled streets and negotiated a tour around the ramparts. Jack vaguely remembered coming here with his father as a boy. It was the typical Burgundy town, bursting with towers, medieval arches and ancient houses with sturdy front doors, often studded with huge handmade nails.

He looked at his watch, realising he must start to consider where he and Nimble would spend the night. They had taken a leisurely drive this far, stopping at small hotels along the way. He had considered stopping in Paris, but he was eager to get to Burgundy before the weather changed. Tom had insisted he get a good mobile phone, with an app that listed places to stay. He'd used it once but preferred just wandering around or stopping at small hotels that looked interesting.

As he tried to catch the waiter's eye, he observed a little drama developing. A young woman had obviously lost her keys and was frantically going through both her handbag and her large bag of shopping. Not finding them, she left her shopping on the bonnet of her car, then disappeared towards the main shopping area. She returned after a couple of minutes, gathered her bags and came into the café. Jack watched as she spoke to the waiter, who reluctantly let her use his mobile. Jack could see that she was not getting any response from her calls. Passing the phone back to the waiter, she started to head outside, but not before placing all her shopping on Jack's table.

'Would you mind if I left them here for a moment?' she asked. 'I need to find a taxi urgently.'

'Can I help?' he replied.

'You're English?' she asked.

Jack always found this remark annoying. He'd been speaking French for over thirty years and whilst it wasn't flawless, he felt that his accent wasn't terrible, yet invariably this happened.

'I'm sorry,' she continued in English. 'For some stupid reason I've lost my car keys. I've searched everywhere. I've only been to two shops, crazy. My mobile's in the car too.' She paused to take a breath and run her hands through her hair. 'My daughter is waiting for me to pick her up from school and I can't contact anyone to help. Are you on holiday?' she enquired.

'Allow us to help,' he replied, indicating Nimble under the table. 'My car is just over there.' He sensed her hesitation.

'Are you on holiday?' she enquired again.

'*Oui*,' Jack replied, 'well, kind of – look, I have a grown-up daughter and two grandchildren, and Nimble here can vouch for me. Come on, let's go. How far is it?'

It was about twenty kilometres, but through the drowsy French countryside it took very little time. Seven-year-old Susan stood at the entrance to the school, her schoolbag hanging wearily from her shoulder. She greeted her mother with some amazement when she saw her emerge from a strange car, but was soon engaged in making friends with Nimble, who sat happily on the back seat next to her as they made their way home.

Home was her grandmother's house, the young woman explained. Her name was Nicole, her daughter was Susan. The girl had an English name because her daddy was English. Her grandmother was Dutch but had married a Frenchman, no, she corrected herself, two Frenchmen, and had lived in France most of her life.

'But she speaks fairly good English,' she remarked. 'She and her first husband, my grandad, lived in England for a while. We're living here whilst my husband is abroad, and I want Susan to speak French.'

'What does Nimble speak?' Susan asked in French.

'Definitely English,' Jack replied, 'but you could try speaking to him in French if you like.'

They approached the small town of Noyers through its carved medieval arch. The main street which ran through the centre was cobbled, and to the left was a large square surrounded by a mixture of stone and timbered houses. The cobbles defied any modern suspension, and the car bounced its way up the main street. They turned right into another smaller square, stopping in front of a set of ancient iron gates. Susan jumped from the car. She grabbed the ring on the gate and turned it, then, using her whole body, opened first one gate, then the other.

'Close them,' her mother cried as Jack drove in and parked in front of a long low house. At one end there was a large tower, obviously older than the rest of the house. It was graced by an assortment of windows and a large wooden door. They didn't enter the house but walked around the side.

'My grandmother will be in the garden,' Nicole explained.

Nimble had followed Susan ahead into the garden. As Jack and Nicole approached, they both heard Susan and her great-grandmother screaming at the dog as he happily chased several chickens through the vegetable patch. Two other dogs were half-heartedly joining in, and a large black cat had already taken refuge up a tree to watch the whole performance. Jack ran quickly back to the car and found Nimble's lead, but by the time he had returned, Susan had caught him. He was sitting next to her, obviously aware he had done something wrong.

'My apologies,' he said in French, striding over to the grandmother with an outstretched hand.

She was tall and slim, with completely white hair piled untidily on top of her head. She removed her gardening glove to shake Jack's hand, then replied in English, 'No matter, my granddaughter said you had saved her life, so I must be eternally grateful.'

'I think that is rather exaggerating the event,' he replied, sensing that he and Nimble were less than welcome. 'I don't think he's had much experience of chickens. Normally he's very obedient, so much so I take it for granted he will behave himself.'

'I am amazed he has never seen a chicken before,' she replied, this time in French.

'Again, my apologies, Madame,' he replied. 'Come on, Nimble, say goodbye to Susan, we must be on our way.'

He turned to Nicole. 'Do you have another set of keys? I can easily return to Avallon, it's not a problem.'

'Certainly not,' she replied, 'you must come in for a drink, and stay for dinner. My grandmother is getting to be a rude grumpy old woman.'

'Yes, please stay,' Susan added. 'Grandma Else is really very nice, she just has a bad back.'

Jack felt embarrassed, but Grandma Else laughed. Speaking again in English, she declared imperiously, 'They are correct, my apologies. If your dog had killed all my chickens it wouldn't have mattered. They are a dirty bunch of girls who seem to lay fewer and fewer eggs. I would have cooked the lot.'

She clapped her hands to shoo them away, but they continued to cluck around her feet, oblivious to the fate to she had threatened them with.

'However, I don't mind being called rude, or even grumpy, but old is a bit harsh. I would remind you, Nicole, I have a few months to go before I am seventy, but even then I will refuse to accept I'm old. As Susan rightly points out, devoid of back pain I am really very nice.'

She swayed a little as she stood, steadying herself on one of the beanpoles she had been trying to pull from the soil. On the ground Jack noticed an old-fashioned walking stick.

'I have a bad back, and Henri my gardener has decided that he is too old to continue working for me. He decides this about this time every year. I am then left with putting my garden to bed for the winter. Now, come in, let's find a drink.'

Jack stooped and picked up the stick, then, handing Susan Nimble's lead, he replied, '*Merci*, I accept with pleasure, but first allow me to take these sticks down for you and stack them against the wall.'

The garden was Jack's idea of paradise. A high wall surrounded it on three sides, with a small gate leading out onto another road, which he later discovered ran alongside the river. There was an orchard of six or seven fruit trees, and a small lawn with a deep border full of fading autumn flowers. An area of flagstones served as a place for a large iron table and a selection of garden chairs. The rest of the garden was given over to a vegetable garden and space for the chickens. Whilst the vegetable garden looked tired, Jack was impressed by the variety of vegetables, herbs and soft fruit bushes it supported. Several plump pumpkins remained to be harvested, and lines of cabbages and Brussels sprouts looked in good shape for the winter.

In parts the old wall looked in need of repair, but everything hung together, supported by climbing roses, ivy, a vine and what Jack thought to be an espaliered peach tree. The autumn weather had been so mild that two tall hollyhocks remained in flower, plus a vibrant mix of dahlias.

Before Jack had left England, he had visited his allotment to pick all the remaining fruit and tidy everything before the ground hardened up. Betty had made jam from the basket of raspberries that he, Tom and Nancy had picked, insisting that the Methodist ladies use it on the scones at the tea after Nancy's funeral. As he stacked the bean-poles against the wall, he noticed a row of raspberry bushes. Closer examination revealed that there were a few fruits remaining, so using a pumpkin leaf as a bag, he collected them and gave them to Susan who had come to find him.

'This way,' she cried, pointing to an open door at the side of the house. 'Grandma says don't worry about taking your shoes off, the floors are already dirty.'

If the garden was paradise, in Jack's eyes so was the kitchen. A large, heavily beamed room, with nothing fitted apart from a deep sink, and a range with a hood above it. Two tall wardrobes had been converted into cupboards, and several shelves housed a selection of kitchen equipment, packets and spices. Two elegant armchairs which had seen better days created a small sitting area close to the range, and a large kitchen table surrounded by several chairs dominated the room. The walls were covered with a selection of art which Jack found intriguing. Very modern abstract pictures fought with old portraits in elaborate frames. In the centre of the table was a pewter pot full of dahlias. To the side there was a tray with glasses, a bottle of wine, plus a plate of sliced sausage and olives.

'Nicole is preparing your room,' Else announced, 'it's far too late for you to try and find a hotel, and as you might have noticed everything closes down in France by the middle of October. We will eat dinner a little later, it is going to be 'pot luck', I think you call it in English. I am preparing a soup, pumpkin and marrow, it's good, you'll like it.'

Jack felt it would be unwise to argue. He sat at the table, feeling the warmth of Nimble's body weigh heavily across his feet.

'What a beautiful house,' he said with true sincerity, 'and the garden is sheer paradise.'

Else turned, and for the first time he was able to see that in spite of the bad back and the stick, she remained an elegant woman. Although she was wearing old jeans and a cotton shirt, he judged that some thought had gone into their co-ordination. She wore brightly-coloured wellingtons, explaining that she had tried but couldn't manage to pull them off.

'When I bend,' she complained, 'my back seizes up. Nicole gets cross because I refuse to take painkillers. I'm afraid if I start taking them it will be downhill from then on.' She sat down and poured them both a glass of red wine. 'I go into hospital soon for a few days. They want to do some examination and possibly give me some cortisone injections. I am obviously not going to grow old gracefully,' she declared to Jack, offering him the plate of sausage.

The conversation continued in half English, half French. Jack explained that Nimble's previous owner had said she wanted to grow old disgracefully, but then found it was too much of an effort.

Later as Jack lay in bed, Nimble on the floor alongside, he contemplated through the haze of several glasses of wine that paradise was the garden, the kitchen, the long delicious 'pot luck' meal. And paradise too was the anticipation of waking tomorrow in this warm and happy household.

When he did wake, he could hear Nicole outside. He remembered immediately that they hadn't sorted the car out. Leaping out of bed, he looked through the window and saw that thankfully she and Susan were getting a lift with a friend. There was no sign of Nimble, but as he continued to gaze out of the window, enchanted by the view of the town, he saw Else walking towards the house. She had Nimble on his lead, with the two other dogs trailing behind. She carried a large paper bag, which he guessed contained bread.

As she approached the house, she looked up and waved, shouting, 'There is no need to hurry.'

They sat over *petit dejeuner* for over an hour, picking up on the conversation that they had started the night before. Else was a good listener, empathetic but not judgmental. He was surprised how much of his life he unfolded to her in such a short space of time. In a very characteristically Dutch fashion, she was direct and unafraid to voice her opinion.

'I like the sound of Nancy,' she observed, sipping her coffee, 'but it sounds to me that deciding to leave your wife Mary is something you should have done years ago.' He wanted to protest, but Else stopped him, remarking, 'Don't misunderstand me, I am sure she is a perfectly nice woman, but being married to a perfectly nice man, which you appear to be, was possibly not the best thing for either of you. I married a perfectly nice and I have to say wonderful man, but it wasn't until I married a less perfect man that I learned how to stand on my own two feet. What is important, dare I say, Jack, is that you accomplish your mission and solve the mystery of your father. If you found out he was gay, would that honestly matter now?'

Jack recoiled, surprised by her directness. 'I didn't say he was gay. Yes, Jean-Baptiste might have been gay, but that doesn't mean my father was. I know there was a rumour that he might have committed suicide because of Jean-Baptiste's death, well, murder, but…'

'So, if you found out your father was gay,' Else repeated, 'would that disturb you?'

'No, I don't think so,' Jack answered, 'but it would be bound to colour my memories of him. I do regret not talking more to my mother about it. She must have been unsure, and troubled by not knowing whether he committed suicide, or it was just an accident.'

'Didn't she ever say anything?'

'No, never. I mean, times have changed so much. I suppose I'm as guilty as lots of people our age of saying yes, I have a friend who's gay, wanting to acknowledge our "right on" attitude.'

'But then are you homophobic, Jack?

He was startled again for a moment by the abruptness of her question. 'No, I've seen the world change, thank goodness, even if things like AIDS became part and parcel of it. But for my mum's generation it was different. I can remember Mum being shocked by the Jeremy Thorpe affair and turning off the TV sometimes when the court case was being reported. But I just thought that was Mum, and quite liked the way she was, well, rather refined. But heaven knows, now I guess she might have felt differently.'

The conversation started to make Jack feel uncomfortable, and he rose from the table. 'Now would you permit me to continue in the garden for the next few hours? It looks worse than it is, and I can start to get it into shape.'

'Of course, and if you can bear a household comprising three females – no, five including one of the dogs and the cat – please stay for a few days. I will make some enquiries about Jean-Baptiste's family if you like?'

'Agreed, *merci beaucoup*,' Jack instantly responded. 'Now, am I to pick the rest of the green tomatoes? I see by your shelves you make chutney.'

'Yes,' replied Else. 'I am the complete grandmother; Susan helps me make jam and chutney, and we knit together, one of the compensations of growing old gracefully.' She reached for a brightly-coloured woollen scarf from a hook. 'Here, wear one of my creations, it's starting to feel wintery outside.'

Jack approached the garden with an enthusiasm he hadn't experienced for a long while. He stood assessing the work that needed to be done. Else had been right: there was a nip in the air, with the possibility of the first frost by evening. In the barn he found an assortment of garden tools, including a lawnmower. He'd leave the lawn until the afternoon, he decided, when the sun had helped to dry it out. Gathering a spade and hoe, he started on the vegetable patch, and later started to cut back the roses and shrubs. When Else called him for lunch he had already the makings of a large bonfire.

Lunch was simple: leftover soup, pâté, cheese and an apple tart. Else had already phoned a friend who she thought might know a little about

Jean-Baptiste's family, having lived in the area all her life. She knew only that the farm had recently been renovated by a couple from Lyon, and before that it had changed hands a couple of times. But during lunch her friend phoned again, having asked several elderly people from the village. She had learned that both parents had died years ago, also the son, but the daughter, now in her late eighties, lived in a retirement home in Tonnerre, a small town north of Avallon. She had suggested they look in the telephone book or ask at the town hall.

'I'm surprised you never researched Jean-Baptiste,' Else remarked. 'He comes up straightaway on Google. He worked under the name of Jean-Baptiste Genoir, and was brutally murdered in Paris in the fifties. The murderer was never found. He was well-known for his ho-moerotic art, but also for a series of paintings he did during the War. One of a young girl was sold a few years ago at auction for several thousand euros. Do you want me to carry on?' she asked. 'I'd under-stand if you'd rather I left it alone.'

'No,' Jack replied, 'it's hard to explain why I never wanted to get to the bottom of it. I remember my father taking the call from Françoise to say Jean-Baptiste had been murdered. It was just before Christ-mas. I can still see my father now, walking back into the kitchen. He looked terrible and he and my mother were very upset. I wasn't sup-posed to realise, and they didn't explain, but I knew something awful had happened.

'They didn't tell me until after Christmas. I remember crying when I sorted through all the French gifts he'd sent me. But at the same time, I was aware that my parents were hardly speaking to one anoth-er. They tried to be cheerful when I was about, but I could sense even at that age that something was wrong. Then in February Dad was found dead.' Nimble nudged his hand, nearly causing him to upset his half-filled glass of wine. 'Why am I telling you all this?' he asked in French.

'Because that's what we do,' she replied, passing him a slice of tart. 'We live our lives, then try to make sense of them, often by relating them to other people. We embroider them a little, possibly leaving things out. I tell myself it's another compensation of age: you reflect on the past, and if you are brave enough you admit where you went wrong.

'I was only nineteen when I married my first husband. He was fifty-six, a professor of history in Paris. I was one of his students, completely infatuated by him. We became lovers, I became pregnant, we were married, then he died at sixty-nine. I was angry when he died, but on reflection I think I was frightened of having to take care of myself. He was my mentor, my best friend. Whilst introducing me to so many things, he also protected me and cherished me like a child. He left me this house, his family home. I'd never really worked properly, just dabbling in art history at university. I married again within two years of his death, a handsome, seemingly well-off young man from a seemingly good family. I knew I wasn't in love with him and when he turned out to be a... what's that lovely English word? Scout?'

'Scoundrel?' Jack suggested.

'Yes, scoundrel. I understood he came from "old money", but that turned out to be "no money". His family were charming but penniless. I blamed him for everything, but now I accept it was as much my fault as his. We divorced very quickly when I realised I might lose this house and what little money I had. I went back to my studies and qualified as an art restorer. It never earned me a fortune, but it gave me an interesting career and supported me and my daughter.'

'And what of the scoundrel?' asked Jack.

'Oh, Bertie. Well, about ten years ago I wrote to him, partly because over the years he had always remembered my birthday. Bitterness is a very bad thing to carry around with you. It wasn't all his fault, we had both tried to use one another. Anyway, he didn't reply to my letter, but just turned up on my doorstep. Since then, we have remained friends. He still is a complete scoundrel. He invites himself to stay, and I usually have to tell him to go. He remains funny and charming, so we tolerate him. Nicole says he's my second child, and my daughter is still angry that I have any contact with him, but as she lives in Australia that's not too much of a problem.'

With an air of 'that's that', she concluded their conversation by standing up and starting to clear the table.

'Thank you for lunch,' Jack said as he too rose from the table. 'I am going to give the lawn its last cut for the year, and then have a bonfire.'

'No, you can't,' Else replied. 'It's Thursday. We can only have a bonfire on a Friday morning, and even then only every other week. It's terribly complicated, and terribly French.' She consulted the calendar on the wall. 'Ah, we can have one tomorrow morning between nine o'clock and noon.'

'What about all those people who are at work on Friday morning?' Jack enquired.

'*Tant pis*,' she replied. 'As I said, wonderfully French.'

By Saturday the garden was transformed and ready for the winter. Henri the gardener had arrived on Friday afternoon, somewhat upset that he had been replaced so soon. Jack found it nearly impossible to understand him, as he spoke so fast with a strong local accent. Else pacified him by opening a bottle of wine, which they all shared sitting outside at the iron table. The sun was just managing to warm the courtyard, but Henri predicted hard frosts from now on, and snow by early December.

On Sunday, Else suggested they went to the local market and then drive to Vézelay, a cathedral town some thirty kilometres away.

'I want to show off,' she explained. 'I've restored some of the paintings in the cathedral. I think you will find it interesting.'

A little more of paradise, Jack thought as they drove from the market to Vézelay. He found Else easy company, and, similarly to Nancy, interested in everything. Their pauses in conversation whilst they drove now felt comfortable, and on the journey home he felt flattered that Else felt no embarrassment in sleeping most of the way.

Whilst they were out, Nicole had taken a message from the town hall in Tonnerre to say that they had found the address of Mme Françoise's retirement home. They left a telephone number, but stressed that they must phone the home prior to contacting her. They had then taken it upon themselves to contact a young family relative who visited her regularly, and had explained that an Englishman was trying to contact her elderly cousin. Later that evening the young woman phoned, and Jack could hear Else explaining Jack's connection with the family.

'She said her cousin had mentioned sheltering a young Englishman during the War,' Else told him after putting the phone down, 'but she didn't seem to know much about the story, and she didn't mention Jean-Baptiste. She's only young, a teacher in Tonnerre, and apparently the only relative to live close. She was a little anxious, as Françoise is eighty and has chronic arthritis. She has all her faculties, but she's very frail. This woman sounded very fond of her – she's visiting her tomorrow and suggested that we join her. If she feels Françoise is not distressed, you could have a brief chat.'

'Amazing,' Jack said. 'I hardly remember Françoise. I do remember she held onto me tightly when we rode in the hay wagon.'

'What will you say to her?' Else enquired.

'I don't know. I don't want to upset her. She might not even remember me. I'll just talk about my Dad and Jean-Baptiste, and my stay with them. I'm definitely not going to pry.'

That night he found it difficult to sleep, pondering what the following day would bring.

The retirement home was pleasantly situated on the outskirts of Tonnerre, with gardens that commanded a splendid view. It was purpose-built, so had very little individuality apart from a large modern stained-glass window. He had accepted Else's offer to join him, and they sat together in the waiting room until Françoise's young cousin appeared. She sat down next to them, explaining that she too was called Françoise. She told them that her cousin had seemed a little confused when she had explained that an Englishman called Jack was here to see her.

'She kept saying, "But Jack's dead, they both died." I explained several times that it was Jack's son, and I hope she understood.'

'I don't want in any way to upset her,' Jack reassured her. 'Do you think it is better if we don't see her?'

'No, no,' she replied, 'she's waiting, she wants to see you. She was adamant about that, in fact she shouted at me very loudly to go and get him.' They all laughed, which helped break the tension.

They walked into a little sitting room, where several other residents were talking with their visitors. The television was on in the background, and the occasional noise of adverts upset the rhythm of the conversations in the room. Françoise led them over to Jean-Baptiste's sister. She was bent forward in her chair as if she might fall out of it, but when they approached, she threw herself back so she could look more clearly.

'So, you are Jack,' she said, extending her long narrow hand. Jack was startled by how lucid she sounded. 'Do you remember me, Jack?' she asked, with a slight giggle in her voice.

Else found everyone a chair, then switched off the television, remarking, 'Nobody is watching it.'

'I remember you,' Jack said gently, touching Françoise's hand. 'We brought in the hay together, rode on the wagon.' He turned to Else to help with the translation, but Françoise had understood.

'It was a good summer that year, a beautiful summer. You're not Jack,' she said slowly. 'You're Jack's son?'

'That's right, I was only nine, my dad and Jean-Baptiste were good friends.'

She edged herself back a little so she could resume her eye contact with him.

'They loved one another,' she said. 'They loved one another very much. Did you know that? It killed them both, my mother said. It was cruel, we were all so young.'

Her cousin bent forward. 'Now don't upset yourself.' Then, turning to Jack, she asked, 'Why are you here? Is there something you haven't told me?'

'Tell the women to go, Jack,' the elderly Françoise shouted. 'Tell them to go. I am not upset. Times have changed. You both go,' she indicated to Else and her cousin. 'Let me talk to Jack's son. He wants to know.'

She hardly waited for the women to depart before continuing.

'They were lovers, your father and Jean-Baptiste. Not for long, but my mother and I guessed. It was no secret that Jean-Baptiste was, how do they say, gay. After Jack left, he went to America, sent money home, we even had a car, but he was never the same. Do you understand?' she demanded.

Jack nodded and she continued. He sensed she was making an effort to speak simply.

'When he invited you to stay, my mother was worried.' She started to cough, as if talking was an effort. Jack fetched her some water from the machine. After she had taken a sip she continued, her voice gaining strength. 'But you mother was going to come, so we thought it would be all right. But then she didn't come.'

'It was a wonderful holiday,' Jack added.

'For you? Yes. But for my brother and your father it can't have been easy. The weather was so hot. Do you remember the thunderstorms?'

Jack flinched, as if he had been hit by something. For a second he closed his eyes, as if he was nine again, frightened of the lightning and the crashing thunder overhead. Frightened by finding himself alone in bed when he had thought his father was there. As if a gap had opened up in his mind, he remembered running from the house across the farmyard, and climbing the ladder into Jean-Baptiste's studio.

As the lightning illuminated the room, he saw Jean-Baptiste and his father asleep together, naked on the bed. Jean-Baptiste had woken. When he turned and saw young Jack standing at the door, he had leapt up, taking him by the hand and helping him down the ladder. Then he carried him across the farmyard and back to his bed.

He made little jokes in half English and half French. He had gone down to the kitchen, coming back with a mug of chocolate. Jack remembered how sweet, yet slightly bitter, it had tasted. He remembered that Jean-Baptiste had cradled him and persuaded him to finish the drink. It all now seemed so clear, so simple, and ultimately so sad.

Jack reached out and held Françoise's hand. 'What happened after your brother died?' he asked, unafraid now to speak of Jean-Baptiste.

She looked directly into his face, gripping his hand. Her voice sounded more robust now. Her French was slow, and whilst he didn't totally understand every word, the sentiment was crystal clear.

'It was a scandal in those days to be homosexual. It was all right in artistic circles, but in a provincial farming family it was a disgrace. My father insisted that we burn all of Jean-Baptiste's paintings. He was a good man, and he loved Jean-Baptiste even though he was only his stepfather, but he felt ashamed. My mother was deeply unhappy, she hid a couple of paintings. And Bernard – do you remember Bernard? Well, he was simple, but he loved Jack, and he took one of the big landscape paintings and hung it on his bedroom wall. My father never said anything, and it hung there until he died.

'We never met your mother. I wanted to meet her. I wanted her to understand. Her name was Elizabeth. I remembered it. Your father used to talk about her all the time whilst we were hiding him. He kept wondering if she had had the baby.'

Her head fell forward again, and Jack beckoned at the nurse who had just entered the room and was about to switch the television back on.

'I am all right,' she declared, 'but go, Jack, you understand now.' She kissed his hand. 'I get tired, but I think that's normal at my age,' she added. 'Come and see me again, in the spring when it's warm and we can sit outside. It's been good to talk. It needed to be said.'

He bent and gently kissed her on both cheeks. 'Take care,' he said, 'and thank you.'

'You're not cross, are you, Jack? Don't judge them,' she threw at him. 'They were both good men.'

'No,' he replied, 'just…' He sought for the word in French. 'I am just relieved.'

Else had explained a little to the young cousin, so they left quickly, promising to keep in touch. Jack drove silently for a while. After a few miles he pulled over, and getting out of the car, he said, 'Forgive me, Else, I need to walk for a couple of minutes.'

It was starting to snow, tiny flakes like ash from a bonfire gently fell to the ground and then disappeared. He felt confused, and a great weariness was engulfing his body. Turning, he saw Else walking towards him. As they met, she linked her arm in his.

'They were lovers,' he said. 'It's a shock. Françoise told me. She said her and her mother had guessed. She didn't seem shocked, just eager to tell me they were good men.' He stopped and looked directly at Else. 'Maybe the thought of the disgrace made my dad commit suicide? My mother must have found out about their relationship. She must have agonised over it for the rest of her life.'

Else was quiet. But when they had returned to the warmth of the car, she said, 'Jack, this is nothing to do with me. We have known one another such a short time. But I would say, hearing about both your mother and father, they were both incredibly brave. If your father did commit suicide you have to think of it as a brave gesture, not to save himself but to save you and your mother.'

For a moment she was silent as Jack started the car.

'But personally, I doubt he took his own life. Your mother sounded so strong, creating a good life and keeping his memory alive. It must have seemed an enormous scandal then, but now, things have changed. Did you ever doubt his love for you? I think not. With your permission, I suggest we celebrate them all by opening a bottle of champagne when we get back.'

The kitchen was an oasis of warmth when they arrived home. Nicole was helping Susan to make Christmas decorations from pine cones and dried orange peel.

'The central heating has decided to stop working again,' she complained as they walked through the door, 'so I've stoked up the range in here. It has a mind of its own, as soon as the weather gets bitterly cold it stops.'

She rose and kissed both Jack and her grandmother. 'How did it go?' she asked.

'Fine,' replied Else, nodding in the direction of her granddaughter, 'but not for…'

'Yes, I understand,' replied Nicole.

'However,' continued Else, 'we are going to open a bottle of champagne, if you think it suitable, Jack?'

'Very suitable,' he replied, bending over to help Susan thread her cone onto a piece of string. 'But first let me do battle with the boiler.'

'You'll not win, it probably needs a service. Our plumber tells me I need a new system every year. Then he works on it for half a day, always managing to repair it. Probably because he knows I can't afford a new one.'

The boiler was situated in the cellar and looked from its size as if it would heat half the village. From the arched ceiling a colony of bats swayed back and forth. On the boiler a small red light flickered on and off, but no amount of persuasion from Jack could get it to fire again.

'How old is it?' Jack asked, returning to the kitchen.

'Probably forty years, or even older,' Else replied, passing him the champagne bottle. On the table was a selection of meats, pâté and cheeses. *How does this happen?* Jack pondered. *Delicious food and drink always seems to appear from nowhere.*

After they had raised their glasses, Else and Susan went in search of hot water bottles. Nicole and Jack remained in the kitchen, with Jack in charge of replenishing the logs burning in the range.

'Will you stay for Christmas?' Nicole asked. 'You know Susan and I leave to join her dad in America at the end of the week. I know it's a lot to ask, Jack, but you did mention you wouldn't want to go back to England. I would be so relieved. Grandma has to go into hospital for a couple of days, and I am concerned that she would be on her own for Christmas. She told you about Bertie, and there is the possibility of him breezing in, but amusing as he is, she would end up trying to look after him.'

'I'd stay with pleasure,' Jack replied, 'but I want to be sure Else is happy with that. I've been here quite a while already.'

'I've found my penguin!' Susan cried, returning to the kitchen with Else, who triumphantly showed the five hot water bottles she had found at the bottom of her wardrobe.

'I've invited Jack to stay for Christmas,' Nicole announced hurriedly, 'and he has accepted.'

Else retrieved her glass of champagne, finishing it in one swallow. For a moment Jack felt she was annoyed, but then she reached for the bottle and topped up first her glass then Nicole's and Jack's.

'Thank goodness,' she remarked, 'I'd have been most offended if he had said no, but just assure me you didn't twist his arm, Nicole.'

'Not at all,' Jack replied, clinking his glass against hers. 'Not at all.'

When Jack awoke the following morning, his bedroom window was covered with intricate ice crystals. It felt too cold to snow. Wrapping himself in an old dressing gown Else had bestowed on him, he descended the stairs with Nimble as his side. He could hear Else riddling out the range.

'I hate the cold,' she remarked as he entered the kitchen. 'I don't know why I am not living in the South. Don't speak to me, my back hurts and I'm in a bad mood.'

'Go back to bed,' he replied. 'Fill up your hot water bottle, I'll see to Nicole and Susan. The roads are going to be icy. Nicole said she is doing the school run; I'll go with her. I can pick up bread on the way back.'

'I've never gone back to bed in my life,' Else declared.

'How very sad. Well, there's always a first time, but if you are going to stand there being a grumpy old woman, put the kettle on. I could do with a cup of tea.'

He looked up and felt the warmth of her smile. It was good to be able to spar with someone without worrying about the consequences.

* * *

Just before Christmas, Françoise died peacefully in the nursing home. Jack and Else were both saddened that they hadn't seen her again, but Jack felt content that he and Françoise had both found comfort from their meeting.

The day of the funeral was grey and cold. At the café afterwards, her young cousin had organised hot wine and cakes for the few mourners who had appeared at the church. Taking Jack to one side, she told him that she had something in the back of her car for him.

'I wanted you to have three paintings by Jean-Baptiste. They are not mentioned in the will, and I don't want the family involved. As I am sure your friend would explain, it's not easy in France after a death, things can take years to get sorted out. If anyone ever asks, which is unlikely, please say that my cousin gave them to you when you met.'

'But don't you want them?' Jack asked. 'They might be valuable.'

'No, I want to honour my cousin's wishes, or at least what I think she would have wanted. When you see the largest, you will understand why.'

Leaving the group, they went to her car. Jack and Else helped her lift out one large framed painting wrapped in paper, and two small sketches.

'This is our secret,' she repeated as they put them into the boot of Jack's car. 'I feel content knowing they are with you.'

When they returned home they looked at the sketches first.

'Early works,' Else commented, 'simple but beautiful; you must have them framed. Unlike this.' They gazed at the large painting which Jack had carefully unwrapped. Two men lay entwined together, asleep under a crumpled white sheet that barely covered their muscular bodies. Their partly obscured faces were illuminated by a flash of lightning.

'You can almost hear the thunder,' Else whispered, placing her arm around Jack. At the back of the picture, barely distinguishable, was a young boy half hidden by the door.

'This is a very beautiful painting. Your Jean-Baptiste had real talent.'

Jack lowered himself to the floor so he could sit in front of the painting and come to terms with what it depicted.

'It's me,' he said, pointing at the child.

'I know,' replied Else.

In typical Else fashion, she wanted to find a place for it straight-away, but Jack protested.

'You have to understand,' he explained, 'seeing a very intimate snapshot of my childhood reflected back at me... well, I'm not sure I'm grown-up enough yet to accept it. One day, maybe.'

So the painting remained where it was, turned to face the bedroom wall.

CHAPTER THIRTY-ONE

I only drink champagne on two occasions,
when I am in love and when I am not.

– COCO CHANEL

The run-up to Christmas was different to what Jack had come to expect in the past. He had no objection to television, providing one was selective, but he hated the endless festive commercials that invaded most homes. For years he had stood his ground with Mary and it was accepted that the television was invaluable just for evenings, but since she had retired she used it as a constant backdrop to all her activities. At the other extreme, Else didn't have a television. Nicole and Susan had one in their rooms, but Else relied on the radio and newspapers, and the odd foray onto the internet, to keep her up to date.

He felt a guilty pleasure in not having to get involved in writing and receiving endless Christmas cards, or decorating the house with a selection of artificial knick-knacks. The main event in Noyers, like most small towns in France, was its market bursting with local produce. Whilst Else pondered about gifts for her family and friends, the main concern was food, and decorating the house with greenery from the garden. Maybe he was fooling himself, he thought, the romance of living in a medieval town in France, but there seemed less pressure, just a feeling of people engaged in doing what they enjoyed.

Else hosted what she described as an aperitif shortly before Nicole and Susan departed for America. An aperitif to Jack involved a glass of wine and a few nibbles, but Nicole explained in France it did involve drinks but frequently was just the run-up to a full-scale dinner.

There were eighteen of them eventually, sitting down at three tables which had been pushed together in the large dining room. A further small table was used for the various children arriving with their parents.

Nothing matched, not chairs, table linen or glasses. Everything was an extraordinary mix of old, well-used items. Jack was in awe of how Else effortlessly decorated everything, illuminating the room mostly with candles and the glow from a large Christmas tree. For the previous few days the kitchen had been a hive of activity, but nothing prepared Jack for the dinner that Else and Nicole served.

Countless courses appeared elegantly from the kitchen. The infamous Bertie arrived from Paris, huffing and puffing like Toad of Toad Hall. Jack was instantly irritated by him, but accepted that this was probably because he spoke flawless English with a public-school accent. He insisted in calling Jack 'old boy', which was nearly the last straw.

But nothing could spoil the evening. The conversation was lively, and whilst he found trying to keep up in French was exhausting, there were enough people who were more than happy to translate when the discussions became too complex.

Else had organised a seating plan, with Bertie opposite her at the end of the table but with Jack at her side. She looked lovely, Jack thought. Normally she appeared to take little trouble with her appearance, relying on her natural elegance. However, tonight she looked sleek and fashionable, her white hair piled on top of her head and secured by black ebony slides studded with stones that glittered and caught the light.

Each course was accompanied by a serious discussion about the wine. All the male guests made a point of explaining not only the wine's provenance but its special qualities.

When he awoke the following morning, he was surprised that his head appeared to be clear.

'Good wine,' remarked Else as he joined her for breakfast. 'If it's good and you don't overindulge, you can guarantee you will not have a hangover.'

'Where's Bertie?' he asked.

'He's already left,' she replied. 'I told him to go. I go into hospital tomorrow and he would have happily settled in over Christmas given half a chance. Anyway, he was jealous of you. I could see that. When he's like that he starts to get pompous.'

Else was in hospital for less than twenty-four hours, returning with strict instructions to rest for two days in bed. Nicole and Susan left, and for the first time Jack felt strangely like the head of the household. The whole of the town had been invaded by model Father Christmases, appearing to climb through upstairs windows. Susan had insisted that she have one, asking Jack to erect it for her. Whilst up the ladder putting it in place, he realised just how much the whole house was in need of attention, particularly the windows. It was too cold to paint, but he organised himself an agenda of small maintenance jobs, insisting that Else obey her doctor's instructions and keep to her bed. His love affair with the house increased as he took pleasure working on it, discovering its secrets amid the ancient stone, metal and wood.

He was amazed how detached he felt from all he had left behind. He had prepared himself for being alone, looking forward to having escaped all the complications of his past life. Just him and Nimble, he had thought, a kind of road movie. But here he was, two months on, living in a medieval village, in an ancient house, with a family nearly as complex as the one he had left behind. So why, he asked himself, did he feel so content?

He knew that Mary had filed for divorce, and he had instructed his solicitor not to contest it. He had made it clear that she could remain in the house for as long as she wished, and he would contribute to the outgoings, but should she wish to sell it, half of the capital was his. On Brian's advice he had left the negotiations of savings, pensions and insurance policies to the experts. Brian had constantly warned him that Trevor would try to influence things and go for the lion's share, but from a distance he found it easier to stand his ground. He kept in touch with both Tom and Brian, checking his text messages every day and resorting to emails when it was necessary. It seemed a world away.

'What do you miss?' asked Else one evening as they sat in front of the fire, cracking walnuts they had collected whilst walking the dogs.

'Nothing,' he replied. 'It's shocking, I know, but there is nothing I miss at the moment that would make me want to return. If that's what you mean by missing. I know I can catch up with friends, Tom, Sheila, within a day if I wanted to. I am concerned about Mary, but we would only continue to hurt one another if I returned. The ache that was my father is partly resolved.' He reached to save a log from tumbling from the fire. Then he had a thought. 'I know. I miss Christmas music. You know, carols. I've looked at the church services, and they don't have carol services, so yes, I do miss that. But I love all this, Else. I feel I have invaded your house. I love the comfort, the candles, the warmth.'

'If you love the house, it accepts you,' Else replied. 'Otherwise it spits you out like Bertie. He hated the house. It made him feel inadequate, things constantly needing doing, repairing, you know what I mean. I always have taken the rather... what's the expression, shabby approach.'

'I think you mean shabby chic,' Jack suggested.

It was late when they went to bed. With all the pre-Christmas entertaining done, they only had themselves to please. The house had four bedrooms, but Else had created a fifth for herself on the ground floor. It was in the oldest part of the house, with heavy beams and an ancient fireplace.

Jack had only been in once, to try to mend the lock on one of the windows that overlooked the courtyard. It was part bedroom, part sitting room, and part Else's workshop. She still continued to take on some restoration work, so there was an area given over to that. There was a sofa and a couple of armchairs in front of a fireplace filled with pine cones. Else had explained she was nervous of using the fire, as the chimney hadn't been swept in years. Several rugs covered the terra-cotta tiles. Her oak bed was covered by a deep red brocade cover that had seen better days, but still retained a sense of grandeur. On the wall behind the bed hung a tapestry that had faded to a dull blue and green. Small areas of it had retained their colour, giving a tantalising glimpse of what it must have looked like when it was first made. A small chandelier hung from the centre of the ceiling, but the room was mainly lit by a variety of occasional lamps. This room, he had thought, was an extension of Else herself, a mixture of the exotic and practical.

As he climbed the stairs leading to the first floor, he heard Else cry, 'Jack, feel the radiator in your room. Mine's cold; it's the boiler again. Do you want a hot water bottle?'

'No, but do you want me to get you one? I'm not surprised, I wasn't confident it would keep going.'

'I'm ok,' she shouted back. 'Look out the window, it's snowing. That means it should get a bit warmer.'

His room was cold, with even Nimble preferring to sleep on a rug rather than the tiled floor. The streetlight at the end of the road cast enough light for him to see the snow descending on the town. It was a Christmas card, he thought, but there was also a feeling of continuity. It didn't take much imagination to conjure up the characters from Else's tapestry with their pointed shoes, elaborate coats and hats, striding below his window.

As he drifted into sleep, his door opened. Just illuminated by the light from the window, he saw Else standing in the doorway. She was clutching a thick shawl which covered most of her long nightdress. Her hair was released from its combs and hung haphazardly down her back.

'Are you ok?' Jack murmured, half raising himself onto one elbow.

'I'm cold,' she replied, not moving from the doorway. Immediately, he threw back the sheets and she slipped into bed next to him, curling her body around him to absorb his warmth. He felt a heady mixture of amusement and amazement. Then he smiled inwardly as he held her close, whispering, 'Are you seducing me?'

'No,' she replied, 'I am waiting for you to seduce me. Don't worry, we are both a little out of practice. What do you English say – Dutch courage.'

When he awoke, the sun was shining through the gap in the curtains. She had gone and so had Nimble. But within minutes the door opened and they both returned. Else was bearing a tray with tea, bread and jam. He didn't articulate his thoughts, but it reminded him of Grace after their first night of lovemaking; she too had arrived the following morning with a tray of tea. He knew he would eventually share the joke with Else, but this wasn't quite the time.

Life became much easier after that. Sometimes they shared a bed, or a room; sometimes they slept alone. Invariably, they shared breakfast.

When Nicole returned, she observed, 'I thought as much,' kissing them both in a gesture of approval.

The old year progressed into the new, with their only disagreement being over the boiler. Without even consulting Else, Jack had a new one installed.

'But I can't afford it!' she protested as the engineer fitted it and took away the old one.

'I've paid for it,' Jack explained.

'What, for services rendered?' she retorted angrily.

He held her firmly in his arms.

'Don't be stupid and unkind. I've lived here several months, and you've only allowed me to pay a token amount. With your permission I would like to stay longer.'

She relaxed in his arms, resting her chin on his shoulder.

'When I left England,' he continued, 'I planned to stay in France for a few months, maybe even longer, I had no plans. In a way I still have no plans, but at least with the new boiler I can feel I have paid my way. Plus keeping wood fires going is hard work. The engineer says the whole system needs replacing with new radiators.' He kissed her ear, and whispered, 'But that can wait until the spring, if you will let me stay that long.'

BURGUNDY, FRANCE, 2016

Jack was tying back the runner beans. He'd asked Brian to send a packet over when he'd discovered that he couldn't buy them easily in France. The weather was perfect, sunshine every day, but the evenings often brought short sharp thunderstorms, with winds that caused havoc in the garden. As he worked along the row tying them back into place, he glanced over the wall and spotted the yellow post van arriving. All three dogs barked, Nimble now being an established member of the pack.

'You have to sign,' shouted Else. 'It's a registered letter for you, Jack.'

Despite the energetic nature of her job, jumping in and out of her van all day, the postwoman was portly, with bright red hair cut in an odd geometric style, seemingly very popular with women in France. As Jack arrived, rubbing his hands on his trousers, he could see that Else was having an argument with her. He could always tell when Else was cross as, unlike the French, who gesticulated, she always pulled herself up to her full height, thrusting her hands into her pockets.

'Sorry, Jack,' she explained, 'Madame here will not let me sign, even though it's to this address.'

'*Pas de problème*,' he replied, and signed in the two places the postwoman indicated.

It was a large manila envelope with an official stamp, but it still came as a surprise when he realised it was his divorce papers.

'I'm divorced,' he told Else. 'They don't mess around, do they?' He sat at the kitchen table with Else opposite. Else didn't reply but rose and gathered up two glasses and a bottle of wine.

'How do you feel?'

Jack paused to stroke Nimble.

'I felt relieved when I found out my divorce had gone through,' Else continued, before he could reply. 'I was in a bit of a muddle at the time and a pile of unopened post had been collecting for ages. When I eventually went through it, I found an envelope a bit like yours with all the divorce papers in it. I'd been divorced for a few months without even knowing. I have an aversion to official-looking envelopes. It's a wonder I hadn't thrown it away.'

He laughed. 'Yes, I am relieved. I hear from Sheila that Mary is doing well, even starting to drive again. Tom said she had phoned and asked him what kind of computer to buy.'

'Well, that's good,' said Else. 'She sounds as if she is standing as you say on her own feet.'

'Two feet,' he corrected, getting up. 'Nimble and I are going to finish tying up the beans, then hopefully it will be time for some of your delicious pâté for lunch. And how about a bit of sunbathing this afternoon?'

As he started the second row of beans, picking the long ones and placing them in a basket, he thought how easily he had slipped into this new life. The garden gave him immense pleasure. Else would often join him, and together they would toil for hours, surrounded by cats and dogs. Occasionally she would sit sketching. She had a fine eye for the absurd, often caricaturing those around her.

Jack wondered how Mary would have reacted to the knowledge he had now acquired about his father. Maybe, he thought, her change of circumstances had opened her horizons a little.

Deep in thought, he was startled by Else appearing on the other side of the row.

'I want to ask you something,' she said, parting the plants so she could see him better. Half laughingly, she went on, 'I want to ask you to marry me. You don't have to answer now. After lunch will do.'

She made to go, but Jack reached across, catching her hair, which today was in a long plait.

'You probably think I am after your money,' she cried, 'but if we are going to live together for, well, who knows how long, I want to be sure that if I die first you can remain in the house for as long as you want. My daughter will understand, but I could never trust Bertie not to try to muscle in.'

'Anything else?' Jack asked coyly.

'Oh yes,' she replied, freeing herself from his grasp. 'You have become my best friend, you are an excellent gardener and handyman, you laugh at my jokes, enjoy my cooking and tolerate the chickens.' She turned, taking his face in her hands. 'And there is no fool like an old fool, as they say. I am in love with you.'

'Are you sure?' Jack asked.

'Typical,' she replied, 'just like a man, always needing constant re-assurance. I am sure,' she shouted over her shoulder, heading for the kitchen. 'I want a proper wedding, with a party, I want to be a bride. But don't rush. You have until lunch to decide.'

For a second he thought of Grace and her ultimatum all those years ago. This time he knew he had no reason to hesitate.

Nicole expressed dismay at her grandmother's forwardness when they told her that evening about their wedding plans.

'But it's just like her,' she told Jack. 'When she gets an idea in her head there's no stopping her.'

Else chuckled. 'He wanted a list of reasons why I wanted him to be my husband, and I forgot to say how lovely he is in bed.'

'What does that mean, Grandma?' asked Susan.

'It means, my darling, he makes the bed very nicely, even fluffing up the pillows.' Before Susan could ask any further questions, Else added, 'And we hope you will do us the honour of being our bridesmaid.'

They decided on a simple ceremony at the Mairie, followed by a grand party in the garden.

When Jack phoned Sheila to tell her the news, he could tell that she was concerned he was taking a major decision far too soon after his divorce. Her own life was in turmoil with Trevor, and she felt she could not emotionally cope with coming to the wedding. However, she promised she would encourage Tom and his girlfriend to be there. Tom, of course, accepted immediately, delighted to be asked to be his grandfather's witness at the ceremony. Brian was dumbfounded and embarked on a series of rather risqué jokes over the phone, until Betty took over, assuring Jack that come what might, they would be there.

As Jack expected, the main consideration was the reception, and what food and wine should be served. Although they had planned on a small affair, when the guest list was finally completed, it was well over a hundred for the aperitif and forty for the dinner in the evening.

'We will need a marquee in case it rains,' Else had guiltily admitted to Jack. 'I'm so sorry, but if I leave anyone in the village out, they will be hugely offended.'

Jack worked constantly in the garden, pruning the dahlias and roses in an attempt to help them reach their final flush of blooms for the end of September. An Indian summer had embraced the autumn, and when Jack and Else walked the dogs, the surrounding forest was vibrant with hues of gold.

Three days before the wedding, they drove to a village famous for its wine. The proprietor was a friend of Else's and was delighted to supply the couple with his very best vintage. On the way home, they stopped to walk the dogs through the forest and up onto a ridge that revealed spectacular views. Beneath their feet a carpet of acorns cracked and splintered as they walked. Jack stuffed his pockets with fallen walnuts, whilst Else gathered chestnuts in her skirt. Much as he loved the landscape, he missed Derbyshire, and looked forward to showing Else his home.

In the distance they could hear the sound of voices, and then a horn.

'Hunters,' Else remarked. '*Attention*, we must be careful. Hunters in France have very little respect for the rest of the population, six people were killed last year. It's no joke. Let's turn back. To be fair we should be wearing yellow jackets.'

As they walked they could hear the dogs, then a couple of loud rifle shots.

'Where's Nimble?' Jack asked as they approached the car. The other two dogs were trailing behind, but no sign of Nimble, who normally never left Jack's side. They called for several minutes, then started retracing their steps.

'You don't think he's been shot, do you?' asked Jack.

'No,' Else reassured him. 'I am sure he was with us when we heard the shots. He might have bolted if he's not used to the sound of guns.'

They searched for an hour, calling him and eventually finding a hunter who denied seeing him. They were both hugely upset, but their guests were arriving that evening from England, and it was imperative they return home.

'We'll phone Francis when we get back. People often contact the local vet if they find a dog, and even the local radio. The problem is that it's not his normal area, I doubt if he'd find his way home.'

Jack was determined not to let Nimble's disappearance affect the welcome he and Else had planned for his guests from England. They dined and drank, and Jack felt immensely proud of his wife-to-be. He could sense Betty and Brian were impressed.

'Bit special,' Brian remarked, 'doesn't look her age. I can see why you voted to Remain.'

'She is special,' Jack replied. 'You wait until you really get to know her, she's very special.'

But under the camaraderie he continually thought of Nimble. When he looked across the table at Else, he knew she felt the same, and on one occasion she whispered, 'We'll find him, don't worry.'

In bed that night he lay thinking of Nancy. For a moment he fantasised that it was a sign she disapproved of his marriage. *Stupid,* he thought, *she would have loved Else. My God,* he kept telling himself, *it's just a dog.*

The following day was charged with preparations for the wedding. Brian supervised the erection of the marquee, Tom and his girlfriend helped Else to lay tables and gathered wild flowers, which they put in a selection of jam jars. Betty joined some ladies from the village to decorate the Mairie. Jack disappeared for a couple of hours to search for Nimble. He returned to the same place, calling his name, straining his ears for some kind of response. To venture too far into the forest was dangerous, he knew, as apart from the hunters it was easy to get lost.

I must take control, he thought on the way home, *tomorrow is our day. He's a dog, I loved him, and he loved me, but tomorrow…* He stopped the car, and though it embarrassed him, he allowed himself the comfort of a few tears.

'Not found him?' Tom said when he returned home. 'When the celebrations are over I'll go looking for him with Jean, at least the weather is warm. He's not going to come to too much harm.'

That night Jack lay next to Else. He feigned sleep, but guessed she was probably aware he was still awake.

Suddenly she jumped out of bed.

'What are you doing?' he asked as he watched her throw on some clothes.

'I've just had a thought. Where we lost Nimble it was only a kilometre from the auto-route. We've looked this side but not the other. He could have just bolted and run across to the other side.'

'That's not easy,' Jack replied, 'there's the central reservations. If he tried, he is probably lying dead somewhere.'

'But where I am thinking of there is a turning to Vassy. He could have followed the road around there.'

'You can't go now, Else, it's our wedding day tomorrow – today. It's 4am. It's crazy.'

'Jack French, if you are going to marry me today, you have to accept that at times I am a crazy woman. Now are you coming or not? Entirely up to you.'

A full moon illuminated the countryside as they took a slightly different route through the forest and over the auto-route to Vassy. The village was small, with just a church, several small houses and a farm. They walked along the main street, whispering Nimble's name. Several dogs barked, and a number of cats observed them with interest.

'It's six o'clock,' Jack said at last. 'We have to get back. You're right, he might be in the area, but he has a name tag. Surely somebody would have contacted us if he was hanging about.'

As they reached the car, they heard the sound of a farmer moving cans around the yard. He was old, and nearly completely bent over with arthritis. Else approached him, and Jack could see by his body language and the way he raised his arm that he was indicating something.

'Jack!' she called. 'He's seen him, says he was hanging around here yesterday. Apparently he shooed him away, he says he doesn't like dogs.'

Just as they were proffering their thanks, an exhausted Nimble hobbled across the yard to join them. He was attempting to walk on three legs, but his tail was wagging furiously.

'You are a miracle,' Jack said to Else, 'a complete angel.'

'Well,' she replied, burying her head in Nimble's coat, 'we'd have got through today, no doubt, but it wouldn't have been complete without him.'

The day was perfect, everything they both wanted. Jack's bride was dressed very simply in a linen suit, her hair caught back with flowers from the garden that complemented her bouquet. They had laughed when he turned to greet her as she approached the Mayor on the arm of Bertie, who had insisted he gave her away. They were both wearing the same colour linen, as was Tom, his best man. Else's only request had been that Jack didn't wear a tie, something she hated, so he had settled for a black silk shirt. Brian had later complimented him on it as the height of French chic, though cautioning him not to go down the existentialism route, something he didn't think he could cope with.

Else had unsentimentally explained later that her suit had been in her wardrobe for years, but her pale cream suede shoes had cost a fortune, and she would consider selling them on eBay if they got hard up.

Susan was perhaps the only person who took the whole proceedings very seriously. Dressed in a cream bridesmaid's dress, with her hair and bouquet reflecting her grandmother's, she added a touch of occasion to the ceremony.

Jack had left Nimble at the vet's, but he arrived later in the afternoon, a huge plastic collar surrounding his head to prevent him licking his injured paw. Susan had adorned Else's dogs with ribbons, and Nimble was given a similar attire, making him look as if he was wearing an Elizabethan ruff.

They ate, drank, laughed and danced until the early hours of the morning, only stopping when the September chill invaded the marquee.

As they curled up in bed, Else whispered, 'I think we should postpone the honeymoon for a few days, until Nimble is better.'

'Yes, I was thinking the same thing. We have all the time in the world.'

'And how about leaving the rampant sex until tomorrow morning?'

'Good idea,' he laughed, 'although I might have a headache.'

He switched out the bedside light, and they giggled like naughty children under the sheets.

CHAPTER THIRTY-TWO

You don't think I'm common, do ya?

– JULIE RITCHIE, *A KIND OF LOVING*

BELPER, DERBYSHIRE, 2015

The police had informed Mary that they were confident she had nothing to fear from her husband, and they suggested she drop the charges and move back into her own home.

Trevor, her son-in-law, nevertheless saw this as a victory, boasting that at least they had taken Jack 'down a peg or two'. He made it clear that he assumed Mary would now file for a divorce, which in turn would facilitate her selling the house. It was imperative, he explained to both Sheila and Mary, that they move things along quickly to enable them to still purchase the much-desired house in Duffield. He waxed lyrical about what an excellent move it would be, suggesting that now that there was no Jack to take into consideration, perhaps Mary could live within the main house to start with, rather than their undertaking the immediate expense of an extension.

For the first time in many years, Mary felt isolated. Brian and Betty had made no contact. Jack had just left a message with Sheila explaining he was moving out, and possibly going abroad. He repeated that Mary could remain in their home for as long as she wished. However, if she decided to sell, he would not prevent her, but she must understand the capital would be shared equally between the two of them. She found it difficult to discuss anything with her daughter, after being reminded on one occasion that she loved her father and would not be alienated from him.

With the tension rising, she decided to return home. In a fit of pique, she rang Brian and Betty to transport her rather than involve her daughter. Betty, she felt, had sounded surprised over the phone, but said she was relieved to hear from her and, without consulting Brian, arranged to pick her up the following day.

The journey home was strained. Brian hardly spoke, leaving Betty and Mary to flounder for conversation that didn't involve touching on sensitive issues. When they arrived at the house Mary was insistent that they stay for a coffee, but half expected them to refuse. To her relief, Betty was insistent that they both came in, 'just to check everything was ok'.

As Mary unlocked the front door, the heat cut through the cold air outside. 'No problem with the central heating, then?' Brian remarked.

Mary bustled in the kitchen, but it felt alien and for a moment she was disorientated. The realisation started to dawn that this was now all her responsibility. No Jack to regulate the central heating, order the oil, pay the bills.

'Don't forget to put your dustbins out,' Brian broke through her thoughts. 'Not sure how you will do your recycling without a car.'

'Sheila thinks I should take up driving again,' Mary replied, 'but honestly that's ridiculous at my age.'

'Well then, you will have to rely on the wonderful Trevor, won't you, Mary?'

'Now stop it, Brian,' Betty interjected, organising the coffee-making around Mary. 'Have you any milk? I can't see any in the fridge.'

'I will not bloody stop!' Brian shouted. 'Of course you aren't too old to drive, Mary, thousands of women your age drive. You passed your test years ago, you just need some refresher lessons.'

'But that was years ago.' Mary rallied. 'I don't like your tone, Brian.'

'Well, I couldn't care a fuck, Mary, if you do or don't like my tone. You've spent your whole life letting other people do things for you, drive for you, garden for you, even bloody shop for you. You're selfish,

Mary, you always have been. You had a lovely bloke like Jack at your beck and call, you two could have been just as happy as Betty and me.' He reached out and touched Betty's hand. 'You even had a baby girl, everything...' His voice shook with emotion. 'You're a fool, all your Sheila's Trevor wants is your money. He doesn't care a fuck about you, or even Sheila, I suspect. He's just like your bloody father, pompous and selfish. And I'll be honest with you, Mary—'

'Stop!' Betty shouted. 'Brian, that's enough.'

'I'll stop when I've finished, Betty, luv. Jack told me he didn't hit you, Mary, and to be honest I never for a minute thought he did. He said he just pushed you away and you fell awkwardly. Did that devious bastard Trevor talk you into lying to the police? Answer me that.'

'Enough!' Betty shouted. 'Go and sit outside in the car. I'll spend a few minutes with Mary. Now go on, and take one of your tablets, I don't want you keeling over.'

Brian hesitated as if to say more, then shook his head, opening the kitchen door gently so as not to aggravate the crack. 'You need to get this sorted,' he concluded.

Later, as Betty and Mary sat drinking their black coffee, Betty not having found any milk, they heard him dragging the wheelie bin outside onto the pavement.

They sat silently for a moment. 'So what do you think, Betty?' Mary asked at last. 'You're keeping very quiet.'

Betty took a deep breath. 'This is my turn to be up front with you, Mary. At this stage in the game it would be wrong not to be. You and I have always been friends, and over the years we've had some good times together. I loved sharing Sheila with you, I always sensed you didn't mind, it helped having to be hands-on at times. But if I'm honest, Mary, I agree with Brian. Maybe he overstated a little, but I'll tell you what I think.' Mary started to reply, but she pressed on. 'Hold on a minute, Mary, listen to what I have to say. You aren't going to like it, but have the courtesy to listen. Believe me, there was an element of truth in what Brian said. I didn't really know your parents, but I guessed you had a pretty poor childhood. But at your age you can't possibly continue to make it an excuse and let it influence the way you treat people.'

'I don't know what you mean,' Mary replied in a whisper.

'Yes you do, Mary. For a start, Jack hadn't seen Nancy for over forty years, and when he bumped into her in the supermarket, well, you know Jack, he was kind and considerate. She was an old lady. An old lady with a dog. We also met her by accident, she didn't seek any of us out. She was funny, self-effacing, a real pleasure to call your friend. We all kept an eye on her over the last three years, but in deference to you we kept mum. Stupid really, she was an old woman. The idea that years ago she was a prostitute was just malicious lies. Yes, she was beautiful, naturally artistic, and we were all a bit envious of her, but she never used any of that to seduce or hurt anyone. She left Jack to protect him. God knows whether it was the right decision.'

Mary remained silent. She reached for a spoonful of sugar, then hesitated before putting it into her coffee.

'Yes, she'd made mistakes like the rest of us, but she had learned from them. She educated herself over the years. Both Brian and I were a bit in awe of her at times, as she was often more well-informed and articulate than we were. At eighty that's not bad. I think she'd always been a reader, since she was a girl. A really well-rounded woman with a great sense of fun.'

'Unlike me,' Mary replied with obvious sarcasm.

She pushed her chair back from the table, then stood up and looked out of the window. She could see Brian sweeping up leaves outside the shed.

'It wasn't easy after all the scandal with my father,' she eventually replied, avoiding any reference to Nancy.

'But Jack supported you, Mary, we all did. I mean, it was obviously a shock to find out you had a half-sister.'

'I called her a little bastard,' Mary continued, 'told her and her mother to get out of the house, dirty little bastard.'

Betty got up and put her arm around Mary. 'I know, love, I know, it's all right. She did all right for herself, went to Oxford.'

'I know, I saw it in the papers years ago. Jack never mentioned it.'

Betty led Mary back to her chair. 'She survived. A friend of mine went to see her recently. She's a solicitor in Nottingham, specialising in women's rights. Well, I think it was her, Grace Ashton, but that's probably her married name.'

The phone rang, but Mary appeared too dazed to answer it, letting Betty take the call.

'It's Trevor, Mary. He says the estate agent is bringing a family around to look at the house this afternoon around three. I didn't realise he'd started on you about selling the house again. Yes, Trevor,' she spoke into the phone, 'I've just told her.'

She put the phone down.

'He says the agent thinks it's exactly what the couple are looking for. He wants you to brew some good coffee and get some flowers around the place. I mean, I ask you, what is he on?'

Brian knocked on the door, shouting, 'It's about time we went, if you want to eat at Dennison's. I've put the rubbish out, taken the recycling stuff, and bagged up the leaves.'

Mary didn't reply. Betty took a deep breath. 'Right, Mary, we're off. You have a bit of a think about what I've said. I'm sorry if we've hurt you, but you have to understand Brian and I care about both you and Jack. Now you think hard and long about whether you really want to sell up. Do you really want to move in with Trevor and Sheila? And I'd get on the phone right now and book some driving lessons. Honestly, Mary, you can do it.'

Mary continued sitting at the table after they had driven away. Half of her wanted to get up and start checking that the house was immaculate, while the other half wanted to remain just where she was at the table in the kitchen. Eventually, she carried her bags upstairs. Putting them on the bed, she lay next to them until the doorbell rang.

That evening, after the prospective buyers had left, she considered her options. The young couple and their two children appeared very keen. The phone rang several times during the evening. She guessed it was Trevor trying to call her.

At half past ten her doorbell rang. She had been sitting wearily by the fire, without lights or the television on, contemplating her day. As she switched on the lights, she heard Trevor calling, 'Mary, are you there?'

She opened the door and he strode into the hall.

'Where have you been, Mary? I've been trying to contact you all day. I thought you might have been with Brian and Betty. The couple made an offer straight away, and can you believe it, agreed to the asking price. They want to be in as soon as possible. There is no chain. They can sign immediately, what a bit of luck. The Homestead is still on the market. They're struggling, I'm pretty sure they'll accept an offer.'

Positioning herself directly in front of Trevor, she suddenly felt a strange inner strength.

'You are a bully,' she started, 'just like my father. I am truly sorry, Trevor, but I don't want to move in with you and Sheila. I will not sell my house. I know I've messed you about, but I'm not sure your motives have ever had my interests at heart. I do hope and pray you don't take this out on Sheila, she has nothing to do with my decision.'

'I don't believe it, Mary,' he cried. 'I thought you were glad to get rid of Jack and move in with us, you've always been very enthusiastic.'

'Well, I'm not any more,' she replied. 'Now please go, Trevor, I have nothing more to say.'

'You bloody old cow. They're right, you are a grumpy, malevolent old bitch.'

'Who are they?' she enquired calmly.

For a second she thought he was going to strike her. Then he swept his arm across the hall table, scattering a lamp and a multitude of china ornaments onto the floor.

'If you continue to do any more damage,' she declared with a new-found dignity, 'I will call the police.'

With that he opened the front door, then, gripping the handle of the letterbox, he slammed it closed. Mary watched with amazement as all the glass silently formed into a dense crystalline pattern of cracks. She touched it, and to her surprise it remained firm.

437

Her immediate instinct was to phone Jack, especially as she now had two doors in need of repair. She knew in the past he would have laughed, taking the opportunity to comfort her. But she had no current number for him, and the blinking computer in his room was a complete mystery to her. Instead she went to bed, clutching a mug of hot chocolate. The phone rang several times, but she refused to answer it. She tried to prioritise her next steps. As she drifted into sleep, she had made up her mind that she would contact Grace.

When she telephoned to make an appointment, Mary accepted a short-notice cancellation, keen to start to take control of her life immediately. She had given her name as Bridget French, feeling that if she revealed her true identity Grace might refuse to see her.

The journey to Nottingham by bus brought back memories of her and Jack going to the Goose Fair. It was shortly after they had been married. He had wanted them to go on his motorbike, but she had refused, saying it was too cold. She recalled that Jack wasn't pleased, but she had enjoyed the bus trip. Many of the houses on the route had been built just after the War and were large double-fronted residences with sweeping drives and well-established, neatly manicured gardens.

'We'll have a house like that one day,' she told Jack. Had he agreed? She couldn't remember.

It was just starting to get dark when the bus pulled into the bus station. It was so long since Mary had caught the bus, she had forgotten that the station had now moved into the shopping centre. Gone was the friendly terminus of her youth; it was now a large modern building, deeply unfriendly and cold.

The offices of Morgan, Briggs and Ashton were situated in the old Lace Market just off the city centre. Everywhere was moderately busy, but the shoppers were beginning to disperse as a gentle but ice-cold rain started to fall. Mary walked quickly, nervous of being late. She stopped a couple of times to ask directions. When she finally arrived, relieved but still nervous, Grace's secretary offered her a cup of tea. The tea was most welcome, and allowed Mary to relax and muster up the confidence to approach Grace for the first time in nearly forty years.

The building was a large Victorian house, one of many that shared a garden space in the middle surrounded by a tall iron fence. Whilst the reception room had been modernised, it still retained its sense of timeless grandeur. As she tried to conjure up an image of Grace, the door opened and she was startled to realise she recognised her immediately. Tall and slim, with that pale skin that complemented the thick black hair she had inherited from their father. She was dressed in a grey tailored suit. The open jacket revealed a red polo-necked sweater and a string of pearls. Her high-heeled black patent leather boots added a touch of playfulness to the outfit.

'My apologies for being late, Mrs French. I see that Margery came to your rescue with a cup of tea. As I'm constantly telling her, I have no idea what I would do without her.'

As she was ushered into the office, Mary felt that Grace was endeavouring to put her at her ease and build a little bond of familiarity before they got down to business.

Her office reflected the rest of the building, but with a few family touches. A pin board displayed photographs of her children along with their various drawings. On her desk was a photograph of her and presumably her husband, and on the wall behind her chair a large watercolour of a flock of starlings silhouetted against a city landscape.

Grace searched for her file.

'Margery has just taken down some details, not enough for me to fully understand why you are here, Mrs French.' Picking up her pen, Grace looked directly at Mary and asked, 'How can I help?'

Mary faltered for a second, grasping at the mental preparations she had made for just this moment. 'My husband has left me, and I would like a divorce,' she replied, knowing her voice sounded unsure.

'Are there grounds for divorce on either side?' Grace asked. 'Adultery, violence, anything like that? Try and fill me in with as much detail as possible. You could, as I expect you know, file for divorce with any number of solicitors in Derby, but I am presuming you have come to me for a special reason?'

'My husband and I had a row,' Mary replied, hesitating as the lie came out again. 'He hit me. I fell over and hurt myself.'

'Has this been a regular occurrence?' Grace asked. 'And did it involve the police? Was he charged, or just cautioned?'

Mary shuddered as she admitted she had called the police at the insistence of her son-in-law.

'What was the outcome?' Grace continued writing notes into a page from a file.

'Cautioned, I think,' Mary replied. She paused, realising it was time to abandon any pretences. 'You don't recognise me, do you?' she asked. 'But I recognised you. I'm Mary French, Jack French's wife. You look a lot like our father, same black hair.' She faltered. 'I'm your half-sister.'

For a minute the room remained silent. Grace rested her head in her hands. Then, looking up, she said in a tone Mary hadn't heard before, 'What are you doing here? Why have you come to see me?'

'Jack and I had a row, he's left me. I want to sort out the past. I need to sort out the past before I can move on. I know it's hard to understand.'

'The last time, in fact the only time we met,' Grace replied, 'you called me a filthy little bastard, and you banished me and my mother from your house. I was eleven, I was only eleven. My mother left shortly after that. If it hadn't been for my grandmother, my life would have fallen apart.'

'Yes, I know,' Mary replied. 'I am truly sorry for that, but it wasn't easy after Dad died. Jack and his mother seemed to take your side, in fact everybody's side but mine.'

'There were no sides,' Grace replied. 'Our father was the bastard. A truly corrupt and vile man. I'm surprised even now you've accepted that we share the same father. We're probably both illegitimate, who knows, and I certainly do not care.'

'But you've been ok,' Mary countered. 'I mean, you went to Oxford, you're a solicitor. It was in the papers. Jack never said anything, but he must have seen it.'

For a moment Grace sat thoughtfully, wondering how much Mary knew.

'Did you know that Jack and his mother gave me an allowance every year that enabled me to go to the grammar school and eventually Oxford?'

This time, Mary sat quietly, clutching her hands together.

'No, I didn't, we never spoke of you. No, they never told me.'

For a moment they stared at one another. 'I must ask you to leave, Mrs French,' Grace eventually said firmly. 'We have nothing to say to one another. I spend my life defending women who have been battered by their partners. I suggest you see another solicitor and continue with whatever you want to continue with.'

'What do you know about Jack?' Mary demanded, rising unsteadily from her chair. 'Just because he sent you money. He and his mother kept that from me. How do you think I feel about that? You know nothing about Jack.'

'Please leave, Mrs French.'

Mary sensed this was her only chance. Why she had wanted to see Grace she wasn't really sure, but the thought of leaving without some kind of amelioration frightened her.

'You know nothing about Jack,' she repeated.

The swirling birds in the painting behind Grace were the only link she had kept to remind her of Jack. He had thought she was young, strong and resilient, but that had been untrue. No matter how angry she had been when they parted, she felt a part of her would always remain in love with him. Her husband had bought her the picture after she had admired it in a small gallery near where they lived. She hadn't shared the relevance of it, wanting to wait until the longing for Jack had totally gone and she could make light of their parting.

Mary's words broke through her thoughts. 'You only knew Jack for a few minutes.'

'Yes,' she replied. A drop of fury began to course through her veins. 'Yes, but then that is possibly when I fell in love with him. Do you hear me, Mary? I fell in love with Jack and he fell in love with me. For six years after I left Oxford we were lovers. A wonderful affair, regardless of the fact he had you hanging like an albatross around his neck. I begged him to leave you, but typically he wouldn't. He couldn't bear the idea of abandoning Tom.'

Mary sank back into her chair. The mention of Tom startled her, as much as the revelation that Jack had had an affair.

'Please leave.' Grace stood up, but Mary remained seated. Grace bent forward and pressed the intercom. 'Margery, please come immediately, I want you to escort Mrs French out.'

Her voice broke and she knew that her secretary would act with her usual sensitivity. Why had she done that? She should have known better. *Good God,* she thought irrationally, *Mary could even cite me in a divorce.* She tried unsuccessfully to recover her composure, aware that she was shaking. Finally she rested her head in her hands, allowing the flow of stagnant tears to flow down her cheeks.

Mary allowed herself to be led from the office, stumbling a little as she walked through the reception area and started to negotiate the stairs. It was only one flight, but she was suddenly overcome by nausea. She felt herself starting to faint, but had the presence of mind to lower herself onto one of the steps. She curled her body forward, experiencing a tingling feeling in her right arm. *I'm going to have a stroke,* she thought, as she fought hard not to lose consciousness. For a second everything blurred, then she felt the warmth of Margery sitting next to her.

'Just relax,' she was saying, 'take some deep breaths. I'm going to call an ambulance.'

Mary clutched her arm, but the tingling had already stopped, and although she still felt sick, she knew she was not going to faint.

'I'm ok,' she said. 'It was a shock, I had no idea, but I'm ok, honestly.'

'What's your name?' Margery asked. Satisfied with the answer, she asked Mary the date, and then, 'Who is the Prime Minister?'

'Which one?' she replied. 'Oh, I see, Cameron.' She let out a nervous laugh. 'You think I might have had a stroke, don't you? Honestly, I am ok, it was just such a shock.'

Margery put her arm around her. 'Worth checking,' she replied, amused by Mary's response. Then she helped her up. 'Now I insist you walk just down to the bottom of the square. There is a tea shop, get yourself a large drink of water and a cup of tea, but most importantly sit and relax for a while. They don't close until six. Now are you sure you are all right?'

'I'm fine,' Mary insisted. She realised she had left her umbrella in the reception, but not wanting the complication of getting it back, she just held out her hand to Margery and thanked her profusely.

She remained in the café until it closed, then walked through the continuing rain to the bus station. She stood for nearly an hour waiting for the bus. Her thoughts were in such a turmoil that she was not aware of the journey back to Derby. Arriving at the Derby bus station, she caught what she thought was her local bus, only to find its route took her within barely five miles of her home. She didn't have the energy to reach an alternative solution, and instead decided to walk the rest of the way. The cold and rain penetrated her body, but she trudged on, letting the discomfort of the walk act as a penance that might eventually help heal her pain.

The realisation that Jack had had an affair, and that she had never for one moment suspected it, filled her with remorse. She didn't feel angry, or even jealous; just immensely sad. As she opened her front door and stepped into the warmth of her home, she started to cry.

She went straight to her bedroom and stripped off her clothes, then, catching a glimpse of her overweight body in the wardrobe mirror, she tumbled into bed. She slept uneasily, waking to a painful tightness across her chest, together with a burning sore throat. Her wet clothes remained in a pile on the floor.

Apart from visits to the bathroom and making herself the odd hot drink, she dropped in and out of sleep for the next two days. When she recovered enough to check the phone, there were several messages from Sheila, the last one saying she was going away for a few days to see Tom. Betty had also phoned, leaving instructions that Mary should phone if she needed anything.

For the rest of the week, she heard from and spoke to no one. Her whole body was in pain, but it was her memories that caused her the most discomfort. Jack's presence still filled the house. For comfort she took one of his sweaters from where it was hanging on the back of a chair and buried her face in it, taking comfort from its feel and the lingering smell of her husband.

Mary had never experienced inertia before, but now it seemed to take her over. She sat for hours just staring into space. Layers of dust, which in the past she would have swept away the moment they settled, remained defiantly throughout the house. The fridge gave off a slightly unpleasant smell as two chicken pieces began to decay. She barely ate anything, but the odd plate and several mugs filled the sink, waiting to be washed. She switched on neither the radio nor the television. Outside noises, as neighbours came and went in their cars, were her only reminder of what time of day it was.

The postman had knocked on the door several times, but she had ignored him. She ignored too all the unopened Christmas cards that accumulated on the mat in the hall. She felt no desire to share her pain with anyone, accepting for the first time in her life that she had to face up alone to the person she had become.

Jack had been her knight in shining armour, reluctant at first, but then offering love, friendship, even admiration if she'd given him the opportunity to show his feelings. All his interests, she knew, she had secretly admired, but had never allowed herself the pleasure of joining in. How many times had she heard herself say, 'Oh, of course Jack only likes classical music,' or 'I don't see what he sees in those foreign films,' all the while knowing that this was her way of saying, 'Look at me, Jack chose me.'

But of course, he hadn't really chosen her. She had tricked him into marriage. She had achieved her goal, won the game, but had been unable to accept the prize. Rather, she had let her guilt fester and ultimately destroy their life together.

DERBY, 1970

She lay on the bed naked, her legs slightly apart. The moisture from their lovemaking still clung to the sheets. Stan leaned on the half open sash window, looking down on the street below. Smoke from his cigarette curled back into the room.

'Poor little bugger,' he remarked, 'he's never got any shoes on, even in the winter. He's out there now without shoes. They forget it's not Jamaica.'

'I shouldn't think it matters today,' Mary replied. 'It's so hot.'

'Bit like you, Princess,' Stan replied, continuing to watch from the window, 'bloody hot.'

Several flies hovered above the bed, sensing the heat from her body. Mary watched them, then covered herself with the sheet.

They had dated once before, on the fatal night she had been accosted by her father, but it wasn't until her brief relationship with Jack had ended that she half-heartedly became Stan's girlfriend. She had gone along with Brian and Betty to the usual Friday gathering in the pub. She had told Betty that it was all over with her and Jack, and he had gone to Toulouse again on business. Whether Stan had been given the information by Brian, or just homed in on her because she was alone, she never knew. But in any case, Stan had spent the whole night chatting her up.

There was nothing really that she found attractive about him. He was shorter than her and stocky, with slicked-back ginger hair. However, his lack of good looks did not hamper his popularity and he was always deemed to be the life and soul of the party. He never seemed to lack a string of girlfriends, all of whom Mary thought of as being slightly common.

But that Friday night he was alone. He insisted on calling her Princess, which she detested as it evoked unpleasant memories of her father. She allowed herself to become a little drunk, enjoying the fact that despite Jack not being there she was still accepted as part of the group. Stan had insisted on escorting her to the bus stop, and then gently persuaded her to accept a lift back in his second-hand Vauxhall Cresta.

What she did remember all these years later was him helping her up the narrow staircase in his lodgings. The room was untidy, lit by a single bulb. He'd held her in his arms. She could feel his erect penis as he gently pressed it against her. She reached forward, fumbling between her skirt and his trousers. It felt thick, firm and warm. For a second the vision of her father in the mirror penetrated her thoughts. Then she collapsed on the bed, pulling Stan with her.

They made love several times that night, reaching finally for one another as dawn broke. The room was not improved by sunlight. Mary thought it was the most disgusting room she had ever been in. Dirty mugs and plates were stacked on a table, a small dressing table was covered in underwear, socks and a mixture of hair creams and aftershave. A couple of times she had groped her way to the upstairs toilet, which was an equally unpleasant experience. On the last visit she had passed Stan's landlady. Without looking at Mary she had shouted, 'Tell Stan I've just made a pot of tea. You're welcome to one, luv, get him to come down and get one for you.'

For the next two weeks, she saw Stan every night, and at the weekends. She felt deeply neglected when her parents were not even curious about her absence. Stan made some attempts to tidy up his room, but it remained in her eyes a sordid mess. On looking back, she couldn't remember ever being nice to him, rather delighting in a continual string of put-downs. He, however, was constantly kind, always trying to please her, make her laugh, anything that might lead to a favourable response.

The last Sunday they had spent together, they had driven to Ilkeston, where he had unexpectedly suggested that they call in to see his parents. He'd rented the room in Derby during the week as Ilkeston was too far to travel each day.

She had anticipated just a Sunday drive, but found herself being driven into a large council estate. All the semi-detached houses looked the same, apart from the individuality of their small gardens. Some were planted and well-tended; others were just dried up squares, supporting weeds and turds from the family dog. Stan explained that all the roads were named in memory of D.H. Lawrence, local lad made good, and that his parents lived on Chatterley Close, near to the Sons and Lovers pub.

Stan briefed her in the car. His dad was a fireman, and his mum worked as a dinner lady. He was their only child, and as he described himself jokingly, the apple of their eye.

'Please don't call me Princess,' Mary had requested as they walked up the garden path. 'You know I don't like it.'

As they stepped into the kitchen, Stan started to make the introductions, but was drowned out by his father announcing, 'Yes, we know who she is, Stan. We've heard a lot about your Princess.'

It was obvious that she was expected. A plate of sandwiches, cake and a tray of cups and saucers were already waiting on the table. Stan's mother bustled around, kissing her son warmly and teasing him about the length of his hair.

The house reflected the family, Mary remembered: warm, cosy and loving, unlike anything she had ever experienced, apart from brief moments with Jack and his mother.

She was treated like royalty, as if it was a privilege to have her stay for tea. With Jack's mum she always felt intimidated, nervous that she might broach a subject she knew nothing about. With Stan's parents it was just the opposite, and she found them easy company. But she knew that however comfortable Stan and his parents' world was, it was not what she wanted.

They stayed for only an hour before she made signs to Stan that she thought it was time to leave. She had graciously complimented his mother on the cake and made every effort to laugh at his father's jokes. But on the way back to Belper, Stan was unusually silent. Without asking, he drove her home, kissing her lightly before she left the car.

Jack didn't contact her on his return, and to her surprise neither did Stan, apart from a cheery wave when he saw her at work.

A month later she reluctantly took herself to the doctor. She longed to confide in someone, her mother, Betty, anyone who would help her in accepting the reality of her situation: she was expecting Stan's child.

CHAPTER THIRTY-THREE

*What you're supposed to do when you don't
like a thing is change it. If you can't change it,
change the way you think about it.
Don't complain.*

– MAYA ANGELOU, *WOULDN'T TAKE NOTHING
FOR MY JOURNEY NOW*

BELPER, DERBYSHIRE, 2015

The phone rang again. Its jolly ringtone mocked Mary as she sat in her armchair, gazing but not seeing out of the front window. She had never shared her relationship with Stan with anyone, or the knowledge that she had once briefly carried his child.

Even with the deterioration of her marriage, she had kept her secret. She had learned very early on that her power over Jack lay in her ability to 'close down' as he called it. To create a wall of silence, waiting for him to coax her out of it.

He had eventually stopped saying 'Come on, Mary, don't sulk,' knowing that she could totally detach herself from everything happening around her. She knew silence caused him pain, and as the years progressed, she revelled in using it more and more. His good humour would frequently win the day, and she would feel a sense of victory as their life resumed to normal, allowing herself to be treated as someone who was recovering from a long illness. But as the years progressed he had found it harder and harder to break through her moods. Her happiness lay not in her home but in her working day.

After leaving Rolls-Royce she had a brief period looking after Sheila. But she disliked being at home all the time and applied for a sales assistant's position in the Midland Drapery, the large department store in the centre of Derby. The building had been purpose-built, with statues of local dignitaries on the façade. Inside was a triumph of elaborately carved swags of flowers and Roman-esque columns. Its brass-trimmed counters on the ground floor gave way to a wrought-iron lift manned by an elderly gentleman in a uniform. Even in the mid-sixties it was fighting to retain its presence, a bastion of gentility in a changing world, but Mary loved it. Within a few years she was appointed as both floor manager and buyer. The key to her success lay mainly with the manager. He was popular with all the staff, but singled her out as an exemplar of good practice.

Each working day she contemplated what to wear, not for Jack, but in the hope that her manager would pay her a compliment. But now, looking through the window, she realised what a fool she had been not to see her redundancy looming on the horizon. It had been ru-moured that the store was being taken over, and the manager had frequently assured her, 'Of course you will be safe, Mary. We couldn't do without you.'

But when the new owners finalised their takeover bid, she found herself at the top of the list of those being asked to leave.

'He says it's because they are going for younger people,' she had defended herself. 'He's very upset, but what can he do?'

'Well, is he going?' Jack asked.

As she gazed out of the window with the phone ringing, she knew it was all true. Deep down she had always known. But that had been her world for twenty years, and when she left there was a gulf in her life that had seemed impossible to fill. On her last day, Jack had at-tempted to comfort her, saying, 'Do you want me to hit that shit on the nose, or shall we go quietly?'

Now, she thought, why, why hadn't she hugged him and relaxed into his care instead of building an even higher wall between them? During some of those years, she now knew, he had taken comfort with Grace. It was a bitter pill to swallow, but she accepted she could hardly blame him.

The phone rang again. This time she answered it. A call from the estate agent, apologising but checking whether the house was still on the market, as the young couple were still very keen and prepared to meet the asking price. As she spoke on the phone, she was startled by her reflection in the hall mirror. She looked totally unkempt, but her face looked slimmer and younger. The younger face seemed to challenge her, and she replied to the estate agent, 'I accept their offer.'

When a few arrangements had been made, she walked towards the front door and gently touched the crazied glass pane. This time it shattered into a thousand pieces. Outside, the world looked cold and uninviting, but she remained calm. Scanning the Yellow Pages, she found a firm that agreed to come immediately to solve the problem.

Whilst waiting for them to arrive, she checked her overburdened answer machine. More calls from Sheila, one from Betty and two from the estate agents. Then, to her amazement, two from Grace. The first was a call from her secretary asking her to phone the office. The second was from Grace herself, saying she understood if Mary did not want to see her, but she felt she must apologise for her behaviour, and was there a possibility of meeting. She would be in Derby at the end of the week, and suggested they meet in a restaurant in town in three days' time. She would book a table and hope Mary would join her. As Mary put the phone down, she experienced a frisson of excitement.

Over the next three days, she was constantly busy. She contacted Jack via Tom to explain that she wished to sell the house, but had decided not to move in with Sheila and Trevor. Using the Yellow Pages again, she organised a course of driving lessons to start immediately after Christmas. With a sense of guilt in breaking tradition with Mavis at the Cut Above, she made an appointment at the most expensive hairdressing salon in Derby, emerging with a short straight bob and some attractive highlights. Not yet slim enough to tackle the designer dress shops, she visited Marks and Spencer. Finding that she had gone down a whole dress size gave her the biggest joy she had experienced for years.

On the evening of her appointment with Grace, she was first to arrive in the restaurant. Grace arrived a little late, looking harassed as she juggled a briefcase, handbag and a file of papers that looked as if they might escape onto the floor.

'I hardly recognised you,' was her first comment. 'Are you all right? Margery was just so angry with me. It was unforgivable, and completely unprofessional. Can we start again, Mary? We are half-sisters, when all's said and done.'

The restaurant was cheerfully dressed with simple Christmas decorations, and outside a tall Christmas tree stood at the entrance to the cathedral, its twinkling lights reflected in the surrounding shop windows. There seemed something strangely cosy about their sitting opposite one another. Their conversation, which Mary had thought might be difficult, was surprisingly relaxed.

'Does Jack know we are in contact with one another?' Grace asked.

'No, Jack doesn't know anything. He's in France, as far as I know. You have to understand, Grace, I'm not jealous of your relationship with Jack, but I'm shocked. Yes, it seems incredible, you can live with someone and not realise what is going on around you. And I am desperately sad I never got it right and made him happy.

'I always deep down accepted that you were my half-sister. It would surprise me if there weren't more half-siblings about. Our father was a truly despicable man, I just felt so ashamed, but I clung onto my pride, daughter of Councillor Blunt. But I know that's hardly an excuse. I can't tell you what a relief it is just to get it all out in the open. I wish Jack was here, but it's good that he's abroad because I need the challenge of sorting myself out. They say it's never too late to change, I just hope that's true. And for the record, I'm ashamed to say I lied. Jack didn't hit me. I just fell awkwardly when he shouted at me.'

They talked until the waiter reminded them that they should order, as their table was only booked until eight o'clock. There was so much to say. Grace asked early in the conversation if their father had ever abused Mary.

'I think he tried.' Mary explained her own experience and that of her friends. 'I've never discussed it with anyone, not even Jack. In truth I think I despised my mother as much as I did him, she just turned a blind eye to everything. When the whole scandal broke after his death, Jack did everything in his power to shield me.'

'He tried it on with me too,' Grace told her. 'I was much younger than you were. I was scared, but I told my grandmother straightaway. I will never know what she said to him or my mother, but he never tried it again. I never really understood why my mother took up with him, she was worth more than that. After he died, she left and went to America.'

Their conversation swung dramatically to one topic after another.

'What of Nancy?' Mary asked. 'Did Jack ever speak of her?'

Grace thought for a moment, unsure who Mary was talking about.

'Oh yes, Nancy, his ex-girlfriend. No, not really, he talked more about Tom. He adored him, I am sure he still does. And Mary, believe me, he talked of you. I was too young and inexperienced to really care about the damage I was doing to your marriage. My view of you was coloured by our meeting that first time, when you called me a little bastard. But don't apologise, Mary, please, it's water under the bridge.'

They agreed to meet again, hugging each other when they parted.

'Mary,' Grace said, 'I see many women in a similar situation to you. You are not old, you look great. I love the new haircut. You can make it with or without Jack. It's scary, I know, but you can do it. Forgive me, but the thing I notice that has changed from last time we met is your voice.'

'Really?' laughed Mary. 'What do you mean?'

'Well, it's hard to explain, but it's softer, kinder, less… I suppose I mean less unsure.'

Mary laughed again, and for the first time since they'd met she felt older than Grace.

'Cheeky, little sister,' she replied, giving her a final hug.

It started to snow. Mary caught the bus back to Belper. When it stopped near the Regal cinema, where Jack had worked since his retirement, she suddenly decided to get off. The board in the foyer was advertising a late-night showing of *White Christmas*. She looked at her watch; only a few minutes to go, but there were still queues of people grappling to buy tickets and drinks. The whole place had a festive ambience, regardless of the crush.

As she reached the counter, she saw an advert chalked on a board. It read:

Desperate. In urgent need of an assistant to work over the Christmas and New Year period. Good wages. Dreadful hours. Eat as many mince pies as you can. Contact the management to discuss terms.

Underneath was a sketch of an exhausted Father Christmas eating mince pies, watching a film featuring a reindeer.

As she bought her ticket, she enquired if the job was taken. The young man looked a little confused, then called his father over.

'If you are that desperate, you might consider me,' Mary laughed. 'I'm completely off mince pies at the moment.'

'Well,' he said, shaking her hand, 'if you are really interested, come and see me tomorrow around midday. It's a Jack-of-all-trades type of job, I have to be honest.'

'Not a problem,' Mary replied. 'I know.'

WIRKSWORTH, DERBYSHIRE, 2016

Gospel sat looking menacingly through the window, his eyes determined to engage Mary, who sat at the kitchen table writing Christmas cards.

'Oh, come on in,' she said, rising and letting the overweight cat through the door. 'No wonder they called you Gospel, you're so righteous.'

The cat jumped onto the table, inspected the Christmas cards, then curled up, purring loudly. Mary stretched across to stroke him. She had never owned a cat before, and the truth was she didn't really own this one. He'd just adopted her when she moved into her new home at the end of the summer.

Last year she hadn't sent a single Christmas card, but this year she had been determined that everyone she cared about received a card. It had been a tough year. She had sold her house, rented a flat, renewed her driving licence, bought a car with Tom's help, and continued to work at the Regal cinema part-time.

When she had finally admitted to being Jack's ex-wife, she was nervous that her reputation for not being interested in the cinema might have preceded her, but as she was genuinely enthusiastic and hardworking, she eventually slotted in and became part of the team. When she turned out the house, selling some of the furniture to the couple who bought it, she had been careful to save all of Jack's books about film, together with his mother's desk, which now fitted perfectly in her lounge.

A new world had opened up for her, as she researched many of the films that appeared in the Regal programme. It wasn't necessarily part of her job, but she found it fascinating. It led her into joining the local library, and finally enrolling in both the cinema club and a reading group. Longing to share all this with Jack was a constant dull ache, only made bearable by her new sense of self-esteem. *Bizarrely enough,* she thought, *I want him to be proud of me.*

Grace continued to keep in touch, advising and encouraging her when self-doubt started to undermine her newfound confidence. Mary kept their relationship private, not even sharing it with Brian and Betty. She sensed that whilst it was precious to both her and Grace, it still remained fragile.

On Grace's advice, she had not rushed into any decision about where she wanted her new life to take her. Sheila had separated from Trevor and was forging a new life for herself and her daughter in Leeds. They spoke regularly on the phone, but were reticent about offering each other advice. Brian had an opinion on everything, whilst Betty unknowingly endorsed Grace's words of caution.

Working in the centre of Wirksworth, she realised how comfortable she felt in this small market town, with its ancient church and stone-built houses. Its main street bustled with all the usual high street shops, and the Dennison's, which Jack had religiously used every Saturday morning, was now only a short drive away from her rented flat. When Ian, the estate agent, phoned to say that he had a house on the market that he thought might suit her, she was somewhat surprised, still being unsure in her own mind what that meant. All she had ever told him was how much she could afford: only two bedrooms, and a small manageable garden. Intrigued, she arranged to meet him at the cinema after the children's afternoon film the following Saturday.

He was a large middle-aged man, who carried his weight somewhat uncomfortably. He had been remarkably kind when she had sold her old house, tactfully sorting out the details with Jack and ensuring that all the necessary paperwork was transferred efficiently from England to France. He and his wife were also members of the cinema club and had taken her under their wing when she had enrolled.

'I'm intrigued,' Mary said when they met. 'I'm longing to know what kind of house you think would suit me.'

'Wait and see,' he replied, leading her down the steep main street and turning right into the back of the churchyard. On the opposite side of the graveyard was a high wrought-iron fence, and behind that a Georgian house. It was not typical of its era, as it was long and low, with the only sense of its period being two small columns and a portico around the door.

'You don't mean Eyam House?' she said in amazement.

'No,' he replied, pointing to the small adjoining cottage, 'Dove Cottage.'

Mary was enchanted by it immediately. The complete fairy tale. The front door, with its solid brass knocker, was only a little smaller than that of its grander neighbour. It was overhung with roses, and the small front garden was a riot of colour. Inside was a small hall with the original wooden staircase, a cosy lounge that overlooked the churchyard, and beyond that a large narrow kitchen that had been extended into the small walled garden. Upstairs there were two bed-rooms and a bathroom.

Mary wandered around, trying to imagine what it would feel like to live here. She had always professed a dislike of old houses. She knew Jack would love it, regardless of the garden being small.

'Why,' she asked Ian and his wife at the cinema club later that day, 'did you think it would suit me?'

'I think,' his wife replied, 'Ian thought you deserved it, and it deserved you. Does that make sense?'

At the beginning of November, Mary received an email from Jack. He explained that Tom had told him that she was now computer-literate. He hoped she did not object to him contacting her this way, but they had an insurance policy which was now about to mature. He had contacted the company but they said they needed all the original paperwork. He suggested that it might be in the old deed box which he had kept in his room. She knew what he meant immediately, having been careful to keep the box.

She replied saying she had found the box, but not the key. She then spent the next half hour trying to decide how to finish the email. *Best wishes, Mary. Kind regards. Yours sincerely.* She settled eventually for *Regards, Mary.* She pressed the send button, content in the fact that they were now in contact again.

'I've just heard from Jack,' she shouted to Stan as he passed the kitchen window. 'Come in and have a cup of tea, you must be freezing.'

She had run into Stan regularly since taking the job at the Regal cinema. He usually arrived with a string of grandchildren, all demanding sweets and ice-cream, which he seemed more than happy to provide. The loss of his wife, Betty had explained, had hit him very hard, but his grandchildren seemed to compensate, and he was frequently to be seen meeting them from school or taking them to various activities.

He had jokingly flirted with Mary from the first moment he'd seen her at the cinema, teasing her about sitting on the back row, and much to her embarrassment calling her Princess. This time she didn't really mind, allowing his kindness and good humour to act as a balm in her new, busy life. He had retired, but did small building jobs for people, which led to his tackling her roof and window frames, which were in need of a little attention.

'Well, I'm not sure I'm pleased to hear that,' he said, removing the cat from the table and onto his knees. 'I was rather hoping you would be my girlfriend again, and then that bloody Jack of yours always seems to get in the way.'

Mary laughed in return. 'He's probably secured a string of French girlfriends by now. But it would be good to see him. There's lots of unsaid things that need to be resolved,' she continued.

'Be careful, Mary,' Stan replied seriously, 'sometimes better to leave the past untouched. When in doubt keep your gob shut, that's my advice.'

For a second she felt nervous. She had never spoken of the child she had carried for such a brief period. She remained silent, taking his advice for the moment to leave the past untouched.

Jack arrived in England at the beginning of December. He had replied to Mary's email to say he had a bunch of keys, but no idea which fitted the box. He thought it was about time he returned, as he hadn't seen Sheila for a long time, and he needed to sort out his allotment. He hoped that she would agree to meet so that they could either unlock or break into the deed box together.

Mary was amused that in his list of priorities for returning, sorting out his allotment featured above the deed box. She was eager that he see her new house, but realistic, knowing that she had not that long ago banished him with the aid of the police from their previous home. The thought of it made her deeply ashamed.

Unsure of her ground, she replied suggesting that they meet at the coffee shop across from the cinema. It was usually busy, but with a little patience one could usually secure a table and two comfy armchairs.

When she approached the café, she could see Jack seated in the corner. He looked different, more French she felt, whatever that meant.

His hair was short all over, which in part disguised the grey, and he wore what looked like an expensive cashmere scarf tied casually around his neck. His reaction to her was exactly what she expected, and desperately wanted to hear.

'My God, Mary, I hardly recognised you.' She had thoughtfully dressed in slim jeans, ankle boots and an expensive duffel coat that Grace had persuaded her to buy. She too wore a cashmere scarf that matched her outrageously expensive handbag and gloves.

'Unbelievable,' Jack continued. 'Sorry, I mean you look wonderful.'

He kissed her on both cheeks. They ordered coffee. She felt strangely shy, but sensing no animosity, she relaxed, enabling them to engage in comfortable chit-chat about Sheila, Tom and her new work at the cinema.

'The box is at home,' Mary explained eventually. 'I really would like you to see my new house, Jack.'

'I can't wait to see it,' he replied, paying the bill and helping Mary on with her coat. 'I'm pretty sure I know the house you mean. I vaguely remember a rather arty American woman living there. She used to come to the cinema regularly.'

Gospel made a great performance of meeting them at the door, purring and rubbing himself against Jack's legs.

'He's a complete pain,' Mary confessed, 'but I do enjoy his company, especially in the evenings.'

She smiled as Jack looked over the house. It felt reassuring to hear him ask questions about plumbing, central heating and the state of the roof. She offered to return his mother's desk, but he was adamant that she keep it, adding that he thought it had found its rightful home.

Mary had prepared a light lunch, some meat, cheese, and to Jack's surprise a bottle of wine. As they sat down to eat, she pushed her plate to one side, saying firmly, 'Jack, there are things that need to be said.'

'Why?' Jack replied, unsure whether to start helping himself to the food. 'What's the point, Mary? It's all water under the bridge. Forgive me for sounding patronising but I am immensely proud of you. I only wish I'd been able to help you accomplish all this. I am truly proud of you.'

She smiled, closing her eyes for a second. 'Thank you, Jack,' she murmured, and for a while they ate and drank in silence.

Eventually, draining her glass, she continued. 'To be completely content, and to move on as they say, I have to tell you one or two things. So please be patient and allow me. I was a dreadful wife. I know one can blame one's parents, and let's face it, mine were diabolical, but I realised rather late on that I can't use that excuse for the rest of my life. I seem to have been bogged down in a quagmire of disappointment, hate and insecurity. Betty and Brian talked to me about Nancy, and it seems unbelievable now that I conjured up so much dislike for her.'

She swallowed uneasily. 'I also have a confession to make. It's not easy for me, and perhaps you're right, it should be left as water under the bridge. But it troubles me, and you have to know that I tricked you into marriage.'

Jack sipped his wine, then topped up Mary's glass. 'Come on, Mary, how do you mean, you tricked me?'

'Because,' she said, engaging his gaze, 'when I had the miscarriage, it wasn't your baby, as even my father thought. It was Stan's.'

Jack put down his wine. 'You mean Stan Fossett? Stan from Rolls-Royce? The one with the rather large wife you never wanted to speak to when we accidentally met in town? She was bridesmaid at Brain and Betty's wedding, the one with the snapped bra strap. Fuck, Mary, what are you saying? I can't believe it. You had it off with Stan?'

'Yes,' replied Mary. 'Whilst you were away in France that time, we had a brief, rather sordid affair. Although to be fair to Stan he was always, well, Stan. Thoughtful and kind. When you returned, I knew I was pregnant. I couldn't make up my mind what to do, and then I had the miscarriage. I know my father, bad as he was, genuinely thought the baby was yours. I'm not so sure about my mother, but she was never interested in anything I did, or didn't do. I deceived you, Jack, I was determined to marry you, and then foolishly I couldn't hold it together and make us happy.'

He reached across the table. 'That's a bit of a revelation, Mary. I'm shocked, truly shocked.' He sat thoughtfully for a minute. 'I admit at first I didn't want to marry you, you were just a replacement for Nancy, we both knew that. But that changed, Mary. When I saw you walk down the aisle, you have to believe me, I felt totally knocked out. I make no bones about it, I had no time for your father, he did untold damage to you and to a lot of people.'

'And to Grace,' Mary said quietly. 'I know about Grace, Jack, we've met and talked, and we are happy to call ourselves sisters.' She could see the confusion on his face. 'Well, perhaps it's time for you to confess, but fortunately I already know that you and Grace were lovers for many years. I was shocked too. In fact it was a body blow. But it served to make me realise that I had possibly driven you to it. I don't believe you found it easy to be unfaithful, Jack, I know that you're not really that kind of man.'

Jack was silent, stunned as much by Mary's acceptance as by the revelation itself.

'Grace and I have had time together,' Mary continued. 'I'm sure we'll keep in touch. She doesn't – well, it's stronger than that, she will not talk about you. I suspect maybe some love remains, maybe anger, but she has stopped being angry with me. She is married and she wants me to meet her husband and children. This may surprise you, or even upset you, but she wants her kids to call me Auntie Mary.'

Jack rose from the table. Picking up his glass, he opened the kitchen door and walked into the garden. A few wintry rays of sunshine touched his back. Mary didn't follow but watched him from the window as he walked slowly around, stopping occasionally to examine a fading flower or shrub. Gospel walked along the top of the wall as if to accompany him as he sipped the rest of his wine.

He knew he needed time to digest all of this. *Do you look back on your life*, he thought, *and think 'If only'?* He wasn't sure; more like 'one door closes and another door opens'.

'Lovely little garden you have here, Mary,' he remarked. 'Needs a bit of cutting back, but it will be wonderful in the spring.' At last, he went on, 'So Grace is fine? She helped me through those years, Mary, with all the problems with Sheila. I wasn't proud of it. Mum never knew.'

Mary felt exhausted. She remained seated. Endeavouring to defuse the moment, she said, 'Enough about me. How are you? What's life like in France? How long are you going to stay over here?'

Jack removed Gospel, who had taken command of his chair.

'I have to be back by the weekend. Else is going into hospital again for a while to have more treatment on her hip. What she needs is a hip replacement, but she's immensely stubborn about whether it is the right thing to do.'

'Ah,' Mary replied coyly, 'so Else is your girlfriend, is she?'

Jack hesitated. A sense of apprehension swept over him. 'Well, not exactly,' he replied. 'She is the same age as us, but didn't you know, Mary? Else is my wife.'

Mary froze. The room seemed to spin for a second. 'Nobody told me,' she whispered. 'Not Sheila, not Betty, not even Tom. She's your wife?' Then, as if the realisation had really sunk in, she shrieked in a tone that Jack was much more familiar with, 'How could you all? Nobody told me!'

But this time he was not afraid, not timid of upsetting her. Racing around the table, he pulled her to her feet, then threw his arms around her and hugged her tightly.

'Nobody told you, Mary, because nobody wanted to upset you, I suspect. I thought you knew. Listen, Mary,' he begged, 'you have made a remarkable new life for yourself. You've done it without me, you have accomplished so much, don't you dare let this spoil it for you. You don't need me any more. And if you did, I would always be there for you, not to continue our marriage but as a loving friend. Else knows that, it wouldn't even occur to her to question it.'

Mary stiffened. Her whole body became rigid, but then she gently relaxed, drawing in Jack's warmth and love for what she knew was the last time. Tears streamed down her face. 'I didn't know,' she repeated.

She sat down at the table, and Gospel instantly sat on her knee. Stroking him gently, she looked up at Jack, and half laughing, she whispered, 'I'm ok, Jack, I'm ok.'

He left shortly afterwards. He knew there was no more he could do. He felt confident she would continue forging a new life for herself.

He wandered towards the river, overwhelmed by the rollercoaster of emotions he had just experienced. It was beginning to rain, not the torrential cold rain that had flooded the river and killed his father, but a light clingy mist that could easily turn into snow. The river was full, swirling under the bridge. It had taken his father decades before, but he still loved it, marvelling at its capricious moods.

As he walked back towards the town his phone rang.

'It's Sheila, I've just spoken to Mum.'

'Why didn't you tell her I'd got married?' he answered.

'Why didn't you, Dad?' Sheila replied angrily. 'You're always the one for the easy way out. I knew if I said anything she'd be upset, and Auntie Betty agreed with me. She was doing so well, honestly I am really proud of her. I knew you two were in contact by email, and I thought you would have said something.'

'You're right. I just took it for granted somebody else would break the news. Is she very upset? I left her about an hour ago and we parted, well, nicely.'

'Well, amazingly she's ok. Shocked, a bit cross with me, but when I told her how proud I was of her and that Tom and Tracy felt the same, she seemed OK. I even said, "You're free now to get yourself another fella."'

'And how did that go down?' Jack laughed.

'Very well. Surprisingly she replied, "Watch this space," so I will,' she laughed. 'I was actually trying to contact you to say that Brian and Betty phoned. They're still on their cruise but wondered if you could stay for a couple more days. They'll be back on Friday. Brian said he's emailed you, but you haven't replied.'

He sheltered for a moment in the doorway of a shop. 'Hold on a minute, reception's not that good,' he shouted. 'Oh ok, I can hear you now. Yes, my email's a bit erratic at the moment, I'm not sure my French mobile likes it over here. Can you hear me? I did explain to them before I left that I had to be back, Else's still having problems with her hip. Reply for me, please, Sheila, and say I'll be in touch as soon as I get back.'

'Ok, Dad,' she replied. 'It was good to see you last week. I'll be over to see you in the spring, I hope. Love to Else.'

Continuing along the high street, he passed what he remembered to be Harry's Newsagent. Mo had returned to Pakistan years ago after his wife had died, and Jack thought he remembered that a cousin had taken over the shop. So he wasn't surprised to see that its windows had been papered over and overlaid with a sign which announced the imminent opening of a 'Gourmet Kitchen Delicatessen'. As he peered through the door, he could hear the sound of banging, and when he turned he spotted a white van outside. Its side panels announced:

Stanley Fossett – Stan of all Trades – You name it, we can do it. Building works, electricity, plumbing, gardening, odd jobs.

As Jack returned to the shop, Stan opened the door.

'Don't you touch my van, Jack French,' he shouted, reaching for Jack's hand.

'Wouldn't dream of it,' Jack replied, 'although I was bit concerned that someone might add "Master of None".'

'Cheeky bugger,' Stan replied, 'you always were a bit of a know-all. Actually, I think it's rather clever. It implies I'm not a true professional. The grandkids wanted me to call myself Stan the Builder, but I thought better of it. Come on in, Jack. I can offer you a cup of tea, a Cuppa Soup or a Pot Noodle.'

A half bottle of milk, a much-used bag of sugar, and a selection of both full and empty Pot Noodle pots rested on and around a square piece of wood supported by an upturned metal bucket. On the ground was an electric kettle, with a long extension lead to a socket on the far wall. The area was almost devoid of anything resembling its former self, apart from a lingering smell of spices.

'Good to see you, Stan. Amazing, all this work and the place still smells of curry. What's happened, have the family sold up?' he enquired.

'No,' replied Stan, plugging in the kettle. 'It's still part of the Raj empire. It's going to be a delicatessen, or "things you never really wanted in small packages at expensive prices", as I always call them.'

Jack laughed, opening up a folding chair that Stan passed to him. 'Does Singh still run the show? I thought it was just a chain of estate agencies.'

'You're joking,' Stan replied. 'To be honest I've only met him once. It's run by a board of directors, it's called Raj Enterprises and they are into restaurants, housing, hotels, all sorts, all over the country. But I'm not complaining, I offer them a good price and they pay up promptly. I think Mo might have recommended me.' He passed Jack a cup of tea and a plate of Jaffa cakes, then continued, 'So how's my Princess? I knew you were coming. I thought, that bloody Jack always pops up just at the wrong minute. I'm sure I'm right in thinking you're going to get back together.'

'You couldn't be more wrong, Stan. I was married last year to a French – no, Dutch woman.'

'Get it right, Jack, not much chance of a future if you can't remember if she's French or Dutch.'

'She's Dutch, she is the same age as me, and she's, well, as the song says, kind of wonderful.'

'Congratulations, Jack,' Stan said, offering his hand again. 'Mary didn't know, I'm sure. Is she upset?'

'Just a bit,' Jack replied, 'more because nobody had told her. But she's changed so much, she doesn't need me any more.'

'Quite right,' replied Stan, lowering himself gingerly on to a plastic garden chair. 'What she needs is me. I've loved her since I was, well, early twenties. I tried to nick her from you but...'

'Yes, I know, Stan, Mary told me. I never suspected anything, you bugger. You always seemed so happy with Lucy. I used to envy you.'

He felt a pang of guilt as Stan replied, having just had the revelation about Mary's pregnancy. It was her secret, and he would respect that. But he did wonder if Stan had known all along, and just kept mum.

'Lucy was a bonny lass, she was kind, a lovely woman, and I loved her dearly. I know we made one another very happy. I was distraught when she died, but the kids kept me going. They even encouraged me to get one of those apps – you know, a dating agency. Apparently they do one for wrinklies.'

'You mean like Tinder?'

'What do you know about Tinder, Jack French?'

'Tom showed me.'

'A likely story,' Stan replied, helping himself to another Jaffa cake. 'Well, I better start mugging up on foreign films, Mary's big into that now since she took your job over at the Regal.'

'Well, you have my blessing, Stan,' Jack replied, aware that Stan looked less than confident.

'Not sure that's going to do any good, but we'll see, we'll see. Now,' he went on, changing the subject, 'it's a bit of a coincidence, I wanted to contact you. I had mentioned this to Mary, but she obviously forgot. Whilst I was clearing out stuff upstairs, I found something in the back of a cupboard. Hold on a minute, I'll go and get it.'

Returning from the back room, he handed Jack a faded plastic bag.

'My God,' Jack exclaimed as he looked at the logo on the bag. 'Thurman and Malin's closed thirty years ago.'

Inside he found three Mozart LPs, each with a handwritten label stuck on the cover saying 'Jack French'.

'Well, I thought they must be yours, Jack,' Stan explained, 'I know you like a bit of the classical stuff.'

'No, Stan, actually they must have belonged to my dad. He must have lent them to Mr Raj years ago.'

For a moment he was transported back to just before his dad died. He remembered holding his hand on a Sunday morning, choosing a paper, sometimes a women's magazine, and always selecting the right chocolate bar for his mum. The smell of curry, the anticipation of the race home they would have on their bikes. If he stopped to search for childhood memories, they could still often be found lingering like phantoms, ready to elicit pleasure or pain.

Without embarrassment he and Stan hugged each other before saying their goodbyes.

'See you again soon,' Jack said, 'you know you are always welcome to come and stay. You'd like Else.'

'You bet,' Stan replied. 'You bet, perhaps I'll bring the little ones. That's a threat, not a promise.'

But Jack sensed his uncertainty. As he continued walking up the hill towards the car park, he allowed himself to think about his father. As yet he still wasn't completely reconciled to the fact that he was gay. Jean-Baptiste's sister Françoise had confirmed it, so there still remained a possible reason for his father to have taken his own life.

He knew he should perhaps have confronted Elizabeth, but as Sheila had pointed out, he didn't like confrontation, and he had always sensed his mother did not want to talk about her husband in any other light than that he was a good father and husband.

He feared he would never be able to hang that painting. it was just too intimate. Else had reluctantly suggested they sell it, and he knew it would go for a good price if they did. Times had changed, and generally for the better, he accepted. It would comfortably hang in many establishments, a talking point, a little avant-garde. But it was too personal. Like the picture of Dorian Gray, it would remain in the attic, or at least facing the wall in the bedroom he now shared with Else.

He reached the car and drove straight to Derby. The countryside was still bleak, but the Derbyshire Peaks, rising above the Derwent, never failed to move him. He opened the car window briefly, knowing he would still be able to capture the smell of moss and dampness that even in high summer penetrated the valley. Most of the mills left over from the Industrial Revolution were now outlet shops or garden centres, all offering the obligatory cream teas and hot food, but there was still something majestic about them.

At every bend there was a sinister sign warning motorists to slow down. He remembered fondly how he had driven along it with Nancy, and then later with Grace and sometimes his grandson Tom in his open-topped TR2. *Not bad memories,* he told himself, *you've not done badly, Jack.* His thoughts turned to Else and what kind of gift he should take her.

He disliked going into Derby. In spite of picking up quickly after the War, in his opinion it was now a disaster. The cathedral quarter where Nancy had lived still held its charm and a plethora of good-quality shops, but the rest was an unattractive mix of cheap outlets and a huge impersonal shopping centre that dominated the town like an alien spaceship that had landed from nowhere.

Even the elegant old Assembly Rooms had been pulled down to be replaced by a brutal concrete concert hall and car park. He headed for the old covered market next to the Guild Hall, which had remarkably escaped destruction. He'd tried buying Else gifts before, but she always told him that she didn't need any more 'things'. But he had soon learned that food, wine or flowers were always received with enthusiasm. He purchased some local beer, two packets of crumpets, a selection of local sausages and a Stilton cheese that came in a pottery jar with the name of Hartington, the Derbyshire village where it was made, on the side.

He had intended to drive down to the coast that afternoon, but as it was now dark he decided to spend the night at a small hotel near the motorway, ready for his journey in the morning. As he switched on the television in his room to catch up with the news, his mobile bleeped. A text message from Mary read: *I understand I have your blessing?!! :)*

He thought for a moment, and then sent a thumbs-up sign back.

He phoned Else to recount his day and explain he was going to be home a day later than anticipated. They both laughed as he explained about Mary and then Stan.

'If they do get married, or live together,' Else said, 'we must invite them to stay, perhaps with Betty and Brian. I could even throw Bertie into the equation, and then we would have a most interesting mix.'

Later Else also sent him a text message – it was just an emoji in the shape of a heart. He smiled. How times had changed; Morse code, radar, the internet and now emoji, little signs to express your feelings. He wondered what his dad would have made of it all.

CHAPTER THIRTY-FOUR

Love all, trust a few, do wrong to none.

– WILLIAM SHAKESPEARE, *ALL'S WELL THAT ENDS WELL*

BURGUNDY, FRANCE, 2017

With its windows and doors flung open, the house remained cool as the stone walls absorbed the heat from outside. Jack struggled a little with the ancient record player in the salon, but eventually, after he had polished the vinyl LP several times, the overture from Mozart's *The Magic Flute* floated through the windows into the garden.

'Bit of the old classical stuff,' remarked Brian.

'It's Mozart,' replied Else. 'And keep still please, I haven't finished sketching you.'

Else sat a little way from the group around the table. From under her ancient sunhat she kept on looking up at the group and then down as she sketched on a large white pad. Her multicoloured skirt was pulled up onto her lap, exposing her brown legs and bare feet, each toenail painted a deep red. The group sat around a large iron table, where the remains of the summer pudding she had prepared was starting to attract the wasps. Jack bent to remove it and take it into the house, but he left the cheeses on the board as Stan and Brian were still helping themselves.

It had come as no surprise when Betty phoned to say that Mary and Stan were getting married in April, on Mary's birthday. 'Mary asked me to let you know. It's supposed to be a quiet affair, but as Stan has four children and at least eight grandchildren of all shapes and sizes, I can't see it being that quiet.'

'I already knew,' Jack replied. 'Sheila phoned last night, apparently Tracy and one of Stan's granddaughters are going to be bridesmaids. I'm truly happy for them both, she knows that.'

'Yes, she does, Jack. She wanted to invite you and Else, and Stan certainly didn't mind, but she has invited Grace and her husband, and she thought it better if… well, it could be awkward.'

'I'm overjoyed she's invited Grace. Who would have thought it, Betty? Give her my love – I mean our love. I know Else wants you all to come over at the end of the summer, if everyone's up for it. I mean, at our age there should be no room for hard feelings. Who knows how long we all have? We might as well start enjoying the fading light.'

Betty had laughed. 'Yes, I know what you mean.'

'Is this Stilton?' Betty asked now, nibbling a bit of her husband's cheese. 'Or is it French?'

'No, it's Stilton,' Else replied. 'Jack brought it back in February, and I froze half of it. Bit crumbly, but I love it.'

'Do you ever put on weight?' Betty asked.

'No,' Else replied, sounding more Dutch than French. 'I'm just a very scraggy chicken. I wouldn't even bother to boil me. When I look at my wrinkles… too much sun, I know, unlike you English roses.'

'Is that one of your dad's LPs?' Stan shouted to Jack, who was still in the kitchen. 'The ones I found at Mo's place? Oh, and incidentally, I meant to tell you, I saw Mo about a month ago. He came into the shop. I was finishing off some electrics. It's open now and doing really well. Anyway, I told him about finding the LPs, about me and Mary, and that we were coming to see you. He didn't seem to know anything about the records, apart from he knew his dad loved classical music. Anyway, he left, got into a very swish car, then about ten minutes later he turned up again. I said to Mary I was really surprised. I stopped work and he bought me a coffee.'

Jack continued to clear the table, assisted by Mary, who vowed she was going to finish the summer pudding if Else didn't mind, regardless of her diet.

'Please do, Mary, I'll only give it to the dogs if you don't, and Nimble is beginning to get a bit fat.'

'Are you listening?' Stan shouted good-naturedly, trying to finish his story.

'Go on,' Brian encouraged him, 'I'm with you. I didn't know Mo was back from Pakistan. I'd love to have seen him.'

'Anyway,' Stan continued, enjoying taking centre-stage, 'Mo said he had had something on his conscience for years. Something about a cardboard aeroplane, I really wasn't sure what he was on about. You were both ten years old, he said.'

Jack emerged from the kitchen, drying his hands on a tea towel. 'Go on,' he said, frowning. 'What about a cardboard aeroplane?'

WIRKSWORTH, DERBYSHIRE, 1956

When Jack left the house, the rain lashed his face. He found it impossible to ride his bike, as the icy wind continued in huge majestic gusts, knocking him this way and that as the fancy took it. Water flooded down the sides of the road from the surrounding hills, unstoppable as it had been for centuries.

As Jack approached the bridge, he could see a double-decker bus ploughing its way through a foot of water. The river had already started to burst its banks, and with that came the possibility of it carrying part of the bridge away, as it had done years ago. He hadn't thought to put on his wellingtons, but his sturdy boots and his old flying jacket protected him as he picked his way cautiously along the narrow pavement to the other side. Two or three cars passed him, sending up waves of icy cold water, which he tried unsuccessfully to avoid.

He felt more tired than he could ever remember. Every waking moment he was tormented by why he had allowed his relationship with Jean-Baptiste to destroy his life. For nearly ten years he had silently borne the shame, skilfully avoiding any suggestions of visiting the family in France. He was angry that Jean-Baptiste had betrayed him, charming Elizabeth into accepting an invitation to a non-existent engagement party. He should have turned the invitation down, he knew, especially when Elizabeth's mother had fallen ill. But young Jack would have been so disappointed.

But he also knew, if he was truly honest with himself, he had wanted to see Jean-Baptiste again. They had parted abruptly, and it had always seemed like unfinished business. Over the intervening years he had accepted that for a brief moment he had desired, loved, wanted him. He couldn't ever explain why. It was irrational, wrong, sordid. And yet when he saw him again that summer, and they joined the family and friends gathering the hay under a clear blue sky, he desired him again. With young Jack running around under the supervision of Françoise, he and Jean-Baptiste were able to laugh and relax, enjoying the physical effort, as their bodies soaked up the sun.

It was crazy, he knew, but he always reasoned with himself that it didn't affect how he felt about Elizabeth. It was as if he was a different person. But how could he ever expect her to understand? He barely understood himself. How could she ever desire him again, even though he continued to desire her?

In the last few days he had come to some kind of a decision, that if she wanted a divorce, he would facilitate it without causing any problems. He would protect and provide for her and Jack for the rest of their lives. Jean-Baptiste was dead; he no longer posed a threat to them. Suicide had briefly crossed his mind, but that was the coward's way. Besides, he wanted to live, if only to watch Jack grow up. He'd find a way.

As he mounted the hill into town, he was relieved to see the lights were still on at the newsagents. *They're amazing,* he thought, *open all hours.* But when he reached the shop, the door was locked, despite the sign saying 'Open'. He knocked, then saw the owners' two young sons arranging sweets on the front shelf near the counter. He knocked again, knowing that if their parents were about, they wouldn't mind him disturbing them. Eventually the elder of the two opened the door.

'Sorry, Mr French,' he said, turning the sign around to say 'Closed', 'mother and father are in the warehouse down the road. Can we get you anything?'

He was always impressed by their politeness, particularly the elder boy, who had a confidence well beyond his years. The whole family displayed an old-fashioned courtesy that both he and Elizabeth found charming.

'Just wondered if you had a *Daily Express* left, the one with the model aeroplane. I promised young Jack one, and I'm afraid I forgot to pick one up earlier.'

'Sorry,' said Mo, the younger of the two. 'They all went straight away, Mr French, everyone's collecting the aeroplanes.'

Jack felt a sense of desperation; such a little thing, but he had let his son down. Elizabeth's cutting words rang in his ears, and he saw again the look of disappointment on his son's face.

'Mo will sell you his,' Singh ventured, 'won't you, Mo?'

The young child looked accusingly at his brother. 'No,' he mumbled, 'I've already made it.'

'That doesn't matter,' Singh countered. 'I am sure Mr French will buy it from you. We can take it to pieces and put it back in the wrapper.'

'Would you do that, Mo?' Jack asked. 'I know it's a lot to ask, but I would give you five shillings for it.'

Mo hesitated, unlike his brother, who said at once, 'Well, actually I think it's worth ten shillings, Mr French. Little Mo is very proud of it as it was the last in his collection.'

Jack was stunned. The old-fashioned courtesy seemed to have slipped away, and here stood a young entrepreneur.

'Ten shillings,' he replied. 'That's a lot of money, Singh, not sure what your dad would say about that.'

'Let's say seven and six,' Singh suggested, seemingly unfazed by Jack's reference to his father. 'Your Jack will be delighted, I'm sure. Everyone's collecting them.'

'Done,' he said. 'but are you sure that's all right with you, Mo?'

Mo nodded, and went to fetch the plane. Then, taking it to bits, he carefully replaced it in the cellophane envelope. When he'd re-sealed it, he reluctantly passed it to his brother, who then offered it to Jack.

'May I ask, Mr French,' Singh asked in a surprisingly adult voice, 'that you don't mention this to our parents? I wouldn't want Mo to get into trouble.' And with that he took possession of the ten-shilling note that Jack offered him, and proceeded to carefully count out the two and six change from the till.

Strangely the whole incident lightened Jack's spirits. He was amused by the brothers, noting that Singh was obviously on his way to mak-ing a fortune. He would keep his promise, he thought, by not telling their parents, although under other circumstances he would have taken Singh more to task. But he accepted he too was culpable, and it was unlikely that Mo would see any of the ill-gotten gains. He slipped the package into his coat pocket, satisfied that at least someone would have a smile on their face when he returned home.

The night had become pitch black. Probably the electricity had failed, Jack thought, wheeling his bike carefully down the hill. As he approached the bridge, he half expected it to have been closed, but it remained open and a car pierced through the darkness, its headlights searing Jack's vision. A wave of water engulfed him as the car passed. Battling against the wind and trying to hold onto his bike, he lost his balance. His foot came down on nothing, and he felt himself starting to slide down the bank just before the entrance to the bridge.

Gripping the bike with one hand, he tried desperately to grasp onto anything with the other, but there was nothing. He slithered unstop-pably through the mud and finally plunged into the torrent.

He fought for minutes, raising his hand and shouting as the current swept him along. At last it threw him head first into a fallen tree that was half-submerged near the bank. Stunned by the blow to his head, he nonetheless managed to grasp one of its branches.

His eyes had now become more accustomed to the dark, and he realised if he pulled himself along the trunk, he could reach the bank. But as he started to heave himself up, he saw the little cardboard plane in its cellophane wrapper had escaped from his pocket and was caught up in a smaller branch only a foot or so away from him. Without hesitating he let go of his branch and flung himself towards it.

As he lunged, the force of the raging torrent shifted the tree. At once it was swept into the centre of the river, taking Jack with it. The model plane bobbed on ahead, leaving Jack entangled in the branches of the tree. Weak from the blow he had received, he tried to fight to escape, but it was becoming harder and harder to keep his head above water…

Finally, the branches released his lifeless body. The river swirled on, at last regurgitating him unceremoniously onto a bank further downstream.

BURGUNDY, FRANCE, 2017

There was silence around the iron table.

'Mo never mentioned the plane,' Jack said weakly. 'I've seen him on and off over the years, and he never referred to it.'

'Yes, he said that,' Stan continued. 'He said it had troubled him, kind of been on his conscience for years. He said that he'd often wanted to tell you, but as the years went by it stopped seeming so important.'

'Well, go on,' Jack said, reaching for Else's hand, which she had placed on his shoulder.

'Well, the day after your dad's death they were at school. Everyone knew that your dad had been found drowned in the river, and when Mo and Singh got home their parents were very upset. They saw your parents as friends, you know, not just customers. They told the kids that the police had been round to check if anyone had seen your dad before he died. But of course they'd said no, they'd closed early and been in the warehouse, and Mo and Singh were watching telly by the time they'd returned home. Mo and Singh didn't want to put them right about their seeing him after that, they thought they'd get in trouble with the police themselves.'

'Little buggers,' Brian chipped in.

'Anyway, that's the gist of it. Mo half apologetically said that Singh never looked back after that where money was concerned. I think he's a bit resentful, he called him the much-admired entrepreneur of the family. I don't mind telling you, I felt as if he was actually a bit upset telling me the story. He sent you his best wishes. I mean, I was surprised he remembered it all so clearly. What must it be, nearly sixty years ago?'

The Magic Flute continued in the background, with the Queen of the Night's Aria.

'My word,' said Stan, 'she's got a good pair of lungs on her.'

Jack turned and, without speaking, walked back into the house. Nimble followed him. Else stood up, laying her sketchpad on the ground. She searched briefly for her shoes, but when she couldn't find them, she gingerly picked her way barefoot across the lawn.

Brian got up to join them. 'Leave them, Brian,' Betty said, 'I think they need a bit of space. If Jack's dad had just negotiated a ten-shilling deal with Singh for Jack's benefit, it's hardly likely he committed suicide, is it?'

'Not sure I understand,' said Stan. 'I did do right in telling him, didn't I, Mary?'

'Course you did,' said Mary. 'Come on, Betty, let's make a cup of tea. They'll be back soon. Brian and Betty know the story better than I do, Stan, Brian will explain.'

Else followed Jack through the house. Her feet felt cold as she walked across the stone floor and into her bedroom. Jack had pulled Jean-Baptiste's painting away from the wall and had rested it against the foot of their bed.

'It's beautiful, Jack,' she whispered. 'It reflects so many things, love, betrayal, rites of passage, even the aftermath of the War. He was a great painter.'

476

Jack put his arm around her. 'You're cold,' he said, drawing her a little closer, 'no shoes as usual.' Then he continued, 'Yes, but I just remember him, and then only vaguely, as being good fun, full of life and humour. He used to tease me all the time. I do remember him and Dad laughing a lot and getting told off by Françoise and her mother for drinking too much. I felt a little embarrassed to see Dad a bit drunk but also excited. He was never like that at home.'

'What they had together was… I would describe it as special,' Else added. 'They were young, and unlike many of their friends after the War, they were still alive.'

'Yes, "special" possibly sums it up,' Jack replied, half laughing. 'But I still can't bring myself to let it share our home. I feel it would always elicit comments, and it'd have to be explained. Although one day I would perhaps like to show it to Tom. He's young, and the world has changed.'

Else moved towards the bed so she could sit down and take her feet off the cold floor. 'I spoke to the little museum in Avallon a while ago and suggested they might like to have it on loan. Don't look shocked, Jack, I knew the painting disturbed you. I know it might sound radical, but I even thought of painting over the young you. However, Avallon said no, they actually thought it was too valuable. Not surprising, they hadn't the right security system. But Dijon Art Gallery got in touch, and whilst you were away one of their curators came and had a look at it. I didn't say anything. Anyway, you were in England at the time, remember, back in February? The curator was impressed by it straightaway. They already have one of Jean-Baptiste's paintings. We should go one day and have a look. He said if ever we wanted to allow them to have it on loan, he was sure the powers that be would happily accept it.' She reached for a pillow and tucked her feet under it. 'It's your decision, but I really don't think you should sell it.'

Nimble put his head on the bed, as if listening to their conversation. His tail wagged occasionally, sensing from their tone when it was a good time to add a bit of encouragement.

'But I believe it shouldn't be hidden away either,' Else continued. 'That's hardly fair on Jean-Baptiste, or your father, and you're right, Tom should be invited to see it.'

They returned to the warmth of the garden and the smell of late summer. Betty poured them a cup of tea whilst Jack quietly outlined the uncertainty that had surrounded his father's death. He knew it wasn't necessary to reveal the relationship between Jean-Baptiste and his father, but in a strange way he wanted to share the full story with them. He didn't mention the picture. That, he thought, might come later.

Mary felt tense, as Stan so often fell into harmless banter to take the edge off a difficult situation. But instead he stood up and offered his hand to Jack.

'I'm proud, Jack, to have been able to pass the message on. And deeply, yes, deeply privileged you shared it with us all.'

As he spoke, Else could be heard juggling a tray of glasses and a bottle of champagne from the house and into the garden.

Jack walked towards her. 'Put some shoes on,' he said, taking the tray and placing it on the table.

She smiled. Taking the bottle and releasing the cork, she filled the glasses and passed the first one to him.

'End of story,' she whispered in his ear. He hesitated for a moment, then, turning towards her, he kissed her gently on the lips. 'End of story,' he agreed.